Prologue

They never could remember whose idea it had been, finally, to buy the ticket.

This was frustrating for them all, not because any one of them wanted to have special claim on the ticket—whatever else they'd forgotten about the night, none of them ever questioned the fact that the ticket had been for all three of them, that they'd split the winnings on the off-chance they won. It was frustrating because it seemed so unlike *all* of them to even think of buying a lottery ticket.

Kit wasn't the type to quote you statistical unlikelihoods, but she *was* one of the most talented observational scientists around, and anyone with a shred of observational talent knew going in for a lottery ticket wasn't altogether sensible. Plus, of the three of them, she was the most practical about money. She still lived in a shitty one-bedroom above One-Eyed Betty's Bar and Restaurant, swearing that she wouldn't buy a place of her own until she had a certain percentage of her student loans paid off and at least a twenty percent down payment for a house. No way could it have been Kit.

Zoe was the most impulsive of their group; she sang karaoke and threw darts with whatever bearded hipster dude at the bar asked her and always ordered the special and also jetted off to exotic locales every year for vacation. But Zoe was also the most successful, and she didn't need the money, and she wasn't the kind of woman to want more of what she already had enough of. Zoe wouldn't have thought to buy herself a ticket.

And Greer thought the lottery was bad luck. She thought lots of things were bad luck, actually—the usual stuff, like black cats and walking under ladders and hats on the bed. But she had other ones too: goldfish, old brooms in new houses, opals, candles with two wicks. Mostly she accepted teasing about these superstitions, but Zoe and Kit both remembered clearly that

Greer had once said lottery bad luck was real—she'd watched a whole show about it on TLC. Greer wouldn't schedule a doctor's appointment on the thirteenth of any month, so there was no way she'd buy a lottery ticket without some real coaxing.

And yet—they'd bought a lottery ticket. There was even grainy surveillance video of their purchase, all three of them at the Seventh Street Quick Mart, looking like they'd had a bit too much to drink (they had—Betty ran a good happy hour), which was embarrassing, but maybe not quite as embarrassing as the fact that they were also purchasing twelve Snickers bars, a bag of Cool Ranch Doritos, and a box of tampons. One of the local news blogs had run a headline under a screenshot of the video: "Gal pals find best cure for PMS is a jackpot." Zoe wanted to sue over that quip, and knowing Zoe, she would have done her hot-shot lawyer thing until the blog was wiped off the internet forever, but Kit—who was more concerned about keeping it quiet than any of them—had reminded her that it would just draw more attention to the whole thing.

What they wanted, once they learned of their winnings—Gary from the Quick Mart called Betty, Betty called Kit, and Kit called Zoe and Greer—was to absorb the shock, to the collect their shares as privately as possible, and to make sense of their new lives.

But that all came later.

What came first was the three of them at Betty's on a Wednesday night, where and when they'd met almost every week for the last four years. Seven total alcoholic beverages, two total plates of nachos, and three terrible days between them, and *someone*, at some point, brought up that night's lottery.

Maybe it was that others at the bar had been discussing it—last week's jackpot had reached record proportions owing to a long stretch of no winners, but a group of twenty postal workers from the next state over had claimed the four hundred million, doing a press conference over the weekend all together, looking stunned and joyful and a little uncomfortable on camera. It was a big news story, and it seemed as if everyone was devoting at least a brief amount of dinner conversation to the life-changing implications of winning that kind of money.

"Six of them said they're going back to work," said Greer, going straight for the newly deposited plate of nachos. "Can you *imagine*? You win four hundred million dollars and go back to delivering the mail."

"It's really only around two-hundred-forty-eight million," Zoe said. "Taxes."

"I'd go back to work," said Kit.

"We know, honey," Greer said, patting Kit's arm affectionately. "It's

When three friends impulsively buy a lottery ticket, they never suspect the many ways their lives will change—or that for each of them, love will be the biggest win of all.

Kit Averin is anything but a gambler. A scientist with a quiet, steady job at a university, Kit's focus has always been maintaining the acceptable status quo. Being a sudden millionaire doesn't change that, with one exception: the fixer-upper she plans to buy, her first and only real home. It's more than enough to keep her busy, until an unsettlingly handsome, charming, and determined corporate recruiter shows up in her lab—and manages to work his way into her heart . . .

Ben Tucker is surprised to find that the scientist he wants for Beaumont Materials is a young woman—and a beautiful, sharp-witted one at that. Talking her into a big-money position with his firm is harder than he expects, but he's willing to put in the time, especially when sticking around for the summer gives him a chance to reconnect with his dad. But the longer he stays, the more questions he has about his own future—and who might be in it.

What begins as a chilly rebuff soon heats up into an attraction neither Kit nor Ben can deny—and finding themselves lucky in love might just be priceless . . .

Books by Kate Clayborn

Beginner's Luck

Published by Kensington Publishing Corporation

Beginner's Luck

A Chance of a Lifetime Romance

Kate Clayborn

LYRICAL PRESS
Kensington Publishing Corp.
www.kensingtonbooks.com

First Electronic Edition: October 2017
eISBN-13: 978-1-5161-0510-6
eISBN-10: 1-5161-0510-9

First Print Edition: October 2017
eISBN-13: 978-1-5161-0511-3
eISBN-10: 1-5161-0511-7

Printed in the United States of America

you and that big microscope until the end of time. The greatest love story of the century."

"I wouldn't," said Zoe, more firmly than perhaps any of them would have anticipated, since Zoe seemed to both love her work and do amazingly well at it. Zoe waved a hand dismissively. "It'd be just—a lifetime of spa treatments and male strippers, I'm pretty sure."

"Jesus, Zoe," Kit said, on a laugh. "Why does your mind always go to male strippers?"

"I think that *Magic Mike* movie rewired my brain."

"At least one of those twenty will do something like that, though," said Greer. "I mean, maybe not the male strippers. But you'll read about one of them buying a six-million-dollar RV and a gold-plated pickup truck or something."

"Judge not, lest ye be judged," said Betty, snaking her tattooed arm between them to refill Greer's beer. Betty winked at them, her trademark move when she served a drink. Betty actually, literally only had one natural eye, the left one a very convincing prosthetic, and all the regulars here had heard a different story from Betty herself on how she came to have it. "I saw that on a fridge magnet," she said.

"Oh, I'm not judging," Greer said, embarrassed, though it's not as though Betty herself had a multi-million-dollar RV or a gold pickup truck. "I mean, people can—you know, do whatever. I'm not judging!"

This was classic Greer—quick to feel as if she'd said the wrong thing, always apologizing. Zoe kept telling her she needed to let her balls drop, but so far this hadn't worked to make Greer any more assertive.

Betty smiled, bright red lips passing over her white teeth. "I'm teasing. So what *would* you ladies do if you won the lottery?"

There'd been a pause, a too-long one, because then Betty had shrugged and said, "Well, you three sort that out while I go serve some more drinks," shimmying away in her vintage dress, little lemon and lime and orange slices printed all over it, her jet-black hair stiff in its pompadour. Except for the tattoos, Betty could've walked straight off a vintage poster, the kind that'd keep soldiers going.

"She must not have heard me about the strippers," Zoe said.

"Seriously, though," said Greer. "What would we buy?"

Another pause, while they all took a drink. Maybe on another day, they would have taken Zoe's lead and riffed on all their ridiculous, overindulgent ideas—the ones where you speculate on how many shoes you could fit in a walk-in closet the size of your current apartment, on whether you could afford a private plane, on the likelihood of being able to purchase some rare piece of historically important jewelry.

But on that day—when Kit had spent two hours cleaning up after a pipe burst in her apartment, when Zoe had, not for the first time, watched a grown man cry at a conference table, and when Greer had, for the third time in a single calendar year, decided to quit a job—not a single one of them was feeling all that overindulgent.

Kit said, "A house," but what she thought was, *home.*

Zoe said, "An adventure," but what she thought was, *forgiveness.*

Greer said, "An education," but what she thought was, *freedom.*

So in the end, it didn't matter all that much who had said, at the Quick Mart, to add the ticket to their bill. What mattered was that the three of them had heard each other's desire.

And not a single one of them was going to see the other waste the opportunity.

Chapter 1

Kit

So the thing is, I haven't quite worked out how to live like a millionaire.

Not that I have much acquaintance with millionaires, really, except for Greer and Zoe, but they're new to the game too. In my mind, millionaires probably do not keep wearing a pair of black pants long after they don't really look black anymore. They probably buy new glasses instead of buying tiny screw kits to fix old ones. They probably do not drive a fourteen-year-old hatchback with no radio, nor do they live in one-bedroom apartments above bars, even really nice bars.

Millionaires also probably do not spend four hours of a workday wiping what was about fifty years of accumulated dirt off lab equipment, because millionaires probably have people they pay for that sort of thing.

I tip a bit more ethanol onto my rag to polish one last spot on the steel creep frame we've recently inherited—it's old, but it'll still do the job for some of our most aggressive stress testing. At this point, it's started to gleam under my attentions, and I get a little thrill of pride at seeing things coming together. This morning when I'd come in, I'd hoped to steal some time on the microscope, especially since in these early weeks of summer, most of the graduate students who use the scopes, untethered from their teaching assignments, are working irregular hours, sometimes coming out of the building rumpled and bleary-eyed at seven a.m. when I'm usually arriving. But when Dr. Singh had asked if I could spare some time getting the lab in shape for the campus photographer, I hadn't hesitated. This lab is where I'd done most of the work for my master's thesis, and it's where I still, almost four years later, train some of the newcomers.

Millionaires like me, I guess, get a little thrill from this kind of thing, and if I wish that some of the graduate students around here shared in my sense of protectiveness about this lab—well, that's okay.

Once I feel the rag slide easily over the steel, I take a step back and turn in a slow circle, admiring my work. I may need to hit the windows one more time—a few are looking a little streaky still. Dr. Singh's lab is the most modest in the materials science department, but damn if I didn't get it the cleanest. It probably won't even make the cut for the photographer, but it's the principle of the thing.

I snort a little, just thinking this. Principles, I suspect, are also part of the reason I have so far been a shitty millionaire. Aside from the fact that I'd lived in a state of near-panic right after the win, begging Zoe and Greer to be the ones to do the Virginia state lottery's mandated press appearance so my name could be left out of it as much as possible, I'd also second-guessed almost every purchase I even thought about making, and consequently made hardly any at all. Three months ago, Greer, newly thrilled by every single college course she was enrolled in, told me I was acting like Silas Marner. Which I found very offensive, once I googled Silas Marner.

But no more miserly Kit, not after today. Today, I'm taking the afternoon off and finally, officially—six months after winning the jackpot—making my biggest dream come true. Thinking about it puts a wide smile on my face, which I can see reflected in those shiny windows I cleaned all morning.

"Excuse me," comes a deep voice from behind me, and it's so unexpected that I jump a little, hitting my elbow on the creep frame I've just finished cleaning.

"Ow," I mutter, turning to meet—oh, only the most attractive person I have ever actually seen in real life, unless something is happening to my vision. I raise a hand immediately to my face, noting the lab goggles I am wearing—right, this is ideal—*over* my actual glasses. I pull them off, the rubbery strap getting a little stuck in my hair, and wince when a few strands come out. Once I've got my glasses straightened, I have another look.

And, yeah. Still the most attractive person I've ever seen, tall and broad-shouldered with sandy-blond hair and a square, set jaw, eyes so blue I can see them even from several feet away, where he's standing in the doorway. I don't usually go for guys in suits, probably because most of the men in my line of work are more the rumpled-khakis or jeans type, but damn. This guy wears a suit like it's his job. Which, it probably is his job, since it's noon on a Friday.

"I'm looking for E.R. Averin." Excellent voice too—deep and smooth, and I had not really realized until this moment that I am so hard up if I am noticing this man's *voice* so forcefully. Maybe there was something to Zoe's constant haranguing about my nonexistent dating life.

"Well, you found her," I say, glad to hear that my own voice, at least, sounds normal.

"I—" He paused, looked back over his shoulder. "I have?"

"You have." He blinks, unbuttons and then rebuttons his jacket. It is awkward to a high degree, and let me tell you what, you don't spend your life around a bunch of experimental scientists without getting a real skewed sense of what's awkward. This guy seems completely thrown.

"You're E.R. Averin?" he says, a little edge of doubt in his voice, and it's at this point that I get almost relieved to know what I'm dealing with. Not for nothing am I the only female—not to mention the youngest—lab technician to ever work in this department, and in fact the only woman working in a lab tech role in the College of Engineering. I've dealt with a lot of dudes who have doubted me.

"I think I've made that clear, Mr.....?"

He has the decency to look genuinely chastened. "My apologies, Professor Averin. I'm Ben Tucker."

He steps forward, holding out his—well, very nice, very large—hand, but I hold up the bottle of ethanol and my rag, shrugging in half-hearted apology. "Hello, Mr. Tucker. I'm not a professor."

"Right, yes. I apologize."

"That's okay," I say, and I almost feel sorry for him. There's something about him, some weary feature behind his handsomeness, that gives me the sense I'm getting him on a bad day.

"Please, call me Ben."

"Okay, Ben. Call me Ms. Averin."

He smiles at that, and I suspect on anyone else it would seem condescending, that smile. But his seems genuine—wide and a little crooked on the left side, chasing a dimple that appears in his cheek. "Right," he says again.

There's a beat of silence, while I take in that smile of his, that dimple. I probably smile back a little, despite my best efforts to look stoic and completely unaffected by him.

"How can I help you, Ben?"

"I'm here representing Beaumont Materials."

I know Beaumont Materials—anyone who works in my field, who does any kind of work at all in materials science, knows about a company that manufactures everything from pipelines to jet engines to those little plastic thingamajigs you can use to hang pictures without nails. But some additional thread of familiarity tugs at my brain. I generally have a good memory, but probably this guy's jerk-hotness has scrambled it. I decide not to try and sort it, and head instead over to the steel storage cabinet where we keep supplies, putting some distance between me and my new visitor. "Go on," I say, appreciating the opportunity to look busy. "I just need to start packing up here."

"We've reached out to you recently, Ms. Averin, regarding the article you and your coauthors published in *Metallurgy International*."

Oh. Oh, fuck, I do remember now what that tug of memory is, and my palms go a little more sweaty beneath my latex gloves. "Ah. Yes. I saw a couple of emails. I don't remember seeing your name, though."

"I wasn't part of the original contact team," he says, stepping farther into the room. "But I read your paper, and I decided I had to meet you, and talk to you about the opportunities Beaumont could offer you for your research."

"I don't want any opportunities from Beaumont," I say, more quickly, more defensively than I intend. I'm immediately grateful for the fact that I'm here alone today—just as I don't want anyone here knowing about the lottery, I don't want them catching wind of Beaumont trying to contact me. When those emails had come in, I'd deleted them almost right away, same as I did with any message from potential employers. I'm happy *here*, and I don't even want there to be a suggestion to anyone around that I'm otherwise.

He smiles again, and—ugh. I need to get this guy out of here; he is terrible for my self-preservation. "I think we got that message from your silence," he says, "but I'm afraid we couldn't let this go without having the chance to tell you what exactly it is we are willing to do for you." He looks around the lab as he says this, and I suppress a wince—all right, so it may be super clean in here, but it is far from state-of-the art, and to a guy coming from Beaumont Materials, it probably looks budget as all get-out. Even after ten years of being here, Dr. Singh was still the most recent faculty hire, and he'd inherited this, the oldest lab, on a side of the building where the HVAC was unreliable and the floors had never been replaced.

"I've got everything I need here," I say, but at that exact moment yet another handle from the already-dilapidated steel cabinet falls off, clattering on the peeling, faded linoleum. "I mean except for functional handles."

Hell. That dimple. "We could take care of that."

"I'm sure you could," I say, hooking a finger through the hole left by the wayward handle and pulling open the cabinet.

"As I'm sure you know, state-of-the-art equipment is the least of what we'd be willing to do to have you on board. Beaumont is working on alloy technologies that relate directly to your research, and we think we could make a real difference working together."

I let out an unladylike snort at this, this cookie-cutter pitch he's giving me. And anyways, I know what alloy technology Beaumont's been pouring most of its money into in the last five years—big oil and big guns—and I want no part of either. My work's always been about figuring out weaknesses in old materials, studying bridge or pipeline failures, figuring out how to make what's already here work better. "I'm not looking to make that kind of difference," I say, setting the jug of ethanol back in its place.

"Many of the scientists we work with have that reaction initially, I can assure you. But Beaumont's packages are very attractive—we're talking a great deal of funding sources for your work. Let me take you to lunch and tell you—"

I cut him off here, bored with everything he has to say, and that's in spite of the fact that I'm pretty sure I could look at him for a good, long time. "Tell me about the nondisclosure agreement you're going to make me sign, so I can't publish research that might hurt your bottom line? Tell me about the devil's bargain this will turn out to be, when Beaumont uses my research to make some product that is horrible for the environment, or that you put on some weapon that you sell to the government at huge cost? Tell me about all the fine print that says you can terminate my contract if I'm not producing patentable material in the next two years? Listen, no offense to you, Ben, but there's a reason I've avoided private funding in the work I do. There's a reason I work here."

"Two of your colleagues here are backed with corporate funding." Don't I know it. Dr. Harroway and Dr. Wagner both have massive corporate support, and there's no kind of fifty-plus years of dirt on any of their equipment. If my lottery money would have made any kind of dent in what we'd need to match corporate funding, I would've donated it all. "And the College of Engineering is exploring avenues for long-term partnerships with industry."

I can feel my eyes narrow at him. This kind of guy was the reason academic research was becoming—was *already*—a patsy for big money. "Let me ask you something about that *Metallurgy International* article," I say, rising to my full—not very full, frankly—height. "What did you think of the technique I used to prepare samples for heat treatment in step three of my experiments?"

It's fleeting, but I catch it, I think: a flash of something near surprise in his eyes, but he so quickly arranges his features into a sly, *I'm-not-ashamed-that-you-caught-me* devilishness that I suspect Ben Tucker never really lets himself get taken off guard. To this, I shrug my shoulders casually. "I don't really blame you, actually. I didn't write it with a corporate audience—with someone like you—in mind. But this is why I'm not interested in working for your company. I enjoy working with people who really know what it is that I do, and more importantly, with people who know what I really want to do with it."

He lowers his eyes for a moment, looking down to where the cabinet handle rests on the floor. Damn, he has long eyelashes, a dark contrast to his light hair, which is actually unacceptable for me to be noticing at this time.

He looks back up and smiles at me. "I like you," he says, and I stiffen in surprise and a fair bit of anger.

Because this is also unacceptable. What does he think, that I'll roll right over and show him my belly, in gratitude for a little male attention? I've known guys like this. I'd taken notes all through general chemistry for a guy like this in my first year of college, stupidly not realizing that for him, the notes were all that I was good for.

"Oh, is this the part where you skate right over the fact that you didn't actually read my paper, and instead tell me I've got 'spunk,' that I'm exactly what Beaumont needs?"

"No. That's me telling you. Independent of Beaumont." He says this firmly, with more conviction than he's said anything else so far.

"Well. I know your type, and flattery isn't going to work, either."

"My type?"

I feel it, right here, that I'm losing a little control over the conversation, but I'm stuck with it, so I barrel on. "Oh, sure. You come in here, with your"—I pause here, to gesture vaguely in the direction of his body—"your suit. And your face, and..." I swallow the rest of it. I want him out of here. I'm afraid someone will come in, Dr. Singh, or any one of the faculty or graduate students who would probably wet their pants at meeting a Beaumont executive who seems to be handing out jobs. "Listen, it's very kind of you to come all this way. But I did read those emails, so I know something about what you're offering. I'm just really, really not interested. And I do, actually, have an appointment."

He takes a deep breath and nods. His skin is golden-brown, a light tan, but I think I see flags of color on his cheeks. This is his fault, coming in here sleek but unprepared, but suddenly I feel a little guilty for being so dismissive. Before I can say anything, though, he speaks again. "I understand. I'm..." he trails off, long enough to run a hand through his hair, before continuing, "...sorry to have wasted your time."

He steps forward a little, holding out his hand. I catch a little scent of something—pine, maybe. Whatever it is, it's not what I'm expecting. With the suit he's wearing, I'd expected some upmarket version of that heinous body spray I sometimes get a whiff of when one of the undergrads is trying to compensate for not-very-clean-laundry. Ben, though, he smells— clean. Natural.

Male.

I take his hand and shake it, forgetting the glove I still have on. He looks down and chuckles a little at the contact, and I try not to be ashamed of the little shiver that chases down my spine at the sound of that.

"It was very nice to meet you, Ms. Averin," he says, and then he turns and leaves the room, as quietly as he'd come in.

For a minute, I stare after him, a little confused, thrown off. I've been recruited before, especially back when I was finishing up my thesis, but never quite that way, never by someone that looked like him. One thing about it was the same, though—that quick-shot feeling of fear that would go through me at the very idea of having to pick up and leave here, start all over again. I can't do that anymore. I've had my fill of it.

I strip off my gloves and shrug out of my lab coat, cast my eyes up at the clock. There's no time for me to be distracted by Ben Tucker or by my disproportionate reaction to his offer. If there's any day when I don't need to feel threatened by an upheaval, it's today.

Today, I've got millionaire dreams to make come true.

* * * *

"It's like a four," Zoe says, peering out the back window to the small, overgrown yard, "on a scale of shithole to ten."

It's Saturday morning, and I've been a homeowner now for less than a full twenty-four hours. I'd spent most of yesterday afternoon at the closing, signing a stack of documents that Satan obviously prepared, and then had made my way over, alone, to take it all in and drop off a few boxes—but also, I guess, to get prepared for this, the morning I was showing my two best friends my new place for the first time.

When I'd first started looking for a place, Zoe and Greer had gone with me to dozens of open houses, had helped me scour real estate websites for prospects. They each had their own opinions about where I belonged— condo, Zoe had said, lobbying especially hard for her own posh downtown building, while Greer said she pictured me somewhere with a big yard, a place to spread out a little.

Of course I valued their opinions. For the last few years, since the night we'd all literally, hilariously, run into each other outside of the entrance to my apartment—Greer walking home from the pet store with a plastic bag filled with water and a single goldfish, Zoe yelling into her phone outside of the yoga studio next door to Betty's, and me, trying to wave a bat outside of the doorway with an old hairbrush—Greer and Zoe had been my confidantes, my cheerleaders, my companions. They were family. But buying this house was so important, so personal to me that I was afraid I'd lose my own voice somewhere in the shuffle, and more than that, I'd known almost since I first moved to Barden and drove through its most historic district that I wanted to live in *this* neighborhood, on this medium-sized city's southern edge, someday. I think I was stalling, really, until I saw one of the Queen Anne style row houses come available, and when one did, I'd gone on my own to the first showing, fully intending to call them, to have them see it another time, once I'd checked it out.

But the house was in rough shape—lots to be done, lots of people to be hired, lots of planning and patience required. I was afraid they'd talk me out of it, and so I'd made an offer that first day, had held off, despite their pleading protests, on showing it to them before today—moving day, when the truck was outside, unloading the boxes that had been picked up from my old apartment this morning.

So if my friends are a little skeptical, it may be because I've made them that way. And also because this house—it probably *is* a four.

Greer tsks, nudging Zoe in the back. "Kit, it's beautiful, really. And don't listen to Zoe. Her mother called this morning and you know what that means."

Zoe waves a hand dismissively. "I'm fine. It's just that my garlic necklace doesn't work through the phone. Anyways, Kit-Kat, I'm totally kidding. This is a great house."

I smile at their gentle approval, but I need, today, to press for more. There's two dudes carrying my mattress upstairs, after all. I am *in* this thing. "You really think so?"

It's a little tough, standing in this kitchen, trying to recapture the calm, joyful feeling I'd had when I'd first seen the house. Then, I'd taken in the flaws, understood the need for many renovations—but I'd somehow *known*. I'd felt a certainty unlike anything else, except for maybe the first time I'd solved a thermodynamics equation. Now, though, I only see the mismatched cabinets, some painted so many times the doors won't shut, the peeling laminate countertop, the floor covered in stick-on tiles. It's like the lab, but worse.

Zoe wraps her arms around me, gives me a smacking kiss on my head before pulling away and heading into the dining room, where Greer and I follow. "I really think so. It's perfect for you. You can make it exactly what you want."

"I can see it now," Greer says, turning in a slow circle around the room. "The light coming in through all these windows, the fireplace in the front room, all this woodwork cleaned up and repainted. You could put this place in a magazine once it's all done."

That idea—it does not appeal, not in any way. This is going to be my safe place, for me and the people I love. Watching Zoe and Greer move through these rooms, pausing over the big, gorgeous bay window at the front of the house, I feel suddenly choked up. *I've really done it*, I think. *I've got a home.*

I lived in sixteen different apartments from the time I was born to when I left home at eighteen. They were all, every one, varying degrees of awful. The first one I remember had no heat, and some nights my older brother, Alex, would light a small campfire grill he'd found in a dumpster and we'd huddle around it, falling asleep leaning against each other. Six of them had communal showers; when I'd go down the hall, clutching a bar of soap and a towel to my chest, Alex would walk behind me, standing outside the door until I'd finished, not letting anyone in. For my entire thirteenth year, I had bed bugs that were impossible to get rid of, no matter what we did. For six months when I was sixteen, we lived next to a mentally ill man who would knock on the door at all hours of the night, shouting that he hoped my father went blind, that he knew I was a whore, that Alex worked as a spy for the Russian government.

The easiest moves were the ones that kept me in the same school district, the same few-mile radius. By the time I started high school, Alex was working, and he could do more to control where we went—but for most of my childhood, I learned to anticipate the upheaval of meeting a new teacher mid-year, a new set of students, a new route to school, everything. My teachers praised me, complimenting me on my adaptability, or, on the occasions when I'd come in having learned more than where the current class was, on how patiently I waited for other kids to grasp concepts I'd mastered.

With each move, my father, stinking of booze and cigarettes, would make promises, telling us this would be the last time. But for the most part, we were mostly invisible to him, especially me—a living reminder only of that desperate time after his first wife, Alex's mom, had died, and he'd tried to recreate the love he'd had for her with a young, quiet waitress he'd met on a riverboat casino.

Good free counseling services in college helped, but it was moving here—working with Dr. Singh, meeting Zoe and Greer, falling in love with this town—that made me feel as if I'd found my stopping place, the place where maybe I wouldn't always have to work so hard at staying put, the place where I could stop obsessively counting sidewalk cracks between my bus stop and whatever crappy apartment building I was sleeping in. To be here, in my own home—to me, it's a miracle.

"God, you're so *lucky*," Zoe says as one of the movers comes in, hauling another two boxes upstairs. "You're going to have hot contractors here all the time. Can I come over? I could hang out while you're at work. I could *supervise*."

I laugh at the way she waggles her eyebrows up and down. "No. You're not going to sexually harass my contractors."

"Spoilsport," she says, watching as another mover climbs the stairs.

"My favorite thing about this," Greer says, leaning against the bay window's ledge, "is that it'll give you something to focus on other than work."

"Yes!" Zoe exclaims, clapping her hands together.

"I'm still going to work, you guys." This is a common refrain, the concern about my working too much. I don't think either of them really thinks I'll ever change, but I suspect it's turned into a sort of shorthand for us all, them expressing affection for me this way, and me secretly relishing their concern. Meeting Zoe and Greer, keeping up with the traditions we'd built over the years we've known each other, probably protected me from what might have been a worrying inclination to work too hard, to let my research consume me. I'd seen the single-minded focus that had overtaken some of my peers, had seen the way work had dictated the lives of many of my professors. One of the reasons I'd made the choices I had—to stay small, to stay on as a lab tech—had been to avoid that fate. Of course, there'd been other reasons too, reasons like the ones I'd told Ben Tucker yesterday.

Unexpectedly, I feel my face heat at the thought of him. That dimple. Those eyelashes for days.

I clear my throat, ignoring these stray, unwanted thoughts. "I am going to do some of this myself, though," I say. "Easy stuff, maybe some of the yard work. And working with the contractors is sort of a job in itself."

"We'll help," says Greer. "Anything you need."

"Anything that doesn't involve me wearing a hazmat suit," Zoe adds, looking suspiciously at a patch of moldy wall near the radiator. "But everything else, obviously."

Right then, there's a little creak and Greer tips forward a bit from where she's sitting. "Oh! Oh, I'm sorry," she says, leaping up from where the sill has separated a bit from the window. We all three look at it, at where the wood is rotting a little, at where another repair will have to be made.

But I have to smile. A problem in my own house, one that I can solve, with my best friends here to help? I don't think I've ever felt more like a millionaire.

Chapter 2

Ben

I've got a job for you, he'd said.

I pull another stack of slate from the bed of the truck, trying not to slam it down onto the pallet, which is what my hands are itching to do.

It'll be easy, he'd said. *Won't even take a full day.*

Another stack, another half-hearted attempt not to be aggressive with it. *We've already made contact several times,* he'd assured me. *The groundwork has already been laid.*

I straighten the pieces I've put down and turn back to the truck bed, still half-full. *Fuck,* I think. *I'll be out here all morning.* I'm restless and pissed, and doing this kind of work should help, but so far, it's not doing shit. I'm mad about yesterday, I'm worried about my dad, and I've been up since four a.m. so I could drive the fifty miles I needed to go to pick up all this slate and bring it back here. It's almost funny—thirty-one years old, and I'm home to take care of him, but my dad still bosses me around this yard like I'm his fifty-dollars-per-week employee.

Strangely, though, I don't feel like laughing.

I hear the muffled sound of my phone ringing from my back pocket, and I already know it's Jasper, because he's called three times since yesterday, and I haven't picked up once. It's hot as hell out here already, only ten a.m., and my arms are tired from all the lifting.

Might as well get this over with, I decide, and yank off my gloves, tossing them on the truck bed before yanking out my phone. Just to make sure, I check the screen before saying, "Jasper, you are an asshole."

"That's some greeting for your best friend, Tucker."

"It's what you deserve. I'm fucking pissed, Jas." I resist the urge to kick at the pallet beside me. Though I've been keeping it together in front of my dad, being back here seems to rouse all my adolescent instincts.

"I'm guessing it didn't go well with Averin."

"You're guessing right."

"Goddammit. Global Chem got to him first," Jasper says, his voice frustrated. Global Chem is our biggest competitor, and we're always chasing down the same talent.

I snort a sarcastic laugh. That would maybe be easier. I could play good cop if I was up against Global Chem. But what happened yesterday—there'd be no way E.R. Averin was ever going to see me as a good anything. "She's not a him," I snap. "I mean, she's—Ms. Averin, she's a she." I sound ridiculous.

"Oh," Jasper says, and I'm surprised to feel annoyed on her behalf. I've been annoyed with myself since yesterday, having blown it so thoroughly with her, but Jasper can take most of the blame on this one, as far as I'm concerned.

"You should have done your research," I say to him.

"That's your area."

"Not right fucking now, it's not. I told you, I needed a couple months here to deal with my dad. You call me, you want me to deal with a recruit that's in town, fine. But you needed to do the legwork."

I exhale a frustrated breath, hunch my shoulder to hold the phone against my ear so I can tug on one of my gloves. I'm too mad to be standing here doing nothing. What I said to Jasper, it's only partially true. I am on family leave while Dad recovers, and Jasper *was* asking me to do a special favor in going out on the job while I'm here. But I'd agreed before I left to stay in the loop, to telecommute as much as possible, and if I'd agreed to go out on a job, I should have been as careful as I usually am when I approach a new recruit. All I had before going to see Averin was what Jasper told me—master's degree in materials science, working as a full-time lab tech at the university, impressive publication record in the area Beaumont was after, high tensile strength metal alloys, the kind of stuff we could use in our building materials division in particular—and the small additional amount I'd scared up through some Google searching an hour before I went in. I should have known something was off there. Everything online about her had been calculated to avoid anything personal—no pictures, no social media accounts, and on her university staff profile page, there'd only been a "No Picture Available" box, and underneath a list of publications so long that I'd had to scroll down twice.

The fact that I'd not taken the time to read a single one was bad enough. But worse was the fact that I'd jumped to conclusions—I'd thought Averin had to be at least forty-something to have that publication record.

And I'd thought Averin was a man.

She was neither forty-something nor a man. I'd thought she was a grad student, honestly. A gorgeous one too. When I'd first seen her, my mouth had gone dry, the tips of my fingers had twitched. It was such a dick move, such a massive error of assumptions that I still got a hot, embarrassed feeling when I thought about it. I may have played it cool when I was standing in front of her—I was terrific at playing that game—but I'd known I had fucked it up, and for some reason, it had felt uniquely awful to fuck it up with her.

"How's he doing?" asks Jasper, and he sounds genuinely concerned.

"He's a stubborn cuss, and he's got me working like a dog. Which I guess means he's doing all right. Doesn't quite have his color back yet, but he's a little better every day."

"You brought him home yet?"

"Yeah. On Thursday." I let that sit, enjoying Jasper's silence. Thursday, the day Jasper called to insist I see Averin as soon as possible, I was helping get my seriously injured father discharged from the hospital, settling him into a house I'd spent the last three days preparing for his arrival, moving furniture and setting up ramps and installing grip bars for his tub and toilet.

Fucking Jasper.

"I'm sorry," he says. "I really am."

Anyone else would probably hear this as lukewarm, barely a gesture. But Jasper hardly ever apologizes, so if he's said it, I know he means it. And I can forgive Jasper for not getting it, I guess—the guy's got no family of his own, and pretty much all he does is work. He laughs off the jokes people make at the office about his being robotic, a machine, but I know that shit gets to him. I know he tries.

"Averin," I say, shifting the focus back to where he'll feel more comfortable. "She doesn't want anything to do with Beaumont."

"Try again," he says, and I have to laugh at how fast he's returned to form.

"I'm serious, Jas. Aside from the fact that I was shit in the meeting, I don't think she's interested at all in what we do." I have a memory of the way she waved a hand over me, where I stood in the doorway. *Your suit,* she said. *Your face.*

"So she's a tough case. But that doesn't mean she's impossible. You've handled lots of cases like this."

I had, actually. In fact, usually, tough cases are my specialty. Two months ago, I closed a guy who'd had his name on four medical patents that

Beaumont wanted to develop. He'd been tenured faculty at his university for fifteen years, making good money, his wife and his kids happy and settled in their town. He had a top-of-the-line lab on campus and grad students that worked hard for him. There was really no reason for him to move on.

Until I convinced him otherwise.

Most people think recruiting comes down to one or two major things— money, usually, is the first one, or location—if you can convince someone that they're going to be moving to a better place, one with more opportunities, or a better climate, whatever. But it's more complicated than that. A good recruiter gets to know as much as he can about his target's life, looks at that life in all its tangled, sometimes piecemeal, and always personal complexity. A good recruiter knows that people might move for money or location, but they stay for all kinds of different reasons—politics, partners, the sports scene, dog parks, whether there's a good local bookstore. Beaumont has branches in seventeen states, and I know them all inside and out. I know the offices and the people who work in them; I know the surrounding areas and the shopping districts and the best places to go to school. I know everything that might turn a recruit on, that might scare them off.

Usually.

"She seems different," I say, stacking more slate.

"Listen. Since we talked, I met again with Greg," Jasper says, his voice serious. Greg is head of R&D, basically our boss, though Jasper and I work with more independence than probably anyone at corporate headquarters. "He's decided Averin is his top prospect. And if we get her, he says he'll let us out of the non-compete."

Holy shit. I drop a piece of slate.

If we get out of the non-compete, Jasper and I have our shot, what we've been working toward for the last seven years. We could go independent, start our own consulting firm—rather than being employed by a single company, doing their R&D recruiting, we go out on our own. We scout talent, we shop it. Sports agents for scientists, basically. We'd work all over the world. We've built up contacts everywhere.

It's the non-compete that's kept us at Beaumont, and if we get out of it, we can make this happen.

If I can get Averin.

"I'll get her." But even as I say it, I think of that firm set to her mouth, that sharp-eyed look she gave me. She looked at me like I'd come to steal the eggs from her nest, and while I'd dealt with targets that were protective of their work, I got the sense that there was something else to the way she'd looked at me as a threat.

"You have a plan?"

"No," I say honestly, picking up one of the shards from the piece of slate I'd dropped. My life is chaos right now, being away from the office and here taking care of my dad. And yet I'd worked my ass off for seven years, for longer than that, really, and all of it had been for this kind of chance. If I need Averin, I'll find a way to get back in her good graces and to ignore the inconvenient and entirely unprofessional effect she has on me. "But I'll make one."

* * * *

I'm back at my dad's place by seven, but it feels like midnight to my body, which hasn't seen that kind of hard labor in years. In Texas, on the road, I work until I'm dead tired, and while I get to the gym almost every day, it's nothing like a day at the yard, which is standing, lifting, pulling, stacking, cranking.

My dad got hurt doing this kind of work, and I'm struck with a fresh wave of guilt. I have that guilt generally, have had it since I left home, but it's not even close to what I've felt since I got the call last week from the hospital. *Your father's taken a fall*, the nurse had said, and I'd had to ask her to repeat it, just to let it sink in.

Sharon, my dad's neighbor and part-time employee at the salvage yard, is in the kitchen, stirring something that smells delicious on the stove. "Potato and leek," she says, as I set my wallet and keys on the counter. "Want some?"

"Thanks, Sharon. How's he doing?"

"I think he terrorized the home health aide today," she says. "He made her take apart some clock he's trying to repair. When I got here, she said he wouldn't even let her do the sponge bath he's supposed to get."

Shit, I think. *Guess I'm doing the sponge bath.* "I'll call the service tomorrow and apologize." It's only for this first week, the home health service, but still, I want to stay on their good side.

Sharon shrugs. "You know, by the end of it I don't even think she minded. She asked where she could leave all the tools so she could work more on it tomorrow when she comes."

I have to laugh, imagining this. My dad is eccentric, no doubt about it, but he's charming as hell too, and he's always getting people interested in the same oddities that preoccupy him. When I was growing up, my favorite days at the salvage yard were when the polished, wealthy clients would come in, looking for something mint-condition, some high-priced sideboard or chandelier. They'd talk to my dad for twenty minutes, and all of a sudden, they'd be devoted to some wreck in the back, something they'd have to put all kinds of money and elbow grease in to restore fully. "You'll hate it for a while," he'd tell them, "but then you'll love it more for hating it."

"You okay?" Sharon asks, handing me a bowl of soup. I accept it gratefully, comforted by the familiarity of having Sharon here. She moved in next door three years after my mom moved out, and at first I was sort of terrified of her. She was six-foot-one and wore old baseball jerseys and jeans almost every day, and within two months of moving in she'd built a garage in the backyard entirely by herself. She and my dad argued about tools and cars and politics, but she was his best friend, and she certainly took better care of me than my own mom did.

"I'm all right. Busy there today."

"It always is on Saturdays," she says. "I'll open and close tomorrow so you can stay home with him. The aide's on the schedule for the morning, if you need to get out at all."

"Sharon," I sigh, once I swallow a bite of her delicious soup, "you're saving us."

"Don't be an idiot. It's just soup. Anyways I usually work Sundays."

"Okay," I say, because I know Sharon. If I thank her too much for this food, she'll probably put a laxative in the next thing she makes me, just to teach me a lesson. I shove in a few more bites, set down my bowl on the kitchen table so I can grab a beer.

"Your mom came by for a bit today," Sharon says from behind me, and I'm glad to have my face stuck in the refrigerator at that moment, so I can school my features. I saw my mom earlier this week, at the hospital, and it was awkward as all hell, as it usually is with us. My parents probably had one of the most amicable splits in the history of divorces, despite the fact that my mom left this house and moved straight into the downtown condo of the partner at the law firm where she worked as paralegal. When dad and I went to her wedding, barely a year later, my dad hugged her and shook Richard's hand, and it was basically as if he was seeing an old friend get married, no hard feelings at all. Sometimes, when I'd have my weekly dinners with Mom, Dad would come along so they could catch up. The best thing about that was I didn't have to do much talking.

"That's nice," I say, popping the tab on one of my dad's shitty beers and leaning against the counter.

"Ben. It *is* nice."

"Sure. That's what I said." Sharon gets along fine with my mom too. Actually, everyone gets along fine with my mom. I'm the only asshole around who holds a grudge, and even though I do my best with Mom—I call her every couple of weeks, I always see her when I'm in town—I still feel as tense and resentful around her as I did when I was a kid. "You should get out of here, Sharon. Get some rest before tomorrow."

"Don't tell me what to do," she snaps, but she's wiping her hands on the towel, heading toward the door. "Henry!" she shouts, that big, gritty voice of hers always a surprise that makes me smile. "I'll see you tomorrow. Don't forget to take the stool softener the aide left!"

I wince, and my dad shouts back, "I'll call you in the morning, let you know if it worked!"

She rolls her eyes at me. "Good luck," she says.

I take another drink of my beer and almost grab one for Dad but remember he's off the stuff until he's not taking his painkillers at night anymore. Instead, I get him a glass of water and head into the living room, where he's sitting in his recliner, a TV tray covered in clock pieces in front of him. His left arm, heavy from the cast he'll be in for the next two weeks, is held tight on his abdomen with a sling, but he's tinkering as best he can with his right hand, which is shaky and pale.

"Dad, come on," I say. "Let's put this away."

"Be quiet or make yourself useful," he says, but I take the tray from him anyways, pulling it toward me before I slump on the couch. He grunts his disapproval, shifting slightly in his chair.

"You want to elevate it for a while?" I ask. In addition to the busted elbow and collarbone, Dad shattered his tibia, and his left leg from the knee down is in a thick, black boot, cushioned by some fancy inflatable bags that are supposed to stabilize the bone, which is now home to a titanium rod and a bunch of screws.

He waves me off, and I can see the effort it's taking him to stay awake. Even in the hospital he fought sleep, wanting to stay as close to his longtime routine as possible: asleep at nine, up at five. I had the best luck in the hospital talking to him until he'd dozed off, and I decide I'll do that here too, just to avoid an argument. If I have to carry him to bed, I'll do it, but it'll probably break my heart in half. Seeing my dad—my strong, unflappable dad—in this condition has been a gut check I wasn't prepared for.

I tell him about my day at the yard, give him a report on the slate I picked up today, which, aside from the piece I broke on my call to Jasper, was in great shape, and would probably do a whole roof on a smaller house, a good profit if we get a contractor who's interested. Talking about the yard, I guess, isn't the best way to make him sleepy, since he looks more alert than he has in a few days. I use the conversation as the grease I need to get him up and moving toward the bathroom, talking as much for his sake as for mine. It's less awkward helping him undress and getting him settled on the toilet when I'm talking the whole time, even when I'm standing outside the door, waiting for him to finish up.

Once I've got him in bed, I make him take his meds, and he leans his head back on the pillows I've propped up—upright sleep for the first days after the surgery, the doctor said, and believe me, I took notes. He looks exhausted by all that bedtime effort. "You're not going to have trouble at work, being here?"

"Dad, we've talked about this. It's fine." I sit in the chair I pulled up by his bed before I brought him home. I'm not leaving until he's asleep. I even bought a baby monitor on Thursday night, but I've stowed it under the bed so he won't know.

"Don't use the f-word with me," he says. "I know you're real important over there at your job."

I think about how important I stand to be if Jas and I can get out of this non-compete, if we can break out on our own. "You had some work yesterday?" he asks.

"Yeah, I went to see a possible recruit. She was—not real interested."

"I thought you go around throwing all kinds of money at people," he says, but he's smiling, teasing me a little. "She doesn't like money?"

"I don't think she likes me."

"Can't say as I blame her," he says. "With that ugly mug you got."

"Jealous, old man?" I tease, and he huffs a laugh. I find myself telling him about my meeting with her, but I'm not even focusing on any of the right things. I skip right over the part where I insulted her by assuming she was someone else. Instead, I'm describing her—I'm talking about the goggles she wore over her black-rimmed glasses, the way I could still see the dark, rich color of her eyes right through them. I'm talking about how she was barely as tall as the steel frame she was cleaning, how she wore a too-big lab coat that had the sleeves rolled up into thick cuffs. I'm not saying anything that has to do with a plan.

"Mad scientist," my dad murmurs, and it's good—he's getting sleepy.

"Yeah," I say, but her lab—it was clean, almost freakishly so, when most labs I visit seem in a constant state of disarray. "She's working with lots of old equipment, which she wouldn't have to worry about if she came to work for us. She broke one of her old cabinets while I was there. The thing looks like it was manufactured during the Manhattan Project."

Dad perks up, rolls his eyes toward me. "What'd she break?" Typical, that this is the detail my dad would seize on.

"Storage cabinet, a steel one. Broke the handle off. She seemed used to it—had a piece of rope as a handle for two of the other doors."

"I got handles for one of those at the yard, probably. Those cabinets are a dime a dozen."

I think about this, wondering what Averin would think if I showed up with replacement cabinet door handles as an apology. Rather than, say, me wearing a dunce cap and having read all her published work, which is what she deserves as an apology. Probably on principle I should also email my women's studies professor from junior year and apologize for exhibiting gender bias.

"Hmm," I say, but I notice Dad's breathing is deeper, and his eyes are closed. I lean back in my chair, wince at the loud creaks it makes in the room.

My dad looks so small in his bed, which doesn't make sense, because at six-three, he's still exactly my height, and he's in good shape from working the way he does. I wonder if it's something about being back in this house, about how when I left eleven years ago, I was still so used to being a kid, used to seeing everything, including him, as bigger than me. It's not that I never make it back here—I do, at least twice a year, and Dad comes out to see me maybe once every two years. But knowing I'm going to be sticking around for a while has changed my perspective, I guess.

"Stop staring at me," he says, his eyes still closed.

"Thought you were sleeping."

"I don't want an audience. Go to bed; you're annoying me."

I chuckle—this is my dad's familiar, cheerful gruffness. I stand, looking over things one last time, making sure there's water by the bed, that there's a pillow under his elbow, that his sling is in the right position.

I swallow a sudden surge of emotion. It's hard not to see this fall as some kind of turning point, some kind of moment of reckoning that means Dad and I have to start talking seriously about what happens in his future. He's only sixty, sure, and even though he's got no plans to retire, his recovery from this is going to slow him down.

Thinking about that now, after the day I've had—after the week I've had, really—feels too exhausting, and anyways, I'm no help to Dad if I'm too tired to see things clearly. I flip off the light and head down to my room, resolved to apply the rest of my mental energy for the night to thinking through what I've got going on with Beaumont, with Jasper, with E.R. Averin. Doing a job here will be a good distraction, will help keep me balanced while I take care of Dad.

But I still switch on the monitor and set it on my nightstand, listening to Dad breathe until I fall into a dreamless sleep.

Chapter 3

Kit

Monday night, tired from the weekend of unpacking and a long day of work, I'm alone in the house, eating takeout at my dining room table that's still got a few unpacked boxes stacked on top. It sounds depressing, but for a girl who's never had a place to call home, right now it feels perfect. I'm happily paging through my favorite issue of the city's weekly alternative newspaper, which I've picked up religiously every Monday since I first moved here. This is the best issue, a once-a-year summary that details what locals have voted as their trusted favorites—everything from eyebrow threaders to heart surgeons. I have this dream—it's ridiculous, really—that someday I'll know enough about this place to call myself a longtime local. To be able to recommend my favorite burger joint or mechanic or dermatologist.

Right now, sitting in my historic house in the neighborhood I'd long ago picked out as my favorite, I feel one step closer. I'm a local somewhere! It feels so good that I laugh a little, the sound echoing in the still bare-walled house.

It's the echo that motivates me to get to work on a little more unpacking. Zoe and Greer had been champions all weekend, helping me settle the most important rooms—the kitchen, my bedroom, the bathroom upstairs. But I'd put off the dining room, eager to work on this by myself. In here is one of my favorite features of the house, built-in china cabinets with arched glass doors on top, cabineted shelving below. Unlike the rest of the house, these look like they've been recently tended to—a fresh coat of white paint on each, the shelving sturdy and clean.

But as I unwrap a few of the cups and saucers and serving pieces I have, it becomes painfully clear that these are neither nice enough, nor copious enough, to fill out those shelves. It's not as if I have family heirlooms for this house. Even if such things existed in my family, my dad would've hocked them long ago for money. It all looks a little sad in there, actually, and I'm hit with a stab of nagging doubt. *You should've bought a condo. You don't have anything to fill this place up with. You're not any good at making a house a home.*

It feels a little cold, a little lonely in here now. I wish I could call my brother. I think he might be the only one who could possibly understand how I'm feeling, the growing pains of settling somewhere permanent, but his last email said he'd be unreachable by phone for the next couple of weeks, a refrain he's been using more often than usual in the last few months, ever since I first tried to talk to him about what I want to do with the rest of my winnings. It's hard to think about Alex, about Alex avoiding me because of the lottery, a pebble in my shoe I can't seem to get rid of.

The china cabinets I'd so admired look too stark now, too white. Plus, they've got these modern, stainless steel knobs for handles, an obvious replacement that doesn't fit the aesthetic of the house, deadening all the historicity of those built-ins.

And it's this—musing on my boring cabinet knobs—that makes me think of him. Of the package I received at work today.

Marti, our department secretary, had delivered it when I was taking a late lunch—basically, this means I was stuffing trail mix in my mouth while doing data entry at my desk. Marti is what Zoe calls my BFAW, my *best friend at work*, which is absolutely true, and probably was even when I was a grad student here. There was definitely a dearth of women in my department, but it wasn't just shared chromosomes that drew me to Marti—she was hilarious and gave exactly zero shits about what people thought of her, and had no problem checking the egos of some of the more notorious faculty.

She'd come in, holding out a cushioned manila envelope to me, her eyebrows raised suspiciously. "Mail call. Some tall drink of water brought this to me, asked me to get it to you." She makes the same sound she makes when she eats one of the Reese's cups from the bowl I keep on my desk, a sort of *mm, mmm, MMM!* exclamation. "I got a hot flash looking at him, and he's not even my type."

Ben Tucker, I'd thought immediately, and I'd tried to look casual as I swiped the package from her. My name—at least the name I publish under, E.R. Averin—was printed across the front, but there'd been nothing else to indicate the sender. "Okay," I'd said, setting it down on my desk, which was a mistake, because however well I've kept the secret about my lottery win from everyone I work with, I'm a soft touch when it comes to gossip of the relationship variety, and me not being curious about some hot guy hand-delivering me a package was very unusual behavior.

She'd crossed her arms and opened her mouth to speak, but I'd been saved by the bell, or, at least, by Dr. Harroway sticking his head in my office to tell Marti he'd broken the copier, again. The man does not understand why you can't put staples through the feeder tray, I swear to God. She'd narrowed her eyes at me, snagged a Reese's cup, and mouthed *Later* at me with what was, frankly, a disconcerting level of seriousness.

I'd waited until I was sure she was down the hall, then closed my door to open the package. Inside had been three brushed-brass file cabinet handles, exactly matching the two remaining I had on the lab cabinet, a business card, and a note:

> *These should fit your cabinet—Shaw Walker, 1959. The university used to order all their furniture from them.*
>
> *I was the worst kind of incompetent on Friday, and I am sorry. Currently making my way through your very impressive backlist, Ms. Averin. You will not hear from me or anyone at Beaumont until I have a better, shall we say, "handle" on things.*
>
> *With apologies,*
> *Ben Tucker*

Damn, I'd thought. *Very good apology.*

I'd put the handles on the cabinet before I'd left work, a little huffy, actually, that they'd fit so perfectly. But I'd tucked Ben's note and business card into my jeans pocket.

I take it out again now, wondering how he found file cabinet handles from 1959. Okay, I might also be thinking a little about the way he'd looked standing in the doorway on Friday, his tall-drink-of-waterness, memorable enough that I'd thought of him quite a few times over the weekend.

His handwriting is bold, straight up-and-down, all capital letters, similar to a drafting hand. I trace the tip of my finger over where he's written my name—*Ms. Averin*. If Ben Tucker could find old file cabinet handles, maybe he can tell me where to find old china cabinet knobs. And also I should thank him. That seems like the right thing.

I tap the edge of his business card against the note. I'm definitely making an excuse to call him—but suddenly it's so *quiet* in here. I swipe my phone off the table before I can think better of it. As soon as it starts ringing, I want to hang up, but then remember that a great crucible of modern technology is widely available caller ID. Have to go for broke, then.

"Ben Tucker," he says when he answers, his voice a deep rumble. It seems to scrape me in the same place it had last week, right at the base of my spine.

"Hi," I say, and immediately slam my eyes shut. *Hi* sounds silly, too informal. I clear my throat and try again. "Hello. This is Ekaterina Averin."

There's a pause on the other end, a little longer than is comfortable for a phone conversation. I think about clarifying, maybe explaining that we'd met on Friday, though if I have to do that, this guy's more incompetent than he'd let on—and frankly, he'd let on a lot. But then he says, "Ekaterina," a little slowly—but he's pronounced it exactly as I do, and I'm grateful for that. Mostly people ignore the first part, the quick, breathy *Eh*, and go straight to *Katerina*. "Beautiful name," he says.

"People mostly call me Kit," I say. "Fewer syllables."

"Okay. Kit, then. But I don't mind the syllables."

"I wanted to call and say thanks for the handles you sent. They were perfect."

"Great," he says, but he sounds—I don't know. A little distracted, maybe? That's annoying—you'd think after everything he'd want to make a better impression. "I'm so sorry," he says, and I think he's about to redo the whole apology again. "Can you just—can you hang on one second? Please." It's the *please* that gets me. It sounds how the word is meant to sound—a real plea for something.

"Sure," I say, and expect him to click over to another call. But I hear the phone being set down, the rustling of clothes, another man's deep voice. And I can hear Ben when he says, "Come on, Dad. You need to take one of these tonight." The other man—Ben's dad—grumbles back, and right when I think maybe I should set my own phone down, maybe I'm hearing something I shouldn't, there's another rustle and the phone is muted. I'm both relieved and disappointed.

It's another minute before he comes back on. "I'm sorry," he says again.

"That's all right—I could call at another time. I didn't realize you'd be busy. Well, that's silly, I should've realized that, it's eight o'clock. It's not like you don't have a life." I clamp my mouth shut. Too much. I'm a terrible phone talker.

He chuckles. "I don't have much of one right now. My dad had an accident recently, and he's a bit of a challenge to—you know. Manage."

"Oh," I say, feeling like the worst for calling. About freaking file cabinet handles. "I'm so sorry to hear that. I can let you go."

"No, no—it's all right. He's okay. He had a fall last week, needed a couple of surgeries. But he's okay," he repeats this part a little forcefully, convincing himself, maybe. "I'm in town to help out for a while."

It's my turn to pause, to draw it out. "And to recruit me?"

"Recruiting you is something that came up more recently. Listen, Kit, on Friday—"

"I got your package. And your note. I appreciate the apology."

"Right, okay. Good."

"I'm actually calling about the handles you sent. About how you found them."

He laughs, but I'm not in on the joke, so I stay quiet. "Well. One of the things I'm helping out with while I'm here is my dad's business. He owns a salvage yard on the south side. Tucker's Salvage."

I've heard of it—in fact, I'm pretty sure Tucker's Salvage is in that local favorites paper I just looked through, but I've never been. "And you guys have old cabinet handles?"

"We have everything. We do architectural salvage, so we've got everything from old building materials to antique furniture and light fixtures. Some stuff we restore, some stuff we sell off as is, some stuff we have parts for. Like your cabinet there."

Well, damn if an architectural salvage yard doesn't sound like just the place for someone who's recently bought an old wreck of a house. "Aha. And—can anyone come by? To have a look at what you have there?"

"You have a need for salvaged parts?"

"I do," I say, and my voice sounds a little petulant, a little defensive. What business is it of his, what I need? Maybe I'll try to go at a time when he's not around. He can't possibly be there all the time.

"I'm there open to close pretty much all this week, and would be happy to show you around."

Shit. "Oh. That's very nice of you, but I don't think it'd be right—"

"No expectations. I won't say a word about Beaumont to you, not unless you ask me."

I lean down and touch the plain, boring handle that's currently keeping place on my beautiful, original, built-in china cabinet. I know there's probably antique handles and doorknobs online, but I'm a materials scientist. It matters to me to hold things, to touch them, to feel their weight. I'd rather see this stuff in person before I buy it. "I guess I could come by," I say, but then quickly add, "I'm really busy though. I could come on my lunch hour, maybe on Thursday."

"I'll make time," he says firmly.

Once we've settled the details—when I'll be there, where to find him once I come in—there's really nothing more to say, but I feel a strange reluctance to hang up. It was nice, for a few minutes, to have his voice in my ear. It seemed to dull the echo I was feeling in the house before I called. But that's ridiculous, completely ridiculous and needy, and also inappropriate given that what I'm most interested in from Ben Tucker is for him to leave me alone about his stupid job offer. And that I get to look at his doorknobs, or whatever. So I say, maybe a little more abruptly than is natural, "Thank you very much. See you Thursday," and disconnect.

I open the music app on my phone and turn the volume up loud. Then I get back to the job of making this place a home.

* * * *

When I drive up to Tucker's Salvage on Thursday, I'm resolved to make it a short visit, frustrated that I've spent too much time since Monday feeling flushed and fluttery whenever I'd thought of Ben, at one point seriously considering asking Marti whether I might be having hot flashes. Plus, I feel a little disloyal—is going to see Ben a suggestion that I'm open to his recruiting? The thought has plagued me, and I've not even told Zoe and Greer about this visit, so determined am I to make this outing a mere formality. I've come a little early, having wrapped up my morning work, and I figure that I'm fulfilling another task. I said I'd be here, and I am, and I'll make it quick.

But when you take one step inside Tucker's, you get the sense that there's no way to make it quick. The building itself is probably the size of a football field, and the space that greets me is sort of a large anteroom—there's an L-shaped set of glass cases, the kind you'd see in a jewelry store, behind which is what looks to be an office. All around me are large, gorgeous pieces of refinished furniture, set out to create aisles and alcoves within this large room. Above me hang pendant lights and chandeliers of all types, some of them casting prisms of light on the concrete floors and along the walls. Along one wall—top to bottom—are shelves lined with labeled bins, the sign above indicating that this is where you search for *Hardware.*

I look down at the crystal doorknob I'm carrying, the one I brought from my upstairs bathroom. I'm supposed to find a match for it in there?

It'd take at least a full day to get through this front room alone, and I can see beyond that the warehouse is full up, and I feel simultaneously overwhelmed and intrigued. I want to look around, to explore this place that's

probably full of treasures, but I don't much feel like doing it around Ben
Tucker. I don't think I should betray that kind of enthusiasm in front of him.

"First time here?" comes a voice from behind me, and I jump, almost
dropping the doorknob. When I turn around, I find myself—well, not face
to face, yet, until I look down—with a man in a wheelchair, his left leg
extended and elevated, his left arm held close to his body in a sling. He
has graying hair and kind, blue eyes, and I know right away that this is
Ben Tucker's father. I've thought of Ben's face that much since last week,
which is probably not a good sign.

"Oh, hello. Yes," I say, "It's my first time here. It's—ah. It's big."

The man chuckles, uses his right hand to move the lever that propels
his chair forward, and then extends it to shake mine. "I'm Henry Tucker.
This is my place."

"I'm Kit. This is wonderful," I tell him, shaking his hand and looking
around again. "I had no idea this was here. I came to look for—"

He cuts me off before I can finish. "For my son? You're the one he's
been telling me about this week." He smiles up at me, a teasing glint in his
eye. "Says you're smart, and also immune to his bullshit."

"Oh. Well. I suppose I am," I say, feeling a little proud of myself under
Henry Tucker's regard. "I'm sorry about your accident," I blurt, and then
feel awkward for doing so. I mean, the wheelchair and casts don't make it
any kind of secret, but maybe he doesn't want to talk about it.

He shrugs the best he can, given the sling. "These things happen. It's
just that when you get old, they happen and you're probably going to break
something. You ever break a bone?"

"No," I say. "I'm a pretty risk-averse person. My brother used to make
me wear a bike helmet when I played kickball as a kid."

That makes him laugh, and once again, I feel that weird surge of pride.
It probably feels good to laugh when you've been laid up, and I'm glad to
be the one who's done it.

"Dad?"

That's Ben's voice, echoing from somewhere in the depths of this giant
building, and I feel a spike of nervous energy. There's a *thunk thunk thunk*,
heavy steps sounding on a metal staircase, but from where I stand, I can't
see it. I didn't even realize there was a second floor in here. I immediately
raise a hand up to my hair, smoothing it, and then I straighten my glasses.
I completely fail at not blushing when I realize that Henry Tucker has
caught me primping, but I clear my throat and give him a side-eye that's
meant to communicate something like *don't make any assumptions, mister*.
But probably it does not communicate that. Probably it looks like I have

lint in my eye.

Ben strides in from somewhere deep in the recesses of the warehouse, and—wow. He looks different. The Ben I saw last Friday was the kind of handsome that made you do a double take, a lean, polished, practiced look that reminded you of high rises and fast cars and dimly lit restaurants. But this Ben—this is the kind of handsome that gets you right in the stomach, that makes your knees feel weak. His dark blond hair is messy, a slight curl at the ends, his face more tanned than it had been when I'd seen him last week, his square jawline shadowed with stubble. His gray t-shirt bears a strip of paint across his right pectoral, which—damn. The man has a chest. And shoulders. You could see it the suit, sure, but in the t-shirt, you could *see* it. I picture, for a flash, my hands spread across that chest.

"Hi," he says, and oh, that smile. Like he's genuinely glad to see me. "I see you've met my dad. Who is not supposed to be at work this week." Ben gives a scolding look down at his father, who waves an annoyed hand in Ben's direction.

"I'm renting this baby for sixty bucks a day just so's I can be right here where I can see you, kid," says Henry, tapping the chair with his good hand. "So you don't go selling any of my treasures on the cheap. *Again.*"

"Dad, that was a good sale. You weren't going to get two grand."

"I could've got twenty-five hundred! This sideboard," he says to me, as if we've known each other forever, as if I'm part of these conversations all the time, "you should've seen it. Mid-century modern, teak. Almost perfect condition—"

"One of the legs was missing!" Ben exclaims.

"It was a small fix! I could've fixed that myself, you know. If you had any sense, you could've fixed it." He grumbles this last part, and Ben rolls his eyes.

I am enjoying myself *immensely.*

But then Ben turns his attention on me, and I drop the smile I now realize I'd had plastered to my face as I watched their exchange. "Sorry about this. We're—you know. Adjusting to all this time we spend together."

"That's all right," I say. "I get it." But I don't get it. I can count on one hand the number of times I've spent any extended length of time with my own father. Mostly it was only me and Alex, and I never got sick of him. Now I feel uncomfortable—I'm the awkward plus-one in this comfortable family moment.

"Dad, how about you go back to the office and keep working through those receipts?"

"Oh, I see. You're giving me *tasks* to placate me. Or else you're trying to be alone here with this lovely lady. This reminds me of the time you were in ninth grade and had that redhead come here after school."

"Jesus, Dad. You are the *worst*."

I laugh, in spite of myself, and then put a hand over my mouth. Ben getting knocked down a peg—by someone who so clearly loves him, where the feeling is still light and jovial—makes me feel a little less nervous here in this big space, in his space. Henry winks at me and rolls away, the mechanized sound of the chair fading as he maneuvers himself around the glass cases toward a back room.

Then it's just me and Ben, and he looks down at the floor and runs a big hand through his hair, shaking his head. "You're early," he says.

"Um, sorry?" I say, but I don't really mean it.

"I wanted—I was going to be down here to greet you. My dad, he's— he can be a lot."

"He's great. He makes a good first impression."

Ben's answering smile is crooked, sheepish. I like it so much that I can't help but smile back.

"So," he says, taking a cautious step toward me. "Hardware."

He leads me back toward the wall of bins, steps away to pull over a ladder on wheels, the kind you see in one of those big-box hardware stores. "Why don't you start by telling me what you're looking for?"

"Well," I say, twirling the crystal doorknob in my hand, "Now that I see how big this place is, I guess I'm looking for a lot. Doorknobs, cabinet handles, switch plates, that kind of thing…to start."

"To start?"

"I'm hoping to find things that are, well, if not completely consistent with, then at least adjacent to the time when the house was built." I twirl the doorknob in my hand again, welcoming its weight, and clear my throat. "I bought a house. Very recently."

He gives me a long look, and I imagine this is not welcome news for him, given his recruiting goals. It's probably much easier to recruit someone who hasn't just purchased a home in an area you're trying to get them to move away from. I expect, maybe, that he'll be less helpful now, because let's face it, I'm sure part of the reason he's had me come out here, despite his promise not to talk about Beaumont, is to show me that he's worth listening to.

"Congratulations." He extends a hand toward me, palm up, and I have this odd moment of confusion, wondering if I'm supposed to shake it, and then he says, "Maybe you could let me have a look at that."

Right. I hand him the doorknob, watch him as he turns it over in his hands, furrowing his brow in concentration. "This is Russell and Erwin," he says, as though I'm supposed to know what that is. "Do you have other pieces like this in the house?"

"Some. It's a bit of a hodgepodge, honestly—there's things like this, and then some, you know, really cheap replacements here and there."

"When was the house built?" He's pushing the ladder down the wall a bit, climbing on the first step to look down at me before going any farther.

"1870. It's a row house, Queen Anne style."

He nods, and I can see his mind working. "This is probably original," he says, climbing up the ladder and reaching toward one of the uppermost bins. I see a flash of his taut stomach and avert my eyes. Reluctantly.

When he comes down, he's holding a bubble-wrapped package, and he sits on one of the lower steps of the ladder so that now I'm looking down at him as he unwraps it. He holds it out to me, an exact match for the doorknob I brought in. Those eyes. "Wow," I say, and am mostly referring to the doorknob.

"I've got a lot more up there. These show up a lot, probably from houses in the area built around the same time as yours."

"That's—that's great. I didn't really count, though, before I came in. And there's all the other stuff I should look for too. I should've made a list, I guess." *But I thought I was coming here as a formality,* I don't add.

"Well, we could start by checking out some of the things that match the style of the house. My dad organizes things mostly by period, so that shouldn't be too hard. And Russell and Erwin did all kinds of hardware, so we could start by looking there…"

And he's off, moving down the wall with his ladder, pulling out bin after bin to set on the floor, and I should say that this is all too much trouble, that I can't stay long, that I'll have to come back another time. But it's easy to get pulled into this orbit, and before I know it, I'm kneeling down on the hard concrete floor, carefully unwrapping filigreed switch plates that Ben says were manufactured right around the same time as the doorknob, and would I also want to look at some hinges? *Hinges?* I think. *Hinges sound awesome, as long as you're still within smelling distance, because frankly, you smell amazing.*

It's like this for a few minutes, Ben crouched next to me, occasionally bringing me another bin, and I feel a giddy sense of excitement about the possibilities of this place, about what I could find here for my house. At one point, I unwrap a hinge—a hinge, who knew?—that features a delicately carved leaf pattern, and in my surprise at the work put into something so largely unseen, I say, "Look at *this*," and hold it out to Ben.

There's this moment where our eyes lock, and we're both smiling, sitting here like we're two kids who found a buried treasure, and I forget all about Ben being such an *idiot* last week.

And then the yelling starts.

Chapter 4

Ben

In general, I don't scare easy. When I was eleven, I found a copperhead snake under my sleeping bag during a school camping trip, and I just backed away slowly and found the ranger who was supervising, keeping an eye on any person who might head in that direction and put themselves at risk. When I was seventeen and stood in front of a judge who was going to make a decision that was going to affect the rest of my life, my hands were as steady as granite, my voice, when I spoke, came out clear as a bell. Even when I got the call about my dad two weeks ago, I'd managed to stay calm, to ask the right questions, to make all the necessary arrangements to get back here.

But when I hear my dad yell, I think my stomach is leaping out of my body, if only to jam itself back down my throat, settling somewhere in the vicinity of my chest. I spring up from where I'm crouched on the floor, dropping a handful of switch plates behind me, and tear toward the office, my mind racing. Surely it's impossible for me to have so many thoughts in the twenty or so seconds it takes me to reach him, but it seems like I have them all: *Has he fallen, how bad is it, will there be more surgery, could it be a clot, a stroke, how could I have let him come here—*

I barely register Kit's presence behind me, not until I barrel through the office door and stop in my tracks, Kit's small frame bumping against me with an *oof* of surprise. My dad's still in his chair, looking as hale and hearty as he has all day, but he's shouting, banging his one good fist against the window overlooking the scrapyard, his face getting redder by the minute.

"Dad, what the—"

"Get outside!" he shouts to me. "Get out there and get that kid!"

I take a step toward the window, and outside across the yard I see a short, skinny kid dressed in tight black jeans and a black hooded sweatshirt, taking bricks off a pallet and hurling them at my dad's truck, the one he mostly keeps on site.

"Shit," I mutter, and hit the pavement.

Jasper and I run most days back in Houston, early mornings where we meet up to strategize, so I'm quick. But it's still weird that with my loud boots on the gravel, the kid doesn't try to flee until I'm almost on him, and I barely have to make a few more strides before I snag him by the back of his hood and pull him toward me, wrapping my other arm around his shoulders to keep him still. I don't realize he's still got a brick in his hand until he drops it on my foot.

"*Fuck,*" I groan, lifting my foot against the pain while tightening my grip against his struggle. "You need to settle down, kid."

He elbows me in the gut, but I'm prepared for that; I've made myself a wall against him. "I'm fucking serious. I don't care how old you are. I will lay you out if you keep this shit up."

"Fuck you," he spits, but he's slumped over a bit now, the fight gone out of him. I loosen my grip and keep a hold of his elbow, turning him to face me. Jesus, he looks young, maybe thirteen? His hair is an unnatural grayish-purple color, swooping over one eye, and his jawline is pocked with acne. I feel like hell, manhandling a kid this way, even if he is a little criminal. And anyways, that look in his eyes—that stubborn, angry stare—I know that look. I *was* that look, back in the day.

"Name," I say.

"I'll tell it to the cop." His voice is unusual, slightly accented, and when he turns his head away from me, avoiding my stare, I catch a glimpse of a hearing aid wrapped around his ear, peeking through his longish hair.

"You'll tell it to me," I say, resisting the urge to raise my voice, "or else you get no help when that cop gets here."

"River."

"This isn't a western, kid. What's your first name?"

"That *is* my first name," he says, and boy, he does not sound happy about it. "And you can save your fucking jokes. I've heard them all."

"I'm not in a joking mood." My dad's truck is a mess, the right fender smashed to hell, the windshield shattered but still in place, which is more than I can say for the passenger side window, which I'm guessing is in pieces all over the front seat. "What the hell did you think you were doing?"

"That's pretty obvious, genius."

Damn, the attitude on this kid. "Well, I'd say what's obvious is that you're looking for some way of getting caught out here, since it's twelve fucking forty-five on a Thursday afternoon and you're making a hell of a lot of noise right outside an open place of business." *Shit,* I think. *Was the remark about the noise insensitive?* Honestly I don't know why the fuck I'd care, since this kid is trying to destroy my father's property. "Let's go," I say, and tug him back toward the entrance. I have no idea what I'm going to do when I get him there. I'm not really sure whether a citizen's arrest is an actual thing or just something Dad used to yell at me when he caught me stealing the Oreos from the top shelf of the pantry.

Kit and my dad are out front, her standing behind his chair. I don't want her to see me dragging a teenager around by the elbow, no matter what I've caught him doing—I probably look like a brute. So I pause and look at him, wait for him to meet my eyes. "You run and I'll catch you," I say, dropping his arm and nodding toward where my dad is. He falls into step beside me, and I see him discreetly reach up both hands and adjust his hearing aids.

In front of my dad, he's not nearly so defiant. He's shoved his fists into the pockets of his sweatshirt and he's not looking at any of us. "What now?" he asks miserably, and I'm already feeling pretty bad about that when I look up at Kit and find her watching him, sympathy and kindness written all over her face. So I *did* look like a brute then. I resist the urge to kick my toe at the gravel, feeling more like a teenager than River probably does.

"I called the police," she says, surprising me. But she's still got eyes on River. "Maybe before they get here you can explain yourself?" She doesn't say it with any malice or judgment—she says it as if she's begging him, really, to have some good excuse for destruction of property, to have something to say that would justify us letting him off the hook. I think if Kit looked at me that way, I'd probably confess sins I'd never even committed, just so I'd be doing what she wanted—she's that persuasive, at least to me. In the warehouse, I'd wanted to bring her every single piece of hardware we had so I could see the look she got on her face when she opened something new.

But River doesn't say a word, and her face falls a little in disappointment.

"I guess he wanted to smash something up," I say, and it's paltry, but the best defense I can muster on the kid's behalf. It's ridiculous that I'm even attempting this, but it's not all that hard for me to feel kinship with an angry adolescent.

Dad scoots his wheelchair forward a little and peers up at River. "What happened to your hair?" He doesn't ask this so much as exclaim it, his voice a boom in the awkward silence.

River's eyes snap to mine, in question, like we're in this together. I shrug. "Better off answering him," I say.

"I—uh. I dyed it."

"Speak up!" Dad shouts, and I wince. This is awful.

"I *dyed* it," says River.

"On purpose?"

River only raises his chin in defiance. My eyes meet Kit's over Dad's head. The corners of her eyes are crinkled in amusement, but her mouth is set tight, fighting off a smile. I resist the urge to smile back. I've still got to play guard dog here, at least until the cops arrive.

"On purpose," River answers.

"Well, it looks ridiculous," Dad says, shifting in the chair. "And you're trespassing. And you busted up my truck. What are you going to do about that?"

River shrugs, and my dad rolls his eyes. "Reminds me of you," he says to me, and Kit really does smile then. *Fuck.* "You got a job?" Dad asks, the force of his stare so strong that River looks back at him. Dad repeats the question.

"No," says River. "I'm only fourteen."

"What's that got to do with anything? I had a job when I was eight." I have to duck my head to hide my laughter. Dad may have worked around the salvage yard when he was eight, but he says this as if he worked fifteen hours a day in a factory. Any minute he'll break out the *I had to make my own toys!* speech he used to give me when I'd tell him what I wanted for Christmas. He did not actually make his own toys, I found out later from my grandpop.

When the police cruiser pulls into the lot, I get a little shiver in my stomach. Jesus, I wish this hadn't happened. It's ridiculous, but I still feel sick as hell whenever I see a police car, in any context. River has kept his *I-don't-give-a-shit* posture, but his skin is pale beneath his weird swoop of purple-gray hair, and I feel so sorry for him that I head over to the cop first.

Lucky for River, it's Sergeant McKay, an old buddy of my dad's who'd been more kind to me than I'd deserved a number of times. He tells me he's seen the kid around before, but never in this kind of trouble, so he'll probably have to take him in. When I follow him back over to where River stands, I feel the kid's dread as if it's my own. I can still smell that police station, if I really think about it. My heart's still hammering with adrenaline, maybe a little residual fear, and I can barely focus on the tense, awkward exchange going on between McKay, my father, and River.

Kit saves me by speaking up, asking whether McKay needs her to answer any questions—she tells him she's really got to be on her way. I see River's eyes slide to her, a little desperately, like maybe she's his one source of protection here, but just as quickly he's looking back down at his boots.

"You go on ahead, ma'am," McKay says.

Kit nods and turns to my dad. "Mr. Tucker, it was very nice to meet you. You have a lovely—uh—store?"

"Come back any time," he says, but he's obviously preoccupied, and I step forward to walk with Kit toward her car, a shitty little silver hatchback. This answers one question relevant to my purposes for Beaumont—Kit's probably not getting paid what she's worth.

"So," she says, but breaks off, her brow furrowing in concern as she looks back at River.

"He'll be all right," I say.

"I mean, I know he totally wrecked your dad's car, but he looks so young."

"Yeah. McKay is a good guy, though. He'll make sure he's taken care of."

She nods, hitches her bag higher on her shoulder. "Thanks for showing me the hardware."

"Well, you're walking out empty-handed. That's no good. You'll have to come back."

The right side of her mouth lifts as she looks at me. Kit's eyes, when you're inside with her, look as dark as her hair, nearly black, but out in the hot sunlight, they remind me of the black cherry stain that used to be my favorite to refinish with back when I worked here—under all that darkness, they're a rich, warm, glowing brown.

"We'll see," she says, and I can see her making the effort to pull herself back in, to become the person I met last week—or maybe she's making the effort to see me as the person I was last week. Her shoulders have stiffened, her chin has raised a fraction. But it's the effort. It's the effort that tells me I've made progress.

Progress about Beaumont, I have to scold myself, as she drives away.

* * * *

My dad and I argue the entire way home, even as I'm helping him maneuver his goddamn gigantic rented wheelchair through the back door. "This house," I say, my teeth gritted, "isn't suited for this thing." I've got to push him over the threshold so slowly to avoid scraping up against the woodwork, and this kind of care is so physically antithetical to the frustration I'm feeling right now that my knuckles have turned white around the handles.

The day went downhill after Kit had left, things with River taking an unexpected turn that started this whole argument with Dad. And there'd been the frustrations of keeping up, of reminding myself of some of the more obscure tasks that needed done around the yard—I'd forgotten that you had to rotate which vents you opened on the second floor throughout the day. I'd forgotten that Thursdays were the days Dad did some online bidding through a private auction site, and he'd had trouble doing it himself one-handed. I couldn't tell how much of my anger at Dad was about what he'd done, or about how overwhelmed I'd felt at everything I'd had to do.

How did Dad handle this on his own, even when he was well?

Sharon's in the kitchen again setting plates out on the table. She looks up at me, and then down at Dad, and says, "I'm guessing today didn't go so well. You went back too early, Henry."

"Don't tell me what's what, Sharon. I've heard it for the last fifteen minutes from this one here," he says, thumbing back at me.

"Oh, yeah?" I say, finally clearing the door enough to shut it behind me. "Why don't you tell Sharon here about the new project you've taken on? Or, wait, that *we've* taken on, since I'm sure I'll have to handle it most days, with you in that condition."

Sharon crosses her arms and looks down at Dad, who at least has the decency to seem slightly chastened. "All's I did," he says, "was help a kid out who's in trouble."

I roll my eyes. "We caught a kid busting up Dad's truck today, and Dad set it up with Sergeant McKay that this kid can work off what he owes at the salvage yard. Starting *tomorrow*." It's this part of the thing, the timeline, that's really getting to me. It was a fight yesterday when Dad announced he was having a chair delivered that would let him come along to work. It was a fight this morning when he kept trying to do work that would risk injuring him again. Now we're adding something else to the plate?

"Oh, Henry," Sharon says, turning toward the oven and peeking in. Jesus, something smells good. I need to hurry up and stop being so mad so I can stuff a bunch of food in my face and get on with the evening.

"It's not going to be any problem," Dad says, wheeling up to his place at the table. "Three days a week, and only in the afternoons. His mother's got him doing some summer school in the mornings."

"You aren't getting it, Dad. Getting you better is the most important thing. You've got doctor's appointments, physical therapy—"

"I said I'd get all that done!"

"No, *I'll* be getting it done. I'm the one handling the yard, getting you back and forth to your appointments. And now I'm the one that's going to be keeping an eye on a teenager with an appetite for destruction."

"He's exaggerating," Dad says to Sharon. I want to bang my head against the nearest wall. Instead, I cross to the sink to wash my hands, then start grabbing silverware for the table.

"Go on and sit down, Ben," says Sharon. "I'll take care of it."

"No, Sharon. You're doing too much for us here already," I say, but as I'm setting out forks, she pulls out my chair and points to it.

"Sit," she says in that way she has, the way that makes you worry you're about to get slapped on the back of the head.

So I sit, and my dad and I stare at each other across the table.

It's lasagna, and thank God for the calming powers of cheese, because I start to relax over the course of the meal. Sharon's taken up talking to Dad about how she's changing out the electrical panel in her house, which distracts him, and soon enough the stress of the day feels a little less close, a little less compressing. I stand and clear plates, now that Sharon's too wrapped up in debating the relative energy-saving virtues of sub-panels to stop me. While I'm loading the dishwasher, though, Dad wheels over and says, "Listen, I'm sorry about the kid."

I slide another plate in, not sure what to say. River is going to be a complication, but if I'm even a little honest with myself, I didn't want to see a kid that young going in either, and if I'm *really* honest with myself, I know damn well why my dad made so much of an effort. A kid like River gets us both where it hurts. "It's fine, Dad. We'll work it out." When I look back at him, I have a quick flash of him in a courtroom, fourteen years ago, holding his old ball cap in his lap, turning and turning it as he watched me come in.

"All right, you two," Sharon says, shuffling us into the living room. "There's a ballgame on in fifteen minutes that we're watching, so long as Henry can stay awake."

"I can stay awake," he grumbles, and that's all it takes for us to be good again, because if there's one thing Dad and I do well, it's forgiving each other.

* * * *

I skip the ballgame in favor of holing up in my old bedroom with my laptop, catching up on work I have for Beaumont. I missed a conference call today that I'd wanted in on, a monthly reporting session on new contacts we'd sussed out for the polymers division, an email marked "Urgent" from Jasper. He's pressing me for a progress report on Kit already, and I send him a quick reply, *Still doing my research.*

Last weekend I'd tracked down all of Kit's publications and had been working through them as best I could in the time I had at night. Jasper's better at the science itself—he double-majored in biochemistry and chemical engineering—but what I am is a good reader, good at picking out details that people overly focused on the data might overlook. When I've made it through eleven of Kit's articles, I know the detail that matters most.

Like most other publications in her field, all of Kit's papers are multi-authored. In the eleven I've read so far, and in the six more I have yet to get to, she's never listed first. The seven most recent papers, I suspect, are written by the same person—that may seem as if it'd be impossible to tell, but there's a quality to these papers that reads differently than most journal articles in the field, a sort of wry, subtle humor that glances at the limitations of other research without directly engaging. The common denominator in all seven?

E.R. Averin.

Even if I wasn't sitting up in my bed with these papers, tangible evidence of her genius all around me, I'd know Kit was smart as all hell, just from being around her at the yard. She had a way of looking over what I'd brought her, a cataloguing curiosity in her expression, and I got the sense she didn't miss anything. Whatever she was holding in her hands got her full attention, and she devoted her senses to the task—she'd run the edge of her fingertip along the filigree of a hinge, tap one of her short nails against a switch plate while she held it up to her ear, then she'd look it over, again, as if memorizing it. It was transfixing, the attention she paid to small things, and a little disconcerting too.

I'd bet all my savings on Kit having done the lion's share of the work that's represented in these papers, which means she's seriously overqualified for the work she's doing now. I know I need to draw her out a bit, to get her talking with me about what she does—it's not going to be enough for me to exploit my connection to a salvage yard that she apparently finds fascinating. I need a way in to her work life—I need to get her talking.

I pick up one of the papers published a couple of years ago in one of the more obscure metallurgy journals out there. This one had presented detailed experimental data on samples of high performance steel, the kind Beaumont uses to manufacture some of its parts for the oil industry. Last year, though, our steel division had started looking into some new research from *Nature* that was supposed to change the kind of composite steel we were using. I do a quick search and pull up the article, scanning it quickly. The details don't matter to me at this point, because I suddenly know how to get Kit talking.

I grab my phone off the nightstand and text her.

Read a paper in Nature that says there's an eight-unit cell crystal in a high performance steel

I tell myself I'm only going to allow myself a minute to wait for a response. If there's nothing, I'll go out and watch the game with Dad and Sharon, see if she's replied later. But it's maybe thirty seconds before I see that she's typing, her texts coming in quick succession, the first what I can only guess is a text-expression of outrage:

!!!

I'm smiling already.

But their samples were electropolished, and they didn't know the position of the particle in the foil. How could they know if it was on the surface or in the middle or on the bottom of the foil? They didn't account for the natural oxide layer that forms on the sample, either. They were probably measuring the crystal structure of a surface layer and not of their particle.

Two texts and I'm way outside my pay grade in terms of the science, but I don't care. I'd read her texts about crystal structure all night—I'm that excited she's talking to me. Another one, even before I start typing a response:

They did all this fancy modeling to back up what they saw on the microscope, but their model is incomplete. They didn't account for the position of the crystal, the surface layers, amorphous layers, or the shape of the particle.

I'm typing back, telling her I've read her paper from two years ago, the one that's dealing with the same stuff as the *Nature* paper, but before I press send her next message comes.

Come back to my office Monday night, 7 pm. I'll show you where they went wrong.

I resist the urge to stand on my bed and pound my chest with victory. Instead, I text her back that I'll be there.

That'll be okay, she writes, *with your dad and everything?*

It's a kindness, I think, that she checks about this, and I feel a strange gratitude for it and for her, for the distraction of these last couple of hours, immersing myself first in her world and then in this conversation. *I'll make it work*, I type back. I stand from my bed, stretch my arms over my head. I need to get out there and get Dad ready for bed. I need to get some rest myself, especially since I'm going to spend a good portion of tomorrow dealing with a sulky teenager. I'm tucking my phone into my back pocket when it chimes one more time.

I know what you're doing, Tucker, it says. I just like showing people my microscope.

I'm grinning, staring down at my phone, but I don't respond. For the first time since I've met her, I think maybe I've got her on the ropes.

Chapter 5

Kit

In the days since I sent Ben a text inviting him to my office, I've alternated between barely acknowledged anticipation and loudly proclaimed dread. When I meet Zoe and Greer for breakfast on Sunday morning, I blurt out the whole story—the fact that I called him about knobs, the visit to the salvage yard, the very fetching way he looks when in pursuit of a young criminal.

"You're screwed," says Zoe, stuffing a huge bite of whipped-cream-topped waffle in her mouth.

We're at the Outcast Diner, one of our favorite spots in the brick-streeted historic district that's adjacent to my neighborhood. Unlike at Betty's, hipsters haven't really caught on here, and other than the three of us, the clientele is mostly of the golden years variety, especially since we come early. We sit on mismatched wood chairs around a small table that Zoe's stabilized with a stack of sugar packets. All around us, on the brightly painted yellow walls, are framed paper placemats that customers have drawn on over years. It's a bit run down, the Outcast, but the coffee is hot and the maple syrup is real.

"I'm *not*," I say, taking a bite of my oatmeal.

"But you *wish* you were," says Greer, and Zoe cracks a laugh, so impressed by Greer's unexpected dirty joke that she gives her a high-five. Greer blushes, because she's adorable.

"You guys aren't helpful. Why did I *do* that? Now I'm going to have to talk to him again, and this time about his stupid job offer."

"Who cares?" asks Zoe. "You're not going to take it, so let him say his piece, and move on." She leans forward and raises her eyebrows. "And by 'move on,' I mean let him touch your…"

"Oh my *God*," I say, and put my forehead on the table. "It's not like that," I mumble, but it is completely like that, in my mind, at least. What was an annoying attraction before became a full-blown crush on Thursday when I'd seen Ben at the salvage yard. There's this—sweetness to him, which I'd noticed not only in his interaction with his dad, but also in the way he'd watched that kid he'd chased down, this leashed protectiveness he'd had for a vulnerable boy who had done him wrong.

And then he texted me about crystal structure.

Zoe is right, of course—not that I'll say that to her—but I know that this really comes down to letting Ben give me his pitch under less tense circumstances than we were in during our first meeting, and politely declining. It's not as if he's the first person I've had to speak to about work. I'd fielded offers from private firms before—nothing as big or prestigious as Beaumont, but still. I'm as sure now as I was then that I'm in the right place, professionally and personally, and so it shouldn't bother me to say that to Ben when the time comes.

And yet it does, somehow—or at least it bothers me to have to confront the idea at all. I went to therapy for long enough to know at least part of what this is about. I don't like change. I don't like the *idea* of change, and however convinced I am about my life now, it's easy for me to feel threatened by any alteration to it. Even the last night I spent in my shitty apartment, I'd cried myself to sleep, thinking of the years I'd spent there, the longest stretch I'd ever had in a single place. I was almost grateful that I woke up with a dead stink bug on my pillow. At least that eliminated most of the nostalgia.

"Sweetie," Greer says, patting my forearm. "You're getting oatmeal in your hair."

I raise my head with a sigh, grab my napkin to clean up. Greer has mercy on me and changes the subject. She's not sure about the classes she's picked for the fall semester, and pretty soon Zoe and I are both wrapped up in talking it through with her. When we stand and gather our things an hour later, I'm lighter, more at ease—it's what we do for each other. It's what I'd never give up about these women. "What's on for the rest of the day, Kit?" asks Zoe, slinging her purse over her shoulder.

"I'm going to try and do some work outside," I say. "Weeding. Either of you two want to help?"

Greer's got a family event, and Zoe bluntly says, "You must be crazy. I just had my nails done." She leans in to give me a hug. "Send us before and after pictures, though."

I spend the rest of the morning in the small backyard, which is weedy and overgrown. But unlike most of the house, there's nothing so bad about it that I can't tackle it myself, and it feels good to be out in the sun, slathered as I am with SPF 50, digging out the worst of the weeds that have grown up around the small garden shed that, same as everything else on this property, has potential to be great, but right now falls somewhere between vaguely shabby and completely dilapidated. Once I've cleared an entire side, I can picture the bed I'll dig out along the edge, the lavender or maybe salvia I'll plant, the cream paint I'll do the shed in. Maybe I'll add small shutters on the windows on either side, add window boxes too. Less haunted house, more dollhouse.

But this dollhouse isn't getting built in a day, and I'm starting to feel a bit like a wilted flower in this heat. Still, I feel good, the accomplishment helping to wear off more of the Ben tension I'd felt this morning. Tomorrow will be *fine*, piece-of-cake fine.

I get myself a glass of ice water and take it out to the front stoop, plopping onto the top step in exhaustion. I try to be out here a bit every couple of days, to wave at my new neighbors as they pass by, getting a sense of who's who on the street. Betty was my neighbor when I lived above the bar, so there was an easy camaraderie. I want that here—the kind of neighbors who'll watch out for your place but who also might invite you over for a cookout. Things are a bit uneven on my street, sure, with some houses fully renovated and some in grim disrepair, but since my place is on the grim side of things right now, I don't judge.

So far I'd met three different homeowners, including Jeff and Eric, across the way, whose house looks as if it was redone for one of those HGTV shows. It's both perfectly current and perfectly historical. When their front door opens and Jeff steps out onto his porch, he gives me a friendly wave and I smile back, warmed by even this small cordiality, this growing sense of my place here. But the feeling cools when I see a tall, broad figure step out from behind Jeff, who turns back to shake the man's hand.

Ben Tucker's hand.

Well, *shit*, I think, standing too fast from where I'm sitting, my water sloshing a bit over the top of the glass to land on my feet. My street is narrow, so my abruptness is enough to catch his eye, and when he looks across the way at me, there's a few seconds where we're just staring at each other, that weirdness that happens when you see someone out of context, like running into a teacher at the movies. But then I see a broad smile spread across his face, and my stomach flutters in answer.

He and Jeff exchange a few more brief words, Jeff giving Ben a firm pat on the shoulder before Ben heads down the steps. I think for a minute that he might get into the truck that's parked out front, but instead, he tucks his hands into his pockets, glancing quickly down the one-way street before crossing to me. He stays on the sidewalk, though, looking up at me, a sheepish quirk to his mouth. "Fancy meeting you here," he says.

"You're not following me, are you?" I say, and his eyes widen immediately, his smile dropping.

"*No.* God, no. Sorry—I delivered some stone to Jeff and Eric this morning. They're customers. I swear to you. I'm not—"

I smile down at him, charmed by his sudden concern. "It's okay. Small world, though, or else your salvage yard gets around."

His shoulders slouch in relief. "We do all right. These older neighborhoods, we get to a lot. And I went to high school with Jeff." He nods up at the house. "So this is your place, yeah?"

I look back at it, stupidly, like I'm checking to see if it's still there, or if I'm at the right address. But really it's just me trying to make sense of how my house must look to Ben. Probably not good. I think of Zoe's shithole-to-ten scale. I am still definitely at a four. "Yep," I say, turning back to him, conveying a confidence I don't really feel. I try to redirect. "How's everything? Your dad, and…that kid?"

"Oh," he says, looking a little surprised I've asked. "They're okay. My dad's busting my balls, of course. You saw a bit of that." I have to laugh a little at the way he says this, the genial embarrassment he has at his father's teasing. "And the kid—his name is River—he's around. My dad's making him work off his debt at the salvage yard."

"Really?" I'm more glad than I thought I'd be to hear this. The boy's pale, stricken face had come back to me more than a few times since Thursday. "That's—that's really good."

"It's really good for him, probably. It's not so good for me, since I can barely get him to say four words sequentially. I think on Friday he called me 'mister,' but maybe sarcastically? He makes me feel like I'm a hundred years old."

I snort. "That's a teenager for you, I guess."

"This is…" He pauses, looks up again at the house, then restarts. "This is a really beautiful place."

"You don't have to do that," I say. "It's not beautiful now, but it will be."

"You forget that I have a unique appreciation for old things," he says. "It's in my blood."

Ben is wearing almost the exact same thing I saw him in on Thursday: t-shirt, dark blue this time, faded jeans slung low on his hips, a brown leather belt that's so worn I can see cracks along the edge from where I stand, and shit-kicking worker's boots that are covered in dust. He's got a ball cap on, low over his eyes, his dark blond hair curling with sweat around the edges.

"Would you want to see inside?" I blurt, and then, in my mind, I dump the entire glass of ice water I am holding over my head. What is *wrong* with me? First I ask him to my lab, now my house? I certainly hope my vagina doesn't have a mind to issue invitations, but honestly the way Ben looks, it's not entirely unlikely that she'll speak up in the next five minutes or so.

His grin should look cocky. It probably *is* cocky, but somehow he wears it well, without malice or intention. He looks—*pleased*, like, what a treat to be asked, what fun to have a crazy almost-stranger invite you into her hot mess of a house to look around. I start to tell him that it's no big deal, he doesn't have to, but he's already opened the wrought iron gate and is coming up the walk, up the steps. "Yeah. I'd love it."

I turn back to the door and for the first time recall that I am currently wearing a pair of old hiking boots, cutoff shorts derived from my most unflattering pair of jeans, and a Harry Potter t-shirt. My hair's too short for a ponytail, so before I'd gone outside I'd pinned some of it back with a few old barrettes. My glasses are probably dirty too, so pretty much I look very similar to the way I did on the playground in elementary school. *Awesome*.

I open the front door and wave Ben in ahead of me so I can quickly remove the offending barrettes. I need a mirror to know if this was a mistake or not, but I do my best to ruffle my hair and make some kind of sense of it.

"Wow," he says, standing in the living room, his hands set low on his hips. He reaches up to take off his ball cap, runs a hand through his hair. It's sticking up everywhere, and this comforts me, given that I'm probably rocking something similar. "This is great. Look at this woodwork," he says, crossing to the fireplace. I'm ridiculously pleased he's noticed this, because it's my favorite thing about the house too.

"It needs a lot of work, I know."

He nods. "Quite a bit on your hands," he says, but I appreciate that he's not patronizing me about it. He walks around, peering under windowsills, crouching to look at the back of radiators, reaching up to run his hands along doorframes, the plaster walls. I'm transfixed watching him, how tactile he is, how focused. It's the hardest thing not to think about what those traits might be like in another context.

I take off my glasses, swipe them quickly on my t-shirt. When I put them back on, he's standing under the archway between the dining room and living room, hands back on his hips, looking at me. "You do need a lot of stuff for this place."

"Yeah. Probably going to give your dad a lot of business, huh?"

He smiles, crooked. "Let's make a list," he says. "Of all the hardware you'll need."

"Really?" This is what I've been thinking about doing since Thursday, but the prospect of doing it with someone, someone who knows a lot about it, makes it seem achievable, exciting.

"Really," he says. "Grab a notebook. We've got work to do."

* * * *

I make a quick stop in the bathroom to pick off the worst of the landscaping that's stuck to me, grab a notepad, and head back out to where Ben is. We start in the kitchen, probably the worst room in the house, me rushing to tell him I'm planning a total redo, happening this fall according to my contractor's timeline.

He gives me a quizzical look, as if he's about to ask a question, but he seems to rethink it, and taps at a bay of lower cabinets along the house's back wall. "These are probably the oldest ones you've got in here," he says. "Maybe 1930s? Too bad about the paint on them." He crouches down, opens a door to peer in.

"I'll probably have to scrap everything. So this room will probably look—you know. Not historical. Maybe I don't really need hardware for this room."

Ben stands and shrugs, looking around. "Maybe. But you could look for antique cabinets. It's a hassle, but possible. Even if you don't do that—those older cabinets are pretty small, not really suited for newer dishes and stuff—you could still get some nice antique drawer pulls, knobs. That stuff'll go on most of the newer cabinetry, no problem. A light fixture, maybe?" He's turning in a slow circle, nodding as he looks around, as if he can see it in his mind. I want to be in there, to see what he's seeing.

"Okay," I say.

"This wall behind the stove was probably exposed brick at some point. You could try and go back to that." Exposed brick? I *love* that idea. I wish I'd thought of it myself.

It's this way for the next hour, Ben and I moving through each room in the house. He's curious, asking lots of questions about what I know about the house, what I like about it, what I wish were different. He knows a lot, but he's not a know-it-all, and he's got a good sense of humor—he laughs easily, especially when I tell him I put a padlock on the door to the crawlspace because of spiders. But it doesn't feel as if he's laughing *at* me. He's just—I don't know. Enjoying me.

We're up in the empty extra bedroom, the one I want to turn into a home office at some point, and I'm sitting on the floor, cross-legged, making a note about how many doorknobs I'd need in here—two for the small closets, one for the door to the room, when it hits me that Ben has been here for a while now, and this can't be what he had planned for the day. "Oh!" I say, a bit more exclamatory than I'd intended. "What about your dad?"

He looks down at me, and I almost lose my breath—he's so *tall*, so good-looking. I *hate* it. "What about him?"

"Well, I mean, aren't you needing to get back to him? Or to work? I can't believe I've taken up so much of your time."

"I'm off-duty for the afternoon. Sharon thought my dad and I could use a break from each other today, so she's with him at the yard while I took care of this delivery and got some errands out of the way."

"Oh. Is Sharon your stepmom?" I don't know why I'm asking, why I'm so curious, but—I *am*. I want to know things about Ben, maybe because he's here in my house, getting to see something so important to me. I want to even the scales.

He laughs. "No. She's my dad's neighbor." His brow furrows for a minute as he looks out the window. "Then again, I guess she has qualities of a stepmom. Or of a mom, really."

"Your mom is—?"

He turns back to me, leans against the wall with his hands in his pockets. "She's around, sort of. My parents got divorced when I was nine, and my dad and me, we're a team, I guess. My mom's not a bad person, but she wasn't much up for being a mom. So I've pretty much always been with my dad, even before the divorce, I guess. Sometimes he messed up, and I definitely did, but we made it work."

"That sucks about your mom." Before I can think better of it, I add, "My mom wasn't around, either. She left when I was, I don't know, three months old, I think? Maybe a bit before." I keep my eyes down, scribble some nonsense in the margins of the notebook, look busy.

"That's young," he says, and though he hasn't moved, I feel somehow that his posture has changed, that it's coiled a bit more tightly than it was before.

"Yeah. My brother was around, though." That sounds sad, sort of *Oliver Twist* sad, so I say, "I mean, you know. My dad too." That's a can of worms I can't believe I've opened here. It's bad enough I've mentioned my freaking absentee mother. I've always been the kind of person who talks, who opens up, who tries to connect with people, somehow. But bringing up my father?

That's pretty new, even for me. He's such a source of terrible guilt and sadness that I hardly ever talk about him, not even to Zoe and Greer, who just think he's kind of garden-variety distant, instead of so screwed up and damaging that I have to make actual, professionally coached efforts to control the way I interact with him. Thinking of it, it strikes me that I'd loved the salvage yard so much in part because I'd liked seeing Ben and his dad together. "I think we've got everything in here, right?"

He doesn't say anything for a few seconds. He's still looking at me, but I'm determined to let this pass. "Right," he says, and brushes past me out the door, to the bathroom.

I stand and follow, feeling awkward and inappropriate. It's one thing for someone to be okay answering questions about themselves, but it's another when you make them feel weird by laying out your own crappy baggage when they didn't ask for it. But when I get into the bathroom, Ben's already talking. "This toilet runs."

"Better go catch it," I mumble, unable to stop myself.

He's smiling as he lets out a dramatic groan. "That is the *worst*, Kit. That's a dad joke, right there."

"You know, what's everyone got against 'dad jokes'? I think they're funny. A toilet running? That's funny! Just picture it."

"What? You're not supposed to picture it. It's just a pun. What is wrong with you?" He's laughing now, and it's so infectious that I start laughing too. "I can't believe a person as brilliant as you laughs at a toilet running joke."

He called me brilliant. I can feel the way my smile changes, from laughing pleasure to flattered surprise—and he's watching it, watching that transformation. I'm standing so close to him in this small room that I can see an answering change in his eyes, and is it—is that something like *hunger* there, something new I haven't seen in his expression before? He's got one hip leaned against my sink, looking down at where I stand in the doorway, neither of us laughing now, and I think, *oh, what if I pushed up onto my tiptoes here, what if I lean right into him*, and then Ben straightens and says, "I'm going to fix your toilet."

And thank God for that, because I was maybe a hair-trigger away from making a fool of myself, stunned stupid by that dimple and those blue eyes. "Oh, no, that's all right," I say quickly. "I'll do it. I'll watch a YouTube video or something."

"It'll take five minutes." He's already headed downstairs, probably trying to politely flee from the doe-eyes I just served up. He returns from his truck with a toolbox, and sure enough, he does fix it in five minutes, betraying no embarrassment about that—*moment*. Instead, he fixes the light switch in the guest room and also resecures the window air conditioner that I have in my bedroom, which he says is about to fling itself off the ledge.

But when the afternoon grows late, he checks the time on his phone and says he really does have to be on his way. He's picking up pizza for him and his dad and Sharon, and since he does the bedtime routine with his dad, he doesn't want to push it too late. Weirdly, I feel a pang of loneliness when he describes these plans, which are probably pretty exhausting for Ben. But since I was planning on eating a Lean Cuisine and online shopping for bathmats, pizza with a convalescing salvage yard owner sounds pretty great.

I thank him, maybe a little profusely, for his help. He waves me off, all handsome nonchalance, but—it was a really *kind* thing for someone to do, and even though over the last hour I'd decided that moment in the bathroom was only a blip, nothing to think twice about, now, out here saying goodbye on the porch, my thoughts go right back there. *Here's this nice guy, this hot as hell guy, who spent the afternoon with you.*

"You're not going to get much time to miss me," he says, his voice low and teasing. "Seven p.m., tomorrow. You, me, and that microscope you like so much."

Oh. I feel my face heat a little in embarrassment. *Brilliant*, he'd said, but of course he'd said that, this guy who's recruiting me for a job I don't want. I'd forgotten, a little. I'd forgotten the guy I met in the suit, the corporate guy with all that undeserved confidence, replaced him temporarily with the Ben who makes toilet repair look sexy. And it's deflating to think I'll have to deal with the other guy tomorrow.

"Right," I say, a little flat, and he seems to hear it, or maybe I just imagine that little shift he does with his shoulders.

"Looking forward to it," he says, heading down the steps. At the bottom, he pauses, looks back up at the house. "It really is a beautiful house, Ekaterina."

I'm too dumbfounded by the compliment, by the way he's said my name, to respond. So I wave and duck back into the house, more than a little confused about the day.

Chapter 6

Ben

I'm on the second floor lining up a bunch of shutters that came into the yard this morning. It's dusty, frustrating work; they usually come in a huge heap, and so you've got to keep an eye out for matched sets. Dad is downstairs teaching River how to run the cash register, which I think is the worst idea in history, so my being up here is probably a smart move. Anyways, I'm distracted, worked up thinking about Kit—about getting to see her again tonight, about the time I spent with her yesterday.

Liking a client is an asset, really—some of my best recruits are also good friends, people I've kept in touch with as they transitioned into their new posts. The way I recruit, it's essential that I get to know people, figure out what's important about their lives aside from the work. But the way I feel around Kit is a liability. Yesterday when I'd seen her outside Jeff and Eric's house, I hadn't thought at all about Beaumont. At first, I'd mostly thought about her legs in those shorts, but even after I'd schooled myself not to look (much), I'd focused on her house, how I could help her with it, what things she could use from the yard, what stuff I could fix easily for her.

Even I knew that was entirely counterproductive. If anything, I should've been warning her about how she was just as likely to bankrupt herself on such a big project as she was to actually enjoy herself planning it. I should've been telling her things that would force her to imagine a different life, one in Texas. But the problem was, it didn't feel like she was a job. It felt like she was someone I wanted to know more about, independent of work. It felt like she was interesting and smart and a little goofy, and she was sexy as all hell, and if I'm not mistaken, there'd been a moment there, up in her bathroom—a moment where she'd looked at me as if she was interested, and I don't mean in the job I'm offering her. I'd resorted to toilet tank repair to stop from kissing her.

My phone rings as I'm slotting in the last shutter, and I'm a little grateful for something that'll get me out of my head. Jasper's voice is impatient, excited. "I need a few minutes. Can you take a break?" We haven't talked much by phone since the day he'd called to tell me about Kit, and I knew he still felt a little guilty about railroading right over everything I was dealing with here.

"Yeah, sure," I say, taking a seat on one of the grated metal stairs headed down to the first floor. "What's all that noise?"

"I'm at Waterwall," he says, referring to the uptown park in Houston not too far from our office. It's only two p.m., so if Jasper's out of the office, something's up. "Your dad's doing all right?" he asks, but it's quick, a formality.

"Sure," I say. "What's up?"

"You remember Hamish Beck?"

"Hell yeah," I say, smiling. Beck was an early recruit for Jasper and me, a German scientist working for a car manufacturer. He was a total nightmare, making insane demands for his contract, one of which included that Jasper and I each drink three tiny bottles of Kuemmerling before he signed. But he was also a genius. He'd gone to Beaumont's Rochester division and designed a catalytic converter that made millions for the company. He'd left Beaumont last year when his contract was up, going out on his own to make money hand over fist for himself, but it'd still been one of our most profitable jobs.

"He's in Houston for meetings, so I met up with him last night."

"So you're hungover, right?"

"Oh, man," Jasper groans. "You don't even know. I'm never drinking again."

I laugh, sorry to have missed it. Hamish was a pain in the ass, but he was hilarious too. Somehow he could always cajole you into doing crazy shit, like singing "Angel of the Morning" at a karaoke bar in Munich.

"Anyways, he wants to invest. I told him about what we've got planned, and he's on board. He says he can name at least fifteen people, right off the top of his head, who could use the kind of representation we'd be offering."

"Oh," I say, with what I know is decidedly less enthusiasm than I should be showing right now. This feels so far away from what my life is at the moment. It's not easy for me to slip right back into thinking through all the complexities of what Jasper and I have planned. "That's great."

"Great? It's fucking incredible, Tucker." He goes on, telling me more about what Hamish is willing to do—and the thing is, it *is* incredible. Hamish is offering enough to fund our entire startup, whereas Jasper and I had been planning for at least a few months after leaving Beaumont to pursue investors. We've both been shoring up our accounts for unpaid time. With what Hamish is offering, we could put all that right into the running of the company.

"You think he's for real?" I ask.

"I'm sure of it. And there's something else too. I think we could get Kristen to come with us."

Now *that*—that's big news too. Kristen is one of Beaumont's attorneys, specializing in H/R law, and we've worked with her in putting together several of our employment contracts. Kristen would be a huge asset to our startup—she knows the law inside and out, and she's great with clients, easy to talk to and completely above board.

"Holy shit, Jasper. How'd you manage that?"

"You're not the only one who can recruit," he says, but there's maybe a little something in his voice. Jesus, I hope he's not sleeping with her. Seeing as how Jasper has never kept a relationship going for longer than three months at a time—not that I have room to talk—I don't want things getting complicated. "I'm not sleeping with her," he says, because I guess my silence spoke volumes.

I take a deep breath, run a hand through my hair. "Things are really moving on this."

"Yeah. So, listen. We need out of that non-compete. Greg is set on Averin—she's part of a really small pool who has what we need, Tucker. Where are you on that?"

I'm at the place where I've seen her in shorts. Where I've noticed that I like the smell of suntan lotion on her skin. Where I've fixed her toilet so I could hang around her for longer.

"I'm on it. I'm meeting with her tonight at her lab."

"Good," he says, and the confidence in his voice, which would normally be a compliment, is an albatross around my neck. "You've got to make it happen."

"Yeah," I say, standing. "I told you, I've got an in with her tonight."

"What's she like, anyway?" Jasper says. This is why I'm better at the actual recruiting. Jasper's taken over a week to ask this question, when really, to be good at this, *what's she like* is the first question you ask.

I surprise myself by not wanting to answer. I don't want him to know anything about her. "You know," I say. "Typical mad scientist." This feels so disloyal. It makes me physically restless to have said it. I thunk the side of my fist against one of the shutters I've slotted in place. But I know that it's Jasper to whom I owe my loyalty; it's to this plan we've been developing for the last few years. It's not as if I'm trying to ruin Kit's life. I'm trying to give her a high-paying job doing exactly what she loves.

I've got to get my head straight before tonight.

* * * *

Kit's not in her office when I arrive a few minutes before seven, but she's stuck a note on her door with an arrow pointing down the hall and what looks to be a hastily scribbled: *Ben, I'm in room 006.*

It's dismal down here, more so than it was upstairs in the lab—even though there's no windows to let in outdoor light anyway, somehow being here when night is falling makes it seem darker still, more institutional. I make my way down the hall and knock on room 006, and after a minute or so Kit opens the door, her smile wide and excited.

"This is going to be *great*," she says, but then she looks me over and frowns. "Oh."

"What?" I ask, looking down at my jeans and t-shirt.

"I thought you'd be wearing—you know, your suit or something?"

"Well, despite our first meeting, Kit, I don't generally want to wear that stuff unless I have to."

She waves a dismissive hand. "I don't care about that. It's just that you'll probably be cold. We keep the temperature low in here," she says, thumbing over her shoulder. I notice for the first time that she's got a bulky, wrap-around sweater on over her clothes. "Wait here."

She comes out of the dark room she was in, letting the door shut behind her, and hustles down to her office. When she comes back, she's carrying a purple sweatshirt that she holds out to me. "Uh, I don't think we wear the same size," I say. That's an understatement. I am huge compared to Kit, to the point where in my dirtiest thoughts I've wondered whether I'd crush her if I ever got her into bed.

She rolls her eyes. "It's a large."

"A women's large?"

"It's unisex," she says, shaking it in my direction. "You're not worried about your masculinity, are you?"

I widen my eyes in mock outrage. "I'm man enough to wear purple," I say, taking it from her and tugging it on. *Tugging* is really the right word here, because this thing is tight all over, especially across my chest and shoulders. I'll probably lose circulation. "This can't be a large."

She has the decency to try and stifle her laugh.

"Does it make my biceps look huge, though?" I joke, flexing theatrically.

"Oh my God. You're an idiot." But she's laughing, those dark eyes bright, crinkled at the corners.

Focus, I scold myself, remembering what's on the line here.

Before she reopens the door, she turns to look up at me, her expression serious. "Have you ever seen one of these before?"

"Seen a microscope? Sure."

She shakes her head. "I mean *this* kind of microscope. A probe-corrected scanning transmission electron microscope."

"In person? No. I've seen images of our microscopy labs, though." In my car, I've brought some of those images, plus lists of all our microscopy equipment, a lot of which I've memorized so I can tell Kit about it if she asks. Her eyes brighten again. She looks so excited to show this to me.

"Okay," she says, as we walk into the anteroom—it's basically a small, dimly lit office, with a set of cabinets and countertop along the back wall and the microscope's LED screen and control panel dominating most of the room. I know enough to know that the microscope itself is behind the door in front of me, and that Kit will manipulate it and watch her images appear from here. "So," she says, pointing to a seat distractedly, and I sit, eager to watch her. "First things first, before I take you in there to see it. The Titan—that's what we call it—allows you to look at anything from 1000 times magnification to *millions* of times magnification. You can image anything from cells to individual atoms. It's incredible." I'm keeping up, but then she says, "You can also use it to manage or measure chemical composition with electron energy loss spectroscopy."

"Uh, right."

"Don't worry if that doesn't make sense right now." She takes out a diagram of what I assume is the inner workings of the microscope and sets it on my lap, wheeling her own chair closer to mine, so that our knees are almost touching. I can smell her shampoo, herby and yet sweet, and—I really need to pay attention. She gives me a brief but—to my mind—still damned complicated explanation about the basic parts of the microscope, how it works, and I impress myself by being able to make enough sense of it to ask a few questions. When I do, she seems to relish it—she does this little bounce in her seat that I find completely distracting.

"So the *Nature* article," she says, and it takes me a minute to remember what she's talking about, to remember how I goaded her into this. "The authors used a high angle annular dark field mode."

"That sounds awesome. Like something from *Star Wars*."

She rolls her eyes. "It's not awesome! I mean it is, but—okay, remember what I told you. The probe on the microscope is focused to a point and then rastered over the sample. The probe hits an atom, and the electrons scatter." Here, she clenches her fists and the spreads her fingers wide, "scattering," I guess, and I can't help but smile at her enthusiasm, at how absorbed she is in explaining this to me. "In a high angle scattering, the way they did it, you're collecting only electrons that hit heavy atoms. But in a structure that contains a high concentration of light atoms such as oxygen, carbon, nitrogen—a lot of information can be lost if you only look at heavy atom scattering."

"Uh-huh."

"*Plus*," she adds dramatically, "since the probe is focused to such a sharp point, the scattered intensity can change as you change the depth of focus of the probe." She looks up at me. "If you make a probe joke, you have to leave."

"I didn't say anything!"

"I sensed it. I sensed the probe joke. I have to show this machine to undergraduates all the time, and you can't imagine the probe jokes I get."

I drop my eyes. "Okay, I kind of wanted to make a probe joke."

She shakes her head, smiling, but continues. "The *Nature* authors were going for maximum contrast, but they're only looking at essentially one layer of atoms. If you want to see more, you have to take a focal series. You have to change the focal point in relation to the surface of the material in order to get a full picture of the volume of the material. It's—okay, say you have a stack of pages. If you only take one page out and look at it, that doesn't tell you what's going on in the rest of the book, you know?"

"Yeah," I say, nodding, because actually, the metaphor helps. Probably I should ask her to go back to the beginning and explain it all that way, but honestly, I like hearing her talk so much jargon. I like how fast she's going, how her body is moving in all these subtle ways—the shifts in her seat, the motions of her hands—as though she's trying to release all the energy she contains.

"And then, there's the sample." From the counter, she takes two tiny Ziploc bags, each with what look to me like very similar minuscule, thin metal disks. But no way, she explains, and for the next ten minutes it's all about the ferromagnetism and sample polishing and the focused ion beam system she thinks they should have used. "This kind of sample," she says disdainfully, holding up one of the bags, "is going to make it like you're looking through a bent mirror and trying to describe the way someone looks."

Kit then explains to me the way she prepares her own samples. "How long does it take?" I ask, and she gives me such a wide smile that I feel my heart trip over itself.

"Well, most people would maybe take two, two and a half hours to do this. But I'm really good. I can do it in one." She flushes, and then says, "Not to sound arrogant or anything."

"You don't," I say. "You sound amazing." And I mean it. She does sound amazing. I've met a lot of scientists, spent a lot of time talking with them about their work, but Kit has this—I don't know—*joyful* quality about the way she talks about it. She loves the science—that's as clear as a bell.

Over the next hour, she takes me in to show me the microscope itself, which reminds me of one of those free-standing panic rooms. It's a big gray box taller than I am, lined with sound absorbers and dotted with various temperature controls that Kit shows me. Then she shows me how she sets up the beam direction, how she changes the magnification. It's interesting in and of itself, the rational part of me knows this. But I also know I'm finding it so interesting because it's *her* telling me, because I feel as if I'm learning some of the most important stuff about her by being here. When I'm sitting next to her at the control panel, watching as she brings up various images on the screen—to me, they're just white polka dots on a black background—I feel strangely close to her, in a way that I know isn't good for the job.

"So, Kit," I say, pulling myself back on course as she's narrowing her eyes at a new image she's brought up. "How come you're down here doing this work at…" I look down to check my watch, "eight thirty p.m., instead of, you know, during work hours."

"Oh," she says, half-distracted, absorbed in her image. "During the day, I'm doing tech stuff, helping other people with their experiments, or doing repairs on the scopes. And I do some instruction for classes too, when I'm needed. So my days are really pretty busy. But after hours I can get a lot of this really cool stuff done on my own." She pauses, looks sideways at me, suspicious. She knows right where I'm headed with this.

"You should have this kind of access all the time."

"I *do* have access," she says, looking back at the screen. "I like how it is here—how I can be involved in a lot of different parts of running the machine. I'm good at experiments, but I'm good at tech stuff too. I'm good at repairs, and I'm good at teaching."

"Right, but—the stuff you're doing here, this has real application potential." I point toward the screen. "You're figuring out what makes this sample a strong metal, right?"

"Right," she says, leaning back in her chair and rotating to face me. "So?"

"We—well, the metallurgy division at Beaumont—we want to know that too. We want to know why that metal is so strong so that we can engineer a metal similar to it, one that's not going to corrode at a high temperature, or when it's wet. You can find that. You can help us build a new fan blade in a turbine engine, or a new..."

"I know that," she says, interrupting me. "I know there's applications for what I do, obviously. But that's not what I'm interested in. I'm interested in the basic science. I'm not interested in having my agenda set by a company's product line. Obviously I'm not against it if my research finds its way to an application stage, but I'm not interested in being the one to put it there."

"But what if you were promised the kind of freedom you're talking about? What if you were working with a team big enough that you could do your experiments, and someone else would take on the business of application?"

She shakes her head. "It doesn't work that way. There's too much interference."

"Kit, you're surrounded by interference here. That's what you just said. You're working on other people's projects, you're showing other people the ropes, you're *repairing* stuff..."

"But I *like* that. I enjoy being a part of other people's projects. Dr. Singh and I—"

"Right, Dr. Singh," I say, finding my stride now. "He's P.I. on nine of your papers, yes?" She looks caught off guard, and I press right on. "I read them all. And you know, I'm going to venture a guess that you're doing an awful lot of Dr. Singh's work."

"Don't you imply that," she says, her response angrier than I'd anticipated. "Don't imply that he's taking some kind of advantage of me. Dr. Singh and I work really well together. He taught me everything. He gives me opportunities that I wouldn't have had because I don't have the PhD, because I'm here as a lab tech. He trusts me completely. He trusts what I know and what work I can do. I'd do anything for him," she says, and snaps her mouth shut.

That's a revelation I can use—her loyalty to Singh. But I'm going to hold it in reserve. I don't want to go there yet. The room feels close, warmer now, even though I'm pretty glad about this purple sweatshirt still. "I don't mean to offend you," I say, gentling my voice. "But if you want those opportunities, why didn't you get the PhD? Why are you here as a lab tech? Kit, you're fucking brilliant, seriously. You could be P.I. on any one of those papers." An idea strikes me. Greg said he didn't want a PhD, but as a bargaining chip, he might relent. "If there was a funding issue for the PhD, Beaumont has job-sharing programs. If you came to work for us, you could start work on a PhD at UT…"

"I don't want a PhD. If I'd wanted one, I would've gotten one. But you don't seem to understand that I'm perfectly happy here. That I'm not chasing something bigger—"

I hold up my hands, feigning surrender. "I understand. But you're good enough that the world's going to chase you, Kit. You have to know that. And I'm only here trying to give you some information, trying to let you see a different version of this." I gesture around the room. "Let me tell you about Beaumont. If you've got no interest at all, then what's the cost of looking?"

"My time," she says bluntly, but there's that look in her in her eye again, that little pulse of fear.

I offer up a crooked smile. "But really, Kit. How bad can it be, to have a little extra time with me?"

She takes me in, suppressing a smile, then rolls her eyes to the ceiling. "*Ugh.* Your *face.*"

"But no suit this time, right?" I ask, gesturing to her purple sweatshirt.

"You can walk me home," she says, already starting to switch off knobs. "That's how long I'll give you to talk about Beaumont, okay?"

"Okay," I say, but I feel like I've just won the Kit lottery.

* * * *

I waste a good amount of my walking time talking about hot dogs, but it is entirely worth it.

When we come out of the basement's building, it's muggy, but clear. I can even see a few stars up there past the city lights. Kit tries to beg off having me walk her once she realizes I have my car, but I tell her we're both going to need the exercise once I take her to eat.

"Eat? It's nine o'clock! Too late to eat."

"It's going to be worth it, I promise," I tell her, leading the way through some of the campus paths until we emerge at its edges, where the university's neighborhood intersects with Shaftesbury Park, a small, run-down neighborhood that always managed a little charm with its food carts. "Behold," I say, spreading my arms wide, "the Wiener Cart."

"Subtle," she says, smiling at me.

"I don't know if that's its real name. I don't even know if it *has* a name. But this is what my dad and I called it. I checked with him to make sure it was still here before I came tonight. Only reason to come near campus, in my opinion, unless you're trying to make the case to a genius metallurgist who's wasting her talent."

Pretty much Kit is ignoring me at this point. She's already stepped up to the cart and I'm fairly sure she just said "hot dog me" to the guy working. I admire her adventurousness, and the fact that she gets pickled peppers on hers. I get the same, pay for our food, and we're on our way again.

"I already knew about the hot dog cart," she says, chewing.

"Shit! I thought I was giving you some of my expert knowledge here. You teach me about probes, I show you the Wiener Cart. There's a symmetry in that, if you think about it…"

"Oh my God. First the probe, now this. And you made fun of my toilet joke!"

We head toward her neighborhood, Kit making an occasional moan of satisfaction, and I decide that I am, despite all the knowledge Kit has dropped on me in the last two hours, actually stupider than I was when I began this day, if I thought watching Kit eat a hot dog was a good idea. I keep my eyes determinedly ahead, trying to find a way to start up a meaningful pitch, but it's taking a minute for my brain to stop ignoring my body.

"What was it like growing up here?" Kit asks, interrupting my thoughts. The question catches me off guard. This weekend, Kit had seemed a little jarred by the brief foray we took into personal things, and though seeing her at the microscope today had showed me more about her than any interaction we'd had yet, we hadn't talked about anything other than her work.

"I mean," she continues, "my friend Greer grew up here, so she's told me a lot. I was only making conversation."

God, this woman. She is fucking *adorable* when she gets shy. "Where'd your friend grow up?"

"The west side of town. Cherry Hill."

I nod, wiping my mouth. "That's a pretty nice area. Good schools out there. I grew up not too far from the yard, on the south side. It's kind of an older suburb now, most of the houses built in the early 1980s. Guess that probably doesn't seem so old compared to a historian like you, though." She smiles over at me, and I take another bite of my hot dog so I stop thinking about how pretty she is.

"I'm surprised you didn't grow up in a house like mine," she says. "Wouldn't that kind of thing be perfect for your dad?"

"I think it's sort of the same as what they say about contractors, you know? Their own houses always need the most work. We've got a lot of old stuff around the house, but I don't think he wanted to do much restoration of his own."

"I can see that."

"Plus he's not a great housekeeper, so it was easier for us to have a small place. And one that had a built-in microwave. Not much of a cook, either." We stop at a crosswalk and I almost reach a hand out to guide her across, but stop myself. *This isn't a fucking date*, I scold myself.

"It must be hard, what you're doing," she says, as we reach the other side. "Taking care of him."

"It's not too bad." And the truth is, it's not. There are definitely bad parts—we're past the sponge bath stage, thank God, but Dad still needs help in and out of the shower, especially with the damned garbage bags we have to put over his casts, and it's still a big punch to the solar plexus when I see him get tired so easily, when his good hand shakes from the fatigue of overcompensating. But I like being around Dad, around the yard. I always have, even when I was a young asshole and it seemed like I didn't. "It's the least I can do," I say. But that's a little too much information, so I take the last bite of my hot dog to keep from saying more.

"You mean because he raised you?"

"Sure," I say, once I swallow. *Redirect.* "Where'd you grow up?"

"Ohio," she says, her voice flat.

"The whole state?"

"Mostly the northeast corner. It was cold and snowy, and that's about it."

I sneak a glance at her, and she's balling up the wrapper from her food, looking down. "You know, if you want warm weather, Texas—"

She looks over at me, scowling, but her eyes are laughing. "You're shameless."

"Listen, Kit," I say, taking her trash and tossing it and mine into a nearby can. "I know the weather's not something that'd get you to Texas. When I first came to you, I'd been told you were good, that you were a top recruit. But tonight, seeing you work—you're incredibly talented, exactly the kind of mind my company needs. The opportunity you'd have there, the equipment, would be unlike anything you've seen before."

"Is this your pitch?" she asks, arching a dark eyebrow.

"It's not. My pitch involves a lot of things—a virtual tour of what your lab would be. A conference call with the people who'd be your team. A review of the salary package that includes a very generous bonus structure, with stock options. A chance for you to be able to ask all your questions, and for me to answer them. This is just me telling you"—I clear my throat before going on—"as your friend, that you should consider Beaumont."

We walk for a bit in silence, getting close to her house now, and I know I won't have time to actually go through this stuff with her, but somehow, this feels right, what I've done here—Kit's eased up around me, even when I'm talking to her about this, and that's major, given the way I've been striking out up to now.

"Are we friends?" she asks, stopping in front of her gate. She adjusts the bag she has resting across her body and looks up at me. The streetlight casts her dark eyes in gold, making it look like there's fire behind them. I've entirely lost my train of thought.

Again.

"I think we are," I finally say. "I mean, I fixed your toilet. I wore a purple sweatshirt in front of you. Also my breath probably stinks right now. So I don't know. I think it's the real thing, Kit."

She rewards me with another smile, then looks toward her door. "I guess I should go in," she says, but she sounds reluctant about it. "If we are friends, maybe you'll help me out if I come to the salvage yard again?"

"Absolutely." This will be another excellent opportunity for my father to embarrass me, but still, the more time I have with Kit, the better.

"Okay. You help me with—you know. My knobs and hinges." She breaks off here to give me a quelling look, and I chuckle. "And I'll listen to your pitch. The whole thing—the virtual tour, the stock options, whatever." She offers up this wavy, all encompassing gesture, which suggests she's not going to take any of it all that seriously. "But it doesn't mean I'm interested, okay?"

"Sure," I say, and she serves me another one of those stern looks, a *don't try and handle me* stare. There it is again, that feeling: I want to kiss her so bad that I can feel it in the palms of my hands, at the backs of my knees.

I watch her go up the stairs, make sure she gets into her house safely. She waves at me through a panel of sidelights flanking her front door. It feels—I don't know. It feels *sweet*, like I've just had my first date with her, like I'm hoping she'll go in there and call a friend to talk about the great guy she's met. But I know, I *know* that's not what this is about.

I pull my phone from my pocket, swipe my thumb across the screen. *I'm in*, I text Jasper, and make my way back to my car.

Chapter 7

Kit

It's Thursday morning and I'm at my desk, clicking through a set of images Ben Tucker sent to my personal email—over thirty-five photos and three videos of the microscopy lab at Beaumont's Houston division. When I'd first seen the email on my phone, I'd told myself that I'd look more closely when I got home. I didn't want to bring up an email about a job offer on my work computer. But then I'd happened to see one of the thumbnail images, and—well. An FEI color *and* spherical aberration corrected scanning electron microscope? I can't be sure, having never been much into the stuff myself, but I'm pretty sure this is how people who are tempted by pornography feel.

Ben hasn't added any commentary to the message—probably he figures the pictures do all the talking, and I guess they do, because the lab at Beaumont looks incredible. It's not just the equipment, either—this is the look of a lab that has a professional, scientifically trained cleaning staff, and it's the look of a lab that has zero cash flow problems. Over the past few days, since Ben visited me here at work, this has been his strategy, mostly. It's not him that does the pitching. Instead, he sends me this sort of thing—pictures, but also papers that have come out from Beaumont's team, an annual budget report for the metallurgy division that looks sizable enough to run a small country, and, probably most convincingly, a link to a TED Talk from one of Beaumont's lead software engineers, a petite woman named Kim-Ly Nguyen who completely owns the room, describing her work on developing programs for remote surgical procedures. I don't know much about software other than what I have to know for the running of the scopes, but it doesn't matter. It's compelling to see someone in corporate science be so engaged, so connected to the *work* of what she does.

It's not that Ben has left himself out of the picture. On Tuesday, I'd gone after work to the salvage yard, planning to spend maybe an hour getting started on the list of hardware we'd drawn up. But one hour had turned into three, mostly because Henry had offered to take me on a tour of the whole place. We'd made our way through the expansive space, Henry wheeling along at my side, talking happily about the different "zones," and as it turned out, my favorite was the same as his, the area toward the back that was lit by vintage chandeliers and light fixtures that Henry himself had restored. Eventually, Ben had joined us there, explaining that he too had been trained to do some of the lighting work, and I'd been transfixed by learning about all the different chandelier parts. The space was warm from all the electric light, the prisms casting ripples of rainbowed pattern along the walls. Ben had enthusiastically described—in more detail than I would have been able to provide—my house to Henry, who'd leaned forward in his chair, nodding, as though this was a really important issue to him. "You don't want to be a slave to the restoration," Henry had said, looking at me. "You want historical pieces, okay, but don't think everything has to be from the same era. You pick stuff that catches you, that speaks to you. It all has a story. It doesn't have to be a story from the same time period."

"Kind of how I can see you making eyes at that mid-century pendant light," Ben had said. "It'd go great in your foyer." Then he *winked* at me. And it didn't even feel sleazy or awkward. It felt the same as pretty much everything else Ben did, which meant that it felt charming and sweet and more arousing than it had any right to.

It was easy to be friends with Ben. That was the problem—he made you feel so welcome, as if nothing at all was an inconvenience or an intrusion or a waste of time, even though I could tell he had his hands full with his dad and the salvage yard. When I'd called him yesterday to tell him I wanted to buy that pendant light, he'd offered to bring it over to my house later, once he'd taken his dad to PT. I'd demurred, making my spin class excuse, but the truth was, I'd really wanted him to come over. I didn't even really care if he had an ulterior motive at that point—I'd just wanted to *see* him.

I was right now wearing the purple sweatshirt, for crying out loud. Because it still *smelled* like him.

There's a loud knock on my partially open door, and I jump in my seat, quickly closing the browser window. It's Akeelah, one of Dr. Wagner's graduate students, her brown eyes wide and frantic. As soon as I see her face, my senses awaken to the dim register of the microscope's warning alarm from down the hall.

"Dammit," I say, and hustle down the hall after her.

Five minutes later, and I'm standing next to the Titan, my hands on my hips, my shoulders slouched in frustration. "Well. Someone's definitely dumped the column."

"It was Akeelah," says Todd, Dr. Wagner's other grad student, and *ugh*. Fucking Todd.

I give him a wary look. "Are you guys running this experiment together?"

"Yes, but..." Todd begins, but I cut him off.

"It was both of you, then. Get a grip, Todd. You know better than that. You're on the same team." Akeelah is looking at Todd in such total surprise that I'm almost sure he's responsible for this, but it's not my job to get in the middle here. I'll try to talk to Akeelah later, when Todd isn't around—I've been in her shoes, surrounded by mostly male faculty, mostly male students, and you learn some pretty hard lessons about the way things operate.

I lean in and have another look—I'm guessing someone impatient took out the sample rod without fully closing the ball valve. I'm probably going to have to take apart the chamber, realign the valve and door, and put it back together. Then I'll have to go through the pretty tedious cleaning procedure for the column. It'll be a day or two of work to do the repair, and a day on either side to get the microscope shut down and restarted. I let out a gusty sigh. I'd hoped to get in here myself this weekend for some scans, but that's not going to happen now.

"Dr. Wagner needs these results by tomorrow," Todd says, his tone impatient.

"Not going to happen," I say. There's no way to do this work more quickly. If Todd paid attention to anything about the scopes, he'd know this.

"We could use the Tecnai," says Akeelah, referring to one of our other imaging microscopes. "We don't really need something so high resolution." I give her a grateful smile. Akeelah is smart, flexible, a quick thinker. She's been here since she was an undergraduate, and I trained her on most of these microscopes.

"Or we could get a faster lab tech," murmurs Todd, his arms crossed over his chest.

Nope, I think. *Nope to this guy.*

"Out," I snap, pointing to the door. "You're out, Todd. Your colleague has given you a good idea to solve your problem. I'd suggest you listen to her. I'm sorry you're frustrated, but I run the show down here, and I'm going to spend my next two work days solving a problem you caused. If you think I'm not doing my job, you can talk to Dr. Wagner about it."

It's sad, but I'm used to the Todds of the world. He's as smart as anyone who's managed to make it into a doctoral program in a pretty specialized field, but he's way too self-congratulatory about it for his own good, and he doesn't have any respect for what makes the knowledge in his field possible. He doesn't respect the equipment, or the people who keep it running. He's flippant and disdainful when it comes to reviewing the work of people who have come long before him. If I'm being honest, before I'd met Ben Tucker, it was the Todds of the world who I pictured as working at places like Beaumont.

Todd shuffles out, and Akeelah stays behind for a minute to say her apologies, which I appreciate, but it's unnecessary. I get it—stuff happens when you're running experiments, and even though I'm frustrated about how this might derail my schedule, fixing the scopes is part of my job, and I don't mind the work. And Todd can go complain to Dr. Wagner if he wants. I know I've earned the respect and admiration of every faculty member here. I know they need me.

But damn if I don't think, for a split second, about those pictures on my email.

* * * *

When I go after work to pick up my new light, I'm feeling a bit defensive, a bit off my game. Wagner did come down to the microscope later, and though he clearly didn't buy Todd's version of things, he did ask whether there was any way I could speed up the process. Dr. Singh, too, was stressed about the repair, especially since it was possible I was going to have to reorder a part. The budget was already a little out of control for this month.

I'd tried to calm both of their concerns, but today had been one of those days that was more losses than wins, and I don't want to be going to see Ben with that attitude. I don't want him to pick up on my weakness, or fear, or whatever it is that's made me think too much about his offer.

The salvage yard is pretty quiet when I arrive, only a couple of cars in the lot, and inside Henry is standing—standing!—behind the display cases, laying out what I think are porcelain water tap handles on a piece of felt for a customer who's looking carefully at each one. I give him a goofy, excited thumbs-up to see him standing, and he smiles, a bit crooked the way Ben does, giving a little lift to the cane he's holding in one hand so that I can see. Ben is nowhere in sight, but Henry must see me looking around, because he gestures over his shoulder to where the office is, waving me back. I feel a little honored to be invited back there, like I'm part of the inner sanctum around here, not any old drop-in shopper. I sort of want to gloat in front of the random customer, but he doesn't even glance up at me.

I was in this office once before, for that frantic moment the day Ben caught River, but now I'm able to take the whole space in. It's really only an office in the barest sense of the word. There's a desk with a computer and three big file cabinets lining the wall behind it, but mostly the large, open space is dominated by a workbench with tools hanging from a pegboard that's mounted on the wall. Off to the side is an old, avocado-colored refrigerator, and there's a small round dining table where Ben and River are sitting, hunched over a book.

"Hi," I say, and Ben looks up at me, his eyes crinkling at the corners as he smiles.

"Thank God you're here," he says, and just like that, I don't really feel all that defensive.

Not so for River, though, who finally acknowledges my presence by looking in my direction and fixing me with a stare that seems to say, *way to crash the party, lady.* I know exactly what Ben means when he says River makes him feel old, because jeez, that look. This is the first time I'm seeing him since the bricks incident, and while Ben and Henry said he was getting along better, getting the hang of things pretty quickly, none of that progress shows in his appearance, which is as slouchy and sullen as it was before.

I walk over to the table and stick out my hand for him to shake. "I'm Kit." He doesn't shake my hand right away, just looks over at Ben, as though for permission.

"River," Ben says, nudging him. I notice he waits for River to look at him before he speaks again. "I told you about Kit. She can help you with this."

I cock my head so I can see the book they're looking at—it's a high school physics textbook, and that's pretty much all the invitation I need to sit down. "You're doing physics already? I didn't get to do this until sophomore year."

"River's in some advanced placement classes this summer," says Ben, looking across the table at me. His eyes look so blue in here, I have to tip my own down to the book again to stop from staring.

"What're you stuck on?" I ask, and again River looks toward Ben first, who nods in my direction. I'm amazed by this change—by how Ben, who practically hauled this kid across the parking lot not so long ago, has managed to earn his trust.

It's not as easy for me, but after forty-five minutes of working with River on his physics homework, I think I've made decent strides. River doesn't talk much, and he does not laugh at my classic "photon traveling light" joke, but he pays attention. At some point Ben leaves the table, telling me that Henry was only allowed to be on his boot for thirty minutes at a time, and though I hear them arguing out there, I stay focused on River, enjoying the easy work of his equations. It's nice, after the day I've had.

Finally Henry wheels in, his face red. "Smalls!" he shouts, and River looks up, apparently used to this nickname. "Break's over. Come out here and help me rearrange some tiles. This jerk says I can't do it alone."

"Dad," Ben says, coming in behind him. "Relax."

Once we're alone, Ben sits across from me and lets out an exasperated sigh, rolling his shoulders. "Jesus, what a day. I remember zero things about physics."

"He seems to like you. River, I mean."

Ben snorts. "Yeah, I mean, he's only been here a couple of times, but he seems to want to be around, which is weird. Today's not even his day to come, but I think these summer classes aren't that much fun for him. He's got a little trouble hearing in the bigger classroom spaces. From what little he's said, I gather he takes some heat from older kids."

"That's too bad." I got my fair share of teasing in school, but Alex's reputation around was usually enough to keep anyone from messing with me too much. "But your dad's up, huh?"

"Yeah, it's progress. Took him to physical therapy yesterday, which he complained about right up until they told him he could put some weight on the leg this week. And then he—he gets a little bit of permission, you know, and he wants to chuck all the rules out the window. If he doesn't follow the rules…" He trails off and lets out a another sigh, rubs his fingers through his hair. "Sorry. He's been—a lot this week." I wonder how it would feel to stand up, to move behind him to rub the tension out of his shoulders. I wonder how it would feel to be the person who got to do that for Ben.

Instead, I say, "It's okay. I didn't have such a great day, either."

"Yeah?" he says, but I don't like it. I don't like that he's said it so cheerfully, that there's a spark of hope in his eyes.

"No need to look so gleeful, Ben. It doesn't have anything to do with work," I lie. My voice is harsh, snappish.

He has the decency to look ashamed. But then he asks, "Did you get my email?"

"Yes," I say, feeling cool, defensive again, and even though I'd come here seeking a bit of respite, now I can't wait to leave. "I'm still not interested. Look, I really only came to pick up the light."

"Right." He stands from his chair, a little slowly. I can see the fatigue written all over his lean, strong body, and I try not to feel sorry about being short with him—after all, he kind of deserves it—but I really, really do.

Before I can think of something to say, though, he leaves the office, and it's a few minutes before he comes back, holding a box that looks way too big for the light I remember. "I packed it for you earlier—you have to use a lot of material for something this delicate."

"Oh," I say, feeling terrible now. "Thanks."

"I could install it for you. If you don't want to call an electrician."

"That's okay," I say, but I don't want to call an electrician, even though I do have a good one that's already done some rewiring in the house. I want Ben to do it, because Ben's the one who'd noticed me wanting this light in the first place.

He nods, his jaw clenched. "I'll just get it out to your car for you, then."

We walk in silence to the parking lot, and it's awkward, Ben maneuvering the big box into my trunk, even after I've put the back seats down. It's a minor thing, but to him it's probably another annoying inconvenience in an already annoying day, and sure I'm pissed at his attitude from before, but maybe I'd been too hasty.

"I forgot to say, I also put some of the bulbs in there that you'll need. A lot of these old fixtures, you're going to need to look for things online, but I left you the ones that we used in the display, and some we had in the back."

I had probably been too hasty.

He's tucked his hands in his pockets. He's looking over toward the yard, instead of at me. "I'd better get back in there," he says. "I need to make sure River heads home soon."

"Of course," I say, sounding starchy and weird. "I appreciate your help. I'll let you know how the light turns out."

* * * *

Improbably, the day gets worse, because almost as soon as I get home, my phone rings, and it's my dad calling. The dread I feel at seeing his name on my screen is pretty standard. Since I went to college, I'd learned to expect bad news from my dad's calls, some new financial catastrophe, or, worse, some new scheme he thought was going to prevent it. But the guilt I feel is pretty new, starting—oh, about six months ago now, when those winning numbers came up.

I take a deep breath before answering, lowering myself to the couch. "Hi, Dad."

"I have a new address for you," he says, and—it just strikes this little chord of anxiety I always have tuned somewhere within my body. I feel it shake down all the way to my fingertips, even though the rational part of me knows that my father having to move again doesn't affect me anymore, doesn't have to change my life, doesn't force me to start over. "Dad," I say, my throat tight. "It's only been six months. I send the checks directly to the management office—"

"I'm not being evicted," he snaps, and I slump back in relief, and confusion. "I'm moving in with my—I'm moving in with a woman. Her name is Candace."

"Oh, Dad," I sigh, rubbing an aching spot on my forehead. It's not unusual for him to be dating—despite the fact that he's lived hard most of his life, he's still a good-looking guy, tall and lean like Alex is, with salt-and-pepper hair, and, when he works at it, a charming smile. For Dad, women were part of the life—he didn't usually indulge in his vices alone. And while none of them tended to stick around long—my mother the exception, but only to get through the pregnancy—they usually managed to be part of some new brand of trouble my dad would get into.

My dad coughs on the other end of the line, clearing his throat, and it's a thick, wet sound that makes me wince—what a lifetime of smoking Camels has done to his health. I wait for him to tell me more about Candace, but really I'm already picturing her from experience. Blond, probably, big hair, too much makeup, lots of jewelry, enough so that it makes noise when she walks. It's no small irony that I make a mental ten to one bet he met her at a casino.

"I met her at church," he says, his voice still rocky and uneven with phlegm. What the…what?

"What kind of church?" I'm glad he can't see my eyes narrow in suspicion. "Just a church I go to," he says, and then he raises his voice. "It's none of your business!"

He's always been this way—volatile, quick to anger, especially when he thinks I'm asking for an accounting of his decisions. "Okay," I say calmly. This is a tactic I've honed over many years—*do not engage*. Maybe I haven't done such a good job of it in the practical sense, seeing as how we're about to discuss where I should send his checks, but I've improved immensely in the verbal communication part of things. "Let me have the address."

He rattles it off, a P.O. Box, and I shouldn't ask, but curiosity gets the better of me. "Where is—what kind of place is this, Dad? An apartment, or…?" I trail off, unsure of how much to press here. Despite everything, despite his almost complete negligence of me for my entire life, I worry over him. I want to know he's at least someplace warm, safe. And I don't want to be sending money to some woman's P.O. Box.

"It's a trailer," he says gruffly. "Nice place." A trailer actually could be

a pretty nice place, compared to a lot of the apartments we lived in over
the years, and I'm resolved not to judge—but at least with the apartments
my dad's been in, I've been able to talk to a property manager, or visit a
website. I've been able to keep some tabs.

"Maybe I could meet Candace sometime. Does she have a computer?
We could Skype."

"Yeah, yeah," he says, but I can tell he's already finished with this
conversation. "Maybe."

I take another deep breath, because I always do, before this part of
almost every call we have. "Have you checked out any of those meetings
I suggested, Dad?"

"I've got to run, Ekaterina," he says, and I nod uselessly, feeling as
defeated as I always do. "You take care," he adds, which is as close to *I
love you* as my father gets.

"Thanks. You take care too."

But he won't. He never, ever does.

I try to get Dad out of my mind while I heat up some leftovers, but I'm
a dog with a bone when it comes to his issues, and I've been worse about it
since the lottery. The only positive here is that I've got a legitimate excuse
to text Alex, who's still dodging me about my proposal. I fire off a quick
message, asking whether he knows anything about Candace, and send an
email too—he's doing a shoot in South America, I think, and his phone
contact might be spotty.

Tomorrow is going to be a long day. I'll get up early and be at the lab
by six so I can start the repairs I need to do. I should probably just eat and
head to bed, but instead, I grab my phone again and send a group text to
Zoe and Greer. *Bring candy*, it says, and within five minutes Zoe has texted
back, *On it*. Greer writes that she'll be over within the hour.

I smile in gratitude, in relief. Then I navigate back to my email and hover
over the message Ben sent this morning, the one with all the pictures. With
barely a hesitation I trash it. Today was lousy at work, sure, but it doesn't
take much to remind me of what really matters. That call with my dad—his
constant wayfaring, instability—is a check on what I've worked so hard
for here. No matter what Beaumont has down there in Texas, it doesn't
have Zoe and Greer, and it doesn't have my *home*. I'll fix the microscope,
keep going with all these renovations, keep focused on all the things here
that have made me happier than I've ever been allowed to be in my life.

And if I spend a little too much time thinking about that pained, tired look
on Ben Tucker's face, well—that's something I can deal with another time.

Chapter 8

Ben

I don't mean to be dramatic, but right now, I can't think of one fucking thing I'd like to be doing less than having lunch with my mother.

I'm at the Crestwood, Barden's oldest and most revered hotel, and home to my mom's favorite restaurant. It's the hottest it's been since I arrived in town, but of course you can't wear a fucking t-shirt to the Crestwood, so I had to walk three blocks from my street parking space in suit pants and a dress shirt, and I can feel sweat rolling down my spine. I rushed to get here, because Dad's PT session for his arm today was running behind, and I had to drop him back at the yard with Sharon before I ran home to change. This afternoon, I'm supposed to meet a contractor at the yard who's trying to replace every single sink and tub in the three houses he's working on, and I doubt we have the inventory.

And—*and*—I fucked up, again, with Kit.

I clench my teeth, take a drink of water, willing myself to relax. It's not easy—since yesterday, the week's really been going to shit, though if I'm honest, things were getting stressful even before that. Dad's PT is really ramping up, and so my days—shuttling him back and forth, coordinating schedules with Sharon and now River too—are more complicated. Even though it's good to see Dad making progress, he can be difficult and antagonistic, especially when the pain is getting to him. Usually he takes this out on me, which is okay, but on Wednesday he'd snapped at the therapist, frustrated by the restrictions she insisted on about his weight-bearing limitations. He'd apologized—I can tell he knows this is unlike him, the frustration, the temper—but I'd felt so bad that I'd sent the office two dozen cupcakes. I have a new appreciation for caretakers of all kinds after only a couple of weeks here.

Plus, there's River, who's almost as unpredictable as my dad. Sometimes, like yesterday when I was trying to help him with his homework, it seemed as if the kid was warming up to me. Other times, like when I told him he needed to head home for the night, it became a polar-vortex freeze out, just complete silence and disinterest. It's not my problem—it *shouldn't* be my problem—but the kid's got trouble, and hell if I'm any good at ignoring it.

The worst of it, though, is Kit. Or the job. Whatever the fuck it is. Yesterday, I'd stepped directly in it. And I hadn't meant to—when she'd said she'd had a bad day, I hadn't been thinking about the job at all. Honestly, I'd been thinking, *thank God it's not just me*. I'd been looking for a little of that harmless commiseration friends do over their shitty days. But despite Monday, and Tuesday, when she'd come to the yard and stayed for the evening, I guess we're not really friends. We can't be, and that's down to me, not her. I'm the one who's put the job between us, and I can hardly admit to myself how many times I've wished over the last few days that that wasn't the case. I wish she'd come into the yard one day while I was working. I wish she didn't know me as a recruiter at all.

But there was no point in thinking that way, so after I'd gotten Dad settled last night I'd sent an email to Jasper, updating him on what I'd learned about Kit so far, letting him know that since the materials I'd sent hadn't seemed to sway her yet, I was planning on digging in to some research on the funding sources Kit's department had more generally. Sometimes this could be a good way to negotiate recruiting deals, to have Beaumont fund some of a university's project agendas. I'd had trouble sleeping afterward, which is why I'm probably taking this lunch break with a little more annoyance than I might otherwise.

"Benjamin!" my mom calls out from behind me, and in my defense I'd probably find that annoying on any day, not just this one.

But I've still got manners, so I rise from my seat to face her, leaning down to brush a kiss on her cheek. "Hi, Mom."

"I'm sorry I'm late," she says, settling into her chair. "My blowout ran over."

I'm not so dumb that I don't know my mom is a beautiful woman, the kind that still turns heads. She's tall and rail-thin with thick blond hair that she has professionally washed and styled twice a week. She was always pretty careful about her appearance. The morning after she'd moved out I'd gone into the bathroom and stared in confusion at the vanity, wondering when my dad had managed to replace it. But it wasn't a new vanity, it was the old one, shorn of all the products she'd kept on the counter. Since she married Richard, though, she's got the means to invest fully, and for her, looking good is part of the gig she has with him, being on his arm, fitting in with his life, his crowd.

"That's all right," I say, picking up my menu, a little earlier than is probably well-mannered. But I already want out of this. I feel the same way I always have around my mom, twitchy and restless.

She orders a chardonnay, arranges her napkin carefully in her lap. "How's Henry?" Even this annoys me. Why can't she just say, *how's your dad?* It's like she doesn't even want to acknowledge that we're family.

"Dad's okay," I say, trying not to be pointed about it. "I don't have long. I need to get back to the yard after this."

"Well!" Her tone is still light. Nothing fazes her, at least not now. "I'd better pick something in a hurry, then." She gets a salad, light on the cheese, no dressing, no bread on the side, no croutons, two lemon slices that she'll squeeze on top. I could've ordered it for her. Despite the fact that I only see her once a year now, and only once a week before that, I know this part about her well.

She tells me about how she's redecorating her living room, how she's going to serve as secretary for the board of the symphony, how my Aunt Christine in Alabama has started wearing a mask at night that's supposed to make her jawline tighter. I nod politely, asking questions where I should, keeping my responses to hers light, neutral. I resist the urge to look at my watch.

"You're tapping," she says, and though she's smiling, I hear a fine trace of annoyance under it. I still my leg—I hadn't realized it, but I'd been bouncing it under the table. I clear my throat, embarrassed. Moving this way—repetitive shaking of my leg, gently thumping my fist against my thigh, knocking my index finger against a table edge—all of it, my mom used to call "tapping." I don't do it anymore, ever, except for on those rare occasions when I'm around my mother.

When I was eight, my mom had taken me to the pediatrician about it, had told him, through clenched teeth, that she couldn't *stand* it, that I was always moving, that I fought her at bedtime, that I ran everywhere, that I couldn't *settle down.* We'd come home with a prescription—and my parents had their first fight in front of me. After that, Dad had started picking me up from school, taking me to the salvage yard with him every day. Later—much, much later, when my dad sat across from me in an orange plastic chair with a guard watching our every move—he'd apologized for this choice, said he shouldn't have fought her, or the doctor, said he'd do it differently, if he could have.

I don't know who was right, between the two of them. The only thing I know is that my dad stuck, and my mom left.

"Sorry," I say, and her face softens. She almost looks apologetic. I'd meant what I said last weekend, at Kit's house. My mother is not a bad person—she can be a little severe, a little superficial, but there's a kindness to her. She picks up feral cats and pays for them to get fixed, finds them homes. She volunteers at a hospice facility, often staying late into the night with lonely patients. She sends an email to everyone in our family—still including my dad—with updated birthdays and contact information, so we can all stay in touch. She's a *good* person. I hate that I have trouble remembering it sometimes.

"Now, Ben," she says, and the corner of my mouth hitches up, appreciating that she's stopped with the *Benjamin* shit. "I know you're busy while you're in town."

Well, this can't be good.

She holds her chardonnay by the stem, twirls it. "It's Richard's thirtieth anniversary with his firm, and I'm having a party for him in a few weeks. Here, actually."

"That's nice," I say, hoping against hope this is not an invitation, just a non-sequitur.

"Obviously I'd love for you to be there."

"Mom, things are pretty hectic, on account of me running the yard, and Dad's care."

"Of course Henry's invited too. He and Richard are friends!" I resist the instinct to snort. But then again, what right do I have? I guess they kind of *are* friends. At my college graduation dinner, Richard and my dad got drunk and Richard told a joke about a carpenter and a turtle that had my dad laughing so hard he'd cried.

"I'll see, Mom."

She purses her lips, looks up at me. "Ben. You know you owe Richard a great deal."

And there it is. There it fucking is. I swallow the urge to snap at her, to say, *It was the least he could fucking do since he blew up our family.* But that's not even true, not really. And anyways, I'm not usually so sensitive about this shit. I'm—I don't know what. I'm hot, I'm tired, it's been a bad couple of days. "If I can't make it to the party, I'll make sure I get in touch with him, okay?" I say, trying to keep my voice calm.

She plucks the napkin from her lap, folds it twice and rests it next to her plate, lifts a hand to smooth her hair. "All right. I'll send you all the information," she says, her voice wounded. I don't know if I should apologize. I don't know what she wants from me. I never have.

We settle up, say our final pleasantries as I walk her out to her car, then head the opposite way toward the truck. It's four blocks I've got to go now, and the back of my shirt is sticking to me uncomfortably. These streets are still so familiar to me, even all these years later. When I got old enough, Dad would let me take the bus from the salvage yard to the historic part of downtown to do light deliveries, and afterward, I'd walk and walk, mapping the city with my feet, burning off the energy that never seemed to leave me. A thought comes to me, unbidden: If I take a left here, walk a mile and a half, cut across the fountain quad that's lined with crepe myrtles, I'd be right across from the building where Kit works.

Instead, I get in my truck and go back to the yard.

* * * *

When I get in, Sharon and Dad are behind the front display cases, and she's helping him get settled in his chair. I pause by the door, waiting to go all the way in, because this is the part where Dad usually gets a little cranky, and I may be the world's biggest chickenshit, but I'm inclined to spare myself the abuse right now. But Dad's quiet, and I catch him looking at Sharon as she lifts his booted leg into the chair's sling. What I see there—I turn my face away, look down at my shoes. Whatever that expression is, it's not part of my understanding of Dad and Sharon together. I know them as bickering, almost sibling-like friends.

I don't have time to think much about it because the door opens behind me and River comes in, nearly running into my back.

"Hey," he mumbles, doing that annoying neck-snap he does, the one that gets the swoop of hair out of his eyes for all of half a second before it falls back again.

"You need a haircut," I say, sounding so much like my dad that I want to slap myself. "What I mean is," I clarify, "your hair is always in your face."

"I like it there," he says, and I have to laugh at the way he deadpans it.

"Are you two just going to stand there and chat all afternoon, or can we get to work?" my dad calls.

River follows me in. "We were talking about hairstyles," I say, nudging River with my elbow. He nudges back, harmless sparring that feels almost cheerfully aggressive. "What I'm saying is, this look doesn't flatter the kid's face."

"Ass," River says under his breath. But the corners of his mouth are tilted up.

"I think it's fine," says Sharon. "Reminds me of that Bieber kid, back before he started buying monkeys and growing inadequate facial hair."

"What!" exclaims River, and it's the loudest he's ever been in any of our presences.

"I'll take you to get it cut later." Over his head, I give a thumbs-up to Sharon, who's already gathering her stuff to leave for the day. I duck into the back to change into the clothes I've brought with me, and when I come back out, River's Windexing the display cases, my dad watching to make sure he doesn't miss any spots.

"How's your mother?" he asks.

"Same as always. Having some big party at the Crestwood for Richard in a few weeks. We're invited."

"Right by the register," Dad says to River, in the slightly louder voice he uses when talking to him. "You missed a spot." He turns back toward me. "A party sounds all right. Do I have to wear a suit?"

"Probably. Why would you even want to go, Dad?"

"Why not? There's going to be a lot of free food. That's my favorite kind of party." I shake my head, pretend to be looking over receipts from the morning. "Ben. We've been over this. I got no hard feelings for Richard. Or for your mother."

"Well, I can't say the same," I say.

"Who's Richard?" River says, and fuck if that kid doesn't seem to hear only the things you're hoping he doesn't.

"Richard is Ben's stepdad. Nice guy, money coming out of his ass. When Ben was younger, a little bit older than you..."

"Dad." I don't think anyone could mistake the warning tone in my voice. "No."

River looks back and forth between us, holding his bottle of Windex and rag. But just as soon, it's as though he decides the curiosity isn't worth it. He turns back, applying himself again to the cleaning. But he's turned so he's facing us, I notice—he's listening, in his way. I can feel Dad's eyes on me, but I don't look over. "You get that light up at Kit's yet?"

My shoulders stiffen even more, impossibly. "No. She's got an electrician."

"She could probably do it herself," says River, and Dad and I both look at him. "She's really smart."

"You're right about that, Smalls. Pretty too," says Dad, and they smile at each other.

"You guys are assholes," I say, and leave them to their cleaning.

* * * *

I spend the rest of the afternoon up in the east wing of the second floor, which is basically a graveyard for stuff we don't know what to do with yet—dump-offs from estate sales we need to sort, mysterious parts that even my dad can't figure out a whole for. In a salvage yard, you get accustomed pretty quick to chaos, to the fact that you've probably got more material than you're ever going to sell, that you're going to get more inventory when you don't want it. If you think too much about it, you'll get overwhelmed, wondering about all this stuff, how it'll ever find a place to actually go.

Today, though, it's a good spot for me to hide out. It's relaxing, I guess, to be pulling out stuff that I'll either put into the inventory or take to the dumpster, or out to recycling. When I was a kid, younger than River and pissed off at the world, figuring out this kind of stuff had been a good way to calm me down, to stop the rising tide of anger and frustration I felt everywhere I went, the one that made me want to punch and destroy. You couldn't be that way when you were pulling out parts of light fixtures or stairwells from different centuries. You couldn't just hold on to things as tightly as you wanted or toss around the pieces you couldn't get to fit. You had to *notice*, pay attention to every little piece, learn how to treat it, figure out whether it belonged somewhere.

About two hours in, when a glint of sun from the skylight winks across the floor, I catch a shock of cobalt blue in a corner, where a stack of old, glassless window frames lean against the wall. At first, I think it's part of a dismantled window, maybe some stained glass, but when I get over to it, I see it's the bottom bowl for a chandelier, hand-carved and in improbably perfect condition.

It's that easy for me to get lost—easier in a practical sense, I guess, than it'd ever been back when I still lived here, because now Google has image search, and for the next hour, that's what I'm doing. First I take a photo of the bowl itself, and it's an easy hit to Baltic chandeliers, so I look at about a hundred examples before I start to trawl the room, looking for other pieces that might match the bowl. The good news is that most of the essentials are around—the neck, the arms, the spindle, the main bobeche. But there's probably thirty pieces I'll have to hunt down, either elsewhere in the yard or online, and that's not even counting prisms. I've only found—inside an otherwise empty lone dresser drawer on the other side of the room—about half of what a chandelier of this size must take.

By the time my dad calls up to me, telling me it's time to get going, I feel calmer, more focused, more ready to deal with work, Dad, everything. And if my mind isn't any more clear about Kit—well. It's something I'm getting used to, at least.

Chapter 9

Kit

By Wednesday, I've finished the major repairs on the Titan, and I'm not ashamed to say I'd done a little victory tour before I'd left work, like, *Fixed it, bitches!*, but, you know. With more professionalism. Still, I pass on Dr. Singh's offer to join him and the family for dinner at his place, even though Ria makes the best samosas in the history of the universe and even though his two young daughters call me Aunt Kit. I'm too tired, my lower back smarting from standing on hard floors for the last three days, my eyes gritty and fatigued. I text Zoe and Greer that they can forget about spin class, and it's a mark of how hard I've been working that neither of them try to talk me into it.

It's been miserably hot all week, so humid it feels as if it's always either about to rain or just has rained, even though we've not had a drop. The walk home is a slog, and when I get there, the painter I've had in all week for the first floor is still finishing up, and the air conditioners inside are cranked up to Antartica, in hopes it'll help things dry more quickly. Guess it's going to be sweating on the porch for a while for me.

I sink down gratefully, take a slug of the glass of water I snagged while inside. I've been getting home late all week, so it's nice to sit here while there's still daylight, even if I do feel as though someone's taken a bat to my neck and shoulders. I idly scroll through my phone, pretending I'm not looking for a specific name.

But I completely am.

Since last week, I've only heard from Ben once, a voicemail he'd left on Monday when I was in the microscope room. His voice was careful, neutral. He let me know that I might be hearing this week from someone on the metallurgy team at Beaumont, someone who was eager to talk with me about my work, and the projects that Beaumont was working on. At the end of his message, he'd paused and cleared his throat, then said, *If you think of it, maybe you could send a picture of the light. My dad's been asking about it.*

If it seems weird that I can remember exactly what he'd said, it will probably seem weirder that I have listened to the message at least eleven times. I've never replied, have never sent a picture—the box with my new fixture is still sitting, exactly as Ben packed it, on my dining room table. I feel bad about the way I acted last week, my sharp response to him and subsequent cold shoulder. Even if he was wrong, I miss hanging out with him. Even after a couple of days, I'd gotten *used* to him.

I shift on the stoop, uncomfortable, pissed I still haven't bought chairs for out here. The front door opens behind me and my painter, a short, bald guy who calls himself Packy comes out, thunking his stepladder onto the floorboards. "Probably going to have to come back tomorrow," he says. "I had to do some extra patching in the powder room, so haven't primed in there yet."

"That's okay." We settle on an arrival time for tomorrow, talk briefly about whether I'll eventually want to redo the paint upstairs too, which is almost entirely covered in old wallpaper. It's a little awkward, actually—I'm trying to get Packy to weigh in, to tell me what *he* thinks I should do upstairs, but I mean, this guy is my housepainter, not my decorator or my friend, and probably he wants to go home. I feel my face heat and thank him. Maybe all the alone time with the microscope is getting to me.

As he's settling his gear into his truck, Jeff and Eric come down the street, walking their dog, and they greet Packy as if they're all old friends, backslapping and laughing, pointing over at their house, which is probably perfectly painted all over. No one is even looking at me up here on the porch, but somehow this makes me feel even more like an intruder, the person at the end of the cafeteria table who no one's talking to. I fake absorption in my phone, feeling relieved when I hear Packy's truck start up with a rumble.

"Kit, right?" calls a voice, and Jeff and Eric are still standing on my sidewalk, looking up at me.

"Yeah—yes," I say, standing and coming down the steps to greet them. "Hi, again." I open my small gate and bend down to pet their dog, a fat little dachshund who's panting with delight.

"How's it coming?" says Jeff, gesturing toward the house.

"Great!" It's too cheerful, and Jeff and Eric don't even know me but they are not dummies. My shoulders slouch a little. "I mean, it's—okay? There's something new to do all the time, I'm finding."

"Oh, yeah. These old houses, there's things you don't even think of that come up along the way," Eric says.

"Your house is so beautiful. I stare longingly at it from my front window pretty much every day. I mean, not in a creepy way. If that sounds creepy."

They both laugh, and Jeff says they're happy to know it has admirers. "Honestly we worked so hard on it, we show it off whenever we can. Actually, we're having a few people over tomorrow evening for a little cocktail hour. You should come by! Starting at six."

"Oh, that's so nice of you. But I don't want to intrude on a party you're having."

"It's not an intrusion. We'd love to have you. A couple of the neighbors from the next street over are coming too. So it's not just Jeff's boring work friends."

"I work in banking," says Jeff, a little dully.

"I work in metals. And most people think that's really boring too." *Except Ben Tucker*, I think, because I can't seem to keep him out of my head for longer than five minutes at a time.

"You think you can come?" asks Eric.

"Sure. Can I bring anything?"

"Just yourself. Eric does all the food and drink for parties. He says if people bring stuff, they upset the gastronomic balance he's trying to create."

"I *don't* say that," Eric says, but I have a feeling he does. They're fun, the way they tease each other, and I figure if all their friends are as easy to get along with, this party will be a nice way to meet new people, especially some new neighbors, which has been a goal of mine since move-in.

We say our goodbyes, and they start to move away, but suddenly I'm struck with a thought, and before I can snatch it back I blurt, "Is it—ah— cocktail attire?"

Eric smiles back at me, looking me over. "We're not fancy," he says, "but I think I draw the line at cargo pants."

I look down at my—yeah. Cargo pants. "Right. Well, I was doing some repair work today. I have other clothes, obviously." This is true, but *we're not fancy* is really of no help in terms of giving me instructions. I don't want to seem any more inept than I am though. I'm trying make an impression here, so I wave them away, as though I'm the type to always go to this kind of party. I am not, of course. Even when I go to conferences in my field, I only go to the social gatherings for long enough to make myself a small plate of cheese and olives so I can take it back to my room and watch cable television in my hotel bed.

But hey, this is millionaire Kit now. And millionaire Kit can at least buy a new outfit for making new friends.

* * * *

Of course, millionaire me cannot buy a new outfit alone, because even I know Zoe's the expert there, and she meets me after work to help me pick out a new pair of skinny-cut, ankle-length black pants and a jewel-green sleeveless top, silky and cut in at the shoulders, which she says makes my arms look great. Also she says the color works because I'm a "winter," whatever that means. I hate her a little for the shoes—I don't have a categorical objection to heels or anything, but these are the kind that feel like someone's replaced your feet with Barbie's.

But at least when I walk over to Jeff and Eric's on Thursday evening, I feel pretty confident. And I'm excited. Since last night involved me eating a bowl of cereal for dinner and sleeping next to an open window to avoid breathing in too many paint fumes, I'm treating this party as a little celebration for getting the Titan up and running. Even Todd had offered his thanks today, though I think Dr. Wagner made him do it.

A note on the door tells guests to come on in, and I'm not even half a step into the foyer before I start gaping—it's gorgeous in here, every detail exactly right. Beneath my feet are hardwoods polished to a high shine, a large, circular rug that manages to look modern and still suit the old feel of the house. The staircase to my left is intricate, striking, with newel caps and small, inset medallions that look hand-carved. In front of me is a huge mirror, surrounded with similarly detailed woodworking, coat hooks flanking either side; beneath it is an old steamer trunk that's been turned into a functional bench. I resist the urge to take out my phone, snap a few pictures so that I can remember this for later, for all the times I'm thinking about how to make my own place look good. To my right, similar to the layout in my own house, is the main living space, and the laughter and conversation is flowing easily.

It's probably rude of me, but at first I don't even scan the people in the room. I'm too busy fixating on the fireplace, the recessed lighting, the crown molding. Holy crap. My house is a two on Zoe's scale, by comparison.

"Kit!" a voice booms out, and it's neither Jeff nor Eric, but—Henry Tucker? He's sitting in a wingback chair set near the fireplace, a plate of food balanced on his knee, his good hand waving me over. My first thought is for Ben—is he here? Did he know I was coming? But a quick scan of the room and I don't see him anywhere, though I'm not sure how Henry would've gotten here on his own. Still, I'm oddly relieved to see Henry. While I know Jeff and Eric, wherever they are, will be great, welcoming hosts, it's nice to feel as if I'm in with part of this crowd already.

I wade through the guests, giving polite smiles as I go, and reach Henry, leaning down a bit to shake his hand. "It's nice to see you again," I say, smiling wide at him as I take in his outfit—he's wearing a faded plaid shirt tucked into—hey, *wait a minute*—cargo pants, his big black boot covering one leg. "You're lucky. They said I couldn't wear my pants like that."

"Sexism!" Henry cries, his eyes bright with laughter. "No, Jeff and Eric are good people. But two changes of clothes in a single day is probably a bit too much to ask of my son, so I think they're giving me a pass tonight."

"Oh," I say, my face heating. "Is he here?"

"Out back," he answers, lifting a crab cake to his mouth. I look up, through the dining room, trying to get a glimpse of Ben out the back window, but I don't see him. "We did the materials for the patio they're having built, so Ben's checking on the progress. I'd do it myself, but guess who's already used up almost all his allowed weight-bearing minutes today?" He pauses and then jerks a thumb at his chest. "This guy."

"Bummer. How's the food?"

He takes a surreptitious look around, lowers his voice. "Honestly I thought these crab cakes had dirt in them. Eric says that's the mushroom oil he puts on top. Also I wanted a beer and he gave me this." He lifts a light green bottle that he's tucked between his hip and the arm of the chair. "He said it was beer, but it tastes like lemons."

I have to laugh at his honesty. "It's a pretty fancy party, I guess."

"First time here for me. But I've known Jeff since he was a kid, and he's bought so much stuff from me over the last five years I figured it was time for me to see the results."

"It looks wonderful. I wish you could show me every single thing that came from the yard that's in here."

His smile is so similar to Ben's that I straighten, only to look up and meet the eyes of the man himself. I don't miss that his graze tracks down for the barest of seconds, tracing my mouth, my shoulders, my chest. In spite of myself, I feel a spark of pleasure at his attention. "I didn't know you'd be here," he says, and it's almost an apology, as though he's embarrassed to find himself here. "I promise."

"No—I—well, I'm a late addition to the invitation list, I guess. I didn't know you'd be here, either."

"Good lord, you two," Henry says. "One of you get me another one of those dirt cakes, will you?" He holds up his plate, and Ben takes it before I can reach out. "Get the lady a drink while you're at it."

Ben and I smile at each other, a little shyly. Henry gives good icebreaker, that's for sure, and when Ben holds out his arm to gesture me ahead of him, I follow. "Listen," I say, once we've passed into the dining room, where the table is laid with an assortment of platters, all the food looking professionally prepared. I turn and set a hand on his forearm briefly, then snatch it back just as quickly. The sleeves of his blue button-up are rolled up, the skin on his forearms warm, tight over the muscles beneath. I only meant to *still* him, I tell myself. I'm not going to go around *touching* him just for the sake of it. He looks down at where my hand rested, then back up at me. "Listen," I say again, regaining my bearings. "I'm sorry about before, last week. I overreacted."

That dimple, right on his left cheek there. I'd like to *lick* that dimple.

"Hey, no. I'm sorry. I was having an off day."

"You were just doing your job." I shrug, and the dimple disappears. His smile is replaced by something blander, less inviting, but still, technically, a smile.

I turn and we load up two plates, one for me and another for Henry, and Ben pauses at the buffet that's set under the back window to pour me a drink. We're quiet, feeling each other out, some new tension between us. I'm grateful when Jeff and Eric come through from the kitchen, greeting me warmly. Before I know it, Ben and I are pulled away from each other, Jeff introducing him to a lithe, glamorous blonde from his office and Eric leading me through an abbreviated tour of the house, with frequent stops to introduce me to other guests, all of whom seem perfectly nice and interesting.

But I'm having trouble focusing on any of it, because my eyes keep seeking out Ben, who'd returned to deliver more food to Henry, the blonde having followed. It seems he's leaned in that same position, against the mantel, for the entire hour I've been here. At some point I'm pretty sure I agree to serve on a neighborhood community board, but it barely registers. Because the thing is—I think his eyes keep seeking me out too. More than once, our gazes have tangled, and I'm always the first to look away.

Despite my distraction, though, this is a pretty good showing for me at a cocktail party. I've done some champion mingling, if I do say so myself. But the introvert in me is starting to cry out in distress, or maybe that's just my feet in these shoes. Either way, I make my way to Jeff and Eric, offering my thanks and compliments before heading over to Ben and Henry again. The blonde smiles politely as I approach, and before I can say anything,

Ben speaks up. "Jennifer, this Ekaterina Averin. She works as a research scientist at the university. Kit, Jennifer's an accountant at Waterfield's."

"Hi," I say, shaking her hand. "I'm really a lab tech. Ben's overstating it."

"No. I'm not," he says, his eyes on me, his voice serious. Jennifer looks back and forth between us, and seems to pick up on something, politely disentangling herself from our little party. This whole evening—it feels strange, uneasy. At this point, I don't even care if Ben wants to talk about Beaumont again. I just want things to go back to the way they were before.

"You get that light hung yet?" asks Henry, and my eyes break from Ben's. Did I say I'm happy with this top Zoe picked out? Because right now it's sealing in every nervous drop of sweat that's forming between my breasts.

"Ah—unfortunately, no. It's been a really busy week. But I will, I promise. And I'll make sure I send a picture."

"Why don't you ask this knucklehead to hang it? I guess he's terrible at conversation when it comes to you, but he can get that light hung in under an hour."

"Dad," Ben says, shaking his head in embarrassment, that same joking resignation that's part of their dynamic together every time I've been around them.

"Oh, I don't want to trouble you all anymore."

"It's no trouble," Ben says.

Henry grunts as he leans forward in his chair, and Ben reaches to grab the four-point cane that's in front of the fireplace. To watch Ben lean down, offer his arm for his father to grip as he lifts himself, stiffen his body against the weight—it's hypnotizing. When Henry is up, good hand braced on the cane, Ben stays right as his elbow, one hand cupped underneath it, but not touching Henry at all. He's watchful, prepared, careful. It makes my heart clench to see the way he does this, the way he's so attuned to Henry's care. I walk out with them, following behind, and we're all quiet as Ben helps Henry descend the steps to the walk, Henry's breathing growing more labored with the effort.

"Holy hell," he says, once he's at the curb. "That was hard! Wasn't worth the dirt cakes and lemon beer, I'll tell you what."

"Told you," says Ben, opening the door for Henry.

I'm not really needed here at this point, but it feels strange to walk away. I don't want Henry to get the sense that I'm in a hurry, and I also don't want him to feel that I've turned his slow pace into a spectator sport.

And I don't want to leave Ben.

My phone rings from the clutch I'm carrying—I thought I'd set it to silent, but at least it hadn't rang inside the party. I use the opportunity to look away while Ben helps Henry into his seat, buckling him in. "Oh!" I exclaim, catching sight of the screen, my voice high and excited. "It's my brother!" Ben looks over his shoulder at me, the corner of his mouth hitching up, that dimple showing again. "I have to take this," I say, even as I'm swiping across to answer. "He doesn't always have reception."

"It's all right," Ben says, closing Henry in.

I pick up, say a quick hello to Alex before asking him to hold on, lowering the phone to my side. I don't even *think*—I just talk. "Ben," I say. "I really could use help with that light, sometime. If you'd still want to."

Full dimple. I know what it means now, when books talk about "swooning." I'm about to swoon right into that dimple.

"I'd still want to."

"Okay, then. Call me tomorrow?"

"I'll call you tomorrow."

I wave at Henry, putting the phone back to my ear. Alex has called, finally! Right now, everything feels so good—well, make that *almost* everything. I balance the phone between my shoulder and ear, lean down to slip off these truly maniacal shoes. And then I'm tiptoeing across the street, Alex's voice in my ear, Ben's laughter soft behind me.

Chapter 10

Ben

My week has gone from shit to sunshine since Jeff and Eric's party, and that's all because I feel back on track with Kit. By Saturday morning I was at her place, two coffees, a box of donuts, and my toolbox in tow, ready to hang her new pendant. When I'd finished the work—I might have drawn it out a little—she'd stepped onto the porch, then down to the sidewalk, then back into the house again, so she could see it from all angles. She'd clasped her hands in front of her chest in delight, and it'd been just about the most successful I'd felt in days.

And then she'd asked me to come out tonight. "I mean, with me my friends," she'd said quickly, her face flushing. "I told them about your job offer, and they want to meet you. Really," she'd added hastily, "they're more family than friends."

The side of me that's working for Beaumont knows this is an opportunity. I'm excellent, I always brag to Jasper, at the kitchen table, at those moments when you're meeting with a hire's spouse or kids, when you're trying to give them an insight into the new life you're offering. It's not quite the same, meeting up at a bar with Kit's friends, but it's something.

But the side of me that has been picturing Kit in that green, silky top from the other night? That side's just happy to get to see her again.

The heat's finally broken, but that's only because it's been raining since this afternoon, so by the time I get to the place now called One-Eyed Betty's—it was a fish-and-chips place when I was a kid—my t-shirt is splattered with raindrops, my hair wet. I run a hand over it as I duck through the front door, scanning the room for Kit. Before I spot her, I hear a voice call out to me. "Ben Tucker! I can't believe it!"

Liz—that's what I always called Elizabeth Trenton, before she became the I guess now-famous Betty—looks nothing like I remember her. She's got her hair dyed jet-black and pulled into a tight ponytail, blunt cut bangs framing her face, and bright red lipstick painting her lips. When she walks over to me and smiles up into my face, I see that she's got black eyeliner painted thick around her eyes, a little cat-eyed swoop to it at the edges. It's such a shock to my system that I say, "Holy shit, Liz."

She laughs, swats my arm. In school, Liz was quiet as a church mouse, her hair a pale brown, her skin freckled and given to flushing, her glasses out of style, one lens thick and bifocaled, the other, thin and clear, just there for symmetry. She got a fair bit of teasing, a lot of kids calling her "three-eyes," since everyone knew about the accident that had taken out her left eye when we were in second grade. Me, I never teased Liz. Our alphabetical homerooms all the way through high school meant I almost always sat next to her, and over the years we became friends.

She fluffs her ponytail and winks at me, and I take in the space.

"Damn, Liz, it looks great in here." It's full up, all the barstools and every table I can see taken, and there's a robust staff milling about, carrying trays full of drinks and food, smiling and interacting easily with customers they seem to know. There's certainly an aesthetic about the place—all the women working share Liz's retro fashion, and the men have beards that probably require some kind of special hair product. Hipsters everywhere, but I'd noticed a lot of this in Barden since I came back—it seems to be a younger, more creative, more vibrant town than the one I'd grown up in.

"I do a good business." I'm happy for the way she says that, so unapologetically confident about her success. Liz used to be the type to immediately cover up all the A+s she got on her papers when the teacher handed them back. "What're you doing back home?" she asks.

"Ah, my dad had a little accident, so I'm helping him out for a while. It's temporary."

It's not that I'd mind catching up, hearing about how Liz transformed this former dump into an urban hangout, but my eyes are already drifting, looking around for Kit. I find her weaving through the crowd toward me, and I feel a quiver of anticipation go through me. She's wearing slim, cropped jeans, and a simple loose black tank top, and I swallow past the lump of anticipation in my throat, the same one I got when I'd first seen all that smooth, pale skin on her arms and shoulders—the skin I try not to notice whenever I see her.

But I always notice.

When she smiles at me, her face looks flushed and happy, maybe a little nervous too. "Hi," she says, and her eyes slide toward Liz's. "Do you two know each other?" There's a little something in that question. I wonder if maybe Kit feels a little—jealous? That's probably too much to hope for. Probably she just feels thrown that she's got me on her home turf and I've already found an advantage.

"We went to school together," Liz says. "First through twelfth grade. Did you know Ben was voted 'Biggest Underachiever'?"

Jesus. That's not something I want her to know. But at least Liz has left out that it wasn't really *all* through twelfth grade. Suddenly I think there's a degree of liability in coming out to a local place with Kit, the off chance I'll bump into someone who'll run their mouth off. Jeff isn't the kind of guy to ever bring up my past, but this bar isn't such a controlled environment.

"No," Kit says, cocking her head at me. "That's not a very nice designation."

"I was voted 'Most Likely to Become a Pirate,'" Liz says, gesturing to her prosthetic eye. "Get it? It was not a very nice school."

"I guess not," Kit says, a little huffily, and I like that she seems wounded and defensive on our behalf.

Liz looks between us, a curious smile on her face, then tells us she's got to get back to work. "You can put him on our tab," Kit calls after her, and hooks her arm through mine. It's so unexpected—and the feel of her bare skin against mine is so electric—that I can't say anything for a second. I just stare down at our linked arms and try to seem nonchalant. "So. Underachiever, huh?" she says, leaning in so I can hear over the noise of the bar.

"Oh, that's—that's not really accurate. Or it is, but…" I don't know why I'm suddenly so rattled, so desperate to explain myself to her. "I had a little trouble with the law when I was young. Just—teenage stuff."

"A delinquent, I see," she says, but she's teasing me, and I enjoy it so much that I don't even care that she's teasing me about something that's pretty awful from my past. "You ready to meet my friends?" She's got a little mischief in her eyes. Maybe she's had a couple of drinks, or maybe her friends have some kind of interrogation planned, and I'm walking right into it. At the moment I don't care so much, because Kit is pulling me behind her, where I can get a good look at the curves of her body, and all I want is a cold beer and to sit right next to her for as long as she lets me hang around.

She turns to look at me right before we reach a corner booth, and I have to snap my eyes up from where they were staring at her ass. I think maybe she notices, but I smile and she smiles back, and—shit, I wish I didn't have to meet her friends right now.

"This is him?" A tall, willowy blonde stands from the booth, her hand outstretched to shake mine. "I'm Zoe Ferris. I'm Kit's attorney."

Kit rolls her eyes. "You're not here in an official capacity, Z," Kit says, and elbows her.

Zoe has a firm handshake, a level, brown-eyed stare, and I'll bet she eats people alive in a courtroom. "I'm Ben Tucker, Kit's recruiter and sometimes-handyman."

This makes Kit laugh, and once Zoe's done sizing me up, she turns back to slide into the booth beside a petite brunette, hair so short she's basically all eyes, a pretty, dark blue color framed with thick lashes. "This is Greer," Zoe says, pointing a thumb at her. "'And though she be but little, she is fierce.'"

"I ordered you a beer," says Kit, sliding in across from Greer and patting the seat beside her. She's different here, more relaxed, as if it's normal for her to invite me to sit right down, as if we've done this a million times before. Her smile is wider, her lips looser, spreading over her teeth easier. I think I might be staring at her mouth, which is not a good thing to do in front of these women. *Fuck.*

"Thanks," I say, leaning back and grabbing the pint. "All right. Let's have it."

To my surprise, Greer starts first, and with an unexpected question. "Did your dad really find a skeleton wearing a Speedo in the salvage yard?"

I almost spit my beer across the table, but I get it down before letting out a laugh. "You grew up around here, huh?"

Greer nods, her eyes even bigger now, and Kit leans an elbow on the table, turning to me. "What's this, now?"

I wave a hand dismissively. "That's all urban legend stuff. You've seen the yard, you know it can be a spooky place. Lots of kids, growing up, they came up with different stories about what goes on there. Famous one here," I say, tipping my glass a little toward Greer, "is about Henry moving some old doors up on the second floor and finding a skeleton upright between two of them."

"With a Speedo?" Zoe says, her face a tableau of disgust.

"I think that part of the story came up later," I answer. "At first it was just a skeleton. By the time I was in high school, kids said my dad put the skeleton in a chair in his office, named it Carl, and talked to it about football."

"Gross," whispers Greer.

"It's not true," says Kit, defensive again, and I realize something about her in this, the way she inclines toward protectiveness. Kit is loyal to her core, and every good recruiter knows loyalty is the toughest nut to crack with a potential hire.

But I don't want to think about that now.

"It's not. But my dad, he eats that stuff up. When I'd have friends come over to the yard after school, sometimes he'd shout stuff to the back of the building. 'Carl!'" I shout, and Kit's already laughing at my spot-on Henry voice. "'This kid out here is wearing a Redskins jersey! You hate them, right?'"

That used to mortify me, but now I'm so glad my dad's as embarrassing as he is, because these women are all laughing, and it's the perfect icebreaker. Greer and I swap stories about the area, about where she grew up, which pool she went to in the summers, whether she preferred ice cream from Dixie's Soft Serve or the soda counter at Rickman's Pharmacy. Kit knows all these places too, and I'm seeing now the hard work she's put into getting to know the city—she's got almost native knowledge even though she's only lived here for a few years. I've lived in Texas since I was twenty-one, and I still don't know the kind of stuff I know about here—which mechanic will pass your car for inspection when you really need new tires but don't have the money, or which high school kids are going to key your car after their team loses a ballgame at your home field.

For the next hour, it's easy conversation and laughter. I learn more about Greer and Zoe. Greer's gone back to college this year, and Zoe's taking a break from her work as a lawyer, though she's cagey about that. The beer is cold and hoppy, and Liz's—Betty's, I guess I better get used to calling her—food is delicious. I convince Kit to eat a jalapeño popper even though she says she doesn't usually eat hot things, and the noise she makes in her throat when she bites into it, her eyes closing in pleasure, forces me to shift in my seat, so turned on am I by the way she looks. I'm trying to be trustworthy, not-corporate Ben, and it's working, but not if I become distracted, horny Ben. Not if I stare at her like I want to kiss her, like I want to taste all that spicy flavor on her mouth.

My thoughts are interrupted by Zoe, who leans both elbows on the table and clasps her hands, as if she's opening a negotiation. "So," she says, looking back and forth between me and Kit before settling her eyes on me. "How'd you get into recruiting?"

It's not as off-the-wall as what Greer opened with, but it still surprises me—I came ready to answer Kit's friends' questions about why I was recruiting her, why she'd have a good life in Texas, why Beaumont would be a good fit. That's kitchen table talk, but this is something different. To Zoe and Greer, at least, I'm Beaumont—me and the company, we're the same.

I take a sip of my beer, set it down and mimic her posture. I feel, but don't see, Kit and Greer exchange a look. "My roommate in college, Jasper, he brought me into the business."

That's not going to be enough for Zoe, who quirks that eyebrow again and signals me to go on. "Jasper's a science guy," I say, and pause to think about how to describe Jasper to people who don't know him. "He's the most focused guy I've ever met—by the time we were sophomores, he had his eye on Beaumont as the place he wanted to land, he knew he wanted to do R&D for a company with that kind of profile. He knew he wanted to search out new tech and bring it to the market."

"That tells me exactly nothing about you."

"Zoe, give him a minute," says Kit.

"It's all right," I say, giving her a grateful look before focusing back on Zoe. "Jasper isn't a great communicator. He sees the tech, or the science, and not always the people behind it. I'm good at that part."

"Kit says you didn't know a whole lot about her when you showed up here," Zoe says, and I smile, because as much as she's making me squirm, I'm glad as hell Kit has her.

"She's right. I got a call to talk to Kit under different circumstances than are normal—I'm around here taking care of my dad, so my approach wasn't very elegant."

"It was fine," says Kit. "I don't like elegant, anyways."

"Your dad's salvage yard," Zoe continues, "That's a family business?"

"It is. My great-grandfather started it, a one building operation over on Main. He bought the land it's on now, and my grandpop built the warehouse itself. My dad and him, they did a good amount of expansion over the years."

"But you work in Texas," says Greer. It's not a question, but behind her statement is something tougher than anything Zoe has asked.

I shift in my seat, feel the weight of the silence while they wait for my answer. "Right, yeah. I'm not planning to take over for my dad. I think he'll sell after a while."

"That doesn't bother you?" Kit asks. It's not lost on me that I'm saying nothing about Beaumont, about what Kit stands to gain from joining the team. But somehow I feel drawn into this with Kit and her friends. It's an important part of my having any chance of convincing her and them of anything I have to say.

I shrug, take another sip of my beer. "My dad, he brought me up in that yard, and my grandpop too, when he was alive. They taught me a lot about the business. But they never pressured me to take over, and I think my dad knew I had to get out of here after..." I trail off here, swallow uncomfortably. Probably I should not have gone down this route.

"After?" Zoe says.

I'm seized by a surge of confidence, or maybe of stupidity. I don't have any reason to keep this a secret. In fact, I have good reasons to be proud of how I came out of what happened. So I lean back in my seat, ignoring the way my back, already a little sticky with sweat, rests uncomfortably against the vinyl booth. "I got sent to a juvenile detention facility for six months when I was seventeen," I say, and Zoe sits back too, crossing her arms over her chest. I give them the facts as clearly and quickly as I can. "I had some minor prior offenses, for vandalism. But one night, I was out with some friends, and we were being stupid assholes and we tried to start a bonfire. We were too close to a building, a residential garage separate from the main house. There was a lot of flammable material in the garage, and—ah. An apartment up top." That was hard to say, harder than I thought it'd be. "The tenant made it out, with some minor burns, but it went up quick, burned the structure down." It's hard to explain the way my mind still works around this issue, around what I'd done—it's this razor-edged panic that slices across me, knowing that I was seconds away from killing someone. In court, they'd called it *recklessness toward loss of life.* I've never forgotten that phrase. Sometimes, I still wake up in the night and hear it echoing in my head, though I can never remember dreaming about it. "I got sent in for arson."

"What about your friends?" asks Kit.

I shake my head. "I took the blame. I lit it. None of them had any priors. It was an accident, but the cops felt there was enough gross negligence to treat it as arson. And they were right. So I went in to juvenile detention while my case was being processed, all that. Eventually, I got out with just probation. I didn't have to serve any time in the correctional facility." I leave out that things hadn't looked all that good, really, until Richard had finally gotten involved. To this day I hated that he got to be the hero, when it'd been my dad that had been there for every court appearance, every visitation day.

"Was it—?" Greer starts to ask, but seems to think better of whatever she was going to say, closing her mouth and fingering the corner of her napkin.

"It was all right," I say, but I'm not going to tell them most of it, about how sad it was sometimes, how lonely and scary it was waiting for a court date, about how there were these sudden, unpredictable outbreaks of violence, sometimes between people you thought were friends, about how much I missed my dad and the yard. "I got my shit straight in there. Studied a lot, kept up with my schoolwork as best I could. When I got out,

I had some things to catch up on, school-wise, so I stayed here, finished up. Did a couple of years of community college and worked at the salvage yard. I made enough to pay back the family whose garage I burned down, paid the tenant's hospital bills, the stuff insurance didn't cover. Then I went to Texas for school."

"Wow," says Kit, and I wish I'd had a more noble story to impress her with. I'm proud of how I cleaned up, but it's not easy to tell people that you'd been the kind of person to do something so incredibly stupid and dangerous. After a beat, she says, "But you could come back now, if you wanted. You could take over the salvage yard. You're good at it."

I smile down at her, and for a second it feels as if we're the only two people in this room. I wish we were. I wish I could ask her if she holds it against me, if she's even a little afraid that I'd once been capable of something so awful. Instead, I say, "I'm good at what I do now. And it's not all that different from working at the salvage yard." I reach into my pocket to pull out the small talisman I've carried with me everywhere since I was ten. I set it on the table. It's a small, octagonal prism, pale green, a half-inch at its widest point. "I found this going through the tear-down we had of an old chimney. Basically it was a big truck full of bricks, and my job was to knock as much cement off as I could, save the best bricks. But about halfway through, I found this," I say, setting my index finger atop it, pulling it back toward me. "It's not worth a whole lot, actually. This kind of piece is pretty easy to find. But it doesn't belong in a bunch of bricks. And it would've been easy to overlook. I just caught it in the right light." I smile to myself, remember running in to show my dad, who told me I should go back through the pile I'd already done, make sure I hadn't missed anything else. "Anyways, the point is, I think of it this way: Jasper and I, we sort through a lot of bricks, and we find the gems. We help them go somewhere where they can shine."

"Kit's the gem, huh?" says Zoe, suspicious as all hell.

"Kit's the gem." I believe it. I believe Kit's getting crushed working in that basement office, buried under the pressures of other people's research and data collection. I believe if she had money and access and independence, she could be more successful than she's ever imagined.

"But—you're not really thinking about this, are you, Kit? About going to Texas?" Greer asks.

There's still no hesitation. "No. I'm not going to Texas." She looks over at me, gives me a half-hearted smile. "But that was a whole lot better than anything you've said to me so far, Tucker."

It's another hour and a half before we leave the bar. The conversation had long since shifted away from work, and I was glad to have the spotlight off, to watch Kit as she interacted with her friends. The three of them told a long, winding story of how they all first met, something about a yoga mat, a hairbrush, and a goldfish in a bag, and they laughed so hard that I'd had trouble understanding some of what they'd said. But I didn't care, because I like watching Kit laugh. She'd had to keep wiping her eyes and catching her breath, shimmying in her seat—everything about her in on the act of laughing, as though it's not so common for her that her body's accustomed to it.

As we step out into the night air, even cooler now from the pounding rain that came down while we were inside, I know two things for sure, and they don't necessarily sync up. First, I know that tonight I made a good impression on Kit and the people she deems most important to her consideration of anything I've been offering her on behalf of Beaumont. Second, I know that Kit's not ever going to leave Zoe or Greer easily. The three of them interact as a family, like they have the weight of a lifetime of shared experience between them. Usually, when I scout talent like Kit, young professionals who are living in the towns where they did a degree or a postdoc, they aren't hugely tied to their geographic location. They may have some fondness for the place, or even good friends or a partner, but they don't have the kinds of ties that make them want to dig in for a lifetime.

Kit is dug in. And Greer and Zoe are dug in right beside her.

"Hey," Kit says, lagging behind while Zoe and Greer walk ahead. They're taking a cab back to Kit's house, and I'm glad she won't be heading back there alone. "I'm so sorry about what I said before. About you being a—a delinquent. That was really insensitive."

She's looking up at me with such sincerity, her brow knit in concern. "You didn't know," I say, tucking my hands into the pockets of my jeans. "And anyways, I was a delinquent. So you weren't wrong."

"I think it's really great," she says, punctuating the *great* with this firm nod of her head, really committing to that particular adjective.

"You think it's great that I'm a delinquent?"

"I think it's great that you...are you. That you're this way now. That you made a mistake and you paid for it, and that you didn't let that mistake determine your future."

It's not a whole lot different from what other people—old teachers, Jasper, even my dad, though not in so many words—have said to me over the years about what I did. But coming from Kit, it feels different. I realize that I want Kit to know the best things about me, and if she has to know the worst ones, I hope she thinks of them this way.

"Thanks." *Fuck*—my throat feels tight. Somehow I always forget what thinking about that night does to me.

Kit looks over her shoulder to where Zoe and Greer laugh at something Zoe has pulled up on her phone. "Ten to one that's a video of a puppy playing with a lemon," she says, smiling. "Zoe loves those." She looks down, toying with the hem of her shirt. "I'd better get going. Thanks for coming out." There's a moment, I think, when both of us are wondering what the right goodbye is. A handshake would be ridiculous now—we're *friends*—but a hug feels dangerous, too big, too close. So Kit gives a wave and a smile, and starts to head toward her friends.

"Kit," I call, once she's a few steps away. She turns to look at me, a question in her eyes. I should not, I should *not* say what I'm about to say, but I guess almost always say the wrong thing around Kit, so at least I'm being consistent. "What I said before, about you being the gem?"

"Yeah?"

"You're that—you're that, anywhere. Even if you don't go to Texas."

I don't stick around to see her reaction. I just turn and hustle to my truck.

Chapter 11

Kit

Over the next week, it's hard not to hear Ben's words in my ear every time I see him—*you're that, anywhere.* And I do see him, a lot. We fall into a strange sort of rhythm, texting about our days, me ending up at the salvage yard or Ben stopping by to show me something for the house. There's an easy, laughing cadence to the way we speak to each other, but we don't shy away from the complexities of the business with Beaumont anymore, either. Last night, we'd debated for over an hour about corporate science—me giving Ben every example I could think of, from the food industry all the way to my own, where shoddy science had led to disastrous results, him offering an equal number of examples of for-profit scientists who'd changed the world, some of them, even, from Beaumont's own ranks. Ben is smart, determined. He knows his company inside and out, and there are times, when he's talking to me about what I could do at Beaumont, that I wish I could be someone else for him, someone who is going to give him a different answer.

But we don't only talk about work. We also talk about my house, about ideas I have, about what's at the salvage yard to help make it happen. On Tuesday, I'd even asked him to come by while I met with the contractor who would be doing the kitchen, and my favorite thing about that had been the way he'd stayed entirely quiet during the meeting—this was my house, these were my decisions, and he'd never let the contractor think any different. Once we were alone, though, we'd gone through the information together, strategizing about what questions I'd ask, what I might change.

Today, though, I passed on Ben's offer to meet up at the yard to check out some new furniture inventory they have in, because all my attention needs to be here, on getting ready for my most important, longed-for guest. My brother is coming.

I'm more nervous than I should be for Alex to arrive, tinkering with every last thing in the house so it's exactly the way I want him to see it. Despite the many miles that separate us most of the time now, despite the strain that's been between us for the last six months, he's the person I'm closest to in the whole world, and I want him to feel about this house the same way I had when I'd first seen it.

And I also want him relaxed, happy—because part of this visit is going to be tough. When our numbers came up, I'd called Alex in tears—tears of panic and relief and guilt, and I didn't even have to explain all of that to him. We'd lived through the same things. He knew why I couldn't just take the luck joyfully, why I had such a hard time accepting it. And because of all that, he'd known exactly what to say to make it okay for me to take the money and move forward. He'd been in Australia then, an extended job he was doing for a conservation trust, and the line had been crackly and unreliable, but he'd stayed on with me until I'd calmed down enough to make some semblance of sense out of having all my financial problems— past, present, and if I was careful, future—wiped out in a matter of seconds.

But as much as Alex was willing to listen to my panic, he wasn't interested in listening to my proposal. Ever since I'd first floated it to him, he'd kept more-than-usual distance. Sure, we'd talked occasionally, standard check-ins we did about our dad, and he'd kept up with the emails we sent back and forth regularly since I'd left for college—short messages, photos snapped, links to interesting articles. It'd always been some small way of staying connected after so many years of being in each other's pockets, or, I guess, me being in his, since Alex had always, always been the one to take care of me.

But six months was the longest we'd gone without him coming to wherever I was for at least a couple days' visit, and even when he'd been in the States for three weeks two months ago, he'd not managed to make it here. And I don't think it was because of his schedule.

I refold the blanket I have draped over the edge of the couch, smoothing it over the arm.

"Hey, Martha Stewart," Zoe says from the dining room, where she's setting out plates. "You need to chill. It's not a head of state."

"I know," I grumble. Her presence is a balm but also another reminder of the stakes of this night. Despite the fact that Alex has been to town a couple of times before, he's never met Zoe and Greer. So tonight, my surrogate and real families are finally coming together.

I look around the living room, feeling pretty satisfied, overall. With the floors refinished and the windows replaced and Packy's new coat of antique white paint on the walls, it's not the crumbling wreck that the rest of the house still is at this point, and just today I'd hung pictures on the wall, including a special one over the mantel that I can't wait for Alex to see. In here, it's got the look of a home—*my* home, and I want Alex to recognize that, to see that I'm getting everything I need. If he knows that, maybe he'll be more open to taking what I'm offering.

I drift into the dining room, smoothing the front of my sundress, and Zoe sets down her stack of silverware and comes over to put an arm around me. "It'll be fine," she says, squeezing my shoulder.

I nod, swallowing a sudden constriction in my throat. "Have you heard from Greer?"

Zoe goes back to setting places, giving me the small comfort and then the distance that I need. "She's on her way. She got stuck working on a group project at the library."

This probably means that Greer was the only member of her group actually working. Greer's one glancingly negative report about college so far is the age difference between her and most of her classmates, the fact that she often took work more seriously than them. But, true to form, she'd never really blamed them. "They're young," she'd told us. "I don't mind, and anyways, everyone makes mistakes." I swear, Greer would give Voldemort the benefit of the doubt.

"Okay. I've got everything set up in Alex's room, and we're set in here, and the food should be ready in"—I steal a quick look at my watch—"thirty minutes, so I think that's about everything." I catch the edge of Zoe's knowing smile, and nudge her with my shoulder. "It soothes me," I say.

Right then, the sound of the house's old mechanical doorbell rings out, and I smile to hear it, wishing I could have caught Alex's expression when he twisted the handle. I know he'd love that old detail about the house as much as I had.

When I open the door to him, it's as if something fundamental shifts in my relationship to this house. I'd thought it was home before, but now, with my brother here on the threshold, I can really say, *hey, this is where I live. This is where my life is.* His jet-black hair is messy and his jaw is thickly stubbled, and he smells a little like airplane when I open my arms and wrap them around his middle, but I've never felt more glad to see him.

"Hey, Tool Kit," he says, squeezing me back before pulling away to look down at me with bright green eyes that I've always envied. I'd only ever seen a couple of pictures of Alex's mom, and she was a knockout, tall and curvaceous and eyes exactly the same as Alex's. "You look too skinny."

I laugh, just with the relief and joy I feel at having him say something so familiar, something he's said to me since we were kids and he'd harass me about whether I was eating the lunches he'd packed for me.

I'm ushering him through the door, grabbing bags off his shoulder and setting them down in the foyer before pulling him into the living room, and I know I'm chattering away, pointing out details about the house that are totally irrelevant at the moment someone is trying to take in a place for the first time.

He hooks an arm around my neck and gently rubs his knuckles over my head. "Give me a minute, huh?"

Zoe comes into the living room to introduce herself, shaking Alex's hand and winking at me. "God, Kit," she says, with no shame in her voice. "All your friends must've had *massive* crushes on him when you were growing up."

Alex smiles, his cheeks going briefly ruddy, and I laugh. "Oh, yeah. *Massive.*" This was partially true, since pretty much every girl in any one of my various high schools went silent and swoony whenever Alex showed up. But not many of those girls were my friends, since I was a temporary fixture everywhere, and anyways, I was too wrapped up in my schoolwork to think about anyone's romantic interests. For a second, I have a distracting flash of imagining how it would've been if I'd seen someone like Ben Tucker in high school, of wondering whether he would have noticed me at all.

I shake my head and refocus. I have no room for thoughts of Ben tonight. Instead, I wait for Alex's eyes to snag on the picture above the mantel, and when they do, I'm not disappointed. He looks at me, then back at it, and I see him take a deep breath. It's the first picture Alex ever developed on his own, a shot he took early one morning after an ice storm had closed nearly everything in town. I still remember him lying on his back in his too-thin coat, pointing his camera up at the sky, catching the clear-blue of it as the backdrop for the ice-encased branches of the lone elm tree that was out front of the complex we'd lived in for eight months when I was twelve, Alex seventeen. Somehow, he'd made it look as if we grew up in pastoral bliss, as if we lived in the kind of place where the wonders of nature could be appreciated. I'd loved that picture since he'd first brought it home to show me, an uncharacteristic gleam of pride in his eyes.

"Looks good," is all he says, but I can hear the catch of emotion in his voice.

Zoe is pretty much allergic to this kind of loaded moment, so she takes over, asking Alex about his flight and his travels while I go grab him a beer from the fridge. I'm glad not to be giving him a full tour right away, since I'll have to do a lot of explaining about the condition of other parts of the house, and anyway, I'm enjoying seeing Alex sitting on my couch, talking and laughing with my best friend.

It's about twenty minutes before the front door opens and Greer comes in, her hair mussed and her cheeks flushed pink, panting out, "I'm sorry, I'm sorry! Traffic was total *shit*, and I had to park three streets over, and then your neighbor's dog was out in the street, and I was trying to chase it down...oh." She stops, noticing for the first time that Alex has stood from his spot on the couch and is watching her with a smile.

"Alex, this is Greer," I say, stepping around him to usher Greer farther into the room.

"I'm sorry!" she says again, her hand fluttering over her forehead. "I don't usually use that kind of language."

"That kind of...?" Alex says, confused, and I laugh.

"Greer, don't worry. Alex has the foulest mouth of anyone I know."

"I don't," he says, a little sharply, cutting me a look before reaching out a hand to Greer. "It's nice to meet you."

There's a little ripple of silence while they shake hands, nothing like the easy joking that seemed immediate between Alex and Zoe. But I'm sure she'll warm up. Greer has always been a little shy around new people, and Alex can be a bit intimidating.

I excuse myself to the kitchen to check on our food, but also so I can have a second to take a deep breath, to take in the feeling that's overwhelming me. This dinner, it's already how I imagine a real family dinner, with food I've made from scratch and in a house that's mine, with people I love talking and laughing in the next room. It's what I dreamed of every day when I was growing up, when Alex and I would sit by ourselves on the living room floor of the apartment and eat hot dogs he'd chopped up and mixed with macaroni and cheese.

I'm still nervous, but right now, I'm so happy I could cry.

* * * *

Things don't really go to shit until much later.

Dinner is great, even though I think I've over-salted the potatoes, and even though Greer has stayed relatively quiet, telling us she's just tired from a long day of classes. Alex has asked about one thousand questions about the house, and Zoe delights in telling him about how I've been getting help from the Tuckers in doing some of the finer points of restoration.

"*Ben* Tucker, from Beaumont Materials," she says, with emphasis. "In case you want to google him. He knows Kit's work. He wants her to move to Texas for some big job."

"I'm not moving to Texas," I say quickly, giving a vague sweep of my hand to indicate the house. "Obviously."

"He's over here a *lot*," Zoe continues, as though I haven't spoken. "I think he's trying to woo her with all these knobs he brings over."

Greer stifles a giggle behind her napkin, and Alex says, "What kind of knobs?"

"Just, you know. Hardware. For the cabinets and doors and stuff. His father owns a salvage yard here. They do a lot with the historic homes in the area."

Alex narrows his eyes at me, then looks toward Zoe. "What's he like?" This is ridiculous, but somehow, it gives me a warm feeling to see his protectiveness toward me.

Zoe opens her mouth to answer, but Greer speaks before she can. "He's very nice. Very helpful and professional."

"Also he's got biceps like a comic book character," says Zoe. "You should see him in a t-shirt."

"I'll pass," says Alex, and I start picking up plates because I can feel my face getting hot. But he's watching me with curiosity.

For dessert I've made a double-chocolate cake with a chocolate-mint frosting, and it's so good it almost makes me dizzy to eat my whole slice. We've relocated back to the living room, where the conversation slows, but comfortably, no one seeming to mind the little silences that pass while we digest and grow tired.

"All right, Kit," says Zoe. "Let's do the dishes so I can go. Obviously I need to get up early tomorrow so I can run the ten miles that will be required to get rid of the cake I just ate."

"No cleanup. I'll take care of it. I want to show Alex around before he collapses totally." I know he's probably tired from travel, and now with a big help of sugar coursing through his system, he's probably due for a crash.

We say our goodbyes, Alex offering to walk Greer to her faraway parking spot, but she demurs, insisting that Zoe will drive her over. She's so adorably flustered at my brother that I have to hold in a laugh. Alex, predictably, has no idea of the effect he has on her, and when he goes in for a hug, Zoe and I share a speaking glance, both of us half-expecting Greer to faint with nerves and embarrassment.

Once they're gone, I exhale loudly and smile at my brother. "Thanks.

For spending time with them, I mean. They're my people here. I never would have made it without them."

"They're great." I beam under his approval. This is part of my dynamic with Alex—he's always been the one I took my report cards to, the one I called whenever I had a paper accepted at a conference.

As we clear plates, I tell him more about the plans for the kitchen, figuring it makes the most sense to start the tour here. He's interested, but I can tell he's grown distracted now that we're on our own, as though he's anticipating what's coming. After what's probably about one hundred consecutive "uh-huhs," I finally break, leaning back against the counter and crossing my arms. "Okay," I say, taking a deep breath, "I was going to wait until breakfast tomorrow, but I can see you're tense, so let's do this now."

"Kit, come on. Let's not get into it."

"It's happening, Alex. It's not something I want to argue about."

He goes back out into the dining room, clearing more plates. But I can still see him, so I press on. "I've already met with my finance guy. Gifting the money gets expensive for both of us, with taxes and everything, but if I set up a trust—"

"No," he says, his movements growing more hurried before bringing back in the stack of plates he's collected. I try to barrel ahead, explaining what I've worked out for the trust, what paperwork he'll have to be a part of, but he interrupts me. "I told you, Kit. I don't want it. I appreciate what you're trying to do, but it's not what I want."

"It's what *I* want. You raised me, Alex. I want you to have half of this money. You took care of Dad on your own when I couldn't, and I owe you this."

"You don't owe me anything. We both take care of Dad now, and I already know you've been sending him more in the last few months."

"Right, but there were years when you were doing that by yourself," I say, already frustrated. This has been a sticking point between me and Alex for years. In college, I tried to send some of the money from my part-time jobs to Dad, and Alex found out and sent it back to me.

"You were in school. I didn't mind doing it." His voice is gruff, impatient. But I *know* he minded. Alex's whole life had been about taking care of our family. He'd worked full-time since he graduated high school, only leaving home to start photography seriously when I'd settled into my first year of college. He'd missed so many opportunities, sacrificed so much for me. I owed him everything—my safety, my education, what little stability I'd had growing up.

"Okay, you didn't mind. But now I can do something for you. This money—it would make your life better. You could get a place, be a bit more stable."

I've been too direct there—I can see it. Alex does not like to be mother-henned, probably on account of his not having a mother to have done it. But I hate that Alex travels all the time, that I don't get to see him except for every once in a while. I hate that he sometimes goes to dangerous places, and I hate that he never seems to talk about anyone he's close to—no friends, no girlfriends, no one except Dad, and that's less about closeness than it is about obligation.

He clenches his jaw and inhales, turning toward the sink to start rinsing. I know he's trying to stay calm, and I decide to give him a minute to cool off, so I go to collect more from the table. When I come back to the kitchen, he shuts off the water and turns to me, crossing his arms over his chest.

"I'm happy for you, Kit. I'm really happy you have this house, and your friends here, and that things are good for you. I know that's what you've always wanted. But stability isn't my dream. It's yours."

"But how do you *know* it's not your dream? How do you know you couldn't be happy if you settled down a little—"

He laughs, a snarky, clipped laugh, shaking his head as though he can't believe what I've said. "I just know," he says, and turns back to the sink.

"Okay, but what if I bought a place for you, something small and manageable, something you could come back to in between your trips? And then the trust could be used to maintain it, and—"

"Uh-huh," he says, his tone still laced with sarcasm. "And where would this place be?"

I'm wringing my hands back and forth over a dish towel now, feeling childish in the way only my big brother makes me feel. But he's pressing up right against the things inside me that are most soft and vulnerable, the things I'm always waiting for an opportunity to say, to make a reality. "Well, I guess it could be anywhere, but I mean, I don't see why *not* here, if you think about it, because, you know, we're family, and—"

"Kit, Jesus," he breathes, setting down a plate too firmly in the drying rack. "No. *No.*"

"No, we're not family?" I tease, trying to lighten his mood, trying to get us back to a place where we can talk without me touching every single one of his nerves. But he doesn't respond, so I say, "Come on, Alex. Please. Please let me do this for you."

"You don't get it. I don't want you to do anything for me, except to keep being okay, keep living your life. That's what I want. I'm glad you have the money, because you can do that, and it'll be so easy now, Kit. It'll be so much easier for you with the money."

"But I want it to be easy for both of us. We both deserve that, to be able to settle into a place and not worry about the next job, the next bill—"

"I don't worry about that. I do fine, better than fine. Maybe you don't understand that."

I don't, really. In my mind, Alex must be struggling to work as much as he does, to be taking jobs in these far-flung places, to be staying in short-term rentals whenever he does have an extended break. "I—well, it doesn't matter. It's still something I can do for you, and I want to. I really—I *need* to do this." Ugh, I feel tears well up a bit, and I swallow them back.

Alex's expression softens. I know he knows what I'm thinking. "You can't feel guilty about this, Kit. You got lucky. You've got to take your luck when it comes."

That last thing—it rings a bell for both of us. It's one of the things our dad used to say, usually right before he'd lose a ton of money and then go on a multi-day bender. Alex turns away, looking embarrassed.

I don't want that hanging in the air, so I go back to my earlier point. "Would it be so bad, though? To—you know. Slow down a bit? I thought if you stayed here for a while, got to know the city, maybe you'd think about—"

"I'm only here for a couple of days. I've got a job next week in Johannesburg."

"But you said you didn't have to travel again until August." I hate the way my voice sounds, a little whiny.

"I got a call yesterday." He's avoiding my eyes, a little too focused on his dishwashing.

I'm angry now, knowing he's lying to me. I march over to where he stands at the sink and shut off the water. "Don't bullshit me, Alex. You've been avoiding me for months."

"Because I knew you'd do this!"

"Do what? Try and share this great thing that's happened to me with my brother? Yeah, I'm being such a *dick*, right?"

"It's not—" he breaks off, clearly frustrated, and passes a wet hand through his hair, making it stick up in all directions. "It's great that you want to share it. But I've told you, I don't need it, and if I took it, you'd just—you'd expect things. You already expect things."

"I don't expect *anything*! Jesus, that's a horrible thing to say!"

"It's not. It's the truth. You want me around, you want me living a life more like *this*, staying in one place, everything easy." He spreads his arms out, gesturing to the house around us, making my pride and joy feel—plain. Insignificant.

"Oh, okay. I'm sorry this is so *dull* for you. I'm sorry it's not a tent in the freaking Amazon or whatever. I'm sorry that I actually wanted to have a home, a place of my own to take care of—"

"Kit, for fuck's sake. I don't give a shit that you wanted this. That's great for you. But don't forget—I did this already. It might've been in shithole apartments with no heat and leaky pipes and cockroaches, but I've got plenty of experience making homes. I made homes for you since the day your mom walked out. I *did* stability. I had to do it, for you and for Dad. I don't want that now. I don't want this. I don't want your fucking money, and I don't want to be tied down to anyone, anywhere. I just—I want to be on my *own*."

This hurts so bad that I wish I could bend over right where I'm standing to catch my breath. But I can see already Alex is registering what's just come out of his mouth, and for a second he clenches his eyes shut before looking at me again, his eyes full of pity.

I don't want his pity. I only want to be away from him right now.

"Hey, Tool Kit, listen, I didn't mean—"

"No, you know what? You did mean it. And you're—you have every right." I'm trying but failing to keep the wobble out of my voice. "I'm tired. You can leave everything, and I'll clean up tomorrow, okay?"

I'm halfway out of the room already, and Alex has tossed something—silverware, probably—in the sink, making a loud clatter. I don't even stop. I call over my shoulder to him that his room is the second door on the left upstairs, that I've put out towels for him in the bathroom. He'll see everything half-done now, without me explaining all my careful renovation plans, but I've stopped caring.

I don't hear him downstairs when I get in bed, even though I listen for a while. Maybe I should be angry at what Alex said, at him throwing it in my face that he got stuck with raising me, or maybe I should be sad for him, that his response to the way we grew up has been to cut himself off from anything permanent. But mostly I feel embarrassed, embarrassed at how excited I was to show the house off, that I was stupid enough to even suggest that Alex think about making this his home base.

It's late, but I know if I call Greer or Zoe they'll answer. Except I don't want them to think poorly of Alex now, not after we had such a good time, and even after what he's just said, he's my brother and I love him, and I want them to love him too. I think fleetingly about the night I asked Ben to meet Zoe and Greer at Betty's—was that the same instinct, somewhere deep down, that I wanted them to like him, to feel okay about whatever I was—*am*—doing with him? I think about calling him, maybe I could think of some question to ask him about the light fixture I want for the downstairs bath, and I know he'll take my mind off this. I know he'll have some funny story about his dad or River that will make me laugh.

But that's ridiculous, to call Ben.

I feel lonely enough to cry, but I don't. I just roll over into a ball and pull the covers around me, naming the elements from the periodic table until I finally fall asleep.

Chapter 12

Ben

"Riv, don't go so fast," I say, stilling the kid's hand as he paws through the tray of loose pieces I've put out for him on the workbench in the office. My dad's out front, dealing with customers, and even though he'd told me I didn't have to come in today, I know weekends are risky for River, easy times for him to get in trouble without his classes. So I'd called him this morning, told him we had to sort through some inventory before Monday. Not true, and I'm pretty sure River knew it, but he'd still shown up at ten.

"You've got to go piece by piece with a tray this big," I say, pulling out a yellowed candle tube to hold up. "See, this might look like junk, but it's from a chandelier, same as the one we worked on last week. No cracks, and the socket's in good shape. We find a bulb for this, and it'll work."

River doesn't say anything, but he slows down, taking out pieces and setting them on a large piece of felt I've laid out. Right now, the way he's ordering things doesn't seem to me to make much sense, but I'm not going to say anything. This is how I learned too—getting a feel for the objects, making my own patterns.

I turn back to my project, frowning at what I've got so far. I'm still missing at least thirty pieces for the Baltic chandelier I'd found last week, but I'm in deep now with it. I'd forgotten how much I enjoyed doing this when I was younger, how much I relished the puzzles of these old, found objects.

I want to call Kit to see if she wants to come over and have a look. But I know her brother is in town for the weekend, and I got the sense she'd planned a full agenda for them. And while we've spent a lot of time together over the last week, I've tried to make sure she comes to me first.

I don't want to crowd her. Or, I do—but it's bad enough I don't have my head in the game lately. Jasper called me on Thursday night, right as I was leaving her place, checking on whether I'd made any progress, and it had taken me a second to realize that I'd spent three hours with her and not brought up Beaumont once.

My dad limps in, looking a little pale as he lowers himself into the chair across from where River sits. His eyes scan the felt, and I feel my muscles tense infinitesimally. I'm hoping he doesn't say anything about whatever nonsense system River has going here, because I want the kid to figure it out on his own. I think he might break when he opens his mouth, but then he just as quickly closes it again, looking up at me with a faint smile.

"Dad, you ought to go home. You look tired."

"I am tired. I'm old," he says, and River snorts. My dad nudges him with his good foot. "Something funny, Smalls?"

To my surprise, River doesn't even blink at the nickname now. In fact, I'm pretty sure he's trying to hold back a smile. Even though I was frustrated with my dad for taking on River, especially right now, when he's still struggling to get better, I can't deny how good he is at this, how calm he is around River, how easy it is for him to make teasing feel the same as a compliment.

"I'm serious," I say. "Get Sharon to take you home so you can rest. I can be here until close."

My dad leans forward and scans River's tray, picking up what I'm guessing is a column from an oil lamp. "Aha," he says, like he knows exactly where that goes. The stupid thing is, he probably does. "Just needed to take a load off. Sharon's out there talking to some idiot about trying to match a stain. I couldn't listen to another second. This guy, first of all, he puts his cold beer right down on his mother's Eastlake side table. A real one too, Smalls, you hear? I'd say 1880, maybe. Now this mother, I doubt she's operating at full capacity, keeping a piece that rare right out in her living space, but I don't judge."

River slides his eyes over to me, and I stifle a grin. The only thing my dad does judge people about is how they treat their furniture.

"So this genius looks online at how to get this water stain out, and you know what he finds?" He pauses dramatically, but River only shrugs. Still, he's listening, I can tell. "*Toothpaste*," Dad says, throwing his hands in the air dramatically. "Toothpaste!" He huffs another exasperated breath. "Now the thing about toothpaste is, sometimes it'll work on water staining, but we're only talking the real old-fashioned kind of toothpaste here, not this fancy shit they sell these days, you hear?"

I go over to the fridge in the corner and pull out Dad's lunch, unwrapping his sandwich and pickle and putting it on one of the plates he keeps on top of the fridge. He's still going on about water stains when I set it in front of him, his color back, and he barely notices me. "Eat," I say, and snag the tray from River, setting it aside. "You bring lunch?"

"Yeah," he says, and digs into his backpack, coming up with a crumpled brown paper bag that he unpacks in front of him on the workbench. Can of Coke, smashed PB&J, a bag of what I think are Doritos in broken, jagged pieces, though I probably haven't seen a Dorito since college, so what do I know. I take an apple and a bottle of water from the fridge and set them in front of him before turning back to my chandelier. "So it's got to be repainted?" River asks, his mouth full.

"Repainted!" Dad shouts. "Ben, he said repainted! What are you *teaching* him back here?" I don't even bother answering, because Dad barrels on, talking to River about wood stain. The next half hour goes this way, and I suspect River is being purposefully ignorant about some things, just to see my dad get riled up. It's good for both of them, and it's good for me too, their soundtrack a nice accompaniment to my work. I'm hanging the pear-shaped prisms I've got for the chandelier on a length of fishing line I've strung up over the workbench, which has the best light for me to check for small cracks or dings in the glass. It feels nice to move my eyes across the facets, to not look at a screen all morning, to not have a phone tucked against my ear.

As though it's heard my thoughts, my phone rings from the pocket of my jeans, and I close my eyes briefly, thinking of ignoring it. If it's Jasper, I don't want to hear it, but it's bad enough I'm dealing with work from here these last few weeks, so I answer, not even bothering to check who's calling.

"Ben Tucker," I say, waving a hand at my dad to quiet down. I think I hear him call me "Mr. Fancypants" to River.

"Hi." It's Kit's voice, and I'm more happy than I should be to hear from her. But even in that one syllable, I hear something I don't like, a stuffy, wet quality to the way she sounds. My body goes from relaxed to alert, and I turn my back to the rest of the room.

"What's wrong?" When she doesn't answer right away, I get even more tense. "Kit?"

There's a big sigh on the other end of the phone before she speaks again. "Yeah—I probably shouldn't have called. But something's gone wrong in the house, and I'm not sure—"

"Is it anything dangerous? Anything electrical? Do you smell gas?" I don't know why my mind is going to this kind of shit; I sound neurotic.

But I hate the way she sounds.

"No, no. It's—this is really dumb. But I think I maybe—made a mistake with something? And now there's a mess, and I'm not sure if I should keep going, or…listen, I'm sorry. I'm sorry to call you on a Saturday."

"I'll come over. Give me twenty minutes."

She pauses, and I hear something on the other end of the line, a repetitive metallic, scraping sound, followed by what might be a muffled curse from her. I haven't known Kit long, but I know I can't just go over, not unless she says it's okay. She likes handling herself, and she probably waited until things were really bad to make this call anyway.

"Okay," she says, after a little more silence, and I didn't even realize I was holding my breath.

"Don't touch anything else," I say, which is ridiculous, because I don't even know what she's been doing.

I disconnect and turn back to where my dad and River sit. My dad's watching me with interest, but River's still making his way through the tray. "You've got your young lady calling you," Dad says. I don't even bother correcting him about this. I'm too focused on getting out of here.

"I can come back to take you home."

He waves a hand. "Go. Sharon'll take me. She's on 'til we close." I nod, and look toward River. My dad jumps in. "Smalls. You're with me the rest of the day. This moron hasn't taught you anything."

"Cool," River says, and I'm out the door, headed to Kit.

* * * *

I barely hear her say "Come in," when I knock fifteen minutes later after a too-fast drive. When I walk in, there's a funny smell of dust and chemicals throughout the house, but I don't see anything out of order right away.

"Kit?" I call out, shutting and locking the door behind me. She shouldn't be in here with it open, no matter what time of day it is. This neighborhood is spotty, but I'll talk to her about that later.

"I'm up here." I take the stairs two at a time, and it's a gut-punch when I come across her in the hallway, huddled with her back to the wall, her knees pulled up to her chest, her face pink and tear-streaked. Oh, fuck, I already hate this. I hate seeing her upset. I'm frozen in place, staring at her, and it takes me a second to register the mess she has around her—there's a propane steamer to her right, shut off, and the floor is lined with plastic. There's a spray bottle and a metal scraper and a trash can and—I squint up at the walls—a good bit of plaster dust.

"Jesus, Kit. What happened?"

"I don't know—well, I do know. I tried stripping the wallpaper, and I did everything right, exactly how I read about. And anyways, I didn't just read about it—I *know* this stuff. I know chemicals, right?" She picks up the spray bottle, gives it a little shake. "But I don't know what went wrong. Now the plaster is peeling away too, and—I don't know! It's a *mess*."

Her head bows, and she brings her hands up to cradle it. That's all it takes for my stomach to cramp in distress, such a sudden, visceral reaction that I move right away, and before I can think about it, I'm kneeling down in front of her amidst scraps of wallpaper, feeling it crinkle and stick to my jeans. "Hey, hey," I say quietly, and probably my voice has never sounded that way, so soft and desperate. But that's how I feel—desperate. Desperate to stop her looking this way.

"I really, really needed this to work today."

"Why today?"

She shakes her head, the movement knocking her glasses a little from side to side. I wonder fleetingly where her brother's gone, but I don't want to press her if she doesn't want to talk. I think if I could just hug her, or set a hand on her knee—touch her in some small way, maybe it would help. But I've never touched her in either comfort or affection, even though I've thought about it every single time I've been in the same room with her, and also lots of times when I haven't been. So instead, I reach up past her shoulder and pull at a strip of wallpaper that's hanging down near her hair. And sure enough, there's small chunks of plaster stuck to the back. I touch the wall, pretty sure of what I'll find.

"You've got some moisture behind this wall, I think," I tell her, trying to break the news gently. It's not the worst thing. Lime plaster isn't so hard to repair, but Kit's got a lot on her plate with this house, and I'm guessing every flaw she comes across at this point is a blow.

And sure enough, she lets out a little hiccup, the beginnings of a sob, and—*fuck*—that does me in. I can't just sit here, so far apart from her. So I adjust myself, spreading my legs wide on the floor around her huddled form. I gently take her wrists, tugging her hands from her face. I wait for her to flinch or stop me, but she doesn't—I think she might even lean in to it a little. Her eyes are huge and wet behind her glasses. "Listen," I say, keeping my voice low. "It's all right. My dad knows every contractor in this town, and he'll get you a deal on whatever the work is. Or I could help. I've done plaster repair before. No charge, I promise." It's a small offer, but I make it as if I'm opening a vein. The way she *looks* sitting there—I'd say or do anything.

"It's not the money," she whispers, leaning back against the wall, closing her eyes. I'm still holding on to her wrists, a little awkwardly, like we're on some strange seesaw, so I let my hands slip down to—well. I guess I'm holding her hands now, and I have to take a breath to steady myself against the feeling of holding even this small part of her. I've known all along I have a thing for Kit. But this thing? This is more than liking her, more than wanting her in bed.

"I won the lottery," she whispers, snapping me right out of my thoughts. I look up to see if she's joking, but her eyes are still closed.

"You what?"

"Yeah. I mean, not like, just now. About six months ago."

"You won the lottery?"

"No one knows," she says, opening her eyes and looking right at me, a warning. "Greer and Zoe know, because we played together. And my brother." Here, she breaks off, clears her throat. "My brother knows. But no one else." I think maybe it's not a warning after all. Maybe it's an offering.

I squeeze her hands gently, letting her know she can trust me. But I don't know what to say now—my mind is reeling. A lot of things click into place—why Kit seems so completely uninterested in the massive salary Beaumont is offering her, how she's got more renovations planned for the next year than most people would do over the course of a decade. But other things—why she bought such a rundown house in the first place, why she does so much of the renovation herself, why she drives such a shitty car—I'm wondering about those too.

"I think maybe it's bad luck," she says. "Greer was worried it was bad luck. And I bought this house, like an idiot, and not a single thing has gone right with it since I bought it."

"Kit, this is a great house. You know that. It's always this way with renos."

She shakes her head again, her hair sticking a little to the wall behind her. "I shouldn't have bought it."

"Don't say that. This place has great bones, and—"

"I mean I shouldn't have bought the ticket! The lottery ticket."

I rub my thumbs across the soft skin of her wrists, trying to calm her. Her skin feels so good, I want to press my mouth there. "It's not bad luck," I tell her. "That's just one of those urban myths. I promise you." *Where do you get off, making her promises?* I think. *You're probably part of her bad luck.*

"My dad is a gambling addict."

Oh. I shift then, turning to set my back against the wall so I can sit right beside her, but I hold fast to one of her hands, and when I stretch my legs out in front of me, I twine our fingers together. She takes a deep breath, and I wait, holding her hand. I'll sit here all night, against this sticky, damp wall, on this hard floor, if I can only make her talk to me.

"I've never gambled in my life. I've never played the lottery before that night. I don't even like to play Monopoly. My dad—he bets on everything. Horse races. Football. Sometimes reality TV shows. He plays craps and poker. And he plays the lottery too, mostly scratch-off tickets. He's dead broke most of the time, and he totally fucked up my childhood, and my brother and I—we tried to get him into recovery for years, but nothing works, you know? *Nothing.*" She kicks out one of her legs in frustration, knocks it hastily into the steamer. "So, I mean, how *gross* is it that I played the lottery, first of all, and then I fucking *win*? I win! He's probably bought thousands of tickets. And I buy *one*."

"You can't think that way. You didn't do anything wrong."

"I'm keeping it from him," she says, her words coming more quickly now. She pulls her hand away, and I feel like I've lost a limb. "I haven't said a word. What about that? Do you think *that's* wrong?"

"No, I don't. I think you shouldn't tell anyone if you don't want to. And I think if he's an addict, he may want something from you, something that's not good for him."

She gives this impolite little snort. I think it's supposed to be sarcastic in tone, but she's been crying and sniffling and so it just sounds sad, defeated. "I send him money every month. Alex and I both have, for a long time. But now—I'm still sending him the same amount. Because if I send him more, he'll use it for stakes instead of for food, instead of paying his water bill. I know I shouldn't feel bad—I know I shouldn't. I used to go to these, you know, Gam-Anon meetings? And people there, they're always telling you how you can't make yourself responsible for someone's addiction. But it's not easy, you know? I want to be able to do something, and I had this big fight with Alex…"

Alex is the brother, I guess, and I've never met the guy but I'd like nothing more than to punch his face for being even partially responsible for the way Kit feels right now. "Is he here?" I say, trying not to sound how I feel, which is restless and pissed.

She slides a glance toward me, as if she sees right through me. "No. We had an exceedingly strained breakfast this morning and then he told me he got an earlier flight out." She shrugs. "It's for the best. He needs his space."

Somehow, I know in my bones what Kit needs, so I go for broke, raising an arm up to put around her shoulders. It's awkward, at first, because she's got to lean forward from the wall to accommodate me, but after the barest hesitation she leans in to me, setting her head against my shoulder, and it's as natural as breathing for me to press my mouth against her hair, to inhale her scent while I hold her close to me. I'm pretty sure my ass is falling asleep on this hard floor, and the baseboard is poking me right in the spine, but I don't give a good goddamn about it. When Kit takes a deep breath and snuggles herself a centimeter closer to me, I feel like I've solved the world's problems.

"This is really unprofessional," she says, after a few minutes of silence, silence where I've been listening to her breathe, feeling the sweet weight of her head on my shoulder, and also trying not to notice the way she's set a hand on my thigh.

I laugh, because it *is* really unprofessional, and after this I have no fucking idea how I'm going to try and get her to Beaumont, but I can't really scare up any feeling about that at the moment—she's the only thing I'm thinking about right now. "Sure is," I say, and she huffs out a small laugh too.

She stirs a little, staying close, but unless she's inhuman, her ass has to be feeling the pain too. I don't want to leave her yet, or really at all, but I'll take what I can get to draw out my time with her, so I say, "Hungry?"

She tips her head up from where it rests on my shoulder. Her eyes are still pink and puffy behind her glasses, but no more tears, and anyway I get distracted by her mouth, which is so close that I could move the barest inch and be kissing her. She'd better not look down, because I am absolutely about to pitch a tent in my jeans. She smiles, the first one I've seen from her all day. "I could eat."

She scrambles up, brushing wallpaper pieces and plaster dust off her butt and thighs as she heads toward the stairs, and I swallow and clench my fists beside me. My whole side is still warm from where her body rested against mine.

"Right behind you," I say, but it takes me a few seconds to pull myself together.

* * * *

I make her a grilled cheese and she cuts me the biggest piece of chocolate cake I've ever seen in my life, and we sit at her dining room table while I scroll through my phone, finding numbers of the local contractors I know. I make her laugh, telling her about my dad and the water-stained table, and I moan over her cake, both because it makes her smile and blush but also because it's a great fucking piece of cake. By the time she's finished off her sandwich, I've already called my dad to get his suggestions for who I should call first, and when I hang up, stuffing the last bite of chocolate cake in my mouth, Kit's tapping her short nails on the table, her eyes narrowed at me. "What?" I say, but it sounds closer to *Bwof?* I think about all the dinners I go on for work, my impeccable table manners at even the most sophisticated places. Apparently you give me chocolate cake and Kit Averin and I turn into a Neanderthal. The fact that I've noticed that her breasts look spectacular in her tank top is, frankly, a further point in favor of this theory.

"Why are you helping me?"

This takes me off guard, even though it shouldn't. My reaction to Kit— my need, since I've met her, to involve myself in aspects of her life that have nothing to do with the job I'm supposed to be doing with her—is not typical for anyone in our situation, and it's especially not typical for me, since in general I've involved myself with women who aren't interested in much more than a night out, a good lay, no complications. I swallow and take a big gulp of my water, shrugging as I set my glass down. "You called. You said you needed help." She hadn't really said this, and I know it, but I'm hoping she won't call me out on it.

"But surely this works against your purposes." I can feel her eyes on me, even though I'm looking idly through my phone's browser again, pulling up the number for the contractor my dad wanted me to call first. "Surely it would be better for you to let everything in this house go to hell as quickly as possible, so maybe I'll decide to give up and go to Texas."

I look up at her. Should I say something about what she's told me, about how knowing she has this money means Texas is probably not a necessity for her, even if this house does go to shit? I don't want to bring up something that I know is tender, hurtful to her. "Surely that's true. But let me ask you something, Kit."

She raises her eyebrows at me, and this is familiar territory, this sparring. We do this well together.

"Why did you call me today?"

She shifts in her chair, looks out the back window. "I don't know."

"Come on," I say, because the thing I like best about Kit is that she doesn't bullshit me, or anyone.

Her chest rises when she takes a deep inhale. "I called because—I thought you'd make me feel better. You *do* make me feel better." She shakes her head slightly after she says this last part, as if she can't quite believe it.

"Doesn't that work against your purposes?"

"I don't have any purposes."

"I mean—your purposes to see me as the big, bad corporate guy. The money guy. The guy you're going to keep saying no to."

She leans back in her chair, crossing her arms over her chest and leveling me with a big, black-eyed stare. Holy shit, though, that tank top. That tank top is my Everest right now.

"Depends on the question," she says, and my mind just—stutters. If she's thinking about work right now, then it's 100 percent fact that Kit has scrambled my sex radar forever, because there's something about the way she's looking at me, something about the way her voice has pitched a little bit lower. I feel like I'm about five minutes away from fucking her on this table, three minutes from getting under that tank top.

I stare right back at her. I watch as a pink flush creeps onto her pale cheeks, right under where the edge of her glasses rest. But Kit—despite the tears before, despite the fact that she's had a lousy go of it today—Kit is tough as hell, and if she means the way she's looking at me right now, she's not going to back down.

I set down my phone and stand from my chair. She tips her head back to follow my movements, to look up at me from where she sits, arms still crossed, eyes still challenging.

"I'm asking," I say, once I'm standing right in front of her, and she likes that. The right side of her mouth quirks up in a half smile.

"Well," she says, reaching up to slip off her glasses, setting them on the buffet that's behind her. "I'm answering."

I'm on her so fast, lifting her out of her chair to set her ass up on the table, and she instantly spreads her legs to let me step between them, and it's this hot, unbearable pause where our faces are inches apart, where I know we're both thinking about how easy that was, how quickly we got to a place where my crotch is pressed against hers. But then I'm kissing her, my hands coming up to cradle her jaw, to tip her face just so, and holy shit, kissing Kit is hot, and sweet, and the way she opens her mouth against mine and slides her tongue across my bottom lip—I've got to stop myself from clenching my hands, from grabbing fistfuls of her hair to bring her closer to me. She's got her hands on my stomach, stroking up and down, and when I feel her grab the fabric in her fingers, tugging, I moan, knowing she feels the same way I do, that desperation to get closer. I want these clothes off, want to feel her skin against mine, and I let my hands trail from her neck down her arms, thinking of how I can get this top off her without taking my mouth from hers.

There's a soft knocking, and I think—*shit, this table*, because it's old, and despite my earlier fantasy, it's probably not a good idea for me to fuck her on it. But—no, it's not the table, because then the doorbell rings, and Kit stiffens and pulls away, her busy hands coming to rest right at my waistband, and I think if that fucking antique doorbell weren't so loud, you could probably hear my dick calling out, *lower! Just a little lower!*

"I—uh. I should get that," she says, but she winces when she looks down, sees the bulge in my jeans. "God. I'm so, *so* sorry."

I can't even form words at the moment. All my higher-order thinking skills have relocated to my balls. I step back from her and she scrambles off the table, snagging her glasses. Her hair is a mess from my hands in it, plus she's still got a few pieces of plaster stuck there in the back, and maybe I got one over on that tank top after all, because it's twisted and bunched up a little, and she straightens it as she walks to the front door.

Once she's out of sight, I turn back toward the table, discreetly adjust myself so that whoever comes in doesn't get sexually harassed just by my existence. Holy hell, I need a cold shower. I settle for another drink of water, a rough pass of my hand through my hair. I don't think I've ever been so turned on in my life from a single kiss.

"Greer is here!" Kit says from behind me, and her voice is so transparently, falsely cheerful that I feel better, more at ease knowing she's as thrown off as I am.

"Hi," says Greer, in that small, sweet voice she has. Greer is no dummy— she knows she's walked into something, and so I make even more of an effort to control my expression, to pretend I'm not going home with the worst case of blue balls I've had since eleventh grade.

"Hey, Greer. How's school?"

Kit gives me a grateful smile, and it's hard not to feel proud whenever I get even a scrap of approval from her.

"Oh—it's okay. It's good. We just started an entrepreneurship unit in my business class," she says. "That's kind of your thing, right?"

"Kind of," I say. Greer is holding her purse in one hand and a few DVDs in the other, and even though I'm doing my best, it's awkward in here. I get the sense that dining room table has something to say. I turn back to it, grab my phone and keys and tuck them into my pockets. "I should go," I tell them, but I'm looking at Kit, and she's flushed and fidgeting. If she asks me to stay, if she makes any move to suggest that she wants me to hang around, even if it's with her and Greer, even if I'm spending my evening sitting on her couch and watching—I think that's a copy of *Predator*, which is unexpected—I'll stay.

But she seems cautious, and I don't want to press her. "I'll make some calls about upstairs," I tell her.

"Thank you. Really."

I can sense that Greer is looking back and forth between us, but she too seems locked in place. I hate the heavy, frozen feeling in the room, and I have to do something.

So I do what feels, weirdly, like the most natural thing. I step forward, setting my hand on Kit's upper arm, where her skin is bare and warm, and I lean down to press a firm kiss on her mouth, a quick, intimate touch, as if I've done it a million times, as if this woman didn't just give me the best first kiss I've ever had. "I'll call you," I say, right against her mouth, then set another quick kiss there.

And then I'm headed toward the front door, calling out a quick goodbye to Greer. I barely hear the way she squeaks out a surprised "'Bye!" before I'm on the porch, already wondering when I'll see Kit again.

Chapter 13

Kit

Monday morning, and no call from Ben, not that I'm waiting around or anything. Not that I kept my ringer on high all day yesterday. Not that I couldn't stop thinking about how easily Ben put me on that table, about how hard and strong he was all over, about how he tasted like chocolate and kissed like a dream.

Not any of that.

It isn't that he left me hanging. He'd texted me Sunday morning to let me know he'd be at the salvage yard all day, filling in for his dad, who'd had a rough night of pain. He said he had a call in to the plaster guy, and he'd keep me posted.

But he hadn't made any reference at all to what had happened, either.

I think of calling him, because I am genuinely a little worried for Henry, who tries so hard to act as if he's not in any pain at all. But if I call to check on Henry, will that seem like I'm really only calling to check on Ben? And anyways, what is Henry to me other than the owner of a business I've been frequenting the last few weeks? Would I be crossing a line?

This kind of thinking—it's not the way I am, not at all, and I'm frustrated with myself and with Ben, and with everything else that's been bothering me since Friday. Alex and I shared a mostly silent breakfast on Saturday, except for when he tried to apologize, again, but I was so desperate not to get into it again that I'd put him off. I'd given him a half-hearted tour of the house before he'd headed off to the airport, and in turn he'd asked half-hearted questions as we moved from room to room. But it wasn't the same, and I feel the pain of our fight as though it's a bruise on my body.

It's tender and fresh and I'm trying to avoid it with every move I make.

So I'm up early, headed in to work by six, hoping I can get a couple of hours on the microscope before most of the grad students show up. The walk is good for me—it's going to be another hot day, but right now it's cool enough that I can move without sweating. The blooms of the crepe myrtle trees that line my street are fat and heavy with dew, and the air is sweet with the smell of cinnamon rolls from the bakery on the corner.

Block by block, I let my mind go to the place where I feel safest, to work and the lab, to where I can untangle problems I know how to fix.

By the time I arrive at my basement office, I'm feeling a bit more myself, and it's at least an hour and a half before I hear signs of life in other parts of the building. I make progress on scanning a couple of my samples, but soon enough, it becomes a busy morning—I help Akeelah with her sample preparation, and Todd, playing to type, refuses my offer of help in positioning the beam on the microscope for his initial scan, but then fucks it up and has to ask for me to fix it anyway. I meet with Dr. Harroway, who was my professor in Intro to Non-Ferrous Metals when I was a graduate student, and show him a new animation I did one night last week for explaining crystal structure to undergrads. He's so thrilled that he asks me to come do a lecture to his class this fall.

I'm eating lunch in my office when Dr. Singh knocks softly, his manner always so gentle and tentative that I sometimes wonder how he has managed to survive in this field, let alone how he's managed to become one of its most respected scholars. He seems entirely comfortable in the background of things, and I think this is why I find it so easy to work with him.

I move a stack of papers from the extra chair I have and invite him to sit. When I first started working here, only two weeks after I'd graduated, I'd struggled to talk to Dr. Singh in any other way than progress reports—as his student, I'd always felt compelled to tell him how far along I was on my experiments, on my thesis. As his colleague, I frequently found myself doing the same, giving him an account of how I'd spent my day. He'd listen patiently until I finished, but then he'd just go straight into what he'd sought me out for in the first place—usually to tell me about a meeting or to ask a question about the microscope—without acknowledging my rambling. Eventually, I got used to the idea that he wasn't checking up on me.

"I have good news," he says, a faint look of displeasure crossing his face as he tries to get comfortable in the chair. It's not going to happen since that thing looks as if it came from an elementary school classroom in the 1980s, but Dr. Singh would never complain. "We heard back from the *Journal of Applied Metallurgy* today. With some slight adjustments, they want to publish our paper."

He says this with the same measured tone that he says everything, but this news is big, and we both know it, so we're sort of dumbly smiling at each other across my desk. We worked for years on this paper, having started it in my final year of the master's program. It has data from some of my most successful work on the microscope, data that I was hoping to save for this kind of publication. I'm so excited that I clasp my hands together in pride, squeezing them tightly to prevent an outburst of actual applause. "Congratulations," I say, and Dr. Singh shakes his head, his smile dimming.

"The congratulations go to you." He's clearing his throat, shifting his eyes downward.

Shit, I think, anticipating what's coming. This is the worst part about academic publishing, that you're going to get asked to change your work so much that it won't even resemble what you'd originally done, that you'd have to sell out your work to get the publication credit. For me, this isn't such a big deal—I'm not faculty, and it doesn't really matter to me or my bosses whether I get publications, so I can tell journals to stuff it if I want. I'd be disappointed, but I'd try again with another journal. Dr. Singh, though, is going up for promotion next year, and his case will be a slam dunk if he gets this publication in this particular journal—going somewhere else could take months. "What kind of changes do they want?" I ask, afraid to hear the answer.

"Very minor," he says, and then repeats it with emphasis, as if to convince me. "It's actually more that—that *I'd* want to make a change."

"Oh?" I'm confused. Dr. Singh has been happy with every draft of the paper I've given him. On the last draft, he'd not made a single change, a fact that had filled me with giddy pride.

"I want to make you primary author on the paper."

My face goes immediately hot, the same feeling you get when you've narrowly missed some kind of disaster, a car wreck or a nasty fall. I've never been first author on a publication, and it's rare for someone in my position to have that kind of professional credit. I say the first thing that comes to mind. "No. No, that's—that's really okay."

Dr. Singh leans forward, tapping his hand on my desk. "Ekaterina," he says, and now I really *do* feel like his student again—the way he says my name is an admonishment. "You cannot turn this down. Aside from it being short-sighted for you do so, in professional terms, I am actually insisting that the change be made."

"But I've explained," I say, and I hear that my voice has gone a little high, a little desperate. "I'm not looking for other professional opportunities.

I'm very happy to be where I am. This position suits me. This is what I want." I look away from his skeptical expression. "The first author thing—it doesn't matter to me. At all."

"Everything in this paper is your work. All of the data. You've written it. Yes, I provided the equipment, and yes, the funding came from my group, but this is your work. It may not matter to you, but it matters to me that I not overstate my contribution."

The hands that I had clasped in celebration before—I'm wringing them now, and I make a conscious effort to stop, setting them in my lap. I want to seem in control here, but I feel panicky and startled, unprepared for this confrontation.

He seems to recognize my discomfort, and takes a deep breath before continuing. "You know very well, Ekaterina, that your work is more sophisticated than every postdoc we have here. It's more sophisticated than some of our faculty's. I know you have your own reasons for staying in this position when you could be doing more, and I certainly benefit from whatever keeps you here. But you were my student, and perhaps you are too comfortable standing behind me, rather than out front, on your own."

"That's not it…" I begin, but he holds up a hand to stop me.

"Maybe not. What keeps you from doing more is not my business. But what is my business is how this article sees the light of day. I'm not comfortable being lead author on a paper that I'm not responsible for."

Someone else might hear this from Dr. Singh and wonder whether there's some kind of embarrassment about the work, some concern that it's not good enough to have his name attached to it. But this isn't it, and I know it—my work is solid, the data precise, the writing strong. I may be doing a job that I'm overqualified for, but that doesn't mean I underestimate my own talent or capability.

"If you have my permission, though," I say, quietly, not sure how I want to finish the thought.

"We have a week," he says, standing from his chair, "to reply to their acceptance letter. You let me know if you accept my terms. If not, I'll decline their offer to publish the article."

He gives a nod, almost a slight little bow, one of many gentlemanly relics Dr. Singh has, before leaving my office, his soft steps fading down the hall.

Lunch seems entirely unappetizing at this point, even the small piece of cake I packed as a treat for myself. I hate that Dr. Singh has changed the rules on me, that he tells me now—when the paper is only a step or two away from publication in such a prestigious journal—about stepping down as lead author.

I feel duped, angry.

But as I move through the rest of my workday, setting up scans for two grad students in Harroway's group, ordering a part for the SEM, running a diagnostic on one of the older scopes we're trying to keep online, I realize I'm less angry at Dr. Singh than I am at the very idea that he brought up, that I could *be doing so much more.* This is what Ben has said to me almost every time he's tried to sell me on Beaumont, that I'm wasting my talent, that I have no vision. And this is basically what Alex said to me too—*staying in one place, everything easy.*

By the time I'm ready to call it a day, I'm doing that thing where you too aggressively pack your bag, too thunderously go up the stairs, too forcefully open the door. I'm fucking *pissed*, actually. Who are these men, anyways, to tell me what I should be doing, what my talent is good for, what's easy? Who are these men to say that I have to live a life where work takes over, where I'm always worried about the next thing? Who are these men who think having vision means making money, making *things*? And who are these fucking men to tell me what's easy? What's easy about becoming a part of a community, about reading the local paper every week, making sure you try something new, even if it's scary and you have to go by yourself? What's easy about making best friends, about forming relationships that are going to last, when someone has your back and you have theirs? What's easy about trying to make a home for yourself, when you've never had one before?

I don't notice anything on my walk home, don't feel the oppressive heat of the early evening, don't even bother to wipe the sweat that I feel trace down my jaw. I don't do anything but march toward my house, feeling righteous and defensive and ready to unleash all my anger on the next person who does me wrong.

And lucky for me, there's Ben sitting on my front stoop, waiting.

* * * *

I'm a nightmare when I'm in this kind of mood, and I know it. I'm alternatively quiet and remote, making everyone around me feel responsible for some unspoken error, or I'm quick to lash out, touchy and argumentative. But as soon as I draw close to Ben, as soon as I see the way his big, rangy body takes up space, the way his hands are loosely clasped between his spread knees, the evening stubble on his jaw—some of the fight goes out of me, so I stop in front of him, managing a grudging, "Hi." Even if the things Ben has said to me over the past few weeks are part of why I'm mad, I know it has nothing to do with what happened today with Dr. Singh.

"Hi," he says back, a smile pulling at the corners of his mouth. He looks—I don't know. Relieved, I guess. Relieved to see me. "Couldn't get a hold of you today, and I had some news, so I thought I'd come by."

I dig into my bag, pulling out my phone. Shit, he *did* call twice. I just forgot to turn on my ringer after my meeting with Harroway. Now I have exactly zero things to be annoyed with him about, which is really ruining my righteous indignation mojo.

"How's your dad?" I ask.

"He's all right. He had PT this morning, and they loosened him up a bit. He's feeling good."

"Good."

"I found a plaster guy for you. He can come by tomorrow morning to have a look."

"I have to work."

"I figured. But if you're okay with it, I can meet him here, let him in. If you're not, no problem. He could come Wednesday after five too."

"Wednesday," I say, because I'm still feeling stubborn, not because I don't trust Ben to be here. Maybe *because* I trust him to be here, maybe because I trust him more than I'm willing to admit.

He leans back a little to take out his phone and types out a quick message before tucking it back in his pocket. "All set."

"That's the news?" This sounds dismissive, sarcastic. I close my eyes briefly, scolding myself.

"Kit." The way he says my name, it's a caress, smoothing down all the hackles I have raised. This should annoy me, maybe, this sense I have that he's handling me in some way, but it doesn't. It makes me want to sit right next to him on the stoop, to settle myself into the same crook of his body where he held me close on Saturday.

"I'm sorry," I say. "It was a rough day at work." I know already I shouldn't say this to Ben, whose job it is to look for ways to exploit any unhappiness I might have in my current situation. But I'm tired of fighting the closeness I feel with him. I had a taste of it Saturday, and I just—I just want to *feast* on it right now.

"I didn't have the greatest day at the office, either," he says, surprising me. "The office" is not how Ben usually talks about work at the yard, so he's got to be talking about Beaumont, and while we've spent an awful lot of time talking about how I might be involved there, in general Ben doesn't say much about the day-to-day of his real job.

"Yeah?"

He smiles up at me. "Yeah. I spoke to my partner about how things are progressing with your case."

I stiffen immediately, noticing now, for the first time, that I'd slowly been tipping forward a bit, leaning in to him as we'd talked. I should *not* trust Ben, ever. I should always remember what he came to me for in the first place. It doesn't *matter* what's happened since.

"Kit," he says again, but it doesn't help this time.

"Listen. This has been a really shitty day. Every time we've talked about Beaumont, I've managed to give you calm, rational answers about why I'm not interested. I don't really have the capacity for that tonight. But my answer is the same. It's no. I'm not coming to Texas. I'm not going to do the job. Ever."

"I don't care," he says.

"You don't—?"

"I called my partner to tell him I'm off your case. I'm not able to recruit you."

I stare at him, unsure of how to process this information. I should be relieved, thinking Beaumont has given up, that I won't have to field any more of their queries. But all I can think is: Does this mean I won't see Ben anymore?

"I'm not able to recruit you because I'm involved with you."

There's a pause, a lull—and I'm so grateful for the sounds of the early evening, for the faint hum of traffic going by a few blocks away, for the cicadas starting their evening song.

"What does that mean?" I'm intentionally vague with my question. Maybe I'm asking what it means for Beaumont's pursuit of me. Maybe I'm asking what it means for him and his job. But maybe I'm asking what it means for him and me. Because when I think of being "involved" with Ben, I think about his clothes on my bedroom floor. I think about all his weight on top of me, that chocolate-sweet kiss.

"It means," he says, looking right at me, looking right through me, really, "that if you say okay, I'm coming in this house with you and finishing what we started. It means I got Sharon to stay with my dad tonight, so I have every intention of taking you to bed and keeping you there all night. It means I haven't stopped thinking about your mouth since Saturday. It means that right now, I don't give one good goddamn about anything other than making sure I have you every way I can before you have to go to work tomorrow."

I make a sound—I think it's probably some combination of a whimper and an *unf*—and lean against the porch railing, trying to catch the breath

Ben stole with that speech, which is actually the hottest thing anyone has ever said to me, and this includes the time my college boyfriend said he thought I'd win a Nobel Prize someday. Ben's posture is as relaxed as it has been since I got home, but there's some kind of new tension underneath, an energy I feel pulsing beneath his skin. "Okay," I breathe, and he stands up before I have it all the way out.

"Inside," he says, and that one word is hotter than the speech. I go inside, Ben right behind me.

* * * *

Being with Ben is a reminder of the limits of my imagination.

Because while I'd thought of this, late at night, alone in my bed, I hadn't had much of it right, other than the fact that I'd suspected it'd be good between us. I hadn't expected that we'd come together the way we are now—greedy, a little clumsy, him against my back as I drop my bag, spinning me around so he can get his mouth on mine, open and searching. I hadn't expected that I'd so quickly wrap my arms tight around his neck, one of my legs hitching up around his hip, and I hadn't expected that he'd so quickly, so fiercely, grab on, pulling my other leg around him so that he could carry me up the steps, our kiss frantic, bumpy, his teeth nipping my upper lip, my tongue seeking his lips even as I reach up to pull off my glasses.

"God, Kit," he says, when we get into my bedroom, "We've got to—"

"Don't. Don't say *slow down.*"

I'm on my back on the bed, Ben a planet above me, broad and strong and so hot that I have to close my eyes for a second, catch my breath. Maybe we *should* slow down. I hear a rustle of clothes and I open my eyes to Ben pulling off his shirt, and it's—*wow*, it's all systems go. He looks incredible, hard packs of muscles on his abdomen, the wide expanse of his chest leading to those bunched, sinewy biceps.

"Off," he says, tugging at my top at the same time his other hand reaches for my jeans, unbuttoning, lowering the zipper. I'd help, but I'm too busy, splaying my hands on his hot skin, arching up so he can remove my top but also so I can open my mouth against his shoulder, taste his salty skin. "Kit, *fuck*. Get your clothes off."

His words bring me back to myself, and I take over, tugging my jeans off before pausing. "Oh," I say, and Ben stops biting and licking at my collarbone long enough to look at me.

"What?" He almost looks panicked, as if we have to stop this he'll actually expire, and I enjoy that so much that I make him sweat it for a second.

"I'm—Well. I'm not wearing, you know. Really sexy underwear."

"Are you fucking kidding? Kit. I don't care." He bends down again, sucks at the join of my neck and shoulder. "I can't tell you how much I don't care. I won't even look. Just—*please*. Get naked." This makes me laugh, the desperate, growly quality to the way he's talking. I hadn't expected him to be this way either, all his calm charm stripped away. It's funny, messy, the way my clothes come off, him pulling my bra off while I push my jeans down, limbs tangling, whispered curses when I remember I have to kick off my shoes. Ben is laughing too, and oh, God—it's so *fun* with Ben, everything is always so fun and easy with him, even first-time sex with him, when usually I feel these whispers of awkwardness being naked with someone for the first time.

There's no awkwardness when I'm bare beneath him, when Ben presses the long length of his body against mine, letting me feel all that hard heat, the cording of muscle beneath his skin. Between us, his erection presses against the soft skin of my stomach, and I'm hitching a leg around his hip, pressing closer, trying to tell him, without words, that I want him *now*. I've never felt this close to coming from what we're doing—deep, hard kisses and Ben's big, callused hand against my breast, his thumb flicking across my nipple with the perfect pressure, perfect rhythm. I break from his mouth, tilt my head so that I can lick up the side of his neck, nip his earlobe with my teeth, and he rewards me with the lowest, sexiest groan I've ever heard. I feel it rumble in that aching, wet place between my legs and I buck against him again.

"It's good," I breathe, in relief, in confirmation, in plain, pure happiness to be here with him now—close, naked, *together*.

He scrapes his stubbled cheek against my neck, all that delicious roughness, drags it down over my chest and licks across to my nipple, sucking it into his mouth and working me over until my breath is coming in quick, reedy pants, until I tangle my hands in his hair and whisper *please*, over and over. "Fuck," he says, resting his forehead against my sternum before looking up at me again. "I don't know where to start with you—I want to do everything. I've thought about this—I want to put my hands on you, in you…" He breaks off, tracing two of his fingers between my legs, around that aching spot where I want him most. "But I want to see how you taste too—and, oh God. I want to know the way you'd feel around my dick…"

"*That*," I say, gripping the back of his neck, tugging him up. "That's what I want, first. Everything else, we'll do later. I *promise*."

He smiles up at me, nuzzles at my breast again. "I'm going to hold you to that. If I can remember you've said it. I don't even remember my own fucking name right now."

"*Ben*," I say, pulling him up for another kiss, wet and hungry. He pushes off me, and despite the warmth of the room, I feel chilled with the shock of losing the heat of his body, even though it's only for long enough for him to grab his jeans and pull a condom out of the pocket. I prop myself up on my elbows, watch him roll it on, loving the way his body works, the way he's heavy and hard, the way he comes back to me, using his hands to spread me wide as he nestles between my legs.

I don't wait for him. I can't wait for him—now that we've started this, it hits me how long I've really been wanting it with him, wanting the chance to be this way together. I reach between us, guide him to my entrance, lift my hips to him, and he's licking into my mouth, grunting his satisfaction, and then—*oh*, he's there, one hard, forceful thrust that tips my head back, that takes my breath away in the most perfect way, and I am *lost* to him. I hear him in my ear—*Kit, So good, You're perfect*—and I think I'm talking back. I think I'm telling him how good it is, how full I feel, how close he has me already, but my body and brain have never felt so disconnected. In Ben's arms, I am only the sensations he stokes in me. I am nothing but sweat and movement and frantic, pulsing *need*, and it's only when my orgasm breaks over me, only when I release a desperate, threaded cry that a single thought breaks through, before I can stop it.

He feels like home.

* * * *

It's later—much, much later, when I've fulfilled the promises Ben didn't forget, and even some I hadn't made—and I'm lying on my side, naked, a sheet tangled about my legs, Ben stroking those rough, blunt fingertips up the curve of my thigh, over my hip, down the dip of my waist, and up, again, over the light, curving bones of my ribcage. He does this again and again, learning that curve, and the way goose bumps chase his caress. My eyelids are heavy, my body sated and tender from everything we've done.

"I haven't been up this late in forever," I whisper. It's lovely to be up this late with Ben. I'm hearing whole new sounds of the house at night, seeing the way light from the moon tracks across my bedroom window. After the second time we'd made love—surprisingly fast on the heels of the first time, Ben still eager, intense—we'd foraged in the kitchen, me swimming in Ben's t-shirt, apologizing for the shameful contents of my refrigerator. But we'd managed with slices of apple and generous pieces from a block of cheddar, peanut butter on toast that tasted so good I'd licked the crumbs from my fingers.

Which Ben found very, very distracting.

"Want to sleep?" he asks, leaning down to press his lips against my eyelids. I murmur my entirely unconvincing dissent, tilting my head up so I can kiss him. I don't want the night to be over. For the first time in the years since I started my job, I consider a personal day.

"You know what I thought, when I first saw you?" he asks, his face pressed into my neck, his voice muffled.

"Was it about my goggles?" I say, pinching his side lightly.

"No, but I loved your goggles. You look great in goggles. Maybe that could be the first dirty picture you send to me, you in those goggles."

"I'm never going to send you a dirty picture," I say, laughing. But then I'm whispering again, in his ear, "What did you think, when you first saw me?"

"I thought, *what a goddamn shame I'm here for someone else*. And I know that's not right, because I *was* there for you. I was just an idiot that day. But I wanted it to be you."

I think we both know the issue isn't who he was there for, but *what* he was there for, and it's hard not to think of it now, as determinedly as I'd been avoiding it for the last few hours.

"Was it bad?" I ask. "I mean, with your partner. Is it going to mess things up for you?"

We're so close together that I can feel him stiffen slightly, but he masks it, rolling on his back and pulling me with him so I'm cradled in in the crook of his arm. He takes a deep breath. "I don't know," he says, tightening his hand on my hip. "Jasper is my best friend too. And we had—there were some plans we were working on, which I've probably messed up. So it's business, but it's personal too." He pauses, then says, with conviction that seems entirely borne of self-preservation, "It'll be all right."

I shift away from him, enough to put an inch of air between us. I'm glad he's being honest, but this is hard too. It puts into sharp relief that what we've done here *can't* only be a simple hook-up. It's not that I want it to be, but it's that Ben doesn't really have a choice now that he's sacrificed something important at his job for this. Even if he leaves to go back to Texas next month and we don't see each other again—a thought that makes my mouth go dry—it's not as if he won't be taking back with him the baggage associated with fucking up his work for me. The sex was incredible, yes, and I like him so much that probably at any moment I could tip right over the tightrope I'm walking and fall into a raging, white water river of love. But to him, what does this mean?

"Kit," he says, tugging me back against him. "Come on. Don't do that. It's my choice."

"Yes, but…"

"But it's"—he lifts his head from the pillow, cranes his neck to look at my nightstand— "it's two thirty in the morning. My higher order thinking skills are compromised. Can't talk." It's my turn to lean down, kiss across his brow, his closed eyes, those high, cut cheekbones, and he murmurs his pleasure, tugging me over so I'm forced to straddle him, and just that quickly I'm wet again, still surprised by the way my body reacts to his.

"What about it being two thirty in the morning?" I ask, rubbing against him, his hands tightening on my hips to hold me close.

"Don't need higher order thinking for this," he says, already reaching for the strip of condoms we'd stuffed under one of the pillows after the first time. "Wait," he says, stilling my hips with one of his hands, looking up at me with a furrowed brow.

"What?"

He lifts up, the motion crunching the stacked muscles in his abdomen. His arm bands around me, pulling me close so my head tips forward onto his shoulder. Then he whispers in my ear, "I'm just wondering if you brought those goggles home."

And it's like that, laughing again, that he takes me one last time, before we collapse into a perfect, heavy sleep.

Chapter 14

Ben

I sleep like the dead, even on this too-soft mattress, but when I wake up to the sound of Kit's alarm, my body still feels completely drained. I'm sacked-out, empty-headed, unable to think about anything but Kit lying next to me, the smell of her sleep-warm skin, the way she looks, her lips still swollen from the pressure of my mouth on hers, a pink trace of beard burn on her chest, probably on her thighs too. I wasn't kidding when I'd said I'd planned to keep her up, but it's not the fact that we've had sex of all kinds for the last twelve hours or so that's got me feeling this way. It's that it had taken a herculean effort to wait so long to come to her. From the minute I'd left her on Saturday, this is what I'd wanted, and I'd barely slept all weekend for thinking about her. But I'd been determined to come to her honestly, determined to deal with Jasper first.

I don't want to think about that now, though. Now all I want is to sleep and eat and fuck her again, not necessarily in that order.

Kit's swiping at her alarm, letting out a string of curses I've never heard her use before. When she finally manages to shut it off, she raises a limp arm in the air, a clenched fist. "You'll pay for this, Tucker," she says, then lets her arm drop over her eyes.

"You're so fucking cute," I tell her, leaning over to press a hard kiss over her mouth.

"Coffee," she whispers against my lips. "I don't care who you have to murder to get it."

I don't have to murder anyone; I just use the coffeemaker she has in her kitchen. But the time finally registers and I realize I need to get home.

I'd promised Sharon I'd be back by seven to get Dad ready for the day. I clean up the dishes Kit and I left behind last night when I'd hoisted her over my shoulder and carried her back upstairs, and pour her coffee into a mug that says *Don't Test My Metal*. She's still in bed, arm still over her face, a slant of morning light angling across her neck, right where I want to lick her. I've never wanted to leave a place less.

"I've got to go, honey," I say, the endearment slipping out before I can even think of it. What the fuck is this. I'm bringing her coffee in bed and talking to her as if we've been married for years, and I fucking *like* it. This makes her sit up, her eyes squinty, her lips puckered with the strain, apparently, of seeing the morning light. Her hair is a *mess*.

"Don't laugh at me," she says.

I set the coffee on her nightstand, lean down and kiss her again, open-mouthed, against her shoulder. I see her nipples peak underneath the sheet she's holding to her chest, and—oh, come on. Five more minutes? I could get the job done in five minutes...

"So Sharon stayed with your dad last night?" she asks, a total boner destroyer, but I suppose I should be grateful. I pick up my t-shirt from the floor, pull it on, set about finding my boots.

"Yeah, but she's got somewhere to be this morning, so I need to get back. And Dad's got more PT today, plus it's River's day at the yard. Busy."

"Hmm," she says, into her coffee. She's not looking at me. She's looking into that mug as if it's got the answers to the universe in it. It hasn't crossed my mind to reassure her—that's at least part because most of my relationships with women have been narrowed by the boundaries I establish out of what I've told myself is necessity. I work a lot, much of it involving travel, and I don't have the time or will to make commitments. I can't remember the last time I've slept next to someone all night, and other than these last few weeks with Dad, I can't remember when I've last had to provide an accounting of my day to anyone who I didn't share an Outlook calendar with. But it's also part because already with Kit I feel I'm *with* her. I feel I'll see her tonight, every night I can, no questions asked.

That's sloppy thinking, though, and I know it—I live in Texas, Kit lives here, and I have no idea what she wants from me, or what we'll be to each other. There's fallout I have to deal with from being with Kit even this once, and snatches of my conversation with Jasper are already coming back to me—first, his anger, then his attempt to find a workaround, finally, my promises to make this up to him, to make sure our plans come off anyway.

I finish tying up my boot, set a knee down onto the bed so I can lean close to Kit, wait for her to look at me. When she does, her dark eyes are wary, cautious, so different from last night. "Kit," I say, against her mouth. The coffee steams up between us, nutty and strong. "I like how that is," she says back, her voice soft. "You saying my name." I kiss her again, letting my tongue move across the seam of her lips before breathing out her name again. "Can I come back tonight?" Her lashes lift, and that warm glow is back in her eyes. "Anytime," she says.

* * * *

I walk into Dad's kitchen at 6:58, thank God, or else Sharon would've had my ass. Dad's at the table, squeezing the strengthening ball he has as part of the at-home PT for his arm and reading out loud to Sharon, who's filling in a crossword.

"Uh, hello," I say, because—I don't know what this is that I've walked into. It looks as if they have breakfast together every morning.

"Good, you're here," Sharon says, standing. "I've got my pap smear this morning."

"Holy shit, Sharon. My ears."

"Oh, save it. People my age still get those!"

"What? I didn't—that's—that's not the point." I move over to the counter, pour myself what's left of the coffee, and close my eyes against the sudden thought of Kit and how I left her, naked and sleepy and smelling of much better coffee than this. Sharon waves goodbye, letting herself out, and the kitchen is quiet but for the faint squeak the ball makes when my dad squeezes it.

"Nice night?" he says, keeping his eyes on the paper, but I can see him smiling.

"Yep," I say, turning my back to reach into the fridge. "We've got to get you ready for your appointment, huh?"

"You know, if you're wanting to be out more—I don't need someone staying with me at night now," he says. "You heard the doc."

I did hear the doctor, late last week, when Dad had passed all the tests determining whether or not he was still a fall risk. So long as he kept the cane by his bed at night, he had enough weight-bearing flexibility to get back and forth to the bathroom, to get water if he needed it. But I still didn't feel comfortable with it. I wouldn't have left him last night without Sharon.

Which—about that. "Dad," I say, keeping my back turned as I pour myself a bowl of cereal. I may be thirty-one years old, but I'm not sure I'd ever have the balls required to have this conversation with my dad face to face. "You got something going with Sharon?"

He barks out a sharp laugh. "Do I 'got something going with' her?" he repeats, laughing again.

I feel my face heat in embarrassment. My dad and I are close, I think, but we don't usually talk about this kind of shit. Once, after I'd moved to Texas, I'd asked him if he was interested in dating—I worried, sometimes, about him growing old alone—and he'd laughed sort of the way he's doing right now. "Never mind," I say, sitting across the table and hunching as far down into my cereal bowl as I can without actually dipping my face into it.

"You got something going with Kit?"

Even her name, it makes my skin prickle with anticipation, heat. "Yeah."

"Well. Then, yeah. I got something going with Sharon."

I blink up at him, just—shocked, completely fucking shocked.

"Since you were about fifteen, I guess," he says, so casual, as if this is not a big deal at all.

"What? Since I was *what?*" Dad's calmly squeezing the ball, and now he's added in some of the slight knee lifts he does for his leg. "I—I can't—how?"

"How? Well, here's how it is, son, when a man…"

"Dad, don't finish that sentence. I beg you." Jesus, if this keeps up, I won't even be able to go back to Kit's tonight. My buddy down there will go on permanent hiatus. "Just—explain yourself."

Dad lifts his good shoulder in a casual shrug. "Nothing to explain, really. You know Sharon's my best friend. Turned into something else after a few years, that's all."

"You've never said a word," I say, feeling a little mad now. "You guys have—*been together* for over fifteen years and you've never said a word to me? Jesus, why don't you live together? Or get married?"

"Live together! You must be crazy. Sharon and me, it's good the way it is, us having our own spaces. We thought about it, once you went away, but I suppose we do best how we are."

"Jesus, Dad. I feel like an idiot. Probably Sharon wants to be taking care of you, and I flew in here like I was saving the goddamn day. Why wouldn't you have told me this?"

"Don't see as how it mattered, right at first, when you were a kid. You were going through a lot back then, anyhow, so it didn't seem right, and Sharon and I kept it pretty casual back then."

I don't dare ask if "keeping it casual" means the same thing to Dad as it means to me, and anyways, now that he's said it, little things about those last few years I was in the house come back to me, and I see them in a new light—a couple of times, early in the morning, when my dad came in the house, saying he'd just been out for a walk, even though so far as I knew he never walked only for the sake of it, or the time I found one of Sharon's baseball jerseys in Dad's laundry basket. "Then after a while," he says, "it seemed it'd be strange to tell you, I guess." He clears his throat. "Sorry."

I take the ball from him, squeeze it myself. "You're supposed to rest after five minutes," I say, because now I'm more embarrassed, both by his obvious discomfort and by what this entire conversation reveals. The truth is, I thought my dad and I were tight—I thought I kept up with him and his life, considered myself a good son to him. But if he's been with the same woman for all these years and I didn't even know? I didn't even *notice*? That doesn't say anything good about me, and this feeling I've had since I've been home—that Dad's life is going by without me, that I was wrong not to have known the kinds of risks he took at work—it's overwhelming right now, settling right into my temples for what I know will be a day-long headache.

"Hey, you got nothing to feel bad about," Dad says. "I should have told you. Sharon and I should have told you. Though she's probably going to tear a strip off me when she finds out I let it slip."

"She didn't want me to know, either?" This hurts too. I feel as close to Sharon as I do to anyone here at home, and I think of the effort it must have taken her, all these years, to keep this from me, to never betray anything other than friendly affection—but mostly annoyance—with my dad.

"Ah, Sharon's private in some ways. Not about her gynecology appointments, I guess, but about other things. Don't take it personal."

Oh, man. But I *have* taken it personal. It's ridiculous, but I think of Kit asking me if Sharon was my stepmom. I was such an unholy terror when I was a teenager. Sharon probably hadn't wanted to be all in for that. After all, even my own mother hadn't.

I swallow down more of my breakfast, pulling the sports section in front of me, but not really registering anything on the page. After a few minutes of silence, Dad speaks up again. "Ben, the thing between Sharon and me, it's how it's always been. She's got her life, and her space, and I have mine. We're as close as we want to be. And you coming here..." He pauses, clears his throat again. "That's what I needed to have happen, after I fell. That was more important to me than anything."

It's my turn to look at him, his turn to avoid my eyes. With his good hand, he's gathering up the scattered sections of the paper, piling them haphazardly into one corner of the table. I don't think Dad's just humoring me. I think it does matter to him that I've come, been here to take care of him, and that takes some of the sting out of this revelation about him and Sharon. "Me too," I grumble, then suck down the last of my shitty, lukewarm coffee. But I suppose I'm still feeling a little bruised, a little resentful, because when Dad asks what exactly it is I have going on with Kit, I only tell him we've got to get a move on, and then we're both going through the motions, another day ahead.

* * * *

While Dad's in his PT session, I stay outside, doing as much damage control about work as I can from my phone. Jasper's in flight to California, headed out for a titanium conference where he'll scout some new tech for the jet engine division. This is for the best, that we steer clear of each other for a couple of days. Sunday had been tense—I'm pretty sure he'd said *you've got to be fucking kidding* about fifteen times. I'd kept clear of the details—so far as I was concerned, all Jasper needed to know was that I'd compromised things by getting too close to the recruit, that I could no longer do the job.

The thing is, it'd never happened to me before, but Jasper and I both knew this kind of shit *did* happen. Recruiters fell out with clients for all kinds of reasons, and it could have just as easily been something else that broke things down between Kit and me, not the fact that I wanted her more than my next breath. So I think we'd both tried to focus on how to go forward. I'd made promises to deal with Greg, to find another way around the non-compete, to talk to Hamish and Kristen too. Jasper and I will go to our separate corners for a couple of days, and when I talk to him next, I'm confident I'll have news to placate him.

I call Kristen, who's already heard it from Jasper and who doesn't seem bothered at all. She's not in a hurry about breaking out. Next is Hamish, who shouts at me through the line like we're using a tin-can phone, but he doesn't give two shits about a longer timeline, either, and tells me he's on board for whenever Jasper and I start up. Greg is going to be a tougher case—I won't go to him until I have other prospects, which will probably take me a couple of weeks to scout given my limited resources here. I know already no one will match Kit, but I also know that's because now, I'm more biased than Greg is when it comes to her. All in all, though, it's Jasper's haste that's putting the most strain on things, and by the time Dad's wrapped up his session, I feel less worried about work overall, if a little more worried about what's got into Jasper.

But it's still a tedious day, because I count the hours—minutes, really—until I can see Kit again. River, now sporting a much more agreeable haircut and attitude in general, helps me with the chandelier, mostly with ordering some replacement pieces online. He's good with tech—I think he's even bringing Dad around to the idea of a new point of sale system, a miracle since Dad still used a carbon-copy credit card swipe until the second decade of the twenty-first century.

Right before close, after River's gone, Sharon comes in, and Dad must've told her about our conversation, because the first thing she does is point a finger at me and say, "It's nothing against you, Ben, us not telling you." Then she adjusts the front of her jersey and says, "I'm taking your father out for dinner and then we're going to a movie. And I'll handle bedtime, so you can go out with your new girlfriend."

There's something I should say here, I think—something about how I'm okay with Dad and Sharon, but she's so determinedly not looking at me that I don't want to make the situation worse, so I settle for the unbelievably immature, "I don't know if she's my girlfriend," which at least gets Sharon to look at my face, if only to roll her eyes at me.

So by the time I get to Kit's, the weirdness of my day—and the fact that I only slept for three hours last night—has taken its toll. If I weren't so hard up for her, I'd probably make the sensible decision to stay away, since I'm guessing I'm not good company. But I'm not sensible, not right now, probably not since I've met her, and when I knock on her door, all I can think about is getting my hands on her, sinking into her, letting myself get lost in her. It takes her a minute or so to answer, and as soon as she opens the door I know why. Her hair is flat on one side, a red mark on her cheek, her glasses a little crooked. "I fell asleep," she says, "on the *couch*," like this is the most appalling thing she's ever done.

I'm kissing her before I'm even all the way through the door, and the way her arms go around me, the little moan she makes at the back of her throat—I'm already hard as a rock, but I ought to slow down, take it easier, because as bad as I want her, I don't want her to think I'm just here for that. So what if I haven't even worked out for myself what I am actually here for, but I know with Kit, it's not just sex. I pull back from her mouth but wrap her tighter against my chest, lifting her a little so I can bury my face against her warm, smooth neck. I take a deep breath. Whatever shampoo this woman uses, I want the smell of it on my sheets all the time.

She shivers against me, and I try not to notice the way I can feel her nipples through her thin shirt, pressing against my chest. "Are you okay?" she asks.

"Weird day," I say, the sound muffled against her skin, and holy shit, it just—*hits* me, I guess, this feeling that I'm so glad to see her, be with her, at the end of this kind of day. It's so striking that I take a step back, put a bit of distance between us. I run my fingers across the creases on her cheek, straighten her glasses.

"Was it—are things bad for you, at work? Because of this? Or is it your dad?"

I think of unloading it—everything I found out today about Dad and Sharon, my plans with Jasper, and the fact that he's suddenly gone attack-dog at them—but, *fuck*. It feels so complicated. I don't know if I'm there with her yet, and anyway I haven't even figured out how I feel about most of it myself. "Everything's good," I say, running my hands up and down her hips, her waist. "Just, you know. Recovering. Some insanely hot woman kept me up half the night."

"I didn't! You're the one…"

I cut her off, kissing her again. "You want to go get something to eat?" I ask. "Because I figure, we're probably not going to get much sleep tonight, either, so we'd better at least keep our strength up."

And if her smile looks a little disappointed at the edges, I pretend not to notice.

* * * *

We go to Kit's favorite place, a sandwich shop called The Meltdown that must've opened in the last couple of years. She orders for me—*trust me*, she says, in this bossy way she has, and for the first time in my life I think about asking a woman to tie me up, but I get my mind out of the gutter long enough to lead us to a booth in the back, where we drink beers straight from the bottle and talk about Kit's house, the plaster worker who's coming tomorrow, the timeline she has for her kitchen renovation.

When our food comes, she takes both of our plates and swaps one-half sandwich for the other, so we each have half each other's. "You're going to *love* these," she says, and I'm pretty sure I'd eat a sardine sandwich if she was the one giving it to me.

"Anyways," she continues, "I wanted to ask Alex what he thought of the exposed brick idea, but…you know. That didn't work out." She furrows her brow when she talks about him, a shadow of that sadness I'd seen over the weekend when she'd told me about his brief visit.

"Have you talked to him again?" I ask, but then I'm taking a bite of my food, and—*fuck*, this sandwich. It's really good. I think I just made a sex-adjacent noise about it.

Kit smiles at my reaction, but then her face falls again, remembering my question. "No. But that's not really that weird, I guess. He travels a lot for his job. He's a photographer." She pauses, takes a bite of her sandwich, but I think talking about her brother has taken some of the pleasure out of this for her, and I'm sorry to have brought it up. After a minute, though, she continues. "When he was here, I tried to give him money." She shakes her head, breathing out this soft, sad laugh. "I suggested that he *move* here. I'm an idiot."

"Why does that make you an idiot?"

She shrugs, takes another bite, and I wait her out. "He's a complicated guy. *We're* complicated, together, I guess. He raised me, from the time I was a baby, basically. I mean, I mentioned the thing with my mother—that's not Alex's mother; she died when Alex was four. And my dad—he's not very reliable, so Alex kind of had to take over."

"He sounds like a good guy," I say, but this is grudging. I don't know two shits about Alex other than I hold him responsible for Kit crying, and I hate the thought of her crying, hated the sight of it more.

"You know when I was twelve, he took me to buy my first training bra, which you'd think would be completely mortifying, but it wasn't. Or if it was, for him, he knew it was worse for me. So he—I don't know. He just *did* it. Marched us right into that department store's lingerie section, asked the woman at the counter to point us in the right direction, and fifteen minutes later, we're out of there. When it was time for me to apply to colleges, he worked doubles so he could pay for my application fees. He drove me to scholarship competitions all over the state. He's always been that way, a problem-solver." She picks up a chip, sets it down, picks it up again. "Or at least he always solved my problems. So it sucks that he won't let me solve his."

"What do you think his problem is?"

That seems to land in a place that hurts her. She sucks her bottom lip into her mouth, her eyes falling back to her plate, and goddamn, this is hard. Maybe I should have kept her at home, taken her to bed again. But Kit waits, thinks, then speaks again. "I guess I don't know. I thought it was money, or maybe I wanted to believe that it was. I think maybe I'm his problem, or at least the fact that I was his problem for so long. He needs a break from me, maybe."

This sends a shock of anger so acute through me that I clench my hand around my bottle of beer. I'm white knuckling this sucker like it's done me wrong. "Then he's an asshole," I say, and I don't even care if I don't have a right to that sentiment, about someone who's known her way longer than me.

"No," she says, so serious that she sets an hand on my forearm, across the table. "I don't want you to think that. I really, *really* don't." She says this as if it matters so much to her, those black cherry eyes right on mine. So I move my arm, take her hand and squeeze it briefly, and she smiles at me, sweet as all hell, and I wish I was sitting right next to her, on the other side of the booth. I don't care how cheesy it would look. I feel restless, unsettled, a little, and I know it's because Kit just—she just puts herself *out* there, telling me this thing about her and her brother, and I'm still dammed up. I try and imagine what she'd say if I told her how I took it about Dad and Sharon. That's new, that imagining—because while I've been told by more than one woman that I had problems communicating, I don't think I've ever thought once about how I might go about doing it better.

We finish our sandwiches and when we get outside, I take her hand and hold it all the way back to her place. Inside her house, up in her bedroom, I swipe at least four of the crazy throw pillows she has arranged on this bed onto the floor, and then I take all the time I didn't take the first time, last night. I lie on top of her, kissing her and learning all the shapes of her through her clothes first, until we're both a little crazy with it, moving against each other like a couple of teenagers, so that when I finally start removing our clothes, piece by piece, it feels as if we've crossed a new threshold. When the skin of our stomachs touches, she gasps, her hands rubbing up and down my sides, her kisses growing deeper, more frantic. I slow her with my mouth, moving down her neck, across the fine shelf of her collarbone, down the center of her stomach.

I did this for Kit last night too, tasted her, felt her come against my mouth before I took her the second time. But I think now it was selfish, some other way for me to *have* her, to make her mine, even for that small slice of time. Tonight—I don't know—I'm trying to give her something, something I can't say, something I don't know how to feel. I pay attention to every hitch of her breath, every line of tension in the muscles along her inner thighs, every clench of her hand in my hair. Despite the tight, pulsing protests of my dick, I focus on nothing but her and the way her body twists when she comes, her back arching off the bed, her mouth open in a silent cry. Every ounce of energy in my body is concentrated on the need to rear up and drive into her, but I don't. I kiss my way up to her stomach again, rest my forehead on her sternum and wait, breathing as if I've run flat-out for miles, just from the desperation of it.

And it's only when she tells me to come to her, come into her, that I can settle down again.

Chapter 15

Kit

"I mean I'm not saying you have to *narrate* it. But I am saying I haven't had sex in eight and a half months, so if you *did*…"

It's Sunday morning, and instead of brunch, Zoe, Greer, and I have met for a walk in Hazleton Park, one of the historic gardens not too far from Zoe's condo. It's a gorgeous day, a perfect, clear blue sky and a breeze that carries the smell of roses from the west garden, and it's finally, finally, not too hot for a mid-day walk. Brunch was out on account of the fact that I'd overslept, waking up after nine with Ben's chest pressed against my back—the way I'd woken up most of the mornings since I'd found him on my stoop six days ago. I wasn't the type to cancel plans for a guy, ever, so I'd been prepared to throw on whatever clothes were closest to me and go to brunch with the worst case of bedhead I'd ever had in my life, but when I texted Zoe and Greer to let them know I'd be late, Zoe had sent a bunch of hot pepper emojis and told me to stay in bed for another hour, that we'd meet up later. Although now I realize the error of my ways. Clearly she thinks I owe her details.

"I'm not going to tell…"

She's not even really listening at this point, just pressing on. "I mean *think* about it," she says. "I could have gestated a *human being* in the time since I've had sex."

"It's only a dry spell," Greer says. "You'll get back out there."

I seize this opportunity. "You know, Zoe, there's some very nice men at the university…"

"Who, like your pal Diego from the English department? Nope."

I have to laugh, thinking back to my one ill-fated attempt to date someone from the university. Diego had been sweet, soft-spoken, but he clearly had some kind of clinical impostor syndrome about being a professor. He smoked a pipe even though he confessed to hating it, and he had at least one sport coat with elbow patches. Then on our third date he'd taken me to a poetry reading, and I'm an open-minded person but frankly I draw the line at Diego doing an open mic rendition of the poem he wrote about the infant trauma of losing his foreskin.

"I saw him kiss her," says Greer, out of the blue, and I shoulder-check her off the path. She laughs, coming back, linking her arm through mine.

"*Tell* me," says Zoe, her eyes going comically wide.

Greer shrugs casually. "Yeah, last weekend. He leaned right in and laid one on her. It looked good to me."

"You guys. I don't need your assessment."

"Because it's so awesome, you mean? Like we couldn't even possibly assess something that awesome?"

The smile I try to hide is the only answer Zoe requires. "God. I'm so *jealous*," she says.

"Jealous and really, really happy for you, Kit-Kat," says Greer.

"Well, we'll see." Suddenly, I feel—not embarrassed, not with these two, but—cautious, I guess. I've spent a lot of time with Ben this week—at my house, at the salvage yard, even one evening spent at his dad's house, where we ate pizza with Henry and Sharon, who showed me an old picture of Ben wearing frog-printed swim shorts over a pair of sweatpants. But in all that time, we've never said anything about the fact that Henry's moving around pretty well now, scheduled to be out of his arm sling full time next week and in a walking boot that allows him to get around pretty easily. There's no way Ben doesn't have to get back to Texas soon, but every time I've tried to talk to him about his home there, his work, how it's going with his partner, he gives me a noncommittal answer, telling me work's fine, everything is fine. I'd press him, but I'm not even sure I want to know. I only want to keep going on this floating, perfect island of Ben—sex with Ben, laughter and conversation with Ben, light home improvements with Ben, just Ben in general.

"So has he given up recruiting you?" asks Greer.

"Yeah—conflict of interest, I guess. Anyways I think I'd pretty much convinced him already that I wasn't interested."

"You weren't even a *little* interested?" says Zoe. "I mean, that thing he said, about you being the gem? That was pretty convincing."

I pause where I am on the path. Greer stays with me, her arm linked to mine, and she seems to know, instinctively, how I'd take this, because she draws herself a little closer to my side. "Did you—did you think I should have been?"

Zoe stops, turns to look back at me. "Kit, you are insanely talented. You love what you do more than anyone I've ever met. All I mean is that it'd be perfectly understandable if you thought about going to do it somewhere where you'd have a lot more opportunity."

"I don't think about it," I say, too quickly for it to be convincing. "I'm really happy here. I don't want to leave."

Zoe's brow furrows in concern, her eyes serious. "I know you don't. And I'd never want you to. God, I'd probably have to be sedated for weeks if any one of us ever moved away. But sometimes…" Here, she breaks off, looks toward Greer, maybe hoping she'll take over, but Greer just looks down at her feet.

"Sometimes what?"

"Well, you know the paper you told us about, with Dr. Singh?"

My face heats. I have to give my answer to him tomorrow, and it still makes me feel edgy and unsure. I don't want to upset the balance I'd created at my job. I don't want to change the relationship I have with Dr. Singh. All this week, I'd let myself be distracted from thinking about it, which was easy enough, really, given what I'd been up to with Ben.

"Just thinking about something doesn't mean you have to *do* it. And putting your name on this paper, it doesn't mean you have to start—I don't know—totally changing the way you do your job. You get to decide what you do with your life, Kit. That's the best luck we got on the day we bought that ticket. And considering things, trying new things—actually letting yourself take credit for something you worked really, really hard on—that doesn't force you to decide one way or another. And whatever you'd decide—even if there was some light sedation involved—it'd be okay. We'd all be okay."

Gah, Zoe's speeches. They always hit you right in your soft parts. I look toward Greer, who nods in agreement. I breathe out a sigh, and we set to walking again. After a minute, I say, "It doesn't always feel that way, though. It feels—I just want to stay in my lane, you know? And if I get in the passing lane, even for a little bit, what if there's no room for me to get back over?"

Greer unlinks her arm from mine, but only so she can grab my hand, squeezing slightly. Then Zoe moves to my other side, grabs my other hand so that the three of us are walking all together along the path—it's silly, what we're doing, swinging our arms as if we're kids in the park, nothing to do or think about but play. "Kit-Kat," Zoe says, after we walk a bit. "You can get in that passing lane whenever you want. With us, there's always room for you to get back over."

* * * *

Dr. Singh is frowning at his computer screen when I knock on his open door on Monday morning, but as soon as he raises his head and sees me there, he smiles the way he always does.

I first met Dr. Singh when I was twenty-one, on a campus visit I'd done in my senior year of undergrad. There were three schools on my list for master's programs, all of them top ten in materials science, all of them with a PhD program too, in case I'd decide to go that route. It should've been an exciting time—I was top of my class, had one of my summer research projects headed toward publication, and had full fellowship offers for all three schools.

But, predictably, I'd been terrified. I'd stayed in Ohio for college, at least close to the general region of my nomadic childhood. I hung out mostly with other students within my major, dated a little, had a boyfriend for all of junior year until he got sulky about how high my GRE score had been compared to his. At the time, it'd seemed I was maybe making my way, finding a community, and the thought of moving on, uprooting everything to go to a new place, had me up late at night, every night, reading everything I could about my prospective schools.

When I'd come here, though, I'd realized quickly that I didn't have the community I thought I did at college, and it was Dr. Singh who showed me that. The first night, he'd had me and the four other visiting students over to his and Ria's house for dinner. We'd all sat around a big dining room table and talked about everything from Feynman's lectures to our favorite movies. The next day, Dr. Singh and Dr. Harroway had taken us on a tour of the labs, then they'd handed us off to some second-year grad students who'd shown us around town. By then, I'd been sold—the facilities weren't state of the art, but we were seeing them during the height of the semester, busy and full of small groups of students, and then I'd loved Barden itself, how much history it had, how many neighborhood enclaves there were, each with its own character. When I'd had my one-on-one meeting with Dr. Singh on my last morning, he'd been the first professor I'd ever had to really ask after the way I went about learning. He paid attention to what I liked best about the science, thought hard about what projects I'd work best on.

When I'd moved here, he'd been a steady, calm presence, giving me exactly the right amount of guidance and freedom. He was an incredible teacher, an ideal mentor, and just a good, kind person who wanted the best for me.

I keep my mind on that as I sit in my regular seat across his desk and tell him that I'm okay with being lead author, and as he clasps his hands together and does this cartoonish victory shake with them, which makes us both laugh.

"I'm so glad," he says. "I thought I overplayed my hand last week, threatening to pull the article."

"You wouldn't have?"

He shrugs. "I wasn't kidding about being uncomfortable publishing it as it is. But it is such good work—it would have been hard to pull it. So I'm so glad you're going this route."

"Me too," I say, and I am.

Last night in bed, as we were drifting off to sleep, I'd told Ben about the paper, and he'd gone from drowsy to awake faster than I'd ever seen, propping himself up on his elbow and asking me question after question. "Do it," he'd said. "You've got to do it. Finally, it'll be you out front!" He'd sounded so proud of me. I hadn't known what to do except to kiss him hard, delaying our sleep for even longer. It may have been Zoe and Greer to convince me to say yes, but it meant something to me to have Ben in my corner too.

We talk about some light revisions to do, and when I turn to go, I notice Dr. Singh looks a little tired. "Everything okay?" I ask.

"Sure, sure. I didn't get the Handel grant, though. So it's back to the drawing board."

"Oh, I'm sorry." The Handel would have covered him and two grad students for three years of funding on his fractography project, and I knew he'd had high hopes. Funding was brutal in our field, competitive, money scarce, and Dr. Singh was selective about the grants he'd apply for—I'd learned a lot of my values about corporate science from him.

"Ah, it's part of the job," he says, but I know it's more than that—of the faculty here, he lags behind in funding, and it's important for his upcoming review for promotion. But he's already cleared his face of any strain, and he's looking across the desk at me fondly. "Ekaterina, I must say, I'm very happy about the paper. Very proud to have my name *after* yours." This is too new for me to be cool and collected about, and I know my face has pinked up. So I'm grateful when Dr. Singh waves a hand and says, "Now wrap up your day early today. Get out there and celebrate."

* * * *

Ben, too, insists that we celebrate. He picks me up after closing down the yard, a bottle of champagne tucked in between our seats in his truck. "Where are we going?" I ask, fiddling with the radio. I find a top 40 station and beam in triumph across the seat at him. He hates it when I pick the music. Last week when he taught me how to switch out the wall boxes for my electric, I'd had a full-on girl group playlist blaring, and Ben had complained so much I thought he'd pull a muscle. "You have the worst taste," he grumbles.

My answer is to sing back, off-key, rolling my window down.

When he can't keep a straight face anymore, I nudge him again, ask him where he's taking me.

"Just this place I know about. You'll love it."

"Is it the science museum?"

"No. I figure you've been to the science museum at least ten times."

"Oh, twenty, probably. I gave a lecture there once, for an exhibit they had on railway construction. It was awesome. I met this man who has two and a half total miles of miniature rail built all around his backyard."

"Oh, you mean George Billingsley?"

"You know him?"

"He was my fifth grade teacher," Ben says, smiling. "I think my dad used to date his sister, way back before he married my mom."

"What? That's so great! That's—I *love* that," I say, and Ben sends me a sidelong glance, curious, so I explain. "I love how you know so many people here, in all these different contexts, you know? From your neighborhood, or from going to school around here, or from people you meet at the yard. I always wanted that, but it was hard to get any traction with the way I grew up. You're so lucky."

"I suppose I never thought of it that way."

"Do you know a lot of people in Houston?" I ask, tentative. I usually strike out on this, but I'm so curious—in Houston, is Ben more like that guy I met in the lab? Or is he this guy too, jeans and a t-shirt, tan, stubbled, his hair still wet from a shower?

He takes a minute to answer, thinks about it. "I know a lot of people through work. Not just my company, but other professionals in the area. I suppose—no. I don't know people the same way there as I do here. But that was a good thing for me, I guess."

I wait for him to say more, but he doesn't, so I reach over and nudge his thigh with my hand. "Because why?"

"Well, because around here, I knew so many people, but as the guy I was. The guy who set fire to a house, the guy who almost killed someone." I shift in my seat, so I'm turned toward him more. "I'm sure no one thought of you *only* that way," I say.

He flips on his turn signal, lowers his speed as we head down a gravel path. "I was a pretty bad kid. Not only that time. I was always tearing shit up, getting into trouble. I'm sure it was exactly only that way."

His eyes are on the road. There's a muscle in his jaw that ticks, and I figure he's done with this topic. I try not to sulk about it—so what if Ben's a bit slower to open up than me? Not everyone cracks themselves wide open the first chance they get. Still, though, he must see some change in me, because he sets a hand on my thigh, warm pressure that gives me that familiar, pleasant flutter in my stomach. I lean my head back, close my eyes, and feel the breeze that's blowing in the window ruffle my hair, caress my face.

I must doze, because when the truck rolls to a stop, we've pulled into a circular gravel driveway. To my right is a massive house, Tudor-style, a little worse for wear with a few windows boarded up, some half-timbers missing from the facade. "Is this a haunted house?" I ask. "Because I am not into that."

He chuckles. "It's the dead of summer, Kit."

"So? A house can be haunted any time of year. Ghosts don't take vacations."

"It's not a haunted house," he says, laughing, getting out of the truck and coming around for me. "It's called the Ursinus Mansion. It's getting restored—it used to be a pretty famous home in the area, way back before World War I, because the house itself was dismantled and brought over from England. Lots of the materials are actually seventeenth century."

"Wow," I say, seeing it through new eyes. It makes me feel immensely better about my own house.

A man comes out from the front door, wearing coveralls and a carrying a big toolbox in one big hand. When he sees us, he offers a casual nod in Ben's direction. "Hey, Tucker."

"Good to see you, man," Ben says, walking up to shake the man's hand. "Kit, this is Rick Jarvis. He's the lead contractor on this restoration."

"Hi," I say, shaking Rick's hand. It's dry and scratchy enough that he could probably do sanding just with his skin, but his eyes are kind, his smile twitching beneath his full beard.

* * * *

I guess he's a man of pretty few words though, because once he lets my hand go, he only looks over at Ben and says, "Out by dark."

"Sure thing. Thanks again."

Rick raises a hand in farewell as he walks over to his own truck, puts his toolbox in the bed. He pauses, looks back over his shoulder at us. "You don't got any matches on you, do you?"

I stiffen next to Ben. I'm ready to open my mouth and defend him, but Ben laughs. "You always were a dick, Jarvis." There's no heat in it, just that teasing familiarity Ben has with his dad too.

"Let's get that beer sometime," Rick says, and then he's in his truck, driving back down the gravel path, the tires popping as he goes.

"That wasn't very nice," I say.

"Ah, Rick's all right. He was there that night. He was a good friend."

"Still," I mumble, pissed on Ben's behalf.

"Anyways, one good thing about knowing so many people around. You're going to get to see this place now, before it opens this fall for tours and all that stuff. You thought your house was a handful, you know?"

I grab his hand, linking my fingers through his. "I can't wait."

We can't go in all the rooms—some are taped off, or covered entirely with big swaths of plastic sheeting, particularly upstairs, where some of the bigger jobs are still underway. But downstairs is breathtaking—the floors wide-planked, textured with hundreds of years of nicks and slight depressions, the walls thick and roughened. The windows that are in are leaded glass. In the largest room, a banqueting hall, there's a panel of stained glass that takes my breath away with its intricate leaf pattern, and I wish I could see it with the sun streaming through. Surrounded by the heavy, cherry paneling that lines the walls, some carved with rosettes, the window makes the room feel like a church, even though so far as I can tell, there's nothing in here that suggests religion. We spend an hour wandering around, Ben telling me what he knows about the construction.

When we're back in the foyer, me looking up again at the huge, elaborate staircase, Ben wraps his arms around me from behind. "What do you think?"

"I love it. Thanks for bringing me. I had no idea this was even here."

"Most people don't, but it'll be a big deal when it reopens. You're getting the insider track here, honey."

I flush in pleasure, both at having this special local knowledge and at Ben's endearment, which seems to slip out occasionally, though he betrays no embarrassment over using it.

"Now come on. Let's go have some champagne and toast your victory," he says, pointing me toward the door. "It's almost dark."

Ben spreads out a blanket on the bed of the truck, hoists me up so that my legs are swinging pleasantly in the warm night air. It smells faintly of sawdust from the house, but mostly out here it smells green, the air carrying with it the slight lemony smell from the magnolia trees that surround the house, their waxy leaves rustling in the breeze. It's the best celebration I can think of.

Ben pours me a glass he's taken from the cab of the truck, giving himself about half as much, and he raises his to mine. "Next stop, *Nature*," he says, leaning forward to give me a quick kiss before we drink.

The champagne is sweet, bubbling deliciously in my mouth. I take another sip and laugh. "Not *Nature*. That's not for me."

I lie back, my feet still swinging beneath me, the scratchy blanket against my skin and the hard steel of the truck bed pressing into my shoulder blades. It's worth it to look up at the sky, orange and pink and purple with the setting sun. Ben steps between my legs, humming his pleasure at my new stretched-out posture, leaning down to kiss that spot on my collarbone that makes me shiver. "Could be for you," he says, against my skin, and I go a little cold.

I prop myself up on one elbow, place one hand on Ben's chest. "I know it could be," I say, ducking my head a little so I can look right into his eyes. "Ben—we're not doing this again, are we?" I mean—we're not doing the thing where we talk about my job, about how I should be doing more, about how Beaumont could help me get there.

He takes a long look at me, those eyes roaming back and forth between mine, over my cheeks, down to my mouth, back up to my eyes. "No. I know. I'm sorry." He pushes away from me, shifts to sit next to me on the bed of the truck. "I think I'm—ah. I'm not being a recruiter here. I'm being this guy who…" He trails off, takes a deep breath. "Who lives in Houston. Who is going fucking crazy thinking about not being with you in a couple of weeks."

"Oh." The way that *oh* sounds, it's not what I mean. It sounds awkward, embarrassed, when really my heart is pounding, thinking about what Ben is trying to say here, *whether* he is trying to say it. But I don't want to lie to him. Beaumont can't be an option for me. It *can't*. I belong here. Even considering something else is a betrayal. "Ben." I take his hand, tugging a little, hoping he'll look over at me. But he doesn't, so I go on. "The night we bought the ticket, of the three of us, I was the only one who said she'd go back to work the next day, as if nothing ever happened. And that's because I love my job, even though it's not at the cutting edge of everything. I know it's not top-of-the-line equipment or a lot of money or a bunch of chances for patents. But I want a full life, a life I chose for myself, a life I didn't let *happen* to me. That's really important to me, that I choose, that I'm not getting shuffled around by circumstance."

Ben looks straight ahead, off into the distance, where a line of trees is lit from behind by the setting sun. He's so still, so quiet. I want him to say something else—I'm waiting for him to say something else. *Tell me it's not about the job,* I'm thinking. *Tell me that I've got nothing to do with the job.*

"Yeah," he finally says. "That makes sense."

I've said what I meant, what I really think, and Ben squeezes my hand and smiles down at me, then leans in to press a kiss to my forehead. "We'll figure it out," is all he says, and even as I'm opening my mouth to talk that over, what *figuring it out* might mean for us—long-distance? Calling the whole thing off?—it's as if he flips a switch, case closed. He's pouring me more champagne and changing the subject, to some story about River setting up a new computer system at the yard, and even though it's fun, and we're laughing and talking—I don't know why, but I get the feeling I've spoiled my own celebration.

Chapter 16

Ben

I'm going to be late picking up Kit for my mother's party, a fact that's not helping with my nerves at all. Right up until I'd actually asked if she'd wanted to come with me, I wasn't even sure I'd make it to the Crestwood. I'd still been manufacturing excuses in my mind for why I couldn't go. But then Dad had told me he was taking Sharon as his plus-one, and since he'd factored into 100 percent of my made-up excuses, I figured I was stuck.

And the thought of my whole Saturday night without Kit—it wasn't an option. Since our trip out to the Ursinus earlier this week, I hadn't brought up Houston again, but the fact that next week marked the end of my scheduled family leave was the ten-thousand-pound gorilla in every room we were in together. It's not as if we didn't acknowledge it. After all, with Dad doing better and my promises to Jasper, I'd been doing a lot more telecommuting work over the past two weeks, and more than once Kit had heard me on the phone, setting up future trips, talking to other clients, arguing with Jasper—who'd not, truth be told, given up on the idea that we could swing getting out of the non-compete if we just kept at Greg. When I'd suggested that we hang in, wait six months to do another review of the non-compete, he'd hung up on me in frustration.

Unless I asked for an extension, I was expected back in the office in nine days, and I have no fucking idea what to do about that—every single thing in my life has been reorganized by this leave time, by Kit, and my one ham-handed volley about Houston on Monday night had gone over like a lead balloon. *A full life, a life I chose for myself,* she'd said, and I've thought of those words over and over. I suppose when I'd brought up

Houston, I'd done it in the context of work, but I'd meant something else. I'd meant me, us—and Kit wasn't going to choose that for herself, not if it meant leaving here, and not, especially, after knowing me so short a time. Truth be told, it fucking hurt, no matter how right she probably was. And though I know I need to try again, to sac up and actually tell her how I'm feeling, I don't know the where or when of it, much less the how. All I know is that I'm going to be introducing her to my mother in the next hour, and for now, I have to put all my energy into not being the total dickwad I still sometimes turn into when Richard, my mother, and I find ourselves in the same room.

"It's the next house," says River, from the seat next to me. I'm late because it'd started to cloud over as we'd finished up hauling in some reclaimed wood, and River riding his bike home sounded no good to me. He'd fought me, dramatically pulling up his hood and tightening it around his face, as if this would be enough to protect him from the elements, but had relented when I'd threatened to lock his bike up for the whole weekend in the back shed. He'd waited sulkily while I changed into my suit in the back office, then told me I looked like a politician when I came out. "The asshole kind," he'd said.

I'd laughed. I get a kick out of it whenever River and I tease each other. It reminds me of how far we've come since that first day he'd called me an asshole. And tried to break my foot.

I'm a little surprised, honestly, to see that he lives in a small but meticulously maintained house, the yard featuring carefully dug flower beds, the front porch lined with brightly painted clay pots, overfull with geraniums. I don't know what I expected, but I guess it was easier for me to think that a kid getting in the kind of trouble River had been getting into would have been living in a place that bore more obvious signs of distress, though I of all people should know better.

"Nice place," I say, pulling into the driveway, but River is already reaching with one hand to retrieve his backpack, the other clasping the door handle. This is straight out of my own teenage playbook, the same move I'd pull pretty much every time my dad took me to school in the Volvo wagon he used to have, the one that had an exhaust pipe held up by a pair of pantyhose.

"Wait. We've gotta unload your bike." River sighs, a heavy, frustrated exhale, and I laugh. "You embarrassed of me, man?"

"No," he grumbles, but he's answered me so quick that I know he's embarrassed of something.

I'm pretty sure I know what that something is when I hear the sound of a screen door bang shut, followed quickly by a woman's loud, almost honking laugh—I'm guessing I'm about to meet River's mom, who I only know as the "strange sorta woman" my dad mentioned speaking to on the phone after River was first caught at the yard. There are other voices too, light, lilting voices also full of laughter, and when I see three women emerge from around the back of the house, I figure I've dropped River off during some kind of party his mom his having.

I give him a sympathetic glance and get out of the truck. The woman who I think is River's mom—the resemblance is clear—is wearing a long, floral skirt paired with a men's dress shirt, tied at her waist. She's got brown hair, same as River's is at the roots, but it's shot through with gray, and it brushes her elbows as she walks toward me. "You must be Ben," she exclaims, her arms already coming around me. I catch River's wince. The poor kid.

"I'm Frances, River's mom." She pulls back from me, keeping a grip on my arm, gently pushing me toward her companions. "This is River's Aunt Vera," she says, and I shake the hand of a short, red-haired woman who has River's same hazel eyes. "And this is River's grandmother, Sue." Sue's about the same height as Vera, but with white hair almost as long as Frances's, and she's got clear blue eyes and a big smile that she's aimed right at River, who's got his head ducked in obvious discomfort.

"It's nice to meet you all. River's been doing a great job for us." This probably doesn't help the embarrassment factor, but it seems like the right thing to say to the kid's mom, maybe grease the wheels for him to get back into her good graces if he's been in trouble.

"That's wonderful, absolutely wonderful!" She lets go of me and heads over to River, wrapping him up and kissing his head. I hear him groan. "He's *such* a talented boy. Do you know, I think it's a gift from the universe that he got in trouble that day. A gift!" She raises one hand to the sky, and Vera and Sue nod.

This all seems a bit crazy-town to me, but it sure doesn't look as if River's neglected, and that's something. I clear my throat, trying to diffuse some of the awkwardness, and nod toward him. "You're back Monday after class, yeah?"

"Yeah," he says.

"Well, I'll let you all get back to…ah…" I trail off, because I'm not sure what they were doing. Maybe a drum circle or something, because I definitely smell incense.

"You should come join us!" Vera exclaims, clasping her hands together. "We're having a bean sprout casserole. Tofu for extra protein!"

I try not to let my expression reveal anything. I've got nothing against bean sprouts, but tofu is how I imagine eating a sponge feels. Plus, I've seen what River packs when he comes to the yard, and there's not a bean sprout in sight, so I'm wondering if he's resigned himself to packing his own lunches in protest. "Oh, that's very nice of you, ma'am, but I don't want to be intruding on your family party."

"Family party?" laughs Sue. "This is a regular Friday night!"

"We all live here," says Frances, in explanation. "And River, of course! I'm afraid he's a bit outnumbered, aren't you, honey? It's a lot of estrogen, I'm sure."

"Not from me," Sue quips. "I'm all dried up!"

River looks like he wants to die, and I bite the inside of my mouth to keep from laughing.

"Let me tell you what," says Vera, reaching over to ruffle River's hair, "He'll make some woman a wonderful husband someday!"

"Vera," Frances says, "that is an incredibly heteronormative thing to say."

"Oh my *God*," River says. "I'm going inside." He stomps away, sullen, disappearing through the back gate. I try to make my face smile politely, but it may be more of a grimace.

"You're about the most heteronormative thing I've ever seen!" says Vera, and is it hot out here, or am I just mortally embarrassed? "Look at you in this suit!"

"Oh, now stop harassing him," says Frances. "Are you sure we can't convince you to stay? River has told us so much about you and your father."

"Which means he's told us about three things," says Sue. "That's a lot for River right now."

"Right," I say. "He's a quiet kid." All along, I'd figured River tended toward quiet because of the way he speaks, but now I think maybe he doesn't really need to fill in much of the space with this crowd. "I really appreciate the offer, but I actually have this party to get to…" When I think of it, though, my mother's party at the Crestwood—a big bunch of celebratory toasts for Richard—bean sprout casserole sounds all right, after all. Maybe I'll call Kit, ask her to meet me here. We can just eat and talk about estrogen with these three nice ladies.

"A date! Do you have a date?" She claps her hands, a mini-celebration for something she knows nothing about. Oh, wow. First, never mind about having Kit here, because this would be worse than whatever's coming with my mom. Second, is this how Frances is with River? Because if I had a hooded sweatshirt on right now, I'd be pulling it up and doing some hardcore moping.

"Yes, ma'am. Something like that."

I quickly grab River's bike from the bed of my truck, grateful when Vera moves to take it from me. They're chattering still, asking questions about my work and I'm not even sure that I give a full answer to anything before they move on to the next question. Even when I'm back behind the wheel, Frances is talking through my open window, thanking me again, inviting my father and I over for dinner next week. I promise to get back to her about that, but I think Dad might have a moral opposition to tofu.

When I finally manage to back out of the driveway, though, I catch a glimpse of River in the front window. He's holding up a piece of notebook paper to the glass, where he's written *Sorry about that* in big letters. I give a quick nod, wave off his concern. But I wonder about the depth of embarrassment River—monosyllabic, shrugging River—must be feeling to actually go inside the house to make a *sign* of apology to me. He's living with three women—three obviously powerful, big-personality women—and no matter how nice they seemed, he's at an awkward age, and probably the yard has been a bigger help to him than I'd considered. When I go, will River keep coming? Will he and I stay in touch? Would Dad be willing to go in for tofu and bean sprouts just to keep tabs on how he's faring?

It's surprisingly difficult for me to think about, and anyways, I have a terrible party to get to.

* * * *

I pretty much forget about whatever shit I'm in for when I pull up to Kit's house and find her waiting on the porch in a black cocktail dress, fitted to her curves, cut wide across her shoulders and dipping down her chest so that perfect stretch of skin is on display, that lift of her collarbone that's her favorite place for me to touch, to kiss. It's a dress another woman would wear with pearls, but Kit wears nothing on her neck, and to me, it's all the more arousing.

I beg her to let me take her inside, skip the party. I'll let her keep the dress on if she wants. But it's a no-go. Kit's been excited for this, and I'll do whatever she wants to keep her giving me that playful smile. She takes my hand as we walk into the hotel lobby—she's been here before, she says. She'd done brunch with Zoe and Greer here a few times, but she's never been to a private party. I want to tell her not to get her hopes up, that it'll be good shrimp cocktail but terrible conversation, but I bite my tongue, on dickwad patrol of myself.

The party's already been going on for about an hour, and so the room is buzzing with conversation. Catering staff circles the room with trays of champagne, small appetizers. Along one wall, an elaborately draped buffet table is laden with heavier fare, including a giant, multi-tiered cake, not yet cut. It's over there where we spot my dad and Sharon. He's looking good, up on his cane, more stable than I've seen him since I've been in town, and while Sharon clearly doesn't care that she's the only woman in this room not wearing a dress, she's made a concession with a nice pantsuit and a silk scarf around her neck. Both she and my dad obviously have a strategy for this—they've piled their plates high with crab legs and oysters. My dad always says that the only way to take the sting out of eating off communal trays is by eating the most expensive stuff that's on them. Since neither of them can wave, they both lift their plates in greeting, my dad winking at Kit.

Kit waves back, then turns her head to whisper in my ear. "It looks so nice in here," she says. "Like a wedding reception." Now that she's mentioned it, it does look like that. The cake, sure, but there's also elaborate centerpieces—white, mostly: big, fat peonies that look pretty bridal even to me—on the tables that are arranged around the dance floor.

Where Richard and my mother are dancing.

This is my cue to say something, to agree with Kit about the room, or to offer to get her a drink, but for a minute I can't get anything out. I have this weird, nonsensical thought: *Is this a wedding for them? Did they decide to redo the whole thing, as if the first one wasn't bad enough?*

The first one, in fact, was very small—"modest," my mom said, when she'd called to ask me to come all those years ago, and when I got older I realized this had been a concession, both to my feelings and to the larger matter of taste, since Richard had proposed to my mother before her divorce from my dad was finalized. At the time, it hadn't felt like a concession. I remember that during the ceremony itself—ten minutes, max, under a rose-vined gazebo in Hazleton Park—I'd picked at a loose piece of skin on my thumb until it bled so much that the cuff of my too-big dress shirt got stained. Dad made a makeshift Band-Aid out of a paper towel and a piece of scotch tape he discreetly pulled off one of the packages someone brought to the restaurant where we had lunch after.

Tonight, my mom looks less like a bride than she did then. She's wearing a dark-red dress, floor length but mostly plain. But the way she's dancing with Richard, looking up at him—she looks as happy as she did for that first wedding, and while I know full well I'm a goddamned grown-up, and that the grown-up part of me is glad that she's got someone who looks at her that way, there's another part of me, deep down, that's howling and kicking like a fucking baby.

I clear my throat. "That's my mom," I say, gesturing to where she dances. Kit wouldn't know otherwise. I'm all Henry, and even if I wasn't, I don't have any of her mannerisms, her bearing.

Kit sucks in a breath. "Holy crap, that's your *mom*? Why didn't I buy a new dress for this?" She takes her hand from mine, flutters both of hers down the front of her dress anxiously. "She looks like a catalog model. One of the really classy ones, I mean."

This makes me laugh, and I'm so grateful for the feeling of lightness that I reach back for her hand. "Don't tell her that," I say. My mom and Richard have spotted us, and they're headed this way. Kit's hand feels small and clammy in mine. "Kit. You look beautiful. She's going to love you." I want to say that it doesn't matter what my mother thinks—it hardly matters to me—but here they are, gliding up to us with this twinned grace that makes it look as if they're doing a professional dismount from that dance floor.

"I'm so happy you came," says Mom, leaning in to brush her lips against my cheek, patting it as she withdraws. "Clean-shaven, much better."

I ignore this, focusing on Kit instead. "Mom, this Ekaterina—Kit. Kit, this is my mother, Laura Holland."

"It's so nice to meet you, Mrs. Holland," she says, shaking my mother's proffered hand before turning to Richard, who introduces himself, bright-white smile in full effect. "This is such a wonderful party," Kit says to him. "You must be so grateful."

"Oh, he is," my mom answers, brushing her hand over the diamond teardrop she's wearing around her neck. When she was married to my father, my mom only wore two pieces of jewelry: the plain gold wedding band that had been my grandmother's, and a cuff bracelet with inlaid stones that my dad had bought at auction, 1930s, Tiffany studios. I wonder fleetingly where it is. No way would my father have taken it back, and so it's probably somewhere in her giant jewelry collection, its aesthetic not really suited to her anymore, if it ever really was. Kit notices my mother's gesture, and her lips purse together in a smile that I recognize as inauthentic, even though it's not an expression I've seen on her face before.

"Well, it's nice to be celebrating thirty years anywhere, I'd say!" Richard says in that chuckly tone he has. "Now what do you do, Kit?"

"I'm a scientist."

"Wonderful!" he exclaims, and I realize that Kit's vagueness was a test, and Richard has failed—he's done nothing to betray any rudeness, but he's the same as he always is, which is to say that he's parsing out his time for each conversation, and even during this short exchange, he's probably already started thinking about the next hand he has to shake.

Before that, though, he turns his attention to me. "You've worked wonders with your dad. Henry seems almost back to normal." We all look over to where my dad and Sharon have taken a seat, their loaded plates in front of them. Dad has a Christmas morning expression on his face about those crab legs, I swear to God.

"Yeah, he's come a long way. The therapy has worked wonders."

"So you'll be headed back to Texas soon, then?" he asks, no guile there— why would there be, after all? He's got no idea that I've been sweating my return since that first night I slept in Kit's bed. I feel her stiffen slightly next to me, something infinitesimal shifting in her posture.

"I'm supposed to head back in about a week," I answer, and even as I do, I notice that I'm not looking at Richard when I speak. I'm letting my eyes shift around the room, a mistake. When I'd first been introduced to Richard, about two months after my mom moved out, he'd been smart enough not to do anything that suggested even a whiff of paternal care toward me. He seemed to know on instinct that he'd never have any kind of role in parenting me, and so he'd treated me as any polite family friend would, if one who tried a little hard. But when he'd gotten involved in my case all those years ago—he wasn't my lawyer, but he'd hired the one who eventually got me out—he'd come to the detention facility to coach me for my court dates, and he got his first and last opportunity to tell me how to behave. *Don't fidget. Look me in the eyes when you answer*, he'd say, over and over, and it didn't matter how gentle he'd been about it. It had driven me crazy.

"Supposed to?" he volleys, because this is what *look me in the eyes* had been all about—communicating confidence in your answer.

So I look at him when I answer, "I'll see how Dad's doing," even though this is entirely a lie. Dad's doing fine—everyone knows it, and anyway, everyone, I guess, also knows my dad has Sharon. But I'm not a kid anymore, and I sell this like it's 100 percent true.

Mom's caught someone in her peripheral vision. She's waving and smiling, and then she and Richard are making their apologies, thanking us for coming, promising to catch up with us again in a little bit. When they're gone, Kit turns to me, this little quirk at the corner of her mouth. "Wow," she says flatly, ironically. "They're sort of—"

"Yeah." It's a relief, I realize, to have her to look at following this exchange, to have her, so subtly, confirm some of the discomfort that's there between me, my mom, and my stepfather. Already this party feels about ten thousand times easier.

"He looks weirdly young, right? Kind of in a cryogenic way?"

Again, she's made me laugh, and I tug her closer, pressing a kiss to her temple. It feels like Kit is on my team. It feels like Kit is really *with* me at this party. "Let's get some food, yeah?"

* * * *

She is, in fact, entirely with me at the party. Somehow, she seems to anticipate exactly what I need here—first, she insists that we sit with Dad and Sharon while we eat (Dad gives her two of his crab legs, which at this point is the same as writing her into his will), and while I slough off my broody temperament, she talks animatedly with Sharon, eventually roping me into it by bringing up River. Kit's delighted anew when she figures out that Sharon used to work with River's aunt, because it's these connections, I've found, that thrill Kit the most. So after we mingle for a while, I give her more of what she wants. During the toasts I lean over, whisper in her ear stories about the guests I know—this one who had a son in my seventh grade class, that one who bought a ten-thousand-dollar antique pie safe from Dad and then later dismantled it with a hacksaw so his ex-wife wouldn't get it in their divorce.

Kit's half listening, I know it, part of her smiling at what she hears, the other part of her thinking of my mouth so near her neck, goose bumps pebbling along her skin. It completely sucks that I can't see her nipples through the material of her dress, but I've got a feeling they're reacting. The last few weeks, I've made a study of Kit, of how I can get her to react to me. Right now, nothing about this party feels awkward, artificial. It's not any of the things I was dreading. It feels fine, a little funny, even, showing her this different side of my family that's always felt so disjointed for me.

"Dance with me," I whisper to her, right in her ear, once the last toast has been raised.

"Oh," she says, turning to look up at me, her eyes wide with surprise. "I think the dancing is just for…?" She trails off, looking to where several other couples have taken to the floor in the middle of the room.

"For the guests?" I smile down at her, this rush of—heat, happiness, *fun*—coursing through me, this way I feel only when I'm around Kit. I've always loved women, have loved getting to know them, have loved sleeping with them, have loved making them feel good. But Kit makes me want everything, makes me want to be her best friend, her safe place, her family, and the guy who can fuck her until she doesn't remember her own name.

"Okay," she says, letting me pull her toward the dance floor. "But I'm not much of a dancer."

"You'll learn," I say, but I don't really mean it, because I don't intend to do much other than hold her body close to mine, just so I can feel her arms around me, her breasts pressed against my chest.

"Your mother's probably going to come by and ask whether we've left room for Jesus between us," she says.

I laugh, drawing the attention of a few of the other couples around us. "She won't." In fact, my mother and Richard are with Dad and Sharon, everyone chatting and seeming to be at perfect ease. But it doesn't chafe the way it normally does, not right now. I realize that for a lot of years, what I wanted was someone to complain to about Mom, about Richard, but my dad had been doing the right thing in always staying above the fray about the divorce. He'd made it possible for us to even have this kind of night, where we're all together. Now, though, to have Kit—it feels as if I have that someone, someone who gives you that little room to complain in, but doesn't hold it against you later.

I have a vision, fleeting, of sitting beside her in my mother's dining room, of getting through a family night with Kit as my partner, of going home with her at night after. Of *being* here, and not for a visit. It's a domino effect in my head, then—what if I was here and saw my mother more? What if I could keep an eye on Dad, on the salvage yard, work with him on some of the harder stuff? What if I could stay in River's life? What if in between—every morning, every night—I had Kit next to me?

Something must change in the way I'm holding myself, or maybe it's in the way I'm holding her, because she leans back a little, enough to look at me. "You okay?"

"Sure," I say, pulling her back to me, breaking the eye contact. But I keep my cheek pressed to her temple, because all of a sudden I feel—I don't know what. I don't want distance between Kit and me. I want her to know me. I want to *say* something to her, say something so she'll know why this night made me tense, so she'll know how fucking freaked out I am about leaving her next week. But because Kit always brings it out in me, some reckless looseness in the way I speak and act, what I end up saying to her is—neither of those things.

"Kit. I'm in love with you." *Holy fuck*, I think, as soon as it's out of my mouth. *What did I just say?* It's too soon for this, or if it's not too soon it's the wrong place, here at this party, where I can't distract her with sex or something else. But even as I'm thinking these things, I also know that I've said something true. Something I wouldn't take back. I think I've loved Kit from the minute she showed me that microscope. Definitely from the minute I found her with wallpaper stuck to her hair.

So, yeah—not taking it back.

Even if Kit has gone still in my arms. Even if she hasn't said anything. "Hey," I whisper, running my fingertips up her spine. "It's not…"

She leans back again, meets my eyes with her own, huge and wet. She's wearing contacts tonight, so my view of them is unobstructed, nothing to keep me from seeing those big tears gathering at the corners. "Don't say it's not a big deal."

"All right."

"Ben," she says, those tears—happy tears, I hope, *God*, I hope— threatening to brim over. "Take me home."

Chapter 17

Kit

I don't say it back.

Not Saturday night, when Ben gets me home and takes all my clothes off in the foyer, then carries me upstairs, not taking his mouth from mine until we're both so worked up that neither of us can say anything at all. Not Sunday morning, either, when he leaves for the yard and I leave for brunch, both of us late again from oversleeping, over-touching, over-kissing.

I don't tell Zoe and Greer.

Instead, I hear him say it, over and over, right against the shell of my ear—*Kit, I'm in love with you*—even though he hasn't said it again, either.

But there's something different there, between us. Long after we'd been home from the party on Saturday, Ben and I had been lying in my bed, warm and rumpled, Ben's hair still sweaty at his temples from exertion, and he'd told me more about Richard, his mother, their wedding, the way it all still got to him a little, even though he'd forgiven her, he'd said, he really had. I had my doubts about that—I didn't forgive my mother for leaving me, and since I couldn't pick her out of a line-up, probably, that was a massive waste of energy. But that's the way it is with parents, I think. You're always hauling around some of that baggage.

And we'd talked about Houston too. It'd been me, this time, to bring it up, to ask him to tell me about his place there. He'd had this look on his face at first, a bit startled, and I wasn't sure he'd answer—except for the brief exchange we'd had on the way to the Ursinus, we'd only really ever talked about Texas in the context of my moving there to work for Beaumont, and I was curious about his life there.

"It's an apartment," he'd said, his voice low, sandpapery, the way it always is late at night or first thing in the morning. "Fifteenth floor of a luxury high-rise where Beaumont owns some units. There's a gym and a Starbucks on the first floor. My best friend—Jasper, you've heard me talking about him—he lives a few doors down. I've got a view of downtown, so I can never get it all the way dark in my bedroom. Most of my furniture came with the place, except for an armoire I refinished my last year here, one my dad kept for me until I got a place of my own. I've got a cleaning service that comes, grocery delivery once a week. There's a pool—it's really big, actually, something you'd find at a resort. People love it."

"Do you like it?"

"I don't dislike it. I don't—I guess I think of it as doing the job."

"Doing the job of what?"

Here he'd rolled onto his back, gusting out a sigh before staring at the ceiling for a long, silent minute. "Of giving me a place to sleep. To eat. To occasionally mainline a season of *The Americans* on a weekend when I'm recovering from travel."

"That's a really good show," I'd whispered back, and we'd both laughed softly in the dark.

It didn't sound like any kind of place I'd want to be, me with my mostly mismatched furniture, my messy piles of home design magazines and scientific journals, my haphazard food supplies. And with this skin, I'd probably blind the guests at a pool. But if it's Ben's place, I'd thought—I should know it. I'd thought that we should talk about my visiting, if we were going to do long-distance, if he really was leaving next week, if we were going to start saying *I love you*, but it'd been late and before either of us spoke again we'd both drifted off.

On Monday morning, though, it's Ben who brings up Houston again, right before I'm about to hop out of his truck to head into the lab for the day. "We should talk more, about my going back. About what we'll do."

"Okay," I say. "I want to do that."

But it's not going to be today, or tomorrow. Today Ben's going back to his dad's to work, morning conference calls all day for Beaumont, and this afternoon he's driving out four hours for an auction in North Carolina, where he'll stay until Tuesday evening when it's over. Both have been sources of frustration with him, so far as I can tell. Last week I'd walked in on a call between him and Jasper, which had sounded decidedly unpleasant—*I told you, we'll deal with it on Monday, now get off my ass about it*—and the auction had been a sticking point between him and Henry. Ben hadn't wanted to go, but Henry hadn't missed this particular auction in fourteen years.

"Fuck," Ben says, clutching the steering wheel. "I don't want to go."

I think, given that thousand-yard stare out the windshield, he's probably talking about both North Carolina today and Texas next week, but I focus on the immediate. "It's only one night," I say. "I'm going to the movies with Greer on Tuesday night, but I'll call you after. You can come over if you want."

"I want," he says, and leans over to kiss me—hard, long, probably too much than is appropriate for outside my place of employment, but who cares. It's right now I want to say it back, *I love you too*, but when Ben pulls back, he preempts me with an "I'll miss you."

So I say that back, instead.

* * * *

It's only a couple of days, but during it I get a glimpse of how it might be if Ben and I were to be apart, to try this thing long distance. He sends me texts from the road Monday night, a couple of pictures—one of a motorcycle gang outside of a 7-Eleven, big, tough guys with handlebar mustaches but one of them is reading a *People* magazine featuring the British royals on the front, and one of the shitty motel room he's booked into, surely a contrast to his usual luxury travel. It reminds me of the pictures Alex usually sends me from the road, but my reaction to these is different. I see Alex's pictures and I feel admiration, or excitement for him. I see Ben's and all I feel is longing.

So when I go to work on Tuesday morning, I'm thinking about this, about how I'd do this with Ben for any length of time. The money I have, it would allow me to travel to see him, to visit him in Texas or to meet him other places. But do we have that yet, that kind of foundation, to deal with a lot of time apart? What's Ben like, really, when he's home in Houston? I know the Ben who takes care of his dad, of River, the Ben who does manual labor at a salvage yard and at my house. I don't really know the Ben who puts on a suit every day and flies all over the world making deals. No surprise, I don't even really enjoy traveling all that much. I hate the cold impersonality of hotels, and I hate being away from my own things. And anyway, I don't know if I *want* to know that Ben—this Ben, the one I've let into my home, into my life *here,* is the Ben I want. Thinking of knowing something different about him, about having to somehow integrate his other life with mine feels as threatening as any of those days I'd come home from school, finding our scant belongings stuffed into extra-large black garbage bags, ready to be moved again.

But thinking about not knowing him at all feels worse.

And that's how this thin, delicate thread of a thought enters my mind—wispy, hard to catch, so much that sometimes I don't even know if I can take it seriously. *Can I imagine living somewhere else, if Ben is there with me? Is Ben* home?

At work I preoccupy myself with tedium. When Marti finds me, I've secluded myself in one of the upstairs labs, sorting through a tray of samples that one of our recent graduates has left behind, apparently forgetting that you could still make good experimental use of leftover materials. She's got this face on that I know well from the years I've worked with her. There's a tight set to her mouth, one eyebrow raised a hitch higher than the other. Probably someone has broken something in the supply room, and my money's on the coffeemaker, since I've got a better history of fixing that than she does.

"Good, you're here," she says.

"Give me five minutes. I swear I'm going to replace the cord on that old thing, fix the short. Or buy a new one, actually. That'd be smarter."

"Not the coffeemaker. I think you ought to come down and talk to Dr. Singh, though."

Something in her voice sends a tiny alarm bell ringing in the vicinity of my chest, a trill that shakes through me. "Is he all right?"

Marti shrugs. "I was hoping you could tell me that. He came out of his office—he's had the door closed all morning—and asked if I could track you down. He was a little short, actually." That's all she needs to say, really, because all of these details are odd—usually, Dr. Singh has his door open all the time, unlike most of the faculty, who keep theirs closed on occasion to keep students from interrupting work time, and usually, when he has a question for me or news to share, he simply finds me himself. And he's never, ever short with anyone. Once when I was over at his and Ria's house for dinner, one of the girls—Asha, always the troublemaker—had taken an extra-large blue Sharpie marker to the living room wall while we'd set the table, and Dr. Singh had barely batted an eye before ushering Asha to the couch, speaking to her in calm, firm tones about what she'd done wrong, settling her into a lengthy time-out before returning to his stack of plates as if nothing had happened.

But now that I think of it, it's Tuesday afternoon, and I haven't seen him since yesterday morning. In general, we're at least passing in the halls or collaborating on something in the lab, or meeting up in one of our offices to talk over some situation with a wayward graduate student. It's a bit weird not to have seen him at all.

"I don't know what it's about," I say, curious but not nervous, not really. When I first started my job here, any time I'd get summoned to a faculty member's office or lab I'd get this immediate, hot feeling of dread—maybe I'd messed something up and not realized it? Maybe I'd done something wrong, out of order, against tradition? But in the last couple of years, I'd gained confidence, gained a better sense of myself and my own work. I trusted what I did, and trusted my ability to defend decisions I made. Marti and I exchange a concerned glance, and I do a quick hand-wash at the utility sink before we head downstairs.

Dr. Singh's door is still closed, and Marti shrugs her confusion before reaching quickly into her desk drawer to hand me a small Reese's cup. "I took this off your desk earlier. Maybe you need it more than me, huh?"

I smile at her, tucking it into my pocket. "Maybe," I say, turning to give a soft knock on Dr. Singh's door.

He's leaned back in his chair, his elbows perched on the armrests, his fingers steepled in front of his mouth. He looks tired, his thick brows furrowed, and barely glances my way when I come in and take a seat in one of the chairs across his desk. "Dr. Singh?" I don't know what else to say—his expression is as glum as I've ever seen it. A scary thought crosses my mind: Did something worse happen with his funding? Is he going to have to leave the university? To think of this place without him—it fills me with an almost breath-stealing panic.

"Ekaterina," he says, dropping his hands and looking up at me, and I know that whatever's happened, it's got to do with me—it's something I've done wrong. He looks so disappointed, and my stomach clutches in fear, all my confidence and professionalism gone. "I received a call yesterday from Beaumont Materials."

Forget clutching. My stomach pretty much drops right out of my body, which has gone ice-cold, stiff.

"I haven't—I didn't accept *any* offer from them," I say, so fast and forceful it makes me sound guilty, though I have nothing to be guilty about.

"That's what I'm given to understand. I understand that you've turned down some very attractive proposals to work in a lab down there, to be involved in some very interesting research projects."

I'm numb with shock, my mind racing to catch up with what's happening here. I think of Ben's conference calls last week, the snappish response I'd walked in on him giving to Jasper over the phone. Has Ben called to speak to my *boss*? Could Ben have done that, the Ben whose arms I woke up in yesterday, the Ben who's just told me he's in love with me? Is this his solution to the distance, or to his work crisis, to go behind my back, to get the person I respect most in the world to go after me about turning down the job?

"I don't want to work for Beaumont. I've been very clear with—them about it."

"I would like you to tell me about that," he says. It's the Sharpie-marker voice he's using, and I find it *infuriating* at the moment. "I would like you to tell me why you do not want to work for them."

"I don't even know why you would have to ask me that," I snap back, angry and flustered. I inhale through my nose, a conscious effort to stay collected in the face of this. "You know I feel very strongly—as strongly as you do—about the pitfalls of corporate science. You know I'm very fulfilled at my current position." I clear my throat, look right into his face. "You know that I have been very happy making a home here, that it's most important for me to stay here."

He looks back at me, considering. Then he says, "And the money is not at all attractive to you?" There's something in the way he says this, combined with the way he's looking at me—it's something that makes me feel flushed, embarrassed, dishonest. It's no one's business what happened to me six months ago, but there's something awful about a friend not knowing. But I had made the decision early on not to tell anyone at work. I'd told myself this was because I hadn't wanted people to question why I'd come back.

The truth was, I hadn't wanted them to think someone else needed the position more than me.

But the way he's looking at me—I have the feeling he knows. That Ben has told him.

"No," I answer. It's firm, decisive. "I do not want to work for Beaumont. Under any circumstances." *Not now*, I add to myself, silently. *Not after what he's done.* My head is a mess. Beaumont, Ben—it's all mixed up, and I feel prickles of sweat on my lower back. If I could just call Ben, see if he has an explanation for this—there has to be something. One part of me knows that Ben would never do this. But there's another part of me, the one that's been turning things over in my mind all morning, that thinks—*you don't know all of him, though.*

"I wish you would have felt that you could speak to me," he says, and it's here where his disappointment is, in my secrecy about the offer.

"I didn't speak to you because I never considered it as a real option."

He nods once, then leans forward in his chair, rests his now-folded hands on his desk. He takes a deep breath before looking up at me. "Beaumont has offered me a funding package for the fractography project."

"They—what? What?" I can't be more coherent about this—this entire meeting has been such a shock, personally and professionally.

"They have some projects that dovetail with my work, which of course I knew. But as you know I had not considered this path, private funding. They feel I could contribute," he says, and breaks off for a pause. "Of course they would need someone from their own team to run oversight."

I expect a sarcastic jab to follow, some snarky commentary on how "oversight" usually means total control, annoying interference at every level, impossible hurdles to publication. But instead, he says, "They proposed that you could do such oversight, should you take on a role at Beaumont."

Oh. It's at this moment that I notice my heart must have been pounding up to this point. I notice because right here, I think it stops for a beat.

A trade.

Beaumont is proposing a trade: funding for Dr. Singh if I go to work for them. Funding for my boss, my advisor, my mentor, my *friend*, who needs the money to keep doing the work that inspired me to become what I am now. The same man I'd said I'd do anything for.

I'd said that to Ben.

For the barest of seconds, I think I might actually get sick, right here on Dr. Singh's desk. Instead, I straighten in my chair, smooth my hands over my legs, take a deep breath to keep myself together. I think about who I was all those years ago, when I showed up to learn in Dr. Singh's lab, when I was full of ideas and energy and nerves, and he showed me how to direct them. I think about how he advocated for me to stay on as lab tech here, how much time he spent talking through the job with me, cautioning me—but not condescending to me—about what it would mean to take on this role when I could be thinking of the PhD, of jobs in the field. I think about the way he accepted my decision to stay on, not pushing or judging, and making it easier, at every turn, for me to form relationships in my new role in the department. I think of the way he's encouraged me, just in the last few weeks, to branch out, to take the lead author credit.

I can't count all the ways I owe Dr. Singh.

"Do you want to take their funding?" I ask.

What he says is, "I have no interest in bargaining your happiness for funding." But what I hear—unfairly or not—is *maybe*. I swallow twice, a third time, that sick feeling back again.

"I appreciate that," I manage.

"Let me be clearer about this, Ekaterina. I wanted to speak to you to find out what your reasons are for not wanting to work for this company. I wanted to make sure those reasons were…*your* reasons. Not reasons that have to do with your loyalty to me. If you do not want to go work for Beaumont, then I don't want you to, either. No matter what package they offer me."

"Loyalty is a good reason for doing something," I say.

"So is ambition. So is wanting to challenge yourself, or to try something new."

"I know that," I snap back, then stand from my chair. What he's said—does this mean he thinks I should take it? "I'm sorry. This is—this has been a shock," I say, which is the understatement of the year, and I say this as a person who won the freaking lottery. "I need some time. I need to..." *I need to cry my heart out over this, over what Ben has done.* "I need to take the day."

He's looking at me with such naked concern on his face that I turn, reaching for the doorknob. I've hardly ever "taken the day." Even on the rare occasions I've been too sick to come into the lab, I've done work from home, called in to walk someone through a scan setup or a repair, kept an eye on my email. But right now, I want to be away from here, to be as far away from Dr. Singh as I can get. To think that he could have this funding, funding that would ease a lot of his professional anxieties, and I'm the one who could solve his problem if only I give up this entire life that has made me the most happy?

It's intolerable.

I don't even make eye contact with Marti as I leave Dr. Singh's office. I'm already pulling my phone out of my pocket, SOSing to the only two people I want to see right now.

* * * *

The inside of Zoe's condo is something straight out of *Architectural Digest*. It's all clean lines and white furniture and fancy glassware that makes you feel at first like you should absolutely not touch anything. But what's funny is that once you know Zoe, you know that she keeps it this way not so you feel you can't touch anything, but so you don't feel you *have* to. It's a place totally free of distraction, of little messes or the chaos of life, and it's the perfect place for me to be right now, crying it out on a stool at her kitchen island, a mug (white, of course) of tea in front of me, steaming up my glasses.

It'd taken me a while to get the whole thing out to Zoe and Greer. At first, I'd been shuffled into the condo and placed in my current seat, Zoe getting to work on the tea and Greer scooting her stool right next to mine, tossing an arm around me so I could rest my head on her shoulder. After a few minutes of soaking in their presence, letting that high-strung initial response loosen, I'd finally managed to tell them about my meeting with Dr. Singh, about how Ben had tried to trade me for money. I'd also managed—and this had been the worst, sobby, choked-voice part of the whole thing—to tell them about what he'd said to me Saturday night, while we'd danced at his mother's party.

At first, it's all the stuff I've come to expect from my friends—we do a sort of shared three-minute shock and awe (*how could he do this*), then we do some collective indignation over it (*what a jerk*), then we do the thing where I cry and they coo and fuss over me and then make promises to defend my honor (*I wish I could punch him right in the dick*). It's pretty much a script we've mastered over our years of friendship, anytime we've been wronged at work or a social gathering, or anytime one of us has gone through a breakup. But this time, it *feels* like a script. We're all going through the motions, because I think we all know there's something bigger happening here, that this is the most upset they've ever seen me.

And maybe this is why we cycle through it a bit more quickly than usual, why we're definitely approaching the stage where we're supposed to get rational, to get to the part where one of them starts giving out the advice that I've come here for anyway.

"Okay, but..." Zoe says cautiously, and I already know I'm not going to like what I'm going to hear. "Have you called him?"

"No," I say, taking off my glasses to wipe them on my shirt. I appreciate, for a few seconds, that the world goes blurry around me.

"Maybe you should call him. Let him explain."

"Let him explain that he basically used me? That he's been sleeping with me and telling me he's not involved with my recruitment anymore? While he's—I don't know what. Gathering information he can use against me?"

"Kit," Greer says. "It doesn't seem that way."

"How does it seem?" I ask, putting my glasses back on, looking back and forth between them. "Explain how I should take this a different way."

"No," Greer says, dropping her eyes. "You're right. It does seem lousy. I just...it's terrible. You seem to like him so much."

I love him, I think, and just as quickly, I think, *thank God I didn't say it back.*

"I'm not defending him, Kit," says Zoe. "But it's worth talking to him. Corporate stuff—it's complicated, fast-moving. This might not be him. Or if it is him, it might've gone a different way than he intended."

I shake my head, unwilling or unable to see how to reinterpret this. I feel so *upended*. That's the best way I can describe it. I feel like I'm going to wake up tomorrow and everything, once again, will be different. Everything will be new and I'll have to relearn things, meet new people, steel myself all over again. It doesn't matter if that's not what's really happening—it's how I *feel*.

My phone rings from my purse, and I ignore it, my doing so another implicit answer to Zoe's suggestion. I can sense them looking at each other as it rings, waiting, but I concentrate on sipping my tea. It would be good to go back to the collective indignation stage—that part at least seemed to stem the surge of tears I keep feeling welling up in my throat, behind my eyes. It's not that I'm never going to speak to Ben again. Obviously, at some point, I'm going to have to be an adult and find out what the fuck happened between him telling me he loved me and him selling me out to his fucking horrible company. But I don't have to make it easy on him, either. I don't have to talk to him now, when I'm weepy and freshly devastated.

The phone goes quiet, but only for the barest of seconds before it starts ringing again, and it's twice more that way before Greer finally slides off her stool and goes over to my purse, pulling it out to silence it. But she must look down at the screen before she does, because she says quietly, "Oh. It's your brother."

I haven't talked to Alex since he left a few weeks back, aside from a few brief emails, him letting me know when he got back to the States, nothing about our fight. I'd wanted to give him time, space—to be on his own, the way he'd said he'd wanted. And I'd been wrapped up in Ben too, the happiness and excitement I'd felt about being with him dulling what I know, at any other time, would be a lot of pain and grief over what Alex had said during our argument. But Alex calling me this many times in a row, it sends a current of fear through my already overloaded system, and I'm off my chair headed to take the phone from where Greer holds it out to me.

I don't even get out a hello before Alex says, "Kit. I've got bad news."

Barely three hours later, I'm on a plane.

Chapter 18

Ben

I wake up to the sound of my phone ringing, and it takes me a minute to register where I am—on Dad's couch, the remote on my stomach. The trip out and back to North Carolina was a slog, even though I'd made some good purchases of building materials—high quality, high resale value, and good for this time of year. But I'd spent extra time sorting transit for it all, and everything had been made worse by the flat tire I got out on one of the backroads I'd used to get to the highway more quickly. I'd finally come in around nine, Dad watching a ballgame on TV, and muttered about needing a few minutes to sit down, but I guess that had turned into a full night of sleep. I jerk to a sitting position and look around, panicked. Did Dad get ready for bed on his own? Did I miss Kit's call?

"Kit?" I say as I pick up, standing to check Dad's room.

"It's Jasper." I cross the living room again, peek into the kitchen. Dad's there, at the kitchen table, sipping a mug of coffee, which he tips to me in greeting, and I breathe out a sigh of relief. He must've got himself ready for bed, got up on his own, made his own coffee—it's huge progress, and I should feel happy, but something in me, again, feels a bit bereft. "You there?"

"Yeah," I say, scrubbing a hand over my face. "Sorry. I overslept."

"You know anything about what's holding up Averin's decision?"

"What?" I say, confused. My brain still feels sludgy, sleep-deprived, unprepared for Jasper's work-ready attitude. "What decision?"

"Singh called me this morning to tell me he'll need a couple weeks before he can give me an answer."

Something goes cold inside me. But it's been a rough couple of days. I must be missing something. "Singh?" I repeat. "Jasper. I don't know what you're talking about."

"Jesus, I thought you were involved with this woman. She hasn't told you?" It's that cold feeling again—I say nothing, waiting for him to go on. "I went to Singh, Averin's boss. We offered project funding for three years, some equipment too."

I have to lean against the doorjamb to keep my legs holding me up.

"Told him we wanted her to come work for us, that she could stay involved in the research he'd do for Beaumont, regular travel back, all that. This guy, he needs the money. He's running last in his department for external grants. It's a good offer."

"Jasper," I say slowly, my brain trying to catch up. "You tried to get Singh to trade Kit?"

"Yeah."

Fuck. Fuck, fuck, fuck. Kit told me herself—she'd do anything for Dr. Singh. If she feels responsible for him missing out on that kind of funding— it'd be terrible for her. *I owe him everything*, she'd told me. "Jesus Christ. I can't believe you—"

"This guy, he's clueless. Kept asking about what we'd be able to do for her, salary-wise, like he's real worried about her? He didn't even know she'd won the lottery."

"What?" I shout this through the phone. "How the fuck do you know about that?" My heart is pounding. This conversation with Singh—if he's gone to Kit with this, she must be devastated.

She must be done with me.

"It's public record, bud. State law where you are, she had to disclose her identity to claim. There wasn't much news about it, because the jackpot wasn't all that big, but I found it."

"Jasper, what the fuck. How could you do that?"

"Do what? I don't know if he'll take it, but he at least listened—I thought I might have him. But then he called me late yesterday and told me something had happened, that Kit would need some more time. He ought to take it—he's not going to get the kind of funding we're offering anywhere else, but he seems reluctant to lose her, so I guess you two have that in common, though—"

I cut him off before he can go anywhere else with that sentence. "I need to go."

"Wait—"

"No." I'm already in my bedroom, grabbing clothes out of a drawer. "You have no idea the shit you've buried me in, Jasper."

"Tucker, come on. This was your idea."

"This was my idea over a fucking *month* ago. I told you I was involved with her. I told you I wasn't recruiting her anymore."

"Well, I told *you*. You're not the only one who can recruit."

"You had me on the phone for two hours yesterday. You didn't say a goddamn word. Tell me that's not fucking shady, man. *Tell me.*" I shout this, slamming my fist against my dresser.

His pause is too long, and right now, I don't give a shit what he has to say anyway so I hang up, immediately call Kit's cell—voicemail. It's the same at her office, and when I call the front office, the secretary tells me Kit's not in. I quickly brush my teeth and pull on fresh clothes, then go out to the kitchen. "Dad," I say, "Can you—?" I don't even know where to start. The salvage yard is supposed to open in two hours. I can't remember if River's coming today. I don't know if Sharon is working. Does Dad have PT today, or a doctor's appointment? Everything I've been keeping straight in my head over the last weeks—it's all gone to shit. I can only think of getting to her.

"I'm fine," Dad says, his brow furrowed in concern. "I'll call Sharon. You all right?"

"No," I say. "I have to go, but I'll call." I pat his shoulder before leaving the house, driving to Kit's as fast as I can. The whole time, all I can think about is everything that has been violated for Kit—her job, which she loves, the loyalty she has to Dr. Singh, the risk of having to leave this place, the privacy she guarded about her win.

I barely remember to shut off the truck when I pull up to her house.

The door opens before I'm even all the way up the steps.

"Zoe," I breathe, and fuck, I wish it were Greer. Zoe looks as if she wants to slit me from neck to nuts. "I have to talk to her."

"Oh, I'll bet you do."

"Is she here? Her phone is off, and there's no answer at work. This was not me who did this, Zoe. This was not me."

"Who was it?"

"It was my partner, he—"

"How did he know to go to her boss? How did he know that would work on her?" And yeah—it's exactly what Jasper said. It's because I fucking told him, when I'd still been keeping him in the loop about what I'd learned about Kit, when I'd still been lying to myself about why I wanted to be around her all the time, why I wanted to know so much about her. I have never hated myself more, and I've almost gone to prison, so that's saying something. "You told her you wanted to be with her, that you loved her.

Do you realize what she thinks?"

"It wasn't about the job, Zoe. That was *never* about the job. I swear to you. I need to see her. I'll do anything for her."

"You tried to just *push* her. Right into the fucking fast lane," Zoe says, and I have no idea what that even means, but at least she hasn't slammed the door in my face yet. It's Zoe and Greer who Kit wanted me to go to, before she'd even really listen to me about Beaumont, and somehow I know it'll be Zoe and Greer who I'll have to get through if I ever want to see her again.

"Please," I say, and it's almost a whisper, how it comes out.

She sends a long, assessing look down at me. I'm grateful to be on these steps below her. I'll get on my knees if she wants me to, but there's something in her expression, some whisper of familiarity or sympathy that makes me think Zoe's been where I am. She's had to beg for forgiveness too. "She had to leave town. Her dad—he's not well."

My mind empties of everything about Beaumont, about what I have to explain to Kit. "What happened?"

"Her brother called yesterday afternoon. Kit's dad maybe had a stroke. They don't know much yet. She flew out to Ohio last night."

"Zoe, Jesus. Do you know where she is? What hospital?"

"I'm not telling you that. I've told you enough."

It doesn't matter. I've listened to everything Kit has ever said to me. I know roundabout where her dad lives these days, or at least where she sends his money. I'll find the hospital closest. I'll go to every goddamn hospital in that state if I have to. I can't imagine her alone right now. I can't imagine not being with her.

* * * *

In my job as a recruiter, I'm on the road for probably 150 days out of the year, and while that's pretty exciting at first, mostly, after a while, it sucks—it's all mediocre food and nondescript hotel rooms and a regular feeling of jet-lagged fatigue. But it's also massive frequent flyer miles, and I use God knows how many to get myself on a flight to Ohio.

I don't bring extra clothes, a toothbrush, anything. I call my dad from the airport, where I drive immediately after leaving Kit's, asking if he's okay for at least the rest of the day and tonight. I call Sharon too, to make sure I haven't dropped the ball on his care in any way, and thankfully neither of them asks much of anything, other than whether I'm all right.

I'm not all right. I'm panicked. I'm not a nervous flyer, ever, but on both of those shitty regional flights I'm a sweaty first-timer, clutching my armrests and keeping my jaw clenched tight. I keep thinking, *what if I don't get to see her?* By the time I've touched down, I'm sweaty, tense all over, and I take a few minutes in the airport bathroom to rinse my face, calm down so I can think long enough to make the calls I need to make.

I luck out, at least, in finding the regional medical center where Kit's father has been admitted, paying an unholy amount of money to a cab driver to make the hour drive there. And I lie like a fucking dog to the receptionist in the lobby, saying I'm family, and it's wrong, but I don't care.

All I care about is seeing Kit.

When I do see her, she's at the end of a long hospital corridor, her small form huddled in the hard plastic chairs that are always an extra cruelty at hospitals. I spent days in an almost identical one, next to my dad. Sitting across from her is a small, plump woman with bottle-blond hair, her hands clasped as if in prayer. And beside her is a tall, lean man with jet black hair and a beard. He sees me first and stands as I approach. This is Kit's brother—despite his height and his light-colored eyes to Kit's almost black ones, there's a similarity to their faces, to the arrangement of their features.

Except on this dude, those features look mean as hell.

"No," he says, walking toward me, putting out a hand. "No."

"I'm Ben Tucker," I say needlessly, because from the look on his face I know already that he's heard everything he thinks he needs to know about me. "I came to be with Kit."

"I'm her brother. And I don't give a shit what you came for."

"Alex," Kit says from her chair, and then she unfolds herself, standing wearily. Oh, *fuck*, she looks so tired. Her cheeks seem gaunt, and the pale skin under her eyes, nearly transparent even when she's well, is purpled with fatigue. I level a look at this Alex person, try to fill it with as much accusation and judgment as I can manage. Why isn't he feeding her, making sure she sleeps?

As if you have any right, I think to myself.

Kit stands beside her brother, setting a quelling hand on his forearm, which I now notice leads down to a clenched fist that he has rested at his side. I'm not immune to such a show of aggression. Part of me wants to take out all my anger, all my frustration, on this guy, this guy who's acting like he's Kit's protector and I'm the big bad wolf come to blow her house down. I feel it close to the surface, that urge, that hair-trigger intensity that was under my skin almost every day of my teen years. But I won't do that to Kit. I won't make this worse for her.

"I'll talk to him," she says, looking up at Alex, who scans her face in concern.

"You don't have to," he says.

"I know. But it'll be faster this way. I'll take care of it." *Faster this way.* Faster, I know she means, to get me out of this hospital, out of her face, out of her life. I feel sick.

Alex nods, then turns to glare at me before heading back down the hall. But he sits a few seats closer than he was before. He's keeping an eye on us.

When Kit looks at me, she's wiped any expression of recognition from her face. I could be anyone. I could be another hospital employee, someone she just wants to deal with and get rid of. "Kit," I say, but even though I've thought of nothing but her since I left home, I haven't thought at all about what exactly I'd say in this moment, when I'd see her, white-faced under these fluorescent lights, looking slight and weary and so, so *finished* with me. "How is your father?"

She crosses her arms over her chest, but it's less defiant than it is an effort to stay warm, or to self-contain, somehow. She's holding the pieces of herself together. "He's not awake yet. We'll know more when he is."

"Has the—is the doctor good? Answering all your questions? Because sometimes it helps if you—"

She cuts me off. "The doctor is fine. She's very helpful."

"That's good," I say dumbly.

"Ben. I don't know how you heard about this, but—"

"Zoe told me." Kit clenches her teeth together, and I know Zoe must've broken confidence, must've done exactly what Kit had told her not to do. But somehow that gives me a strange sort of hope, that Zoe would do that, that she'd believe in me enough to tell me where Kit was. "Don't be upset with her."

"I'm not," she snaps, then takes a deep breath. "But listen, this is a family matter. And I know you've come a long way, but—I'd really prefer that you leave."

I search her face for something, *anything*, to tell me she's lying, to me or to herself.

"Kit, you have to know—"

"No," she says, an echo of her brother. "I don't."

She's right—she doesn't have to listen to me, to my explanation about Jasper, about how I'd told him stuff about Singh before I was involved with her, before I knew where this was going. Here, in this place, I doubt she cares, or at least I doubt she can let herself care, not until her father is out of the woods.

"Just let me be here with you. I'm so worried—"

"You know what, Ben? I'm sorry about that. I'm sorry that you're worried. I know that's hard. But this isn't about you. This is something that's going on with me, and I get to pick who I want to have around. I get to choose. And it's not you. It's really, really not."

"I'll do anything," I say. "I'll wait outside, if you want, or I'll—what if I check into a hotel? And you can call, if you want to—" It's me who breaks off here, something cruel twisting in my chest. This is familiar—I have done this before. I have begged this way before, a long time ago, and it was the worst day of my life, worse than the day I got arrested. Half of me doesn't care—half of me wants to keep going with this until I've lost any shred of dignity I have left. But the other half of me? Something ices over, a soft frost, and I feel my spine straighten.

Kit looks at me, hard, a flash of something in those dark eyes. But then she lowers them, shakes her head slowly from side to side. "I'm not going to want to. I don't think—I'm not going to want to see you again, okay? What happened with Beaumont, and Dr. Singh, that's really terrible, and I'm going to have to sort through that later, when things are…" She doesn't finish this thought, and I know why. There's a sort of superstition that steals over you when you're in the hospital with someone you love. You're always looking for wood to knock on, always wanting to say *don't jinx it* to any doctor or nurse who promises recovery. Her chin trembles for a split second, and I reach for her, instinctively, but she turns her body just so. Just so that I can't get near her. "But I don't have to sort through much to know that I can't trust you," she says. "And right now—all I've got energy for is the people I can trust."

I can feel it, right then, my throat closing up—not for me. It's for her, for the way she looks so small, and so in pain. I swallow, once, twice, to force the feeling down, and it's ugly, the feeling that replaces it. That soft frost, it's hardening into something else, something I don't want Kit to see. I'm rooted to the spot, though. Looking at her, I can't bear the thought of walking away and leaving her here.

But I don't have to.

Because Kit walks away from me.

* * * *

Someone other than me, someone with a bit more optimism, or someone who didn't actually see that look in Kit's eyes when she saw me, may have stuck around, waited it out. But not me.

I don't get a hotel room. I don't stay overlong at the airport.

I go back home.

It feels like it's been the longest day, like it should already be tomorrow, but Jasper's call had come in early this morning, and in the end, I'm off my last flight before midnight. I don't drive home right away, though. I drive to the salvage yard. At this time of night, it's as dark and menacing as all the kids used to think it was. I let myself in, disable the alarm, and head straight back to the office, where I've been working on the Baltic chandelier. It's maybe half assembled now, the largest pieces in place so that it can hang straight from the hook I've put it on. Every day I've been here, I've worked a bit on assembling more of it.

What I want to do, what my instinct is: to pick up the baseball bat my dad keeps under his desk—from before he had an alarm for this place—and smash this chandelier to hell. To watch all the pieces shatter, hear the sound they would make, feel the crunch of them under my boots.

What I do instead is take it off its hook, less gingerly than I should, and carry it upstairs to the east wing, the graveyard, where I first found it. I don't bother rehanging it. I set it on the floor, its layers collapsing into themselves, the prisms tinkling against each other, against the ground. I go back to the office, pick up the tray of spare pieces I have gathered on the workbench, and carry this upstairs too. Again, I resist an urge—to scatter these all over, to make it next to impossible to find all the pieces again in this mess. Instead, I set the tray beside the broken-bodied chandelier. Maybe River will come up here sometime, find it, and start in on it instead of me.

I stand in that room for a long time. And I don't do anything but live out all my aggression in my head. In here, there's tons of stuff to destroy, to smash up, to grind into dust. My body is still, but coiled—I can imagine the release I'd feel in picking up those window frames, breaking them over the top of the dresser in the corner. I can hear the wood split, can feel splinters that would go into my hands and arms from the impact. I could tip that dresser right over, and it would make the most satisfying *thud* on this floor. It would shake everything in here. It would feel really, really good.

But I don't do that anymore. I haven't been that person in years and years.

Still, I can't shake the sense that what I did with Kit was pretty close to what I'm imagining—I smashed up the room of her, of us. I went in reckless that first time I'd met her, and I'd been reckless about my involvement with her—I waited too long to get myself off her case. I didn't tell Jasper enough when I finally did. I fell too fast, too hard, told her I loved her too soon. I barreled into that hospital, didn't have the right things to say. I acted like the brash, feckless kid I'd grown up being, that I'd worked hard to leave behind.

After a while, I go back down the steps, reset the alarm, lock up. I'm so tired that I hardly remember the drive back to my dad's, but I'm dreading getting into bed, closing my eyes and seeing Kit there. So it's a minor relief that my dad's waited up—I may not feel ready for talking, but at least it gives me an excuse to put off the tossing and turning I'm sure to do all night.

He's in the recliner. He's got the TV tray of clock pieces pulled up again, but this time, he's using both hands—the left one's shaky, pale, a little smaller than the other one, but other than this, Dad looks almost like his old self, as if I've never been here at all.

Fitting.

"Up late," I say.

"That's my line, kid."

I sit on the couch across from him, scrape a hand down my face. "I fucked up, Dad."

"Let's hear it," he says, keeping his eyes on his clock pieces, his hands busy.

I give him an abbreviated version—what I'd told Jasper about Kit and Dr. Singh when I'd still been working on her case, what Jasper had done with the information without telling me first, what Kit thinks now about me and her, about why I've been with her. "Now her dad's sick, and today I—I flew all the way there, tried to be with her. I tried to tell her it wasn't me who did this, with Beaumont, but…"

"She's probably not in the mood to hear that," he says, matter-of-fact. "Probably she's too worried about her dad to hear anything you've got to say."

"I know," I say, dropping my head back.

"Maybe you ought to have stayed. Got a room nearby, in case she needs you."

In spite of myself, I lift my head up to cut him a sharp look, but only because he's floated the idea I was too chickenshit to do myself. "I'm not going to fucking stalk her, Dad. She said she didn't want me around."

"Tough thing, that."

Holy shit, I am not in the mood for this. I am not in the mood for my dad's weird, monkish approach to advice, where he says hardly anything at all and I'm supposed to sort out the answers in the silence. "I don't think I'm right for her, anyway," I say. "She's pretty settled in here, with her life, and I'm headed home in a few days. Long distance wouldn't have worked. It was a temporary thing. We don't—we don't really fit."

He snorts, half laugh, half scorn. "Don't be an idiot, Ben. I was married to someone I didn't fit with, and what you've got with Kit, it's not that. Maybe you're not going to be able to work it out with her, but don't say some damn fool thing about you not fitting with her. You know you did."

I do know I did. But right now, I want to go on lying to myself about it. I want to pretend I'm going to get on a plane on Sunday night, fly back to my life in Houston, sleep in my king-size bed with its two pillows and extra-hard mattress and not think about Kit at all. I want to pretend that it'll be easy, at some point, to just check-in, make sure she's okay, and then go on with my life as if I'd never fallen in love with her.

As if I'd never thought at all about living a whole different life, for her.

"So you're going to leave, then," he says. I look over at him, at where he's still got his eyes down on the clock. Despite the words, he's not said this with any judgment, and that's how he's always been. He'd been the same when I'd announced I'd go to Texas, when I'd told him I'd be staying there once I'd taken the job with Beaumont. I always wondered whether he thought I should have stayed, taken over the yard, been closer to him. But he's done fine without me. He's had a whole life without me, with Sharon and his work. He loves me, but he doesn't need me here.

"We ought to turn in," I say. I rise to go over to Dad's chair, still shadowing him a little as he pushes himself up, even though now he uses all the stability training he's got from the trainer.

When he puts his good arm around my shoulders as we walk, I know he's trying to take care of me now.

Chapter 19

Kit

For the next three days, my life is stale coffee, shitty hospital food, and long, loaded silences with Alex and Candace, punctuated with the occasional interruption of a doctor or nurse. Alex and I have checked into the hotel nearest the hospital, separate rooms, and Alex didn't even bother arguing with me about paying. At night, one of the three of us stays in Dad's room, the others scattering to our respective corners. I sleep better upright, in the chair next to my father's bed, than I do for the two nights I'm in the hotel room—there, it's too quiet. I'm too alone. After the first day, the immediate danger to Dad had passed, and that left room for everything else—for thoughts of my job, of Dr. Singh. For thoughts of Ben.

If I'm lucky, Ben will never know what it cost me to send him away. To not collapse into him, inhale his familiar scent, press my whole self against his warmth and cry until I couldn't anymore. But the truth was, while I was terrified about my dad, I'd still been in a sort of numb, unprocessed shock about it. The real thing that had been keeping me on the verge of tears was what had happened with my job, with what Ben had done.

Candace is what I pictured, back when Dad first told me he was moving in with someone, except maybe her hair is even more enormous, teased up in the front in such a way that I want to take photographs and study it for scientific purposes. But over the last two days we've spent together in my dad's cramped hospital room, I've learned a few things about Candace.

They're not the normal things—where she works or whether she's got kids of her own, or how long she and my dad have been together. The mood in the room has been too tense, too somber to strike up those kinds of conversations. But they're important things, I think. Candace takes notes when the doctors and nurses come in, because, she tells me and Alex, it's easy to forget when there's so much information coming at us. When she leaves for an hour to take a shower, she comes back with an afghan that she'd made for Dad as a gift. It's his favorite, she says, and even though it is completely hideous, she is obviously correct, because my father, who hardly opens his eyes, still manages to clutch that afghan between his hands like a child. She also brings in a small radio, tunes it to a station that plays "golden oldies," and lets it play softly from the table next to Dad's bed. And she watches him—not with the furrowed, tense, vaguely angry attentiveness that Alex seems to radiate—but with a patient, focused concern, her hands often clasped in her lap.

It's these things that make me think I should make an effort to know her in a more complete way. I haven't even spoken to Dad about her, other than that first phone conversation we'd had weeks ago, but I have the sense from watching her these last couple of days that she's not temporary. By Saturday afternoon, the worst has passed—the doctor tells us that Dad's stroke was minor, and during the few hours a day he was awake, he'd been passing benchmark tests, though he's got lingering aphasia—language difficulties—that may or may not clear up. We've heard long, frightening lectures about my dad's risk if he keeps smoking. A counselor has come by and spoken to us about managing his withdrawals. But it's all less pressured than those first few hours, and so while Alex is out picking up lunch, I decide to try for conversation with Candace that's not about my father's immediate care needs.

"So. You met my dad at church."

Candace looks up from the Sudoku puzzle she's been doing. She's got a book of these and has done them periodically throughout our time here, and up to now, I've preferred that to her trying to make conversation. "Is that what he told you?"

Oh, fucking great. I should have known better. The craps table is my dad's church. I don't say anything in response.

"Well, I suppose we did meet at church. Our meetings are in the basement at St. Christopher's."

"Your—what meetings?"

"Alcoholics Anonymous meetings. You didn't know?"

"I know my dad's an alcoholic. Among other things. But I didn't know he went to meetings."

"We met there, well, I suppose about eight months ago now…"

"Eight *months*?"

"Aha," Candace says. "Well. Your father attends meetings. And he's sober, or at least he has been for the last five months—he had a few stumbles early on. But I don't know that he's necessarily accepted many things about the work. Such as making amends to the people he's hurt."

"Right."

"And I know he's hurt you, Ekaterina." The way she says my name—it's too harsh, starting with an *eee* sound.

I look at my father in the hospital bed, sunken cheeks and gray stubble, sleeping heavily. I don't want to talk about this when he's there, in this state. It feels disloyal. But I guess I've opened a can of worms with Candace, because she's got no such compunctions. "He talks about you kids a lot. About mistakes he's made with you both."

He doesn't talk about it with me, I think, but I don't say this. Instead, I opt for a re-direct. "Why did he move in with you?"

"I asked him to," she says placidly. "The place where he's been working is closer to my place—"

I hold up a hand. "I'm sorry. He's been working?" At this point, it feels as though she's angling for me to be disloyal, to get angry, dropping these revelatory bombs about my father's life that I know nothing about. My father has had jobs before, off and on, but not since Alex and I left the house for good. Given that Alex and I both have been sending him checks, it would've been nice to know that Dad himself could have supplemented.

"Yeah, at a dry cleaner in town. Four days a week, and before this happened he was going to start learning how to run some of the pressing machines."

"Well, that's—that's just great, I guess." I shift in my chair, reach for the remote that's on the windowsill. Mostly we've kept the TV off in here, but right now I don't care what awful thing is playing. I only want the distraction.

"He's been saving the money you and your brother send him, for the last six months or so."

I have to look at my dad again, to remind myself that it's colossally shitty to get angry with a man in a hospital bed. It only half works. "Well, Candace, that's really great for him. Maybe he can use it on his hospital bills." Even as I say this, I know it's ridiculous. I'll be paying every one of those hospital bills, and I wouldn't have it any other way.

"He wanted to give it back to you on the one-year anniversary of his sobriety." Maybe this should make me feel warm and fuzzy inside. Maybe I should be celebrating the fact that my dad was in a place to think of this kind of gesture. But it makes me so *mad* to hear this, to hear that he's been going along, getting better at his life, making some grand gesture plan for me and Alex when all we'd really want was a bit more kindness from him. Maybe it's progress, but it's still selfish. It's still 100 percent the dad I know, him choosing whatever feels good in the moment. It feels to me like a bet he made with himself, rather than a real commitment to change.

"Do you know he has a gambling problem?" I ask, and it sounds so harsh, so snappish. As if I'm trying to *assert* myself in front of her, to get back at her for all this knowledge she has about my dad with something of my own, even if it's something terrible.

"I do know that. He hasn't gambled since the night he took his last drink."

"You ought to make sure about that. He can be really sneaky about it. And he never lasts long."

Candace gives up a little cough—she's got that smoker's raspiness too. "You're a good person to be here, Ekaterina," she says, surprising me. "My own kids, I put them through a lot, and I don't think they'll ever forgive me. I'm not here to defend your father to you. That's work he has to do himself, and I know he's not doing a good job at it. But I think he was trying."

I don't know what to say to this. This is—it's all such a *mess*, this thing with my dad. It's chaotic and conflicting and terrifying. I hate that he's sick, and I hate that I'm so scared about that, about the thought of him dying. But I'm angry with him too—about the last eight months of him getting his shit together and yet still being mostly difficult and recalcitrant with me and Alex, about all the years before that when he wasn't even trying to get his shit together. I'm angry that I don't trust a single thing Candace is telling me, that I don't trust her or my father, and mostly that this distrust might say as much about me as it does about them.

"Hey," says Alex, coming in with bags of food from the bagel shop down the street, and thank God for that, because however strained it is between me and him right now, it's not worse than the situation I've worked up with Candace.

"Why don't you two take your food outside and eat?" she asks. "It's so nice out there today, and we've all been so cooped up. You two go first, and I'll go once you get back."

"You sure?" Alex says, right as I'm saying, "Oh, no, that's okay." We look across the room at each other, and I roll my eyes and push myself up off the chair.

"You'll call us if the doctor comes in?" I ask.

"Of course," she says. Alex crosses the room to give her one of the sandwiches he's brought, then pauses to take a look at Dad. He straightens the bedclothes around my dad's sleeping form—quick, efficient, again that vague frustration with everything. It's this that gives me an unwelcome flash of Ben. A few times, Ben had told me how hard it was, sometimes, to be his dad's caretaker, how stubborn and willful his dad could be, especially during the long recovery process. But in front of Henry, Ben was patient and gentle, never condescending. You watched him and thought, *he doesn't want to be anywhere else but here.*

It's not fair to judge Alex by these standards. Beneath my brother's gruff attentions there's a kindness, or at least an awareness of my dad's humanity. Sometimes I forget that Alex had years with Dad before I came along, that his relationship to him is different than mine, and I'll bet this whole experience is hard for him in a different way. It's been tentative with Alex and me, these last few days, and I'm suddenly seized with an urgent feeling that I have to fix this, whatever this is between us, because we're family, and my father's sick, and ridiculously, maddeningly, without Ben, I feel more alone than I have in years.

* * * *

We find a mostly quiet spot on a wood bench that's set under a huge horse chestnut, its leaves fat and summer-green. The air is muggy, the sun too bright, but it all feels good. I hadn't realized how tired I'd gotten of the dry hospital air, the fluorescent lights. We both sit crooked to the side, so we can lay our food out on the expanse of bench between us, and it reminds me of our many living-room picnics, messy and haphazard, but somehow comforting.

"Thanks for this," I say, once we've both taken a few bites, and once I feel desperate to break the silence.

He shrugs his acknowledgment, wipes his cheap paper napkin across his mouth. "How's the house coming along?" he asks, and I know this is his peace offering, this attempt at conversation.

"It's all right. I had some unexpected repairs to do upstairs," I say, swallowing back a fresh wave of pain when I think about the plaster, about the day Ben first kissed me. "But it's all set now. Should be starting on the kitchen pretty soon." Even as I say this, there's unwelcome, stomach-turning thoughts about whether I'll even be in the house, whether I'll have to pick up and move to help Dr. Singh.

"That's great."

It's my turn, but this is harder than I thought. I'm out here to try and make things better, but I'm still mad about last month. I'd been so excited to show Alex every single thing about my house, to get his input, to have him be excited for me. Now I don't want to talk about the house at all, and especially not with him. Whether that's me protecting something that matters or me punishing him is too complex a problem for me to sort out on such little sleep.

We dither our way through various other dead-end topics—what we think of Dad's doctor, our shared impressions of Candace, even, God help us, the weather. We've both balled up the trash from our meals and I'm packing it all back into the bag for disposal when Alex stills my hand and says, "Tool Kit."

I have to look down, give my eyes a minute to fight back the wetness that springs up there. "Yeah?"

"I need to tell you I'm sorry about last month. For everything I said, and for leaving the way I did."

One of those tears snakes its way out anyway, and I swipe at it, frustrated. There's no one else like Alex in my life, who can make me cry this way—I want so bad to be tough in front of him, to make him proud of me, to stand up to him when the moment warrants it. But with Alex, I've always been the weak link, the kid, the one he has to take care of, and I have a trigger-tear response to him. I want to tell him that he *should* be sorry, that what he'd said had really hurt, and that while I may have messed up, offering that money, all I'd really wanted was a chance to tell him how important he is to me. But I know if I try to say all that, my voice will be weak and tear-soaked, so I settle for a simple, "Thanks."

He takes the bag of trash from me, stands to take it over to the can along the sidewalk. I guess we're done here, so I gather my purse, but Alex comes back, sits beside me, slinging an arm along the back of the bench. He looks out toward the parking lot, and he's quiet for so long I think he's not going to say anything, that he maybe wants to enjoy the quiet for a while—or he's giving me a minute to collect myself. "You know I take a lot of risks in my job," he says. "That job I was doing, in South Africa, it was for a series on prison overcrowding. About the violence there, the TB outbreaks they've had."

There's a hard knot forming in my stomach while he talks. I know the kind of work Alex does, but he rarely tells me himself about it. I usually find out later, when I see pictures he's got a credit on, and by then I know he's safe, out of danger.

"Are you okay?" I manage.

"I'm okay. But when I was there, I thought—I've always thought of myself as a pretty tough guy, doing these jobs. That's what I've gone after, since I left home. Nothing familiar."

"I know," I say quickly, not wanting to hear a retread of this, not wanting to have him try to explain what he meant in a nicer way. "I heard you. And I understand why you'd want that, after everything."

"I don't think you do. I think it's actually you who's done the harder thing, the braver thing. Chaos is what I was used to. And chaos is what I've stuck with, just a more intense version of it. And this way, I can watch it happen from behind my camera, but I don't have to try and clean it up for anyone. What you've done, Kit—you're the bravest person I know. The way you put yourself out there with people, the way you've made a home there. You've done exactly the thing neither one of us had any training to do."

"But you made…"

"I didn't," he says, cutting me off. "I know what I said last month, but I didn't really make homes for you. I kept us afloat. And I'm not saying that wasn't good, especially for a kid, but I didn't do what you've done, ever. So I'm sorry. And I'm so fucking *proud* of you." This part, he punctuates it, thumping the edge of his fist against his thigh.

Well, *shit*. He's going to have to wait a good long while longer for me to talk again, because my one rogue tear has turned into a flood, and I have to sit forward, rest my elbows on my knees so I can cradle my face in my hands. Alex moves his arm from the back of the bench, rests a warm hand on my shoulder and squeezes. In that small gesture, I feel everything Alex has ever done and wanted for me. I feel all the unconditional comfort and support, the selflessness it took for him to wait for me, to wait until I grew up enough for him to go out and live his life. Alex has always been everything our dad couldn't be.

But maybe I haven't been. Maybe, despite what I'd said to Alex when we'd fought, I *had* expected something. I had been thinking of myself and what would feel good to me. I wanted to give that money to my brother on my terms. I'd wanted to make his decisions for him.

"I'm sorry too," I tell him, when I've caught my breath again. "I'm so sorry about the money."

"Kit," he says, before I can go on. "I told you, you can't feel bad about the money."

"No, I'm sorry for trying to force the money on you. The truth is, Alex, I'm always going to keep some of that money for you." I shoot him a quelling look when it seems he might protest. "Because you're my brother, and nothing would make me happier than being able to help you out sometime, if you wanted me to. But if you never want me to, that's okay too. It's okay so long as you're happy. So long as you're living a life you feel good about."

"I am," he says. "For now, I am."

"I'm glad." And I *am* glad. I miss him, but I'm glad. And maybe for the first time, I realize that it's possible to feel both at the same time.

"We're okay, Tool Kit?" he asks, using the hand at my shoulder to shake me, gentle and coaxing.

I lean in to it, reaching up to pat his hand. "We're okay."

It feels good, this conversation—like having something lost returned to you, unexpectedly. But I still feel as if something huge is missing, some big sucking hole that's actually inside me. Despite how Alex sees me, I don't feel very brave right now. I still feel like I'd walk all the way home just to get away from this hospital and this situation with Dad and with Candace. I wish I was in my own house, or on the microscope. I wish more than anything I hadn't sent Ben away—that he hadn't given me a reason to.

"Is it that guy?" Alex asks, because this is how well he still knows me. He knows I'm not all right. "Because it's not a problem with you, that you don't want that job. It was a shitty thing he did." Alex knows the bare minimum about what happened with Ben—at some point, on that first morning, before Ben himself had shown up, Alex had asked, in one of our bland attempts at conversation while we waited for Dad to wake up, what had happened to the recruiter Zoe had mentioned. "I started dating him," I'd said, "And he went around my back and tried to have me traded to his company." Almost immediately, I'd felt a wave of guilt, and tried to take it back. "Well, I mean, I think that's what happened," I'd added, but the damage was done. I'd ensured that full freeze-out Ben got from Alex when he showed up.

I close my eyes against the thought of Ben's face, the way he'd looked at me. *I'll do anything*, he'd said. "You know, this thing with Dad and Candace," I say, changing the subject, or at least I think I'm changing the subject.

"Yeah." He says this on a resigned sigh, and from that sound I know he shares every single one of my doubts.

"She knows he's a bad bet. She knows he's got a drinking problem, a gambling problem. She knows he's not even all that great at recovery."

"It's early, though. He might get better at it." It's surprising, this generosity, maybe another sign of how we relate differently to our father. Maybe Alex had held out hope for longer with Dad, while pretty early on I'd learned to keep all my hope focused on my brother, the guy who actually got things done for our family, the guy who never messed up.

"I mean, I don't get it," I say. "She's got a drinking problem too. Why would she go in for someone who could screw up her own sobriety?"

"Different kind of bravery, I guess," says Alex.

"Or stupidity."

"Or that."

"Ben made me think about moving to Texas," I blurt. "For a second, I thought, *hey, maybe it wouldn't be so bad, if we were together*." It isn't remotely the same, what Candace is risking for my dad, and what I thought fleetingly about risking for Ben. But damn if that conversation with her didn't make me think of how *weak* I was with Ben, about how the first time he got me into bed I'd thought, *this is home*. I knew better than that—I knew that despite what people say, no one person can be your home. Home was complicated, layered. Home was people you loved but also places you knew well and liked to go to, things you had around you that made you feel safe and comforted. Home was too much for one person to be to anyone. Look at what it had done to Alex, for all those years he had to be a home for me.

Alex starts to say something, but I don't even let him get a word out before I rush on. "That's stupidity. Everything I've worked for? My friends, my work. Everything I built on my own there? *Stupid*."

"I don't know what to say, Kit. It's not always stupid to want to be with someone, not that I'd know much about that. But this guy—not this guy, not if you can't trust him."

"If I don't take the job, I might be screwing over my friend. My mentor."

"If he's your friend, he'll understand that you don't want to take it. You don't owe him anything." He pauses, seems to consider what he's said. "You don't owe him as much as what you're considering, I mean."

"He gave me a shot. He's given me this job that I've loved. He's welcomed me into his family."

"Kit," Alex says, moving his arm to wrap around my shoulders. "You must not have heard me before. *You* did all that—you made yourself the kind of person someone would want to take a shot on. You made yourself the kind of person someone wants in their family. That's not going to change because you don't take a job."

I don't know whether Alex is oversimplifying it, but right now, I don't really care. I want to believe that things can go back to the way they were before this thing with Beaumont blew up in my face. Before, I trusted my life, the choices I'd made in it. I felt so settled for once—I'd finally had control over what was in front of me. I felt safe. And I hated that Ben had made me wonder about those choices, about that control, even for a second.

The truth is, I don't know what Ben really had to do with Beaumont's offer. I don't know whether I can trust him. I trust Alex because he's the only family member I have that had any hand in raising me. I trust Zoe and Greer because I've known them for years, because they always show up for brunch and break-ups and random bitching sessions. I trust Dr.

Singh because he's always on my side, because he's let me do what I love under circumstances I can handle. I just—I don't *know* about Ben, not for sure. I don't know what he'd say if I gave him a chance to explain about Beaumont and the offer to Dr. Singh.

But maybe, the problem is that with Ben, I can't trust myself. I can't trust myself to see the big picture, to see what's best for me. When Ben is in front of me, I think about *him*—he becomes the person I'd let myself be shuffled around for, the person who I'd risk home for. And I can't do that, even if the thought of never seeing him again makes me feel as though someone's stuck needles right through my ribs, puncturing my lungs, making it impossible to breathe. That feeling, it'll go away after a while. It has to.

"We'd better go in," I say, and I'm off the bench, headed back to that hospital room before Alex can stop me.

Chapter 20

Ben

When I first moved to Texas, I didn't miss anything at all about home. I'd worked so hard to leave. I'd had my mind set so completely on a different future that I think I had actively worked, in my last year there, to de-color the world around me, to see everything as flat, dull, dead-ended. I'd gone to Austin and immersed myself in it. I declared Texas barbecue the best, I rooted for the Longhorns, and I drank Texas whiskey. When I moved east to Houston after college, I ignored the claustrophobic feeling I got from all the highways and high-rises and plunged into the city's corporate life. I thought of home not with disdain, but with a sort of detached nostalgia. I thought of it as my dad's home, but not my own.

But now, I miss everything. I miss the way the air there is heavier, wetter somehow, even on a dry day. I miss the sound of the drawl in people's voices, different from the quicker, rougher twang I hear in the native voices here. I strangely miss the musty, damp smell of the salvage yard, the dusty feel I'd have in my clothes at the end of the day. I miss the fried rockfish at Betty's. I miss my dad and River, so much that I've called Dad every day since I've been back. I say it's because I'm checking on him, seeing how he's feeling now that's he's supposedly back to full strength, but we both know I'm only trying to stay connected.

And I miss Kit like nothing I've ever felt before in my life. For the first few days, I'd called her, once a day, leaving her a short message each time, asking after her father, asking if she was taking care of herself. But she never called back, and I knew with a certainty that she wouldn't. I got a text from Zoe yesterday, shorn of detail: *Her dad is going to be okay. She's home.*

I have a hundred questions, but I don't ask any of them. Her text, I know, is a generosity I don't deserve.

What else I don't deserve? That I see Kit every night in my dreams. Whether this is a consolation or not, I haven't decided. The sight of her in the hospital—the flat, emotionless way she'd told me to leave, the way she'd walked toward her brother, not once looking back at me—at least that's not what I see in my sleep. At night I see her next to me in bed, her black hair webbed across the white sheets she had in her bedroom, laughing up at the ceiling at something I've said. Or I see her spin joyfully atop the stool she sits on to look on her microscope, rhapsodizing about the fracture pattern she's found in her sample. I see her underneath me, her head tipped back, the long, pale stretch of her throat begging for me to kiss, to lick, to suck.

I wake up every day, my dick hard and aching for her. And I don't have to do anything to relieve the pressure, to take the edge off. All I have to do is lie there, let the reality wash over me again that Kit and I are over, and soon enough it's my heart that's aching, not my dick.

So probably it is not so much a consolation.

I go to work. I go through the motions. I don't ask if Jasper has heard from Singh, or from Kit. I schedule six scouting trips for next month, because I think it will distract me, but deep down I know it won't. Last week I signed a recruit for Greg, for the polymers division in Seattle, but I'd judged the guy for folding so quickly. I thought, *Kit would never. Kit would ask a hundred more questions. Kit would have laughed in my face.* At night I run the streets of Houston, because I can't face the state-of-the-art gym in my apartment building, all its sleek, industrial newness. I run until I'm exhausted, until my throat burns and my legs shake, until I know my body will have no choice but to sleep. I'm exhausted, edgy, not fit for human company.

Friday, I shout at an intern who spills a coffee on the quarterly report we're going over in a meeting, and I don't even have a chance to apologize to him before Jasper barks an abrupt, "Outside," at me across the conference table.

I follow him out of the room to his office, which is right next to mine. "You have a lot of fucking nerve," I say to him. "I'll apologize to whatshisname in there, but you don't police me around here, Jasper."

"You're out of line. I know you're pissed at me, but we have a job to do here."

"Yeah, the job. That's your big concern."

"You know what, Tucker? Fuck you. I'm sorry for what happened with you and this woman, and for the part I played in it. But I—*we*—have years invested in this company, not to mention on what we'd planned to do in the future. I didn't do anything different than what you've done dozens of times. I used your playbook. You told me you couldn't do the job with her, and I let that go—but we never agreed she was off the table."

"I told you I was involved with her." It's weak. It's so, so weak, and I know Jasper won't let me get away with it.

"And what difference does that make? I'm sorry, but you get in and out of your involvements with women pretty regularly. Good on you for pulling back from the deal once you realized you wanted to fuck her, but…"

"Jasper," I say, cutting him off, so angry I can barely see straight. "You don't talk about her that way. I'm dead goddamn serious. She's not mine, and I'm probably never going to see her again, but I'm in love with this woman. Don't talk about her that way. Or at all."

He crosses his arms over his chest, looks at me for a long moment. "I'm sorry. But you should have told me it was—you should have told me that you were serious with her."

"And you would have left it alone?"

He lets out a breath. "I don't know, man. I really wanted out."

I don't know what to say to this. I should have told him—if I'd been thinking about the job, if I hadn't immersed myself so completely in my life back home, I probably could have seen that Jasper would try what he did. Getting out of the non-compete—before I left Houston, that would've been the most important thing to me too, but I'd barely thought about it once I'd started seeing Kit. Honestly, I'd barely thought about it even before I'd started seeing her—once I was home with Dad, everything about the job felt different. Everything about *me* felt different.

"Ben," Jasper says. "I fucked up. But I did think—I thought I was doing what was best for us. What we both wanted."

I don't know if I can forgive this, even if I do own my share—my negligence, my reticence to tell Jasper everything. Over a decade of friendship, but I wonder if for me, Jasper will always be the reason I lost Kit.

"Singh didn't take the offer," he says, and my eyes snap to his before I cast them back toward my shoes, feigning disinterest. But I am desperate to know something, *anything*, that is even related to Kit. And hearing this makes me realize that as unlikely I'd known it was, I'd been nursing some small hope that maybe, possibly, Kit would come to Houston. That she'd be here, and I could try and win her back. Here, she'd need me; she'd be on her own. It's a terrible thing to think, and I know it—but I miss her so completely that in my darkest moments, I turn to this kind of selfishness.

"Did he say why?" I ask, embarrassed. I know I sound desperate.

"No." I hear a little remorse in his voice. He feels fucking sorry for me. This is awful.

"You need to know something," he says, as I'm headed out the door. I stop and turn back, see him take a deep breath. "Us going out on our own—I still want that. It's going to take longer now, but we can do it. But I only want that if you do. And if you don't..." he trails off, looks out the window. "If you don't, that's all right too. So—let me know where things stand, when you figure it out." This is Jasper telling me, in his carefully neutral way, that for him, we're still friends. That nothing that's happened over the last month has to get in the way of that.

I give a brief nod, and leave his office. Then I walk straight to mine, grab my things, and leave for the day. It's early, only four thirty, but I'm guessing after my stellar performance at the meeting, no one's going to miss me anyways.

I go directly to the bar on the corner, fully intending to drink myself into a stupor. For the last two weeks, I've stayed stone-cold sober, thinking I ought to be sharp if she called, if I had to leave suddenly.

But she's not going to call.

I'm nursing my second drink when I feel a hand on my shoulder. "Hey, stranger," says a voice from beside me, and there's Gina, leaning in for a quick kiss of my cheek. As she settles in on the barstool behind me, I can think of nothing else but the complete unfamiliarity I feel, the strangeness of Gina's reddish brown hair, of my body in this suit, of the bluish light of this bar. "You've been gone *forever*," she says, signaling the bartender.

I'd forgotten, I guess, that Gina comes here every other Friday, on the weeks when her kids are with her ex. It's where we always used to meet for drinks and conversation about work—Gina does PR for one of the refineries—and then almost always a trip back to my place, where Gina never stayed, on the off chance her kids needed her at home. It had been, for the three or so months before I'd gone back to Barden, a fairly regular hookup, and though we'd never been anything but friends with benefits, I'd still called her to tell her I'd be away for a while, to wish her the best—to end it with her, which she'd been entirely indifferent about.

She orders a martini, three olives, takes off her jacket and drapes it over the back of her seat.

I could do this, tonight. I could drink enough to take the edge off. I could take Gina to my apartment and fuck her on every available surface in there. I could do the reckless, stupid thing and break another tie to Kit, the tie that makes her the last woman who I've touched, kissed, slept next to. But my leaning back from Gina—it's automatic. I don't even notice I'm doing it until I see a little the little wrinkle at the bridge of her nose.

"Sorry," I say, taking a sip of my drink. My standard in this bar: gin, no ice, a twist of lemon peel. It tastes horrible now. I miss the shitty beer my dad keeps at home. "Haven't been out in a while."

"How's your dad?" she asks, when the bartender brings her drink.

"He's all right. Thanks for asking." I realize I have no interest in telling her anything at all about my dad, about my time at home, about anything. I'm so checked out, and it's completely unfair to Gina, who's doing nothing but being the polite friend she's always been. "How've you been? Kids okay?" I ask this even though I've never met her kids, and we hardly ever talked about them. Gina wasn't interested in anything that involved from me, and the feeling was mutual.

"Kids are good," she says, keeping her eyes on me as she takes an olive from her martini and pops it into her mouth.

I feel nothing. I feel like I won't feel anything ever again.

"Gina," I say, and in her name I'm trying to tell her everything I don't want from her.

She smiles over her drink at me before setting it down. "Ben. It's fine."

"I'm sorry. I've had a rough—I'm not at my best."

"What happened?"

I shrug. "Got knocked on my ass by love. Fucked it up, of course. Now I'm back here, pretty much hating everything."

"Been there," she says.

Gina's a good friend, a good person—she had a shitty divorce and an even shittier custody battle, and I'll bet if I sat on this stool and got sloppy drunk and told her all about Kit, she'd listen. I'll bet she'd give me cocktail napkins when I'd cry, and I'm not even ashamed to say, I could probably get a cry going without being sloppy drunk.

But I don't want to tell anyone about Kit. It's over and it's awful, but somehow saying nothing about it is an effort at protecting the part of Kit that I'd failed to protect before. Somehow I tell myself that I can hang on to her longer if I keep her to myself.

I set a fifty on the table, for me and Gina, for the bartender I'd rudely barked my drink order at an hour ago and get off my stool. I lean down and brush a kiss on Gina's cheek, a polite, friendly gesture that still makes my skin feel tight with wrongness. "You're still gorgeous, G," I tell her, pulling back and putting my suit jacket on.

"Ben," she says, as I'm walking away, "take care, okay?"

I nod and head out, seeing nothing and no one around me as I make the long walk to my apartment, and there's nothing and no one there, either.

* * * *

I wake up the next morning, late, to the sound of my phone's video call ring. I'm in no mood to answer—I drank too much last night, having stopped off at a corner market on my walk home to buy six cans of lousy beer, and my mouth might as well be full of sand. Sensible Ben would have had two glasses of water and a couple of painkillers before bed, but if I remember right, there'd been a moment where I'd thought of it, and then decided I'd deserved the hangover.

Even though I've pretty much lost hope on the Kit-calling-me-back front, I'm too conditioned to check the screen, just in case.

It's River's number, and I scoot up in bed, glad that I've got a t-shirt and shorts on.

"Hey," I say, wincing as I see myself in that little corner box. I look like shit.

"You look like shit," says my dad, who's standing behind River, the windows of the salvage yard's office visible behind them. The kid has entirely lost the lavender hair color, but he's replaced it with a few bright red tips at the front. It looks ridiculous, but whatever. We're all entitled to being fourteen, I guess, and anyways, I'm too grateful for the call. It's the first time I've talked to River since I've been gone. He doesn't hear all that well on the phone, and so I've had to settle for texts or updates from Dad.

"Hey, man," I say to him, conscious of the way my mouth moves, making sure he'll be able to follow me. "How's classes?"

"Summer session ended yesterday. I got a B-plus in physics," he says, plain as anything, but there's a little quirk to the corner of his mouth that tells me he's proud.

"That's great. Now you're a free man." I pick up the phone and take it with me to the kitchen, awkwardly holding it out in front, but I've got to get some water in me. Even this little bit of conversation feels impossible around the dryness of my mouth and throat.

"Still got another month here," he says.

"Oh, it's some big chore, huh?" Dad shouts, too loud. He's terrible at FaceTime—this is why we never do it on our own. "You know it's Saturday, right, kid? That's supposed to be your day off."

Even with the crappy picture, I don't miss the flags of color on River's cheeks. "Your dad sucks at social media," he says, by way of explanation.

I swallow down another few gulps of water, wipe my mouth with the back of my hand. "That seems like a given, Riv. What are you up to?"

River shrugs, does the hair toss for hair that's not there anymore. "I set the yard up with a Twitter account."

"What a bunch of nonsense!" Dad shouts again, and River reaches up to adjust his hearing aids.

"It's a good idea," River says, looking at me now, and the way he goes to me for approval—it gets to me, makes me feel ten feet tall and terrible, all at the same time. "Most local businesses are on there, and they're already following us back. Plus, those auction sites you guys use, they're on here, and it's a better way of watching what's coming up for bidding."

Fuck if I don't feel a little streak of pride, hearing River talk about yard business. And a little bit of envy too. "It's a great idea," I say. "Dad, do what River says." River doesn't quite *beam*, but he definitely looks happy, proud.

We talk for a bit about yard business, mostly me trying to ignore the pounding in my head while River and my dad talk about customers, new stuff they've had coming in. They ask me about work, and I offer the most mundane, disinterested answers. I'd rather hear about them. From all these miles away, it feels comforting to have this piece of the yard, and of Dad and River, with me. "We gotta go, Smalls," Dad says, too loud still, then turns to look at me. "Closing the yard for a couple of hours to go to River's house for lunch." He puts a finger up to the side of his head, twirls it to indicate what he thinks of River's mom.

"Dude," River says, pointing toward the screen. "I can see you *right there*." But he's laughing a little, a pattering huff to his breath. Suddenly I want to be at that crazy lunch more than anything. The day ahead of me feels formless, empty—just computer work and whatever I keep on the TV as background noise.

River gets up and goes out of frame, so my dad looks down through the screen at me. He's got this furrow in his brow, a look I remember well. I'd given my dad so many years of brow-furrowing shit before I'd left home. "Miss you, kid," he says, and it takes me so much by surprise I almost drop the phone. My dad has never told me that before, not even when I first left home.

I clear my throat, once, twice, a third time, even though it's still dry as the Sahara in there. "I miss you too." For a second, we're just looking at each other in our little boxes, me and Dad. He looks the way I hope to look when I'm his age—sure, he was hurt, but he's still strong, still healthy. He was my hero my whole life, and he still is.

"I'll call you later," he says, still furrowed up in the brow, and I know he knows I was out drinking last night. I know he'll call to make sure I'm not doing the same tonight, that I'm not out doing something stupid.

"Yeah, all right."

"Hey, Ben, wait," River says, coming back into frame right as I'm reaching to press the button to disconnect. There it is, that ten-foot-tall feeling again, because River's actually never called me by my name before. "Yeah?"

"Tell Kit about my B-plus, okay?"

Terrible feeling, back again. "Sure, man."

Once the screen has gone black, I lean forward, my forearms pressing on the cold granite countertops. From here I can see the whole living space of my apartment, pristine and un-lived in, except for where I tossed my suit jacket on the arm of the couch last night. I can hear, barely over the quiet hum of my refrigerator, the city sounds outside. I wonder whether Kit misses me, or whether that look in her eyes at the hospital telegraphed exactly how easy it was for her to cut me out of her life.

I don't want to be here anymore, I think, with a clarity that is completely uncharacteristic of the hangover I'm sporting. I want to fly home today, hear my dad tell me in person about the lunch with River's family, maybe watch a ballgame with him and Sharon. I want to open the salvage yard tomorrow and start working on that fucking chandelier again. Mostly I want to sit on Kit's porch until she talks to me. Until she lets me back in that house again—her home, her place. But I know I can't. I know I have to slow down, think of my responsibilities. Yesterday, Jasper was right. I've worked a long time toward the goals he and I had set together, and no matter what, I'd been unfair to the job, and to him. I'd done what felt good in the moment, hadn't talked about the hard things, and because of that I'd hurt someone I'd loved. I'd possibly fucked up a friendship.

Back when I'd left home all those years ago, I'd told myself I'd finally figured it out—I'd seen that garage go up in flames, scared sick, and I'd sat in that detention facility for months, thinking over how bad I'd screwed up, how dangerous I'd been. And I told myself I'd do the grown-up thing: get serious about school, keep my head down until I could get out of town and start over. It's not as if I'd made a terrible decision—I'd learned a lot, made friends, been successful, seen the world. But I'd missed things too— missed home, and my dad, and the business that was part of our family. Back then, I didn't—couldn't—see any other way.

I decide something then. Being with Kit, seeing her choose everything so carefully for her house, watching her with her friends, sitting with her through the sadness she'd felt over her brother, hearing her talk about her colleagues and her work—all of that, I realize, taught me something I hadn't really managed to teach myself in all the years I'd been out here on my own. Kit was deliberate about her life, her choices, even when they weren't perfect or easy to make. She'd been lucky, winning that jackpot, but she didn't rely on luck. She *didn't* let life just happen to her. She wasn't reckless or one-track minded.

So for once, I'm not going to be, either.

Chapter 21

Kit

When it's been a month since I've seen Ben, when I've worn out all my memories of him in my house, in my bed, even those brief times he was with me at work, I go to the salvage yard.

I've been back for a couple of weeks now, my dad settled into the trailer with Candace, and Alex opting to stay in Ohio for a month or so to keep an eye on things. I'd offered to stay too, had winced at the thought of Alex being there on his own, but he'd insisted. "You need to get back, Kit," he'd said. "You need to be home."

He was right. I did need to be home, and anyways, I think Alex needed to be in Ohio, or, at the very least, needed to be in one place for a while. At work, things have been slow, a summer lull, Dr. Singh and I adjusting to the awkward aftermath of the Beaumont offer and our subsequent conversation about it when I'd come back to town. "I need more time," I'd told him, the first day I was back in the office, and he'd said, "I don't think you do." We'd gone to lunch that day, a winding, two-hour affair at a Chinese buffet which provided a perfect opportunity for breaks to plate-reload when the conversation got hard. I'd told him my reasons for not wanting the job—the professional and the personal reasons, though I'd left out everything about Ben. And Dr. Singh had told me he hadn't wanted to take the money, that he was nervous and unsettled by the contract requirements anyway. I told him about the lottery. I told him I understood if he wanted someone else to have the job. And he told me there was no one else who could do the job the way I could, and the whole department wanted me on board for as long as I was happy.

Once we'd settled the bill, I'd asked him, hot-faced and fidgety, who it was that had called him from Beaumont, but deep down, I already knew the answer: not Ben.

That evening, I'd made an offer to my contractor to move up my kitchen renovation, and then I'd added, on a reckless whim, a contract to work on my upstairs bath. Basically, I've made it very, very difficult to live there comfortably, and so most days I've stayed with Zoe or Greer. I know I'm lying to myself about why I've done this. I say it's because it'll be better to get the major renovations done before the school year starts up again. I say that since money isn't really an issue, I might as well pay for the rush jobs, even though this kind of spending is entirely out of character for me. But really, it's because I'm rattling around in that house, too upset to be alone with my thoughts, missing Ben so much that I'm restless with it, unable to sit still. I suspect Zoe and Greer know this too, though they don't say anything.

So going to see Henry at the salvage yard—I say it's to look into the restored clawfoot tubs he has—is only one of the decisions I've made since I've been back that has more to do with Ben than I'm willing to admit.

It's Sharon who's out front when I arrive, and judging by her face, I've not been missed around here, or at least I'm no one's favorite. Somehow, even when she says hello, her lips seem to stay pursed, displeased. She asks how I've been but it seems pinched and obligatory. If anything, this oddly makes me like Sharon even more—I don't think Ben quite realizes it, but Sharon watches him as if he's her very own. At the Crestwood party, Sharon had flushed with pride when Ben had told her that she looked nice, a genuine reaction that seemed so different from the way Ben interacted with his mother. But I still don't relish the thought of being under her gaze, and she also seems relieved when I ask for Henry.

He's in the office, at the workbench, working on rewiring a light fixture that right now is only a small bulb on a wire, but I've been around here enough times to know it probably goes to something beautiful and unique and old. At first, I hover in the doorway, unsure if I'll be able to handle a similarly chilly reception from Henry. I think if I do, it might break me, might ensure that I never come back here again. But when he turns, there's a familiar light in his eyes, and he stands from his stool to greet me.

"Look at you!" I say, noticing that he'd been able to stand without his cane, without using the table for leverage.

"Still can't walk without the cane," he says, smiling. "But I'm up and down mostly on my own now, especially if I'm up high enough. Feeling pretty good."

"I'm so glad," I say, still staying in the doorway, still unsure.

"How's your father doing?"

"He's doing better. He'll be okay, I think, so long as he takes care of himself a little more."

"Good of you to go there to be with him," Henry says. "It makes a real difference."

I barely manage a nod to this, look down toward my feet. I don't know if it made a real difference to my dad that I was there, not how it mattered for Henry to have Ben. I'd arranged to take care of expenses, and I'd done my best to get to know Candace better, to steer clear of any ugly topics between me and Dad. But he mostly seemed embarrassed by my presence, once he was more awake, and the only day I saw him relax a bit was the day Alex took me to the airport to fly home. Ben is so lucky to have Henry. I wonder if he knows that.

"Come on in," Henry says, gesturing toward the small table where I once sat with Ben and River, talking about physics. "Keep me company while I do up this wiring."

"Sure," I say, but then quickly add, "I mean, I really came to look at some bathtubs." I don't want him to think I'm doing what I'm really doing, which is checking up on him, mining for any information I might be able to get about Ben.

But Henry sees through me, same as everyone else does, I guess, and waves me in. "Sure. I can show you some if you give me a few minutes on this."

I settle in at the chair facing his workbench so I can watch him tinker—it's hard to believe that when I met him, he was in a wheelchair, his arm bound close to his body. We sit like that for a while, quietly, comfortably, and it's such a contrast to the uneasiness I felt in Ohio, even in spite of the awkwardness of the situation between us. It's that comfort, I think, that emboldens me now.

"How's Ben?"

Henry's hands barely pause in his task, but I'm watching him so closely that I notice. "He's all right. Working a lot."

"Yeah," I say dumbly, as if that's to be expected, as if I know Ben's work habits in Houston so well. "Well, I'll bet he's glad to be back."

Henry's response to this is a hum of something—not assent, but not disagreement, either. I wish I hadn't asked now. It's spoiled the easy silence that was between us before. When I'm about to excuse myself, tell him maybe Sharon can show me around, he speaks up.

"You know, when he was a boy, about a week after his mother moved out, he snuck out in the middle of the night, took his bike."

I stiffen in my seat a little, bracing myself. When I was with Ben, I'd been desperate to hear stories from when he was a kid. I'd shared things—embarrassing, sometimes sad things—about the way I'd grown up, but Ben had kept things close. I don't know if hearing this now is what I want or what I shouldn't want.

"I about went crazy with worry," Henry goes on, seemingly unaware of my discomfort. "Back then, I did a lot of that with Ben. He was always in trouble. He finally showed up at home a few hours later, didn't say a word, just sat in a chair while I screamed my head off at him." Henry pauses, stretching his left hand, fingers out and in, wrist back and forth. "That night Laura calls, all upset, asks how he's doing. She told me he'd ridden his bike to where she'd worked, waited outside for her until she showed up. Begged her to come back, promised he'd be a better kid. He cried his heart out, I guess, and Ben wasn't much of a crier, ever. She had Richard bring him home, but Ben insisted on getting dropped off a few blocks away."

I think about how Ben makes his living, about how every aspect of his business is about saying the right thing to get someone to come with him, about how he'd never, not from that first day we met, managed to say the right thing to me. That night at the Ursinus, and after he'd said he loved me, I'd wanted him to say something about the two of us, about how we could be together, but he'd never quite managed that. He'd never put *himself* out there. I think, horribly, about that moment he stood before me in the hospital: *I'll do anything.* "That's…terrible," I manage, around what feels like a big ball of cotton swelling in my throat.

He shrugs, swallows thickly before clearing his throat. "It was my idea, to have Ben. I pushed and pushed. And after, I could see Laura wasn't happy. She wasn't so happy before, probably, but at first, we had something. I was stupid, young. I thought a kid would make us closer, how we'd been before. Worst thing I ever did, and that's the truth—trying to force her into a life she didn't really choose for herself."

I wonder if he's told this to Ben, if what I'd said about not getting shuffled around by circumstance and about choosing for myself, had rung some kind of painful, pealing bell for him. He'd been so quiet after that.

"Ben's the best thing, the best thing of my life, and I don't regret him, not for one second. But I'm sorry for Laura. I'm sorry that my wanting Ben cost her, and forced her to do something I know she feels bad about. But it was the right thing, for her and for him. She loves him. But she couldn't be a good mother to him, not that way. She had to choose something else for herself."

We sit in silence for a few minutes, Henry tinkering, me thinking. I don't know for sure why he's telling me this, telling me something I doubt Ben knows himself. The quiet grows almost comfortable again, against all odds, against the fact that I don't have any real reason to be here, any real tie to Henry anymore. "I don't think it's right. I think she should've chosen him. Even if she didn't stay with you, she could've—been around. Been a mom to him," I say.

Henry sets down his tools, turns in his chair and looks at me. "Don't think he ever let her, not after that day. He never asked her for anything again. Everything she ever gave him—her attention, a gift, her help when he got into trouble—she had to force it on him. Cost him a lot to go to her back then. He's been—well. He doesn't like to ask after what he wants, not much since then."

Aha, I think. *This is why he's telling me.*

"He doesn't get off the hook, Henry. For not telling me about what he'd done with Beaumont. He doesn't get to say—*you* don't get to say that it's hard for him to open up, and have that be enough." But even as I say this, I wonder: What would have been enough? What would have been enough for me, in that moment, when Dr. Singh had told me about Beaumont's offer, when I'd felt small and scared and like Ben was going to take everything good in my life away from me?

"I'm just telling you, Kit. I expect he feels as bad as he can feel now, about how it happened with you. I know that boy same as I know my own self, and he's crazy about you. But don't think he'll come back. I don't know if he has it in him anymore."

And that's the worst of it, what Henry has said. Because hearing it put this way, with this kind of finality, makes me admit to myself that I want him to come back, that I'm waiting for him to come back and try again. That's what I've been doing, tiptoeing around work, avoiding my house, constantly telling Greer and Zoe I'm fine. I'm *waiting*. I'm waiting for him to call or to show up here, to talk to me about what went wrong with Beaumont, to *sell* me on him and on us. For all my talk to Ben about choosing for myself, I'm not choosing anything right now. I'm waiting for more options to present themselves—I'm waiting for him to present himself, again, the right way this time, some way that's going to convince me to go all in, to not be freaked out by tying myself to someone else, someone who could really have an effect on all my future choices.

But if he doesn't come back…

Henry slaps his hands on his knees, casual change-of-subject time, and says, "Ready to see some of those tubs?" Like he hasn't just punched me right in the gut with this story of little boy Ben, trying so hard and failing, to get someone to choose him.

An hour and a half later, I've picked out a slipper-style clawfoot tub and Henry's promised he can switch out the feet, since the ones that are modeled after lion's paws give me the creeps. I stall because I hope he'll say something else about Ben, but he doesn't. When I leave, I don't go to Zoe or Greer's. I go home, and wander through the wreckage of the kitchen renovation, getting a good look at that brick wall that's being exposed behind the place where the stove will go. I wash my face in the downstairs powder room. I go up to my bedroom, but only to bring down a pillow and extra blanket for the couch, which is where I'm going to sleep. Or not sleep, as the case may be, since I lie awake staring at my ceiling for hours.

Until I make a choice.

* * * *

A week later, I'm in Houston.

It's seven o'clock at night and still ninety-three degrees. August, I've heard, is brutal around here. I'd given myself all of today to wander around the city, to follow a few suggestions from a local I'd talked to on the flight, and from the person who served me coffee at the hotel Starbucks this morning. I'd gone to the Museum of Natural Science and spent too much time in the exhibit about minerals. I'd eaten lunch at a Tex-Mex place that had no air conditioning, but amazing food. I'd walked around a park called Discovery Green, studied a map of the city while sitting on one of the park benches, skyscrapers looming behind me. When I'd gone to leave, walking through a shady grove of pine trees, I'd spotted a sculpture, a big bronze-cast heart mounted on slats of wood. From a distance, the heart looked roughed-up, lumpy, but up close, embedded in the heart, were tools—an axe, a hammer, other things I wasn't quite sure about. It was called *The House*. I'd snapped a picture before heading back to my hotel to change for my meeting with Jasper, which I'd insisted on having in the hotel restaurant. I'd insisted on a lot from him, actually, including complete confidentiality, but he hadn't balked at any of it.

Jasper tells me many things during our two-hour conversation, but the most important is that the Beaumont corporate offices are where I'm most likely to find Ben. He works late these days, especially when he's not traveling. In fact, Jasper tells me, I'm lucky to be catching him this week, because the last two, he'd done three trips, all in different time zones. He watches me with a careful, measured suspicion, and at first I think this is because he distrusts my out-of-the-blue interest in talking more about Beaumont. But as we talk, I realize it's because he distrusts my interest in Ben. When he stands to shake my hand at the end of our conversation, he holds it a beat longer than makes sense for a business meeting, looks at me through deep brown eyes that reveal nothing. "End of the hall, fifty-eighth floor," he says. "Good luck." And then he strides away, not looking back once.

So here I am, wandering a long corridor of sleek, frosted glass doors to darkened offices. Every once in a while, the space opens to a large conference room, and midway down there's a lounge space with low, modern black leather sofas, two impossibly thin, mounted televisions, both off. I imagine they stay mostly on during the day, stock prices trolling along the bottom of the screens. Up ahead I can see a door open, light streaming out, and I pause next to one of the sofas, set my hand on its cold surface, steady myself in these insane, soul-destroying shoes. This entire outfit is borrowed, from Zoe. I think I look ridiculous but also like I completely belong here. Suddenly, I think: *This was a stupid idea, this whole gesture. You should have called him. You didn't have to go through all of this.*

But when I close my eyes against the nerves, I see Ben, and this steels me anew. I can't wait to see him in person. I can't wait to be near him, finally. I have no idea how this will go, but just that I get to *see* him—it counts for something, and it gives me the courage I need to keep walking.

He doesn't hear me walk up to his open door. He has earbuds in, and his hands are typing furiously on the laptop he has set up on the glass surface of his desk. There's a blue necktie heaped next to his arm. He's wearing a white dress shirt, the top button undone. I am heart stoppingly pleased that he has not cut his hair, which curls a little across his brow, and his jaw is stubbled, the way I'm used to seeing it. Behind him is the sky turning purple-orange, some of the city lights starting to twinkle on.

Before I think to do anything—clear my throat, knock on the open door, offer up a *hello*—he raises his eyes to where I stand, and there's a brief second when he doesn't do anything at all. He only stares, his eyes a little unfocused from the screen of his computer. And then just as quickly he stands, jolts from his desk, really, and the motion yanks the laptop up from the desk, the earbuds out of his ears. "Shit," he says, saving the laptop from a dive off the ledge, untangling the earbud cord from where it's gotten stuck in his belt loop.

"I'm sorry!" I say, too loud in this quiet office, and holy crap, is this awkward. I grip the handle of Zoe's briefcase tighter even than I had before, when my knuckles were already white with it. "I'm—I didn't mean to startle you."

"What are you wearing?" he asks, his brow furrowed.

"What?" I say, though I've heard him perfectly. I just don't know how to start the conversation from this point.

He waves a hand in my direction, a gesture that encompasses everything from the neck down—my fitted, black blazer, the silky, dove-grey camisole underneath, the knee-length pencil skirt that matches. "A suit?" he says, that brow still slammed down across his eyes.

"Oh. Well, it's Zoe's. I know it's not really my—"

"You look beautiful. I don't care what you're wearing. You're a sight for sore eyes." It's so honest, how he says it, but he stays right where he is, behind his desk. He's tucked his hands in his pockets, his fingers clenching into fists beneath the fabric.

"I met with Jasper today," I say, rushing it out. I just want those hands out of his pockets. I want them on me. "To hear his pitch."

I can see the surprise on his face, the confusion. He looks up past my shoulder, maybe looking for Jasper, or someone who can explain this to him, but it's only me here. "But you said no. Singh called and said no."

"Right, yes. But I decided I should give it a fairer hearing, from an—an unbiased party. And you know, from a place where I wasn't so—reactionary. Where I could listen."

He looks at me, down at his desk, back up at me. "I don't—"

"I'm still not taking it," I say, and watch as his shoulders slouch a little. Is that—is he disappointed, or relieved? It doesn't matter. I still need to get through this. "It's not right for me. It's not the kind of work that's right for me. Something else might be, somewhere down the line, but it's not this. But with you, I started to get all mixed up about it. Whenever you talked about the job, or about Texas, after a while, I didn't know whether you were talking about work or about us, and I got—I got scared. About risking everything I'd worked for."

"Kit," he begins, but I stop him with a shake of my head.

"I know my own mind on this. And I choose to be where I am for now."

"All right," he says, and before he can say anything else, I walk farther into the office, set my briefcase on the chair in front of me, reaching in and pulling out the portfolio I brought along, the one I'd spent the last week preparing. I open it, remove its most important contents—a manila envelope, no marks on the outside, nothing to give it away. I set it down on his desk, then push it toward him with my index finger.

"I brought this for you." At the moment I'd like to back right out of here and find the nearest closet or bathroom stall or, I don't know, under a desk would do in a pinch, because I am so, so nervous about this. I hadn't known, not for sure, whether I'd use these—when I'd come here, I'd promised myself I wouldn't make the final call until I listened, really listened, to what Jasper had to say.

But I'd hoped I'd get to use them.

Ben looks down at the envelope, then up at me, his eyebrow quirking. "Should I—?" Everything is still so tentative with us. I hope so hard that it's not this way much longer.

"Yes, please. Open it."

He takes his hands from his pockets, sits down again, and scoots forward to pick up the envelope. It feels as if it takes him forever to pinch up those little metal tabs, to slide his finger along the flap, to pull out the stack of photographs enclosed. "Alex took them," I say, to fill up the silence. "He—ah—I asked him to spend the day in town."

I know every photo in that envelope. I spent hours choosing each one from the set Alex took at each place. I study Ben's face as he goes through them.

The first, a picture of the hardware bins at the salvage yard, taken from below. Alex had done this one lying on his back, like the photo in my living room, and the effect was to make the wall look enormous, endless.

Second, also from the yard, a picture of the lighting room. I'd chosen one that was a little blurry, ethereal, orbs around each lit bulb.

Third, River, cheeky in black and white (his choice), holding a brick and looking right at the camera, unsmiling but not angry, a look of challenge in his eyes.

Next, Henry, bent over the pieces of an antique clock, his face a mask of concentration. Sharon, camera shy, a blurry form behind him.

Fifth, a crowd shot: Betty's on a full night, Zoe's outline barely visible at the bottom of the frame as she throws a dart, and Betty's tattoos a bright mural in the center as she carries a tray.

Sixth, the front porch of my house, now newly painted, two white wood rockers facing the street.

Seven through fifteen—a few more of my house, that exposed brick wall, the begonias I've planted in a pot that sits on the back stoop. Some of the city, including one I took of Alex getting a hot dog at the Wiener Cart. Another of the elaborate doorway to the Crestwood hotel.

And finally, me.

I'm on my front stoop, a picture Alex took while standing above me. It's close, tight on my face. My hair catches at the edges of the print, my eyes look right up at the camera—through my glasses, and through the goggles I'm wearing over them.

Ben smiles. I can see his dimple peeking out, but he keeps his head determinedly down.

The silence is so heavy I can hear my pulse thrum. Still looking down, his voice ragged, a little choked, he finally says, "Have you come to recruit me?"

He looks up at my silence. My throat is too tight to answer, so I nod. He gets up from his seat, but gathers up all the pictures first, holding onto them at the edges like he's not ready to let go yet. Then he comes around his desk and stands in front of me, one hand coming up to my neck, his thumb touching under my chin, so he can tip my face up to his. "Kit," he says. "I was coming to you."

"What?"

"I guess Jasper didn't say. I'm leaving Beaumont. I'm giving up my partnership with Jasper."

"Your partnership...?"

"I didn't tell you about that before, but I should have, and I will. I'll tell you all about that. I did everything wrong before, with you. I went too fast, and I'm sorry about that. But I'm doing it right this time, Kit," he says, and in spite of what he's saying about *too fast*, he's talking faster than I've ever heard him talk, messy and disorganized and it's so, so perfect. It's Ben without anything in between us. It's not Ben being charming or funny or anything else but honest, and this time, he's not stopping himself or backing off. "I put in my notice here, but I'm tying up all my loose ends, and I'm working with Jasper on an exit strategy for him, and our colleague Kristen too. That's going to take some time, but they—they're going to do well. They deserve to do well. I'm going to work at the yard—well, if my dad will have me. I haven't told him yet, but I've thought about it a lot, and it's what I really want to do, to be in the business with my dad. Or I'll do something else if that doesn't work, or if I need to make more money, whatever I need to do. I've got a couple of places I've been checking out, apartments not too far from the university—I mean not because I wanted to bother you or anything, just because it's a good location. I was going to come to you, ask you if you wanted to go out sometime..."

"Ben," I say, setting my palms on his chest, stilling him, my heart squeezing at the deep breath he has to take after that haphazard speech. "You didn't go too fast. I love you. I want to be with you. I want you to come back and be with me, and if you didn't want to do that, I was going to try and sell you, but if it didn't work, I was willing to negotiate..."

"You don't have to sell me," he says, setting the pictures down and tugging me to him, wrapping his arms so tight around me, lifting me so that he can bury his face against my neck. "You never have to sell me. Holy *fuck*, I'm so—I'm so happy you're here." He kisses me then, my shoulder, my neck, the spot behind my ear that gives me goose bumps, working his way to my mouth, as he talks to me, telling me how he's missed me, how I smell so good, how he's thought of me every second. When he kisses me, it's perfect—it's *us*, hot and sweet and the way it always is between us. Ben is tugging at the buttons of my blazer, moving me so he can back me against the desk, lift me onto it, and I want that, want to spread my legs so he can step between them, but Jesus, this pencil skirt. It is really tight. Nothing is going to happen unless I scoot this sucker up to my waist and put my bare ass on this desk. I mean, I am really turned on, but let's be honest, not enough to keep myself from picturing the prints my butt would leave on glass.

"Ben," I whisper against his mouth. "I don't think we should do this here."

He pulls back, rests his forehead against mine, and breathes out. "I'm sorry. Too fast, I know. We should talk more, and figure things out."

"No, I mean—we should go somewhere where I could get this suit off."

He exhales on a laugh. I feel the air of it on my chest, ruffling the delicate fabric of my camisole. It feels like happiness, a new beginning. "Kit," he says, almost a whisper. He's not looking at me. He's kept his head down, and I'd make a joke about him peeking at what little cleavage I have on offer in this top, but I can sense something about Ben, in the way his fingers flutter against the backs of my knees, in the way his breaths are a little reedy. So I wait for him, stroke my hands up and down his arms, relishing the feel of him again after all these weeks apart. "Thanks for coming to get me."

"Anytime," I say, my throat tight again with emotion.

"I'm going to mess up, I'm sure. I've never done this before. I'll do things that are going to make you really mad or annoyed."

"Ben," I say, squeezing his forearms, once, twice, until he looks up at me. "Anytime, okay?" Ben is part of what home means to me now—he's not everything, but he might be the biggest thing, and he's going to change every careful arrangement I had set up in my life, but for once I'm so excited about that prospect. I can't wait to see what'll happen.

"I'm so lucky," he says, almost a whisper.

"Nah," I say, pulling him toward me for a quick, hard kiss. "But you're about to be."

Epilogue

Ben

One Year Later

"Rain is good luck for weddings, though," Greer says, looking out from the dining room into the backyard, which is puddled and muddy, sheets of rain still falling from the sky, streaming down the windows.

"Tell it to the bride," says Zoe, and I snicker, checking my watch.

Forty-five minutes until this thing gets underway, and the storm isn't quitting, so I'm guessing we're all going to have to cram into the living room. It's a good thing it's a small group, and I wave River over so that he and I can start pushing furniture out to the sides of the room. He's wearing ripped jeans and Converse, a blazer his mother bought him at the Salvation Army, and a vintage-looking *Tucker's Salvage* t-shirt underneath, which he'd designed sometime last year in spite of my father's repeated protests that we'd never sold anything new at the yard, ever. He's brought a date to this—a quiet, pale-faced girl named Amy who has a streak of her mostly white-blonde hair dyed hot pink—and I can tell, when he moves to the other side of the couch to heft it up, that he's trying to impress her. Greer lights candles on the mantel. That's where we'll have the minister stand, and Zoe takes the big basket of rose petals that were planned for post-vows tossing and scatters them from the bottom of the staircase to the fireplace, a makeshift aisle that I'll have to sweep up later.

It's not perfect, but it'll be fine. With the candles and rose petals, it at least looks the part of a place you could get married. I check my watch again, and Zoe nudges me. "She'll be here," she says.

"I know," I mutter, but I'm nervous, sweaty and tense under my suit, which feels heavy and unnatural on my body these days. I'm not quite used to Kit's travel schedule yet. When she's gone, I sleep with my phone turned up on high next to the bed, and I check flight plans, making sure her connections run smoothly. She teases me about how I'd made my living traveling all over the world and now get "fussy" when she does even a short trip up the eastern seaboard for the private consulting she's been doing for the last six months. It'd been her idea, the consulting, and I'd at first thought she'd meant the kind of work I was most familiar with—visiting corporate labs, lending her expertise on various materials or equipment. But Kit, I don't think, will ever be interested in that kind of science. Instead, with Jasper's help, she'd taken half time at the university and has been doing educational rep work for the manufacturers who make the microscopes themselves—running training sessions, reconfiguring the way they operate their schedulers, maximizing experimental time for faculty and graduate students, offering suggestions for undergraduate education on experimental equipment. She'd gone back and forth a bit, before those first few trips—*maybe I shouldn't do this, I don't even* like *travel*—and I'd listened patiently, every time.

Because every time, Kit got on the plane, and made the best of it. Kit was trying, with her work and with me, not to be afraid anymore, not to cling so hard to the familiar, to let herself explore different parts of herself without worrying that something would be taken away. She's talked, over the last couple of months, about wanting to teach, about how she might make that a reality. But she's as committed as ever to this place, her hometown, she's started to call it. Last weekend she made me spend two hours with her filling out some kind of survey for a local paper about our favorite spots.

I check my watch a third time. Maybe we shouldn't have planned this for this weekend. The schedule is too tight now that there'd been a flight delay that had kept Kit away an extra night, and despite her new willingness to get out there and make a different path for herself, she relishes coming home. Sometimes, we spend whole weekends without leaving here, eating and talking and puttering around with various house projects, making love late into the night, early in the mornings before falling asleep again.

I've never been so happy in my life.

"Ben!" my dad hollers from upstairs, and I turn to hustle up, finding him in the guest room standing in front of the full-length mirror there. "Tie this," he barks at me, holding out the pale yellow necktie he has for today, the one that's supposed to match Sharon's pantsuit, though since she hasn't let us see it, we'd only made our best guess at the department store this week.

"Relax, Dad," I say, taking the tie from him and looping it around my own neck to make a loose knot that I can pass over his head.

"Relax? You try getting married at my age! I haven't had this much flop sweat since I saw you come out of your mother's..."

"Dad. No," I say, contemplating self-strangulation for a brief moment.

"I fainted then, you know. Do you think I'm going to faint down there?"

"You won't faint," I say. "Sharon'll hold you up, anyway."

Sharon had proposed to Dad three weeks after I'd moved back from Houston—"all business-like," Dad had told me, but she'd also told him that she was never going to have him go in the hospital again and not be his next of kin, and anyways, she loved him and it was about time they made it official. The day after, Dad and I drove to an auction in Pennsylvania to buy her a ring. Since so far, they were both keeping their houses—"I said I wanted to marry him, not clean up after him!" Sharon said, but Dad thought she'd change her mind—Kit had offered ours as a neutral spot for the wedding, an idea that had seemed to hold more appeal for Dad and Sharon than something at city hall.

"You got the rings?" Dad asks, as I tug the tie over his head, tightening it around his neck.

"Yeah," I say, touching my pocket. Two wedding rings in there, and one that I've been holding onto, since that auction in Pennsylvania—a dark green emerald, surrounded on all sides by tiny diamonds of varying cuts, marquise, round, tapered baguettes—a starburst around a verdant planet. I'd never seen anything like it, and had decided right then it was the ring I want to give Kit, sometime, when the time is right.

"Jeez," Dad says, wiping his brow. "How much longer?"

"Seventeen years and now you're in a hurry!" shouts Sharon, from our bedroom next door, where she's getting ready. My mom is helping her. She brought a makeup bag the size of my toolbox, and as weird as this whole situation is, somehow, it feels right that my mom's in there, helping out with this day. Richard is downstairs too, having spent the last hour trying to talk Zoe into joining his firm, and while I've been getting along with him better these days, I have no problem admitting that I thoroughly enjoyed watching her turn him down flat.

"Ears like a bat, that one," Dad says, smiling.

"I'm happy for you, Dad," I say, setting my hand on his shoulder, looking at both of our reflections in the mirror. He puts his arm around me too, squeezing my shoulder back.

"You're my best friend in the world, kid," he says, looking into my reflected eyes. "And I'm real glad you'll be standing up with me today." I swallow back that damned lump in my throat, look down, check my watch again. "Me too," I manage.

The door slams downstairs, a little titter of applause that I'm guessing is from Zoe and Greer. "So, she made it," Dad says, shoving me away playfully. I give him one final pat on the back, tell him to be downstairs in ten, and call through a timing update to Sharon too.

Kit's at the bottom of the steps, handing off bags to Zoe and Greer, running a hand through her hair, jet-black with moisture from the rain. Her face is flushed, her brow furrowed. She's complaining about the flight, the taxi service that took too long to get her here—and then she looks up and sees me, and for a minute, everything stressed and flustered disappears from her face, and it's only the two of us in this house, smiling at each other in relief for her being home and excitement for the day and happiness for being back together. I kiss her behind her ear when I get to the bottom step, tell her she's got ten minutes to change, and watch as she bounds up the stairs, laughing at the way this day has turned insane already.

* * * *

Later, after we've watched my dad and Sharon exchange vows they wrote themselves—including a surprisingly lengthy diversion from them both regarding promises having to do with my father's work hours—and after we've eaten piles of catered food and made toasts and drank too much, the rain stops, late afternoon sun peeking out from the clouds that make their way out of town. While we'd only invited a few to the ceremony itself, the after-party has grown considerably, and so we've spilled out into the house's outdoor spaces too. Some have taken off their shoes and squelch happily around the muddy backyard, others drink and talk on the front porch, still others, including my mom and Richard, reluctant about the damp, stay inside, where River's date has turned herself into something of a DJ for the event, though I have not recognized a single song she's played through her tinny portable speakers. Sharon and my dad danced together, right there in the living room, as if they'd done it a hundred times, and as it turned out, they had—my dad sheepishly admitted they'd taken classes together for the last ten years.

When I see Kit duck into the kitchen, carrying a few discarded champagne glasses, I follow her in, wrapping my arms around her from behind, pressing my nose into the join of her neck and shoulder. "You smell so good," I tell her.

"I smell like an airplane," she laughs.

"Nope. You smell like yourself, right here. Right on this skin here." I kiss her there, open my mouth and take a small, surreptitious bite. Her nipples peak beneath the fabric of her dress, and I can't help but press myself against her, loving the small sound she makes in the back of her throat as she arches her back a little, pressing into me.

"Too crowded in here," she says, but her voice is low, husky. She turns in the circle of my arms, wraps her arms around my neck, and kisses me, damn the crowd. She tastes like champagne, sugar from the cake we ate. Like Kit and like home. "Missed you," she says, and I murmur it back.

It's getting too heated in here between us, not suitable for public consumption, so I pull back, reaching up to trace my hands down her bare arms while I do, clasping her hands in mine when I get to her wrists.

"I can't believe we had a wedding here," she says, smiling up at me, those brown-black eyes lit up from behind. "In this house!"

"Nothing broke, either," I say, and I'm only half kidding. We'd done so much to this place since Kit had moved in all those months ago, and since old houses were full of unexpected challenges, some of that had been unplanned, inconvenient, supremely ill-timed. All of it, though, every single thing about it, had been fun, had been Kit's and my way of making this place belong to the two of us, of making it our home. When she'd made the offer to Dad and Sharon, I'd been a little surprised, actually—we'd been working so much on renovations, on various repairs, that we'd not even managed a housewarming of our own, and I'd worried the wedding would steal some of her thunder about the house. "You're really all right," I say, tugging her toward me a little, "that we did this here?"

"Of course," she says, a little line of concern wrinkling her brow. "Why wouldn't I be?"

I shrug, noncommittal. "You don't feel...I don't know. That you're having your space invaded?"

She tips her head back, laughs a little—the sound is half-relief, half-happiness. "No," she says, looking back at me, stretching her arms out wide, my hands still clasped to hers. It's as if she's giving a hug to the entire house. "This is people I love. This is family. So no, I don't feel that way at all."

I lean down to kiss her forehead, her cheeks, another hard press to her mouth. It *is* family. But I can't wait to be alone with her again. "Besides," she says quietly, right against my lips. "I'm thinking of this wedding as practice."

"Practice?" I ask, and that ring is burning a hole in my pocket.

She gives me a crooked smile, all mischief, a smacking kiss on my chin before pulling away. "Practice, Ben. For whatever comes." Then she winks at me, twirling away, calling to Zoe and Greer for a dance, and I stare after her, stupid and stunned and more settled in my own skin than I've ever felt in my life.

I tuck a hand in my pocket, trace my finger over the ring, feeling the same way I've felt since the first time Kit said yes to me.

Like the luckiest guy in the world.

Luck of the Draw

Keep reading for a sneak peek at more lucky chances!

Coming soon from Kate Clayborn and Lyrical Press

Prologue

Zoe

Like most of my dumb ideas, this one came from the internet.

Okay, the internet and insomnia.

Fine. The internet, insomnia, and wine.

I'd been lonely that night, stuck inside in deference to the miserable end-of-August heat and humidity: almost every day culminating in rolling thunder, heat lightning, flashes of pouring rain that did nothing to cool the air. My two best friends, Kit and Greer, were both unavailable for my proposed let's-get-drunk-and-do-a-puzzle night. Kit was with her boyfriend Ben, all newly reunited and too cute by half, and Greer had just left for a week-long Hawthorne family vacation—and I was still unwilling, over eight months since I'd quit in a blaze of jackpot-winning glory, to call up any of my friends from my former firm. Or maybe I was realizing, finally, that they hadn't really been friends at all.

Lonely, a little drunk, and only a laptop for company? Truly, it was a recipe for disaster—or I guess for watching pornography, but instead I'd decided to try, once again, to get something going with my long-promised lottery-win project. *An adventure*, I'd told my friends on that night we'd bought the ticket, staking my claim for what I'd do with the cash. I'd imagined an around-the-world trip, something to take me away from everything familiar, something that would be different enough that I'd come out a whole new Zoe—more perspective, more peace, more *something*. But every time I'd tried to make a decision, every time I said to myself, *today, you plan your trip*, I'd been paralyzed.

"I don't know what's wrong with me," I'd said to Greer one night as we'd strolled through the travel section of the bookstore, a place—along with the gym, the park nearest my house, and my friend Betty's restaurant—where I'd spent an embarrassing number of hours since leaving my job. "You're in school. Kit's bought the house. You're *doing* it, doing what you said you'd do, and I'm just—stuck." Utterly and completely *stuck.*

"It's a big change," Greer had said. "Your whole life was your work. It takes time to recalibrate, right?" She paused, narrowed her eyes at the shelf in front of her. "Recalibrate is definitely a word Kit would use. I think I've been having dreams about her microscope. Let's buy a bunch of these books and see if we get any ideas."

But the books hadn't helped. Greer's gentle encouragement hadn't helped. Kit and Betty sticking labels to the dartboard at the bar with various place names on it hadn't helped (especially because I have superb aim). I was in a rut. I'd only ever felt this way once before in my life, and back then I'd dealt with it by doing something so insane and reckless that I knew I had to tread carefully, lest I fuck up my life or someone else's again.

Maybe I'd been approaching it wrong, I told myself as I opened my laptop, smooshing myself into the corner of the couch, a sad, furniture-assisted cuddle that was the best I could get in my single state. Maybe I needed to stop thinking about a schedule, a set-in-stone path for this trip, and instead think about—inspiration. Pictures of places I wanted to see. Travel *vibes*, not travel *plans.*

So I'd navigated to some feel-good lifestyle site, the kind that shows you a bunch of food you should be cooking and crafts you should be doing to make your life fuller and happier and also more suitable for display on your Instagram. Never mind that my cooking is rudimentary and my last craft project was a noodle-jewelry box I made in third grade. Never mind that I don't even have an Instagram. Something about the *possibility* of such a lifestyle soothed me. So there I was, clicking through a bunch of filter-heavy photos of artisanal kale and hand-woven hammocks and fingerless-glove clad hands wrapped around huge, latte-filled mugs, forgetting, once again, all about my longed-for travel vibes.

Looking back, I wonder if I'd not only been drunk, but also perhaps stunned into some kind of nectarous, curated-lifestyle coma. Because why in God's name would I, Zoe No-Time-for-Bullshit Ferris, click on a picture of a "gratitude jar"? But there it was: a rustic-looking Ball jar, weathered pastel slips of paper with rough-hewn edges folded and tucked inside, and, so far as I could tell, several strands of completely useless pieces of jute twine wound around the outside. The idea was, each day, you'd record a good memory on a small slip of paper, fold it up and put it in the jar. Then, when you're feeling low, you just extract one of those little shabby-chic scraps of joy from your jam jar and get on with feeling grateful about what life has handed to you.

Well. I certainly have well over a million reasons to be grateful, don't I? So why don't I feel any joy? Why can't I just *get on?* *Maybe*, drunk-lonely Zoe had thought, *I need the* jar.

Of course, I didn't have a jar, or twine, or antique-looking paper. I had a Baccarat Tornado vase and a stack of Smythson stationery. And somewhere between me cutting my cardstock into squares (not rough-hewn, are you kidding, I wasn't that drunk) and actually putting pen to paper, the real idea—the *dumb* idea—had hit me.

What I need is a guilt jar.

It suddenly seemed so clear. It was the guilt that was keeping me from doing the trip, or from doing anything, really, since I'd taken home my share of the winnings. It was the guilt that was always there, ever since I was nineteen years old, piling on year after year. But now that I wasn't working seventy hours a week, now that I wasn't scheduling my free time down to the second, now that I'd been the beneficiary of the kind of luck I knew I didn't deserve—I actually had time to really wallow in it. Sure, the wine wasn't helping, but that night, I was brutally honest with myself: *you've done wrong. And you need to fix it to move on.*

After that, it'd been easy. On those little scraps of cardstock, I'd recorded my failures, starting with the comparatively minute.

The time I made Dan cry at work.

When I snapped at the Starbucks barista for not knowing my regular order.

When I parked in one of those "For New Moms Only" *spots at the grocery because I had menstrual cramps and it felt close enough.*

Forgetting my assistant's birthday (2x).

Avoiding eye contact with the homeless man who always sits outside Betty's, even when I give him money.

On and on, until it'd gotten trickier, until I'd had to get to the truly painful ones. The ones I just confined to names. First—names from the cases I was having such trouble forgetting. Then—names I wouldn't ever forget:

Dad.

Mom.

Christopher.

At first I wasn't exactly sure how the guilt jar would work. The gratitude jar was for contemplation's sake, but the problem with my guilt was that I contemplated it pretty much every fucking night of my life, and so if I was going to get any joy out of this thing, I was going to have to do something other than just *look* at my recordings. I was going to have to fix what I'd broken, or at least I was going to have to try.

Thanks to the lottery, I had means.

Thanks to my unemployment, I had time.

And that jar, it was going to give me the *will*.

Chapter 1

Zoe

I choose a Wednesday morning to draw my first guilt slip.

That's far enough away from the night I came up with the idea to give me perspective, but not so far that I seem as if I'm avoiding it. I try not to be weird about it, but the slip-drawing does take on this ritualistic quality, even though I'm wearing monkey pajamas and an anti-aging face mask. The worst thing about leaving my job since the lottery win has been what's happened to my days—or, I guess, what's *not* happened to them. Before, when I was working, my days were so regimented that they were almost comical. Once I asked my assistant to set a timer every time I went to pee, just to see how many minutes my bladder was costing me (too many, so I cut back on coffee). Now I spend a lot of time drifting around, wondering what to make of my time, wondering whether I'll ever go back to some kind of work, wondering how I managed to become the kind of person who isn't working at all, who hasn't worked in well over half a year.

But the guilt jar, much as it contains my most painful flaws, is giving me a sense of purpose I haven't felt in a while, and so I put it in the center of my dining room table and take a seat, setting my mug of tea in front of me. There's a familiarity to this setup, sort of similar to the Sunday mornings I'd get up early and work on briefs before meeting Kit and Greer, and I try and let that familiarity blanket the contrasting feeling of unease. The steam rising out of my mug isn't helping; the vase is starting to take on magic cauldron-like qualities. Maybe one of those slips is going to fly out and hit me in the face.

I take a deep breath, cut the bullshit, and reach in.

And…well. Not that a lottery winner is going to get a lot of sympathy here, but rotten luck that I couldn't have drawn the Starbucks barista first. Instead, I've drawn a name—or, rather, two names: *Robert and Kathleen O'Leary.*

Damn.

I saw a lot of unhappy people in conference room four, to be honest, but I don't think I'll ever forget Robert and Kathleen O'Leary. Their settlement mediation was the last I'd sat in on, and I like to believe that even if I hadn't won the jackpot that night, it still would've been my last day at Willis-Hanawalt. That I would have said to myself, *no, enough is enough*, and never gone back again. They'd been gray-haired and slight, Mrs. O'Leary barely over five feet, her husband only a couple of inches taller—though between the two of them, he'd been the more diminished, the more fragile. Mrs. O'Leary's eyes had been puffy and red, but focused. She'd tracked the conversation with a sad, knowing acuity—well aware her lawyer was outmatched, well aware that whatever money she walked away with, she'd never get what she really wanted.

An admission of guilt.

But Mr. O'Leary—he'd barely been more than a bodily presence. At one point, I'd wondered if he'd had a stroke, or some other kind of catastrophic medical event that kept him from moving or speaking. I still don't know. But I do know that he cried—silent tears that tracked down his cheeks, dripped off his jawline onto the conference table.

What a performance, my boss had muttered, when the O'Learys had finally gone.

I swallow thickly, rubbing the slip of paper between my fingers. It's so uncomfortable thinking about those days when we were doing the settlements; how clear I'd been that something was off; how many opportunities I'd had to say something. And yet I think about those days a lot, too much, when—as my guilt jar is reminding me—I should be *doing* something.

And so I do. I grab my laptop, spend a few minutes getting the information I need. I take off the mask, I shower, I dress carefully. When I walk out to my car, I'm doing so with purpose. When I drive, I keep the radio off so I can focus, so I can keep that little slip of paper in my mind.

The O'Leary house is a small, brick rambler, tidy at first glance, but there are signs of neglect—the two clay pots on the front porch are full of leafless, tangled twigs, the bushes that line the bed underneath the shutters are shaggy, a few aggressive limbs of growth reaching up past the windows. The left side of the iron railing leading up to the front porch is listing to the side, two newspapers still in their bags beneath it.

I think, briefly and nonsensically, about whether I'll pick up those papers when I knock on the door, whether I'll have to start by saying, *Oh, hey, I picked up these papers that were here*, and it's this stray, silly thought that finally gives me pause, pause that I should have had about ten thousand more times before I got here: if they aren't picking up their papers, maybe they aren't around, or maybe they don't open the door for anyone. Maybe they don't want to be bothered.

And it hits me: they *wouldn't* want to be bothered, not by me of all people. Even if they don't remember me, I'll have to explain in order to apologize. I'll either be poking at a festering wound or reopening one that could only be, even under the best of circumstances, barely healed. I grip my steering wheel, so hard that it hurts my fingers, in plain, simple frustration at myself. The real me—the smart, sharp, ambitious me, the me who proofreads everything six times—that me would've thought of this. Instead, I've come over here thinking only of my own guilt, my stupid internet jar and my stupid, lazy sense of purposelessness.

If I really mean to make up to people, I have to do better than ambush them with apologies that they may not even want to hear.

My hand is back on the key, ready to back out and go home where I can rethink this.

But then the front door opens.

It's not Mr. or Mrs. O'Leary there, that's for damn sure, because this is about six-feet-two of muscled, fully alert dude, his thick, dark brown hair messy, his square jaw stubbled.

And he definitely does not look happy to see me, though I suppose he'd have that in common with the O'Learys.

It's still possible, I tell myself, to turn the key, wave an apology as if I've found myself at the wrong house or something. But there's something that stops me—something about the way this man stands so still, watching me, and something about the heavy, guilty fatigue I feel when I look back at him. Maybe this man knows something about the O'Learys. Maybe he can help me get some of this fucking *weight* off.

So I take my keys from the ignition, *inhale, exhale*—even doing the noisy puff of breath that my yoga teacher is always suggesting—and get out of the car. My heel wobbles a bit on the cracked pavement, and I steady myself on the top of the car door before shutting it behind me, smoothing the front of my dress, which is another terrible choice I made this morning. It's a gray herringbone, sleek and tailored, a jewel neckline and sharply-cut cap sleeves. It's a dress I'd wear to work, a dress that makes me look as cool and detached as I probably did on that day. It appalls me how little I thought this through, what a massive, selfish mistake I made this morning. I think of making a new slip, later: *bothered a man at his home, because of my narcissism.*

"Hello," I manage, surprised that my voice sounds very close to the way it always does when I meet new people, which is to say: it sounds detached and professional, when I came here to be anything but that. When I came here to show them that I do, in fact, have a heart.

A heart that is beating so fast that I suspect this man can see it pulsing in my neck.

"What can I do for you?" he asks, and however harmless the question is, however polite-seeming, it is clear he does not mean it to seem so. His voice is gruff, clipped. He stands, feet slightly apart, arms crossed over his chest, like he's here working security.

"I was looking for Robert and Kathleen O'Leary," I begin. "But I believe I've—"

Before I can finish that, before I can say *I believe I've made a mistake,* he cuts me off. "They moved."

It's him that's made the mistake now, because I've lain awake so many nights wondering about what has happened to the O'Learys, to other families I ran mediation for, that I am now desperate to know more. Did they take the money, buy a home somewhere beautiful, somewhere away from the place that must remind them of terrible grief? Do they live a better life? Have they been able to move on, at all? That little shred of information— *they moved*—makes me curious enough to keep pressing.

"Do you happen to know where they went?"

"I do." It seems as if—I don't know what. It seems as if he's made himself bigger somehow. He is looking at me like I am something unpleasant he stepped in.

"I guess I'll have to be more specific with my questions," I say, annoyed now. My concern is for the O'Learys, and this man is becoming an unnecessary roadblock.

"Guess so," he grinds out, but then he shifts slightly, his hands tightening around where they are crossed, at the join of his elbows. And then he says, "I know who you are. And believe me, they would not want you to find them."

I swallow, once, then again, suddenly feeling hot and sick. I should've had something to eat before I came, something light that would settle my nervous stomach. My eyes lower, automatically, an old habit that I had fully eradicated in my adult life, when I made my living off being completely unflappable. I am torn between wanting to ask how he knows who I am and wanting to turn back and get in my car, to pretend this morning never happened.

"I'm their son," he says, and my eyes snap up, taking him in with renewed interest. My first thought is automatic, innocuous: how can this—this *giant*—be the son of the two short, ruddy-skinned couple from conference room four? My second is more painful: *their* surviving *son.*

"I apologize for bothering you," I say.

"You didn't," he says, firmly. The sentiment is so clear: *I am not worth him being bothered.*

I offer a small nod, turn my back to return to my car, to put this entire mistake behind me. *A guilt jar.* What a fucking joke. What a perfect encapsulation of the worthless person I've become. I feel so strangely unwell. It's hot out here, the still-muggy heat of a southern September.

When I have my shaking hand on the car door, he speaks again. "If you have business with them, you need to take it up with me. I don't want you trying to contact them. They've been through enough."

And haven't you? He was your brother, after all, I think, surprising myself.

I turn back to face him, my spine straightening, even though I am desperate to fold myself back into the safety of my car. "I came to apologize. That's it. I can see it was—" I have to pause, take a deep breath in response to his forbidding expression. "I can see that was a mistake."

"Can't imagine your firm would be happy about that."

"I don't work for them anymore," I answer, as though this might magically change his opinion of me.

"I know. I heard you came into some money."

If it was possible for me to feel sicker, I didn't know until just now. Kit, Greer, and I had all agreed on privacy when our numbers came up. The state required a public disclosure of identification, but the jackpot had been comparatively small, the most interesting part of the win being the grainy security video of the three of us buying the ticket, which I'd buried as best I could with some threatening legalese. Greer and I had helped shield Kit—who'd had bigger reasons for keeping it quiet—by doing the small, state-lottery required press conference. But that didn't even make the news, and other than a brief clipping in the local paper, which had identified us by first initial and last name only, we'd flown under the radar. He would've had to go looking.

"Listen, I came to apologize to your family," I say, the effort to keep my voice steady almost herculean. "That apology extends to you. I can see you're not interested, and I'm sorry for that, too. I'll leave you alone. I would appreciate the same courtesy." It's a warning. If this guy has been sniffing around my private life, he'll find out there are limits to my guilty conscience. I don't deserve to be stalked, for God's sake.

He makes a derisive noise, half-snarl. "Believe me, I don't care to know anything more about you than I have to. Your former secretary told me. Without prompting."

Ugh, Janet. Probably because I forgot her birthday (*2x*, per my guilt jar). And made her time my bathroom breaks. Still, my brow furrows in curiosity, wondering what dealings he's had with my former firm. He'd certainly never been involved with the Aaron O'Leary settlement before. But I stifle this curiosity. It seems my sense of what's appropriate has picked this moment to return. Would that it had a better sense of timing.

"Well," I say. "Again. I am sorry for bothering you."

"Are you on some kind of apology tour?"

Good god, this man cuts like a knife, doesn't he? Or am I really that transparent?

"Something like that," I manage.

"For your next stop, I'd say show up in something other than a Mercedes."

I am torn, at this moment, between two instincts. The first is to fight back against this man's ire, to cut him down to size, to push back against his scorn. That Mercedes is four years old, after all, bought not with lottery winnings but with my own salary, the salary I earned for billing the most hours in the entire firm in my first year on the job.

But the second? The second is to stand there and take it. To invite more of it, in fact, because…because in some sick, dark corner of me, it feels good to have his scorn. It feels as if I earned it as much as I earned that Mercedes. Maybe more, because I question every single billable hour I worked for Willis-Hanawalt. It's not easy to be here, to have someone look at me this way. To have to face such naked animosity, all of it directed at me. It's not easy, but it's what I feel like I deserve.

There's a long pause while I stand, frozen, caught between these two instincts, while he stares right through me. He's pinned me to the car with that gaze. In another context, I would find this man so sexy as to make me weak in the knees. But right now, I'm just—weirdly, uncomfortably, weak in the knees, fuzzy-headed and still over-warm. I have a distant memory, suddenly, of the senior partner at Willis-Hanawalt coaching me the first time I went before a judge. *Whatever you do, don't stand there with your knees locked*, she'd said. *You'll faint dead away from the nerves.*

I think I set a hand to my forehead. I think I hear him say, *Are you all right?* I think he moves closer to me.

But then, everything goes gray around the edges.

And then, it all goes blissfully, forgivingly dark.

* * * *

When I come to, my first sight is of lace curtains, yellowed but beautiful, delicate and fluttering before an open window. I jerk up, instinctively, and hear the man's voice, lower now, no trace of anger. "You're all right," he says. I'm inside the rambler, sitting in a dusty rose velveteen chair that is both hideously ugly and incredibly comfortable. "Oh god," I mumble. "Was I out for long?"

"Maybe two minutes." He's kneeling in front of me, a black duffel next to him. "My name is Aiden. I'm a paramedic. Do you know where you are?" I stare down at him, bewildered at this new information. *Aiden. Paramedic. Probably carried me in here.* But I realize I need to answer, if I don't want things to get more awkward.

"Ah—I'm assuming I'm in your house?"

He nods, sets his hand gently on my wrist. "Good. Do you know what day it is?"

I tell him, respond to his question about the year, the approximate time. He looks so different now, his face placid, his body curled into a protective posture at my feet, though he only touches me in that one spot, one warm hand on my wrist, two fingers touching the soft inside of it. *Taking my pulse*, I realize, but he presses on with his questions.

"Do you know how you got here?"

I can't help but smirk. "Well. It started with this jar," I say, but my mouth flattens when he looks up at me, quick and concerned. "No—no, I mean, sorry. That was a joke. I got here because I was making an inadequate, ill-considered apology in your driveway. And I guess I fainted."

"All right. Is it okay with you if I check you over a bit?"

"I think I'm fine," I say, scooting forward a bit in the chair. "I didn't eat today, and I—I think I was a bit nervous."

If he weren't sitting so close, I don't think I'd catch the slight crinkle of tension in the corners of his eyes, maybe something close to remorse. But that's ridiculous—it's not him who has to feel remorseful. "I'm sure you're fine," he says, and god. I bet he is really good at his job—calm and careful, no sense of panicked urgency. "But I really do need to check you over."

I offer a weak nod, and he quietly sets to work. First, he takes my blood pressure, reads it off to me, tells me it looks good. When he removes a stethoscope from the bag, I stiffen, thinking there'll be a moment where he has to try and get into my dress somehow, but he seems to know. "Just going to listen over your clothes, all right?" he says, and I nod again. I watch him from beneath my lashes as he does it, his eyes lowered, his face serious. After a minute, he tips his chin down, says, "Sounds good." Then he takes out a small, flat, egg-shaped device, a digital screen on the front. "I'm going to prick your finger. A little pinch. It's going to tell me what your blood sugar is."

I don't like needles, of any kind, and it probably shows, because he squeezes my hand gently and says, "Look only at me." That would probably work in normal circumstances, because he's so good looking, and so calm, so *good* at this. But this isn't normal. Ten minutes ago he looked like he'd buy tickets to my public humiliation.

It's a little pinch, just as he says, but he frowns down at the screen. "Fifty. Tell me when you ate last?"

"Last night, at dinner. Around seven p.m."

"Can you remember what you had?"

"A small salad. A piece of chocolate for dessert."

"You don't eat breakfast?" His voice has changed now, not quite hostile, but not quite the soothing, softened offerings of before.

"I do eat breakfast. Usually. But—it's like I said. I was a little nervous. I drank a cup of tea. I should've had something. I realize that."

He stands, turns his back toward me and walks down the hall, to where I can see glimpses of a kitchen—a line of oak cabinets, an almond-colored refrigerator. I can hear him moving around in there, and while he does, I scan the room, which is similar in aesthetic to this pink chair, and those lace curtains—feminine, old-fashioned, and very, very lived in. I wonder whether Aiden actually lives here, or if he's just staying here. If Mr. and Mrs. O'Leary have moved, maybe he's checking in on the place, or—

He comes back in, a glass in one hand and a small glass bowl in the other. He crouches back in front of me, hands me the water. "Are you sick to your stomach?"

I shake my head. "No, I think maybe I was, but only in the heat out there. I feel okay now."

"Have a few sips of this, but go slow." While I drink, he pulls a plastic honey bear bottle from his back pocket, squeezes a bit into the glass bowl, and then takes a small spoon from his other pocket.

"Those aren't part of your regular supplies, I take it?" I ask, between sips of the cool water. Already I feel better, physically. It's just the incredibly awkward emotions I need to be treated for now.

"No," he says. "Got this from the kitchen. I want you to take a spoonful or two of this honey. I know it's sweet, but it'll help the immediate issue with your blood sugar."

"I really am okay." I set my hands on the armrest, readying myself to leave.

His voice is forceful, gruff again when he replies. "This is the bare minimum you're going to do for me, before I let you go. Or I'll call the squad." I take the honey.

He backs away from me at this, leans against the jamb of the open front door, arms crossed again, and watches me closely. The honey makes my teeth ache, and I have to set a hand over my mouth so I can discreetly lick at the corner of my mouth, sticky with it. But within seconds I feel oddly restored, not quite normal but almost so. "I think I'll go," I say, standing slowly, expecting a head rush that doesn't come. "Obviously I am very grateful for your help. And very sorry to have inconvenienced you more."

"It'll be more of an inconvenience if you walk out of here and faint again, and then I get sued for not ensuring you got standard of care."

I know, of course, what he means—Willis-Hanawalt does medical malpractice, too, and a paramedic could get sued for negligence. He's made contact with me, a patient, and I did not deny treatment, and technically, he should have to turn over care to a person of equal or higher qualification. But I want out of here so bad that my mind is ahead of these rules. I spot a phone on the coffee table and gesture to it. "Is this yours?"

He nods, and I pick it up, walking it over to him and holding it out. "Turn on your video camera." When he makes no move to take it, I swipe a finger across the screen, see the menu of apps. "You should have a password on this," I mumble, opening the camera and flipping the screen so it points at me. I back up, extending my arm so my face fills it, happy enough that I at least seem to have color in my cheeks. I use my thumb to press record.

"I, Zoe Ferris, assert that I fainted outside the property at 631 Old Crescent Road in Barden, Virginia. I was treated at the scene by paramedic Aiden O'Leary. I was informed of my condition. I understand that there are possible medical consequences for not seeking additional medical treatment. At this time I am refusing further medical advice and/or transport to a medical facility by the aforementioned paramedic." I hit the record button again, stopping the video, then open the file and make sure the time and date were saved before handing it back to him. "Okay?" I say.

Something has shifted in the way he looks at me, something speculative and interested. Less like I'm a pile of dog shit, and more like I'm some odd, nonthreatening species of insect he's never seen before. "Why did you really come?" he asks.

I take a deep breath, look out the door to where my car sits in the driveway. "I'm sure you have no reason to believe me. But I had intended to leave my job even before I—well. Before I came into the money you mentioned. That doesn't excuse how long I stayed. It doesn't excuse anything, really. Your family went through something terrible."

He lowers his head at this, adjusts his booted feet on the wood floors, which creak beneath him. "My parents moved to Florida. I still don't want you to contact them. But that's where they are."

"Are they happy there?"

He looks up at me, and I'm on the bottom of his shoe again. I hear everything he's thinking in that look. Of course they're not fucking happy. Their son is dead.

"I'm sorry," I say again, uselessly. "I realize there is nothing I can say. Nothing I can do." I look at him one last time, offer a brief, placating downward tip of my chin before setting my fingers on the screen's door handle.

"There is nothing you can say." Blunt and honest. I almost admire him for making sure he sticks it to me, in the end. For not making it easy on me. "But there may be something you can do."

My hand stills and my head bows, almost as though I'm waiting for a benediction. I *want* him to tell me what to do, and I am not, maybe strangely, maybe naively, afraid at all. Aiden is angry, but he's not cruel, or at least this what I tell myself. All the possibility of that damn vase feels like it's in this room with us, and I think maybe, *maybe* it wasn't such a terrible idea after all.

"Marry me," he says, and it's a wonder I don't faint all over again.

Acknowledgments

First, foremost, forever: thank you so much for reading. I hope you loved reading *Beginner's Luck* as much as I loved writing it.

The phrase "beginner's luck" is, in some ways, an apt descriptor of my own path to becoming published as a novelist. But just as Kit's story aims to show, "luck" is really only ever one part of the story, and in my case, that is especially so. The truth of the matter is, whatever luck or talent I have is only one very small part of the story of writing this book and bringing it to readers.

The rest is about the many people I have to thank.

Kit's story is so much about friendship, and I want to say that my friends—women who live far and near, women who do all kinds of important, interesting work in and outside of their homes, women who are brilliant and funny and kind and supportive—are the inspiration for this book, and much of what is best about Kit, Zoe, and Greer is from them. I cannot name them all here, but to each, I offer my gratitude for being such generous, encouraging friends.

To Amy and Elizabeth, I offer special thanks for being my first beta readers, and for maintaining the delicate balance of cheerleading and criticism that the job involves. To my mom, my first and very best friend: you are the most inspiring woman of them all, for a hundred reasons big and small. Thank you for (weirdly?) saving all the stories I ever wrote—that box of elementary school scribbles was always a reminder of a part of myself I would want to get back to someday.

I have benefitted from the generous advice of many writers, especially Eloisa James, who gave of her time throughout the process of my writing this book (and getting it in front of readers), and who is a model in all things. Thanks, too, to Sally Thorne, Laura Florand, and Jenny Crusie, whose emails—at various stages in this process—were of immeasurable help to a novice writer.

My luckiest break in this entire process was having this book read by the lovely and talented best-agent-ever, Taylor Haggerty, and I am so grateful for her confidence in this book and in me. I am similarly fortunate to work with Esi Sogah, who has understood, from the very beginning, what meant most to me about this book, and her keen eye has made it so much better. I am additionally grateful to both Taylor and Esi for being so fun and funny—they make collaboration a joy. Thanks to everyone at Kensington

Books and Lyrical Press for making *Beginner's Luck* what it is in its final form. I am especially grateful to Christa Desir for thorough copyediting, and to Tammy Seidick for her tremendous cover design.

Finally, for my husband: at an important moment in this story, Kit speaks for me when she says no one person can be "home." But I say that having lived in many places with you, and always, you have been home's most defining feature. You are my safest place, my favorite everyday moment, and the home we've made together is what made it possible for me to imagine the home I made for these characters. Thank you, always.

Meet the Author

Kate Clayborn lives in Virginia, where she's lucky enough to spend her days reading and talking about all kinds of great books. At home, she's either writing, thinking about writing, or—during long walks around her fabulous neighborhood—making her handsome husband and sweet-faced dog listen to her talk about writing. Kate loves to hear from and connect with readers—follow her on Twitter, on Instagram, and on Facebook. You can also email her at kate@kateclayborn.com.

CPSIA information can be obtained
at www.ICGtesting.com
Printed in the USA
LVHW02s2315050618
579762LV00001B/71/P